2/15

THE
KILLING
SEASON

THE KILLING SEASON

MASON CROSS

PEGASUS CRIME

NEW YORK LONDON

THE KILLING SEASON

Pegasus Books LLC
80 Broad Street, 5th Floor
New York, NY 10004

First Pegasus Books hardcover edition February 2015

ISBN: 978-1-60598-690-6

10 9 8 7 8 6 5 4 3 2 1

Printed in the United States of America
Distributed by W. W. Norton & Company, Inc.

For Alison M. Bell

If you know the enemy and know yourself, you need not fear the result of a hundred battles.

—*Sun Tzu*

They wanted to know why I did what I did.
Well, sir, I guess there's just a meanness in this world.

—*Bruce Springsteen*

DAY ONE

PROLOGUE

The first thing you should know about me is that my name is not Carter Blake. That name no more belonged to me than the hotel room I was occupying when the call came in.

It was nice without being too extravagant. The room, I mean. It was a city-view deluxe in the northwest corner of the seventh floor of a midpriced metropolitan hotel. I liked the room. It had served me well in the eighteen days I'd been staying there. The city itself was pleasant, too: not too big, not too small. A comfortable environment in which to work.

In much the same way, I'd grown comfortable with the name Blake in the last couple of years. To me, names are a lot like hotel rooms: You pick one that suits your purposes, inhabit it for as long as is feasible, and then move on when the time is right.

Although it was not quite five a.m., I was wide-awake when my cell phone buzzed, having given up on sleep a couple of hours before. Some nights are like that. I hit the button to pick up and held the phone to my ear, not speaking.

"Blake? You there?" The voice on the other end of the line was tired, and cranky about it. It was also familiar.

"What's going on?"

"As of right now? Who knows. What's important is what happened two hours ago."

I leaned forward on the wooden chair so I could look

through the gap where the curtains didn't quite meet. The lights of the city twinkled back at me. I knew I was expected to take the bait, so I didn't, not directly.

"You know, I've been busy."

"Yeah, I know."

"Was looking forward to a rest."

"You're in luck. Because a change is as good as a rest, right?"

I paused, thought it over, then said, "Where?"

"Initially? Illinois. Chicago."

I glanced at my watch, the luminescent points on the dial glowing softly in the predawn gloom. I had a car in the garage beneath the building. This time of day, I could make Chicago in three hours. Maybe two and a half.

One final question needed asking. "Black, white, or gray?"

There was a pause, and I could sense the owner of the voice on the other end of the line grinning.

"As the driven snow. You'll like it."

I sighed and leaned back in the chair again, relenting. "All right," I said. "Tell me what happened two hours ago."

1

The moon hung gigantic and full over the expanse of fields as they rolled by like a calm ocean. Late October, northern hemisphere. That made it a hunter's moon.

Wardell breathed a philosophical sigh at the thought as he stared out at the night through the small, mean window. Out here in the darkness, the moon burned bright enough to dazzle if you looked directly at it, lit the world up enough to see everything for miles. A pity, then, that there was nothing to see but fields. Miles and miles of orderly nothing, right to the horizon. He kept looking anyway. Thinking his thoughts and letting his body sway with the rhythm of the vehicle as it rattled along the deserted highway.

Despite the lack of variation, or perhaps because of it, Wardell liked the view. It was ... *serene*. Serene was definitely the word. The moonlit fields reminded him of a line from the Simon & Garfunkel song "America." As a rule, he didn't like pop music, but "America" was one of his favorite tunes. It was a story about two lovers setting off on a voyage of discovery, starting out with youthful optimism and ending in emptiness and disillusionment. Wardell liked the sentiment.

That Simon & Garfunkel song was as close to contemporary

5

popular music as Wardell's tastes ventured, just another detail that had set him apart from the Cro-Magnons in his old unit. Most of the other men had displayed a depressing uniformity in their musical tastes: mainstream hard rock and rap. Nickelback and Kid Rock. Loud, anodyne trash like that. He was quite sure they'd mocked him behind his back for the music he listened to, for the expensive coffee he drank, for the books he read. But not to his face. Nobody ever said anything to Wardell's face, and if they did, they made that mistake only once.

He smiled at the pleasant memory and looked down at his hands, flexing them to kill a nascent cramp. Then he reached up with the right hand to scratch his full beard, having to lift the left along with it, of course.

Clarence, the skinny, sick-looking man beside him, was asleep. Or pretending to be asleep; Wardell didn't care which, as long as it meant he had peace and quiet. Clarence had attempted small talk when he first sat down and had kept at it longer than most people did when you pointedly ignored their conversation openers. Eventually, Wardell had shut him up by giving him the stare. The stare always worked, conveying the message that this was positively the last chance for the beholder to avoid serious physical harm. The trick was to absolutely mean it.

Clarence had come close to testing that by apologizing for being a talker, but he'd gotten the message; he was quiet now, and that was the main thing. That and the fact he'd had sense enough not to fall asleep on Wardell's shoulder. Instead, he was hunched forward over his own hands in a position that could not have been comfortable.

It was unusual, although not completely unheard of, for Wardell to have a traveling companion. It was even more un-usual for him to be making a trip without an accompanying

6

convoy. He'd been transported almost as modestly before, usually on the occasions when they didn't want to draw attention to his movements; but he couldn't recall a time exactly like this. One vehicle, no escort cars, no outriders. Perhaps they didn't think he merited the attention anymore. Perhaps his entourage had fallen victim to budget cuts; this was a midterm election year after all. Or perhaps it was just evidence that his fame had receded far enough that the powers that be didn't need to be seen to care quite so much.

Wardell turned his gaze back to the window, the song continuing to play in his head. Silently, he mouthed along with the refrain.

I've gone to look for America.

America. He hadn't seen much of it, not nearly enough.

Having had the luxury of time to think things over, he realized now that he'd been thinking too small back then. Confining himself to one hunting ground, one city. Only now that the opportunity had passed did he see what he should have been doing all along. He should have embarked on a quest. Town to town, state to state, east to west. Surging ever onward like a forest fire, burning his name into the hide of the country. Building to something big. Something that had been denied him. He closed his eyes and said the name quietly.

Juba.

He flexed his hands again, adjusting the position of the handcuffs so they didn't abrade his wrists too badly, then rested them again on his thighs. The muscles there were firm and toned. Solid, like the rest of him.

Most men in Wardell's current position let themselves go. They gained weight, became soft and flaccid, smoked as many cigarettes as they could get ahold of, slept sixteen hours a day. They did that because they'd been broken; they'd decided, *What's the point?*

Not Wardell. He'd kept up his fitness regime from his days in the Corps, and in the last five years he'd only intensified it. He started every day with sit-ups and push-ups—twenty reps of twenty each and then one-handed push-ups, a hundred on each hand. His mostly free schedule allowed ample time for an afternoon session of the same and one more before lights-out. He walked ten miles around a fifteen-foot circumference every day. The advantage of such a predictable route was that he could read the whole time, keeping his mind in shape as well as his body. Because he knew what the other men did not.

Wardell kept going because he knew that keeping going *was* the point. They hadn't broken Wardell in the five years they'd had him, and they wouldn't break him in the two weeks he had left. Tonight was the first time he'd missed his evening's workout in a long while, and his body ached for the routine the way a junkie's aches for a fix.

It might be too late to do things right, to go back and carry out his work on a grander scale, but that didn't mean he had to meekly accept his fate. Those dozen witnesses who came to see him die would find a man who was going to meet his Maker looking *good*. He wondered who would be there. The governor, probably, and maybe Stewart, the man who'd brought him in. That prick Hatcher would be there for sure. And Wardell would stand up and he'd use his allotted time to the full and he'd look each and every one of those gawkers in the eye and tell them he'd see them in hell. And he'd make them believe it, too.

The trick was to absolutely mean it.

Caleb Wardell might have dropped off the national radar, but he'd make goddamn sure that the last people he saw remembered him.

His body listed forward a little with a reduction in road

speed, snapping him out of his thoughts. Instinctively, he looked ahead. A pointless reflex. This wasn't a tour bus; it wasn't as though he could crane his neck out into the center aisle for an unobstructed view to the driver's cabin and the road ahead. Instead, he moved his head closer to the window, jamming sideways against it, closing his left eye to try to see ahead with just his right.

Three hundred yards along the straight road, he could make out a pair of unmoving taillights. Even with the moonlight, the angle made it impossible to discern what type of vehicle they belonged to. A figure was silhouetted against the red glare, waving them down. An apparent breakdown. Wardell kept looking. Tried to see farther down the road. The heavy transport van accommodated him, swaying a little to the center of the road, away from the stationary vehicle as though obeying Wardell's will. The stationary *car*. It was definitely a car. A sedan, a bloodred paint job showing in the transport's headlights. Farther up the road, a black shape blocked a patch of sky. A farmhouse? A barn?

They were in the middle of nowhere, and it was the middle of the night. There had been no buildings and no side roads in miles. They hadn't passed another vehicle in a half hour. Now there was a breakdown and a building all at once.

The transport van picked up speed again. The driver hadn't been where Wardell had been, but perhaps he wasn't a complete idiot. They passed the red car and the waving man, giving them both a wide berth. The man stopped signaling before they reached him. He ignored the driver and watched the tiny side window as it passed. Wardell locked eyes with him for a fleeting second. He didn't look disappointed or even angry that they hadn't stopped to help. He looked very calm, very focused.

They were still gaining speed, and the barn—it was a

barn—was coming into view. It was an old structure. Solid construction, thirty feet high, gable roof. Wardell had acquired an almost subconscious habit of assessing every environment in which he found himself with a professional eye, deciding where the best vantage points were from both an offensive and defensive point of view. The barn was a good spot both ways. The best spot he'd seen on this road, certainly.

They were fifty yards from the barn now, and Wardell could see it was built close to the road itself. Perhaps the farmhouse it had once belonged to had been bulldozed to make way for this thoroughfare.

Something was about to happen. He was sure of it.

He trained his eyes on the roof, at the position he would have chosen, right next to the weather vane. Something didn't look quite right with the line of the roof, almost as though—

Something big, solid, and absolutely unrelenting slammed into the left side of the vehicle, the opposite direction from where the barn sat. The van was pitched horizontally off the road, and then the world flipped upside down and sideways. For a moment it felt like Wardell was floating in zero G. Then gravity's pull reasserted itself with an angry bump, and the transport van came to rest on its side.

Sounds, smells, noises, pain all jumbled together in a confusing mess of white-noise sensation. Wardell heard shouts, gunshots from multiple weapons, then somebody moaning. The scents of gasoline and sheared metal mingling with smoke. Wardell could taste his own blood. He was shaking his head, trying to sort everything into the correct order. And then there were big hands grabbing his shoulders, dragging him from where he lay and out into the cold moonlight.

The fresh air helped, cleared his throat and his eyes, let him begin to get a handle on things. The barrel of a gun was pressed into the back of his skull as he was pushed, stumbling away from the wrecked transport van. He glanced to the side, registered the bloody bodies of the two marshals up front, a yellow construction digger jammed a couple of feet deep in the crumpled wreckage of the transport van. Then he caught a smack to the head.

"Move it."

Wardell got the message, looked straight ahead. The man had spoken with an Eastern European accent—evident even from just two words. Russian maybe. That was odd. Wardell couldn't remember killing any Russians. He was marched twenty paces off the road, and then his legs were kicked out from under him. He managed to get his cuffed hands up in time to break his fall. Clarence was not so lucky, arriving a second later, face-first in the field dirt. He yelped and rolled over, his nose spouting blood. He didn't say anything, which meant he was smarter than Wardell would have given him credit for. He just looked up at the three men with guns. Two of them grabbed one each of Clarence's arms and dragged him away from where Wardell was kneeling.

Wardell recognized the guy on the left arm from the phony breakdown scene. The one dragging the right arm wore a brown leather jacket over a black turtleneck sweater. He was a little shorter than the other two and gave out boss vibes despite his evident willingness to help with the manual labor. The one who stayed with Wardell was built like a bear. Almost as hairy as one, too. He wore a tight red T-shirt in defiance of the temperature and cradled a pump-action shotgun. A Remington 870, that old standby.

"Good to see you again, Clarence," Turtleneck said in accented English, ignoring Wardell completely.

Wardell glanced at Clarence, taken by surprise, suddenly indignant. This was about *him*?

11

Clarence was staring up at Turtleneck, his hands conveniently brought together in supplication by the cuffs. He took a series of sharp breaths, as though building up the courage to speak. "Don't kill me," he said. The broken nose meant that it came out as *Dod't gill be*.

Turtleneck snorted, feigning amusement. "Not just yet." Russian, definitely.

Without warning, the one who was built like a bear took a step forward and kicked Wardell full in the gut. He had just enough time to tense his stomach muscles to avoid serious injury, but he doubled over and coughed a few times to make it look good. He wanted them off their guard.

"What about this one?" the bear asked Turtleneck. Similar accent but thicker.

"None of our business. Take care of him."

Wardell was still bent over, and saw the bear step toward him again as the other two turned their attention back to Clarence. He was going to kick him again, put him on his back so that he could take a clean shot at Wardell's center mass. Mistake.

Wardell caught the swinging foot in his cuffed hands, braced his own feet on the hard-packed ground, and pushed upward. The big man yelped and toppled over backward. Wardell followed him up and over, came down with all of his two hundred pounds on one elbow dead center to the larynx. The satisfyingly visceral crunch let him know he was done with this one. He was on his feet with the shotgun in his cuffed hands while the other two Russians were still reacting. He squeezed the trigger, and Turtleneck's chest disappeared in a red mist. Wardell pumped the slide on the shotgun, the cuffs ripping the skin on his forearms, and charged, yelling. The charge was both instinctive and practical: It made him a moving target and unnerved his opponent.

As it turned out, the final Russian's nerve was solid, but his aim was lousy. He got off a shot, but it came nowhere near Wardell. Wardell brought the shotgun level, having to angle his body sideways to do it within the limits of the cuffs, and blew the top four-fifths of the Russian's head off. The truncated corpse toppled forward like a felled tree. The last gunshot gave the illusion of echoing for longer than the first, and then the silence descended again and the hunter's moon beamed down, impassive.

Wardell started to jerk another shell into the chamber and winced as the cuffs rubbed the fresh scrape on his left wrist. He turned his head to look at the wrecked transport van, wondering if the keys would be on one of the dead marshals or if he'd have to get creative.

"Th-thank you," a weak, shell-shocked voice croaked from behind him.

Wardell's head snapped around. He'd forgotten all about Clarence. It was easy to do. The skinny man was still on his knees, shuffling forward, his eyes glassy with a mixture of trepidation and hope. Those eyes reminded Wardell of a pet rabbit he'd methodically starved to death as a boy.

"Those guys, they would have—"

"Evidently," Wardell said, cutting him off. He wasn't particularly interested in who, what, or why.

Something in his voice made the other man shrink back, his eyes widening. "You're not gonna shoot me, are you?" Clarence said, a nervous we're-in-this-together-brother smile breaking out on his face.

Wardell looked down at the shotgun and at his bloody wrist, then back at Clarence. He smiled and shook his head slowly. Then he swiveled the shotgun in his hands and rammed the butt into Clarence's face.

Clarence dropped without so much as a squeal, and

Wardell adjusted his grip on the gun again, turning it into a club. He brought it down across the middle of Clarence's face, feeling bone and cartilage give way. He hit the same spot another three times and felt the facial bone structure crumble completely on the third strike. He lost count after that, stopped thinking. Kept pounding until what had been Clarence's head was just mush and matter and fragments.

He stopped when his arms started to get tired, letting the adrenaline seep out of him like an ebbing tide. As his pulse returned to normal, Wardell looked down at himself with disgust. He was a mess: covered in dirt, sweat, and blood. A lot of blood. Some was his own, most was Clarence's. It made him want to retch. He hated being unclean. He hated a mess.

Five minutes later, he'd located the keys to his handcuffs on one of the dead guards and shed his orange prison jumpsuit. He used it to wipe down his arms and face as best he could and discarded it, evaluating his sartorial options. Mess had practical drawbacks as well as aesthetic ones: the clothes belonging to the last two Russians and Clarence were absolutely unusable. That left the big guy.

Shrugging, he stripped the Russian and pulled on his pants and T-shirt. It felt like wearing a circus tent. He paced back to the wreckage and surveyed his choice of weapons. The dead guards had both been carrying Smith & Wesson semiautomatic pistols. The driver's was still in its holster.

He crouched down and looked inside the crushed cabin, at a spot between the front seats. What he saw there made him wonder if a long incarceration could knock your perception of time utterly out of whack, because this was surely December 25th.

There was a Heckler & Koch PSG1 rifle with a telescopic sight strapped there, within easy reach of both driver and passenger. Good for picking off escapees like himself, he guessed. Good for lots of things.

It was a thing of beauty, as powerful and precise as anything he'd used in the desert. *More* precise, in fact, because it was specifically designed for law enforcement and did not require the compromises for weight and durability necessary for military use.

Wardell made a pretense of weighing up practicalities and logistics before giving in to his desire and taking the rifle. It would slow him a little more than taking one of the Smiths, but not much. Hell, it was what he was trained for. It was meant to be.

That was when Wardell remembered the barn roof. He looked back up there, saw only a straight black line against the dark blue night sky. There was no one on the roof, probably never had been in the first place.

There was a line of trees a quarter of a mile south. Wardell slung the rifle under his arm, cast a final glance at the barn roof, and then he was gone.

Gone to look for America.

2

5:06 a.m.

Nine minutes after the phone call began and seven minutes after it ended, I had showered and shaved and was opening the closet door.

I selected a single-breasted charcoal suit, off-white shirt, and Italian shoes. Nothing flashy, even though the full ensemble had cost roughly the equivalent of a small family car. There were another three identical suits in the closet. I closed the door on them; I could pick them up later.

I dressed quickly and strapped on my shoulder rig. I opened the drawer in the bedside table and took out a Beretta 92FS and its detached magazine. I checked the load of seventeen nine-millimeter Parabellum rounds, slid the magazine home, racked the slide, clicked the safety on, and put the weapon into the holster. I slipped my jacket on top and walked across the hotel room to a small writing desk, on which sat the other three items I would need. The first was a wallet containing an even thousand in cash, a driver's license in the name Carter Blake, and a platinum Amex card. The second item was a Dell Latitude laptop in a leather carry case. Finally, there was a set of keys for the car in the basement garage.

I reached for my cell phone and my hand froze. The phone had a screen saver that selected random images from memory, refreshed every fifteen minutes. It had chosen a picture I hadn't seen in a long time: a twentysomething woman with strawberry-blond hair and long eyelashes smiling at the camera and shielding her eyes from the sun. In the background, you could make out the curve of a Ferris wheel. Astroland, Coney Island. It's not there anymore. It was the only picture of Carol I kept.

I tapped the screen to kill the image and pocketed the phone.

Less than fifteen minutes after my cell had buzzed, I was behind the wheel of the car and on my way to Chicago.

3

The FBI building was located at 2111 West Roosevelt Road. It was a long slab of glass and concrete, ten stories high and wider than it was tall. It loomed behind a neat waist-high steel fence, on a perfectly level lawn that stretched out to meet the sidewalk. The sky had begun to lighten, but for the moment, the streetlamps and the lights illuminating the exterior of the building continued to burn.

I pulled through the main gate in the fence and stopped at a barrier. A uniformed security guard approached me as I rolled down the window. I told him my name was Blake and that I had a meeting with the special agent in charge, and he nodded as though he'd been expecting me. He touched the brim of his hat and waved me through as the barrier rose.

I checked my gun in at reception in exchange for a laminated visitor's badge, passed through a metal detector, and was escorted up to the tenth floor by an unsmiling agent who responded to my pleasantries with the occasional grunt. I was shown into an expansive office with a great view of the city at dawn. There was a big desk in front of the window. Behind the desk sat a man.

He was younger than I'd expected, perhaps not even fifty. He wore a top-of-the-line Brooks Brothers suit, button-down shirt, dark tie, rimless glasses. His jet-black hair was emphatically slicked back, with no attempt made to disguise the fact it was receding.

He made no effort to stand up and did not offer his hand. There was a thick file on his desk.

I stood at the doorway for a moment. The unsmiling agent who'd brought me up stepped back into the corridor, carefully closing the door behind him.

"Donaldson," I said, by way of hello.

"That's right. Blake, isn't it? You got here faster than I'd expected."

"Traffic was light."

"First time in Chicago?"

"First time in a long time."

Donaldson leaned forward in his chair and put his hands on the desk, as if to signal we had successfully negotiated the small-talk portion of the meeting. I took the hint. "So, you need to find somebody."

He paused a moment, as though reluctant to go further. "This information cannot leave this office."

"It's okay. I'm not on Twitter."

He didn't smile. "Do you know who Caleb Wardell is?"

The name was familiar, even though I hadn't followed the original case particularly closely. If you attain a certain level of celebrity, your name kind of seeps into the mass consciousness. "Of course," I said. "The sniper. But he's in jail, right?"

Donaldson said nothing.

"I see."

"He escaped from a prisoner transport van this morning. It looks like there was some kind of ambush, possibly Mob related. Wardell was caught up in it and managed to get loose."

"And you want that situation rectified before anybody finds out."

"In a nutshell."

"Can I ask a question?"

"Of course."

"Who recommended me?"

Donaldson's lips widened a quarter inch on each side of his mouth. I took it for his attempt at a smile. "Let's just say it was the kind of recommendation that's unwise to turn down."

"But you don't have to like it."

He sighed and stood up, placing both palms on the desk. "Look. Don't get me wrong. I can use all the help that's available. We're putting together a task force, and it's been suggested that you have certain specialized talents that might do some good, whether my people like it or not. And chances are, they're not going like it."

"That's okay. I have extensive experience with not being liked."

"I'm glad to hear it. I'm bringing the task force leads in for a briefing in an hour. Do you think you can help us?"

I nodded slowly. "You're aware of my terms?"

"I believe payment has already been discussed with your ... agent."

"Yes, but I have three rules before I take a job," I said.

"I'm listening."

"Number one: You pay me half up front, half when I catch your man. Number two: I work alone. I won't be coming into the office nine to five. I won't be joining the team for beers once we put this guy back inside. If you're buying me, you're buying an additional resource; that's all."

"And number three?"

"Number three is that if you're paying me to catch your guy, you're paying me to do it my way. My way is whatever works best. Sometimes it's entirely legal, sometimes not. What I need from you is an assurance that any reasonable steps I need to take in the course of my work that may be in technical violation of the law will not result in you going after me."

Donaldson's mouth was open to interrupt, but I held up a hand.

"I'll let you decide what's reasonable. I'm not asking for a blank check here."

His brow creased and he looked away from me, out the window. I walked forward five paces and took the seat in front of the desk. "It's a great view," I said, just to fill the silence.

"It's a great city, Mr. Blake."

"Spiritual home of the Bureau, right? This is where Hoover got started."

Donaldson turned back to me. "You know your history. Mr. Hoover built us up from nothing."

"And Mr. Dillinger helped him along a little too, of course."

His face was totally impassive. I couldn't tell if he was amused or offended. I extended my right hand across the desk. He looked at my hand as though he were a bomb disposal expert working on a type of device he hadn't seen before. "I decide what's reasonable?"

"That's what I said."

Donaldson studied me for a moment. Then he reached out and shook my hand. "Welcome aboard."

4

9:05 a.m.

Despite her best efforts, Special Agent Elaine Banner was late.

The call had come in just after eight o'clock, summoning her to an emergency meeting with the SAC at nine sharp.

That meant she'd been forced to leave ten minutes into the first PTA meeting she'd managed to attend all year. Another discarded obligation, another letdown for Annie. She didn't suppose this one would register as high on the scale as the time she'd had to fly to Indianapolis on Annie's birthday, but she knew the small disappointments added up all the same. The guilt was a constant, nagging presence. Banner had actually thought it would be easier once Mark moved out, but that illusion hadn't survived long.

There was one slender compensation for her lousy work–life balance: Her abrupt departure had not attracted the usual smug head tilts and smiles from the other mothers. They all knew what she did for a living, and she knew they'd all read the feature that had appeared in the *Times* last year, after the Markow case. Even as she hustled out the door, she sensed her departure send a frisson of vicarious excitement through the classroom: Annie's FBI-agent mom leaving abruptly following an urgent phone call.

After that, all that lay between Annie's school and the Chicago headquarters of the Federal Bureau of Investigation was a city of three million in the midst of rush hour. All things considered, Banner thought as she pushed through the opaque glass conference room doors, five minutes late was respectable.

The room was bright, spacious, and sparsely furnished. Just a long boardroom table, some chairs, and a coffee machine in the far corner. There were four men already in the room: two spaced apart with their backs to the door, two sitting closer together on the other side of the table. She recognized the latter pair as Assistant Special Agent in Charge Dave Edwards and the SAC himself: Walter F. Donaldson. They were mismatched. Edwards was sixty, heavyset, wore a cheap suit, and was sweating despite the season. Donaldson, though he had seniority, was younger and dressed with style and care.

The two men on her side of the table had turned to look at her as she entered. She didn't recognize the guy sitting farthest from the door, but the one closest to her was Steve Castle. *Damn.* Castle was in his late forties, but despite the gray streaks in his hair, he could pass for a decade younger. The look on his face said that he didn't think five minutes late was at all respectable.

"Sorry I'm late," Banner said, taking the seat nearest the door.

Edwards and Donaldson murmured pleasantries; Castle looked at her in stony silence. The fourth man smiled briefly, but with warmth. He looked ... *nondescript* was the word, she supposed. Average height, average build, dark hair, a clean shave. Good-looking, she guessed, but nothing special. The kind of guy you'd find it difficult to provide a distinguishing description of if you had to. He wore a nice suit but no tie, so she knew he wasn't Bureau, if nothing else.

Banner took all this in with a glance, then turned away. She noted the table was entirely clear except for a neatly squared pile of photographs, facedown in front of Edwards.

"Now that we're all here," Donaldson said, the merest trace of a South Boston accent in his delivery, "I'll get straight to the point. We have a situation."

Banner looked on, nodding. Of course they had a situation. She just wondered what variety of situation. Perhaps the president had changed his mind again about visiting the city before the midterm elections.

Donaldson turned his head to Edwards like a news anchor handing over to a junior colleague for the spade work.

Edwards glanced at Banner and then at Castle, as though ensuring they were both paying attention. "This morning, around three a.m., a transport van carrying two prisoners from USP Marion to the federal correction complex at Terre Haute was ambushed on a county highway, about ten miles out." Edwards stopped to take a breath, as though the sentence had been an exertion. "We have a coordinated mixed scene out there, our people assisting local law enforcement. Looks like there were only two marshals on board, both killed. There was no escort. We're still trying to find out why, given the status of the passengers."

"Who were they moving?" Castle asked.

Edwards looked a little peeved at being interrupted. Which was disingenuous, Banner thought, given the pregnant pause he'd left there. Edwards leaned back in his chair, which creaked. "We believe the target of the attack was this man." He held up one of the pictures: a glossy eight-by-ten color mug shot of a weedy, balding man of about forty, the hint of a wry smile at the corners of his mouth. The nameplate he held at chest level spelled out MITCHELL, C. J. in blocky letters.

"Clarence James Mitchell. Photograph taken about four months ago. He'd been awaiting trial on charges including racketeering, aggravated assault, and rape."

Banner studied the picture. The Bureau's involvement made sense already, given the racketeering charge, and so did Edwards's interest: She knew his background was in the Organized Crime section. But why were she and Castle there? Neither currently worked OC. She shot a glance at Castle, who looked like he was also in the dark.

"Mitchell was due to turn state's evidence on one Vitali Korakovski," Edwards continued, "one of our high-value targets in the Russian Mob. We've confirmed that the three men who carried out the ambush were Korakovski soldiers."

Banner tilted her head in surprise. How could the number

23

and identities of the attackers have been established so quickly without any surviving witnesses? Unless ...

"What do you mean 'were'?" she asked before she could stop herself. He'd stressed that word a little too much.

Edwards smiled. Evidently, she seemed to have hit on the right moment to ask a question. "I mean they're not anymore, Agent Banner." He held up three more photographs, one by one. Vivid color close-ups of dead men's faces, snapped where they lay in a barren field. All except the last one, who didn't have a face, or much of a head. "Zakhar Radev, Nikolai Kosygin ... and we're reasonably sure this one was Vladimir Labazanov," he said, introducing the photographs. "Three tier-one badasses, all taken out by one man who started out unarmed and handcuffed."

Banner was suddenly aware that Edwards was talking exclusively to her and Castle, ignoring the fourth man, who was listening with interest, but not reacting as if to new information. *He's been briefed already, whoever he is*, Banner realized.

Castle sat back in his chair, incredulous. He waved his left hand at the mug shot of Mitchell, now lying discarded on the table. "You mean to say *this* guy did *that*?"

Edwards looked pleased with himself, obviously enjoying drip-feeding the information this way. He shook his head slowly, producing another photo. Banner saw Donaldson wince and thought it was less a signifier of squeamishness than of mild embarrassment, like somebody had made an off-color joke that had lowered the tone of a dinner party.

"Clarence James Mitchell, photograph taken around four hours ago," Edwards said matter-of-factly. "Somebody hit him with a heavy blunt object—probably the butt of a shotgun—and kept hitting him until his face caved in. Then they pounded the mess into the ground a little more."

"Who was the other prisoner?" Banner asked distractedly. She was absorbed in studying the photograph, morbidly fascinated by the juxtaposition of the mess of pulped flesh, splintered bone, and brain matter with the smirking mug shot she'd seen a minute earlier.

Edwards didn't say anything. He looked a little disappointed at Banner's reaction, like he'd expected her to close her eyes or shudder or run from the room screaming. She was glad to disappoint him, but it hadn't been deliberate. Bloody crime scenes didn't faze her; they never had. Everyone told her that that was unusual, that it should take time to become desensitized, but for whatever reason, it was an adjustment she'd never had to make.

Donaldson put both palms on the table, wordlessly indicating to Edwards that he would field the question. He glanced at Banner and Castle before speaking. "This is where we come to our problem. It transpires that the second prisoner was fairly ... 'high value' himself." He nodded at Edwards without looking at him as he reused the phrase. "This second man killed all three Russians, most likely in self-defense, and then killed Mitchell, most likely for the sheer hell of it. He's armed, he has military training, and we don't have clue one where he's headed.

"I guess it would be redundant at this point to say he's a highly dangerous individual, but he's also highly motivated to stay free. He was scheduled for lethal injection in two weeks."

That explained why he was being moved to Terre Haute, Banner realized—Haute being the location of federal death row. And that meant the prisoner had to be ...

"Caleb Wardell?" Castle said. Banner thought it sounded like a question, but then she realized it was just that he wanted to be wrong.

Donaldson sighed as Edwards held up the last photograph from the pile.

"Caleb Wardell," he confirmed flatly.

The photograph showed the head, shoulders, and upper chest of a lean, yet powerfully built man in an orange jumpsuit. Neck muscles taut. Charles Manson beard. Cold, expressionless eyes.

"Jesus," Castle said.

"The sniper?" Banner asked.

"The same," Edwards confirmed.

Castle and Banner exchanged a look, both knowing why they were here now.

"He killed twenty people last time," Castle said.

"Nineteen," Edwards said defensively, as though Castle were exaggerating the problem.

"And we want to make sure that doesn't happen again," Donaldson said. "Wardell was doing federal time. That means the Bureau's got it with immediate effect, not once it's had time to spiral out of control. The two of you will be heading up the task force."

"Great." Castle's tone was completely neutral.

Banner kept quiet. She'd sensed this coming and, despite herself, was exhilarated. Sure, it was a tall order, but it was the kind of tall order that made careers. The kind of tall order that could help her on the way to where she wanted to finish up in twenty years or so.

Donaldson let Castle's comment pass. "Agent Castle, you worked on the original case here in Chicago. I understand you were there when they got Wardell. Agent Banner, you recently distinguished yourself on the Markow manhunt. I have every confidence that we can run this fugitive down before the media gets ahold of the story."

Banner looked up at Donaldson as he casually dropped

that last element in. It was like being told you had to climb Everest tomorrow. Oh, and by the way, you'll be doing it blindfolded.

"The media doesn't have this yet?"

Head shake from Edwards. "They know that a prisoner transport van was ambushed and that two marshals were killed. We're holding back the rest as long as we can. That's why we need Wardell back in custody before anybody knows he's escaped."

"Good luck with that," Castle said. "They're going to have some pretty good hints as soon as Wardell decides to brush up on his old hobby."

"We think we have some latitude," Edwards said. "Wardell's psychotic, but he's not an idiot. Effectively, he's just been granted a stay of execution. He'll want to keep a low profile, maybe try to head for Canada. He's not going to start shooting random civilians again if he thinks he can get away clean."

"Which will make it harder to catch him, not easier," Banner pointed out.

Castle nodded agreement. "And he's trained in evading capture, even if we knew where he was headed."

"You caught him last time," Edwards said.

Castle looked at him for an uncomfortable few seconds, then spoke slowly, as though explaining something to a slow four-year-old: "*I* didn't. I was just there when we got lucky."

Donaldson sat back from the table, signifying his desire to move the discussion on. "I'm placing Agent Castle in charge of the task force. Agent Banner, you'll be secondary lead. Both of you will report directly to Assistant SAC Edwards or to me, no one else. I believe we have the best possible people to lead on this right here in this room." As he finished speaking, Donaldson shot a glance at the fourth man, whom

Banner had almost forgotten about. He'd somehow faded into the background as they'd been talking.

She looked at him now. Castle was looking, too. The man's expression remained impassive. Their inquisitive stares seemed to be absorbed by him with as little impact as a scream into a soundproofed wall.

"And exactly who do we have in this room, sir?" Castle asked, not taking his eyes off the fourth man.

The man let the question linger in the air for a moment, then said, "My name's Blake. I'm here to assist you."

5

9:22 a.m.

Nobody said anything for a moment. Four pairs of eyes settled on me, waiting for me to elaborate.

After it became clear I was leaving it at that, Agent Castle repeated what I'd said, slowly. "You're here to assist us."

I looked back at him. *Every time*, I thought. *Every time it's like this*.

Edwards, the fat one, didn't need the nod from his boss this time.

"As I tried to emphasize earlier, this manhunt is high priority. *Top* priority, in fact. The director has briefed the president, and they're both very keen to see this wrapped up as quickly as possible."

Castle looked back at him. "I bet they are. Especially a week before the midterms."

Donaldson shot Castle a glance that told him not to push

it. Edwards cleared his throat. "Bearing that in mind, we're bringing in all the expertise we have available. We've been allocated the services of Mr. Blake here, who's somewhat of a specialist in this particular area."

I watched Edwards with interest as he spoke, wondering how a guy like this had risen to such a senior position in an organization that, throughout its history, had placed so much importance on appearance. The stereotypical FBI agent is sleek, clean-cut, snappily dressed: Fox Mulder in *The X-Files*, or Anthony LaPaglia in that other show. Banner, Castle, and Donaldson all fit the bill. To me, Edwards looked more like a used-car salesman.

Castle had opened his mouth to speak, but Banner, who had been watching his complexion darken, butted in first, her tone carefully diplomatic: "With all due respect, sir," she began, addressing SAC Donaldson, "do you think this is a good idea?"

"Many hands make light work, Agent Banner. Isn't that what they say?" Edwards interjected before his boss had had a chance to respond, and neither Donaldson nor Banner looked like they welcomed the gesture.

I watched Banner's face as she arranged her thoughts. I decided she was probably trying to resist the easy comeback, the one about too many cooks. Instead, she said, "Everybody here knows the challenges of coordinating an effective task force, liaising with other agencies. Isn't bringing in a private operator just going to complicate things further?"

"So he's what," Castle said, "a bounty hunter?"

"Mr. Blake is on board in an advisory capacity," Edwards replied. "He'll be outside of the chain of command." From the look he shot Donaldson and the way his brow had furrowed since the discussion turned in this direction, I guessed that Edwards wasn't 100 percent happy with this arrangement.

"I'm not a bounty hunter," I said, addressing Castle. "I'm just somebody who's good at finding people who don't want to be found."

Agent Banner was leaning toward me now. Her long, shiny dark hair was tied back in a ponytail, and the gray skirt suit should have looked stuffy, but somehow it flattered the curves of her body. Her dark, dark brown eyes were sizing me up.

You always want to make a good impression on a client; that's just good business. I told myself that explained why I suddenly found myself wanting to get a passing grade.

"And in your ... advisory capacity, Mr. Blake, what would you suggest is our best course of action?" Her tone was even, betraying none of Castle's heavy skepticism. I didn't doubt that the skepticism was there; she was just a little more polished in her approach.

I looked at my watch. It was approaching nine thirty, which meant that our quarry had been on the loose for just over six hours. A quarter of a day. *Every time*, I thought again. Every time I worked with government agencies, I encountered this problem. Territory. Professional pride. Perceived loss of authority. I wondered if the slight was particularly pronounced for an FBI agent, far more used to being on the other side of the equation: swooping in to take the big case out of the hands of some backwoods cop. Which, of course, had already happened here. But I doubted any of them would see the irony of that if I pointed it out.

"We're wasting time," I said. "So I'm going to lay every-thing out for you: I'm not here to take your case away. I'm not here to show you how to do your job. I'm not here to take the credit. I'm here to offer my skills and get paid in return. All right?"

Castle opened his mouth to say something, but Donaldson,

obviously tiring of the delays, cut him off. "You're leading the task force, Agent Castle. That hasn't changed." He shot Castle a lingering look that supplied the unspoken coda: *but it could*.

Castle sat back in his chair. He looked like he was mentally organizing his worry list and deciding that, for the moment, this new element wasn't near enough to the top to dwell on any longer.

In the break in conversation that followed, my eyes were drawn to Wardell's mug shot, lying where Edwards had dropped it on the table. Like the name, the face was reasonably familiar. Or rather, the likeness was familiar. I guessed it was the picture they must have used on the front pages and the nightly bulletins around the trial.

But was that really what had drawn my attention back to the picture? There was something about the eyes. Something from the past that I couldn't quite put my finger on . . .

"Is there anything else we need to know at this time?" Banner asked Donaldson, snapping my attention back to the present.

"Not at this time," Edwards said.

Donaldson smiled coldly, wordlessly signaling that the meeting was over.

"Then he's right," Banner said. "We're wasting time. Let's get moving on this."

As if to underline the point, Donaldson's phone rang—a brief businesslike chirrup. It was an almost retro tone, like the way cell phones sounded in the nineties.

Donaldson tapped the screen and held the phone to his ear. He said his name and paused while the caller spoke. Then he took a sharp breath. He stood up slowly, turned around to face the plate-glass windows overlooking West Roosevelt Road, ten floors below. "When?" He paused again and swallowed after hearing the response. "How many?"

Edwards's jaw tensed as he watched Donaldson's face. Banner and Castle shared a glance. Donaldson cut the call off without saying anything else.

"There's a mall in a town called Cairo, about twenty miles south of the crime scene. Somebody just shot a deliveryman in the parking lot. Witnesses didn't see anyone approach him. They say he just fell down."

6

9:57 a.m.

Too soon, that was the problem. Too soon, or too early.

Wardell glanced at the sign as he passed it by at a scrupulously legal fifty-five miles per hour. Truck stop five miles, bus station seven, it told him, which meant that the truck stop was five and a half minutes away, give or take. Good. He needed to make a phone call, and he needed to change. Wardell was hardly slight in build, but the Russian's clothes were almost comically big on him.

A white car emerged from behind a bend in the road ahead and sped past. White, but not a police car. That reminded him that he should probably change the car as well, come to think of it. A pity—the Ford Taurus had only fifty thousand miles on the clock. It was a smooth ride and had reasonable trunk space. He even liked the color.

What had he been thinking about before the sign for the truck stop had distracted him? There were so many distractions on the outside, so many colors and lights and signs and

. . . variations. It would take some getting used to. Oh yes—
too soon, that was it. That was what he'd been thinking: He
had broken his long fast too soon.

Wardell regarded the killing of the fat delivery driver as
an embarrassing failure. It had taken two shots to kill the
man. *Two*. The first shot to the chest had missed the heart,
catching the driver midway between that point and the left
shoulder. Luckily, the guy had been too confused to fall
down, giving Wardell the opportunity to place the second
bullet on target and finish the job.

Two shots.

Sure, he could make excuses. He was out of practice, naturally, and firing an unfamiliar weapon cold-bore, but still . . .
he'd jumped back in too soon, acted too early. That had to
be the problem. He ought to have bided his time, put a few
hundred miles between himself and that field where he'd
left dead men like unharvested crops. The PSG1 from the
prisoner transport van had come with a full twenty-round
detachable box magazine. Not a lot of ammunition in the
scheme of things, but for a former United States Marine Scout
sniper it was plenty. He ought to have hunkered down in
the woods somewhere, spent a while investing some of those
rounds using deer or squirrels for target practice, gotten
properly acquainted with the weapon.

But then again, that's exactly what they'd have expected
him to do: play it safe, lie low, slink away like a chastised
schoolboy smarting from a punishment. No, that didn't
figure into his plans.

He thought back to that first shot. Visualized the ritual:
breathing in and out, regulating his heartbeat, selecting the
target, taking aim, squeezing the trigger. In the mental recon-
struction, he finally found himself able to admit what it was
that had made him miss. It hadn't been a lack of practice, or

33

even the new weapon. It had been something that Wardell had not encountered in a long, long time: fear. Fear that he'd lost it, that he wouldn't be able to make the shot.

Fear was the cold sweat that had prevented him from blanking his mind, the nagging voice that had whispered in his ear and broken the ritual.

But when that first round had gone a little wide of perfect, something had clicked back into place. All of a sudden, there was an urgent, time-sensitive task before him. A job to be finished. And so his mind had cleared and he'd waited for the next space between breaths, made a microscopic, instinctive adjustment, and put the second bullet where the first should have gone: right through the fat man's overworked heart.

He still had it; of that there was no doubt. The next one would prove it.

Wardell flicked his blinkers on and slowed to make the turn into the truck stop. It was a small, down-at-the-heels operation. An expanse of cracked and pitted concrete surrounding a series of squat, one-story buildings: a diner, a gas station, a convenience store. The buildings looked like they'd been thrown up in the midsixties and left to their own devices ever since, the only cosmetic update the rising gas prices on the sign. Wardell's eyes scanned the lot and the buildings, surveying the location for warning signs. He saw none, but still, he'd seen more inviting premises in Baghdad, post-shock and awe.

He made a wide, slow circuit of the lot. It was all but empty: three big rigs, a smattering of cars, no people in evidence. He parked the Ford at the far end facing a grassy slope and a line of trees. Almost, but not quite, the farthest point from the main buildings. He twisted the ignition key, cutting off both the engine and the radio midway through a local news report.

34

He'd been listening all the way down, flitting from station to station, looking for news. The death of the fat man hadn't made any of the bulletins yet, not even the local ones. That was no surprise. In Wardell's experience—and he had a lot—it generally took two, three hours minimum for a one-off murder to make the news. Less for the latest in an established series of killings, of course.

But there was no mention either of his escape, and given that more than seven hours had elapsed, that *was* a surprise. He should have been the lead story on every channel by now. His prison mug shot should have been flashed across the morning papers and on the news channels and the Web since the early hours. The fact that it hadn't been indicated that the cops or the feds or whoever were sitting on the information. They probably thought they could run him down before anybody noticed.

Wardell smiled, musing that his freshest kill would most likely cost some middle-echelon public servant his job. Not the guy who'd actually decided to cover up the escape, of course, but probably the next link down the chain of command.

"Hoping I'd keep out of trouble for a day or two?" he said aloud, adjusting the rearview mirror to examine his reflection. He shook his head slowly. "Sorry, boys."

Looking into his own cold blue eyes, it occurred to Wardell that this was the first real mirror he'd seen in half a decade. It was less forgiving than the shiny plastic in the prison. It showed the new wrinkles, the occasional lines of gray in his straggly beard. The eyes had stayed the same, though. He'd never picked up the glaze of defeat and regret that he'd seen in the other long-term inmates.

The media blackout wouldn't last much longer; he was certain of that. And so a change in appearance was necessary.

He fumbled in the glove box and came out with a pair of sunglasses. They were feminine in style, but not overtly so. The frames were dark brown and conservative. They would pass. He'd have liked there to have been some kind of hat, too, but he was out of luck on that score.

Not that it particularly mattered, of course. Covering his tracks had once been a necessity. Now it was more like good practice, something that would allow him to operate more freely. He'd be traced to this place—Lord knew his current appearance was memorable enough—but he knew how to make the trail go cold from this point. Until the next kill, of course.

He got out of the car, locking it using the key remote, and walked toward the gnarled knot of buildings. It was cold, and there was a light but nagging breeze. He felt the over-sized clothes flap around his body like some kind of gown.

He passed the diner and stopped at the convenience store, pushing the glass door inward and hearing a little bell toll at his entrance. At the far end of the store was a female clerk behind a counter. She was small and doughy and frump-ish—could have been anywhere between twenty-two and fifty. Her gaze lingered on Wardell for a second longer than average. Which was about right for somebody looking at a man with clothes three sizes too big, a bum's beard, and DIY bandages made from clothing strips on his wrists and forearms.

Wardell watched her for signs. She didn't gasp. She didn't look down to compare his face with a recently received police wanted sheet.

He nodded to her and moved into the store. He made his way from section to section, efficient but not hurrying. He selected a first aid box and a men's grooming kit, which included a pair of nail scissors, and also a razor and a can of shave gel for sensitive skin. He found the section that sold souvenir clothing to tourists and selected a pair of jeans in his size, together with a lime-green T-shirt with a hot-pink motif. Lastly, he stopped by the chilled section and chose a sandwich—tuna on rye—and a caffeine-free Diet Coke. He didn't like any substance that affected his moods, coordination, or reaction time.

He was turning toward the counter when a red and black jacketed book, one of many similar paperbacks on a swivel stand, caught his eye. He grinned and plucked it from its slot. It was called *Summer of Terror: On the Trail of the Chicago Sniper*, by Sheriff John Hatcher. He thumbed through it, smiling at the memories evoked by the glossy pictures in the middle. He raised an eyebrow when he saw the picture of the house Hatcher had bought with the proceeds of his celebrity. He wondered how much Hatcher would relish a rematch, given that he appeared to be taking all the credit for stopping him the first time.

Wardell shelved the idea for later and put the book back. His ultimate goal was still the same, but it wouldn't do him any harm to line up some warm-up targets, aside from the one he already had in mind.

He approached the counter, letting the clerk see him up close now. She was trying not to stare, but was plainly curious. No doubt about it: He'd be identified later. If he hadn't been already, that was. If he had been, there was a cheap ballpoint pen tied to the counter with a length of string, and that would be all he'd need to resolve the immediate problem. Wardell studied the clerk's face until she looked away. He was reasonably convinced he hadn't been recognized. That was good. Wardell hated a mess.

She scanned the items he placed on the counter, raising an eyebrow at the green shirt, and told him how much it came to. He took four tens from a brown leather ladies' wallet and paid, giving her a knowing smile. That puzzled her.

You'll be telling the grandkids about this moment, girlie, Wardell thought as the woman returned his smile with visible unease.

7

10:13 a.m.

The truck stop's public bathrooms were cold and filthy and they stank. But they were also deserted, and they had sinks and running water. Real mirrors again, too.

Wardell stripped to the waist and washed up in one of the sinks. It was porcelain, not stainless steel like the one in his cell. There was a choice of chilled or scalding water, but he managed to achieve a balance by blocking the drain with paper towels and filling the sink. He ducked his head in, soaking his face and beard and holding his breath. He held it for two minutes, enjoying the sensory deprivation.

After years of holding his memories in check, he let them flood back in. Toward the end of his submersion, as the pounding in his temples rose to a crescendo, he could almost hear the gunshots echoing across the years. He remembered blood and heat and dirt. He remembered pulling the trigger again and again, seeing the blood spray up close, hearing the cries of pain and fear. And he remembered being interrupted.

Slowly, he raised his head out before expelling a long, slow breath. He'd been thwarted twice now. Once over there and once in Chicago. He felt like a bowstring, pulled taut and then held interminably. This time, no one would stop him.

Some target practice first—and target practice was an end in itself, as far as pleasure went. And then some scores settled, to send a message as much as anything else. And then the finale. Before they'd caught him, he'd planned on hitting a mall or a movie theater or a subway station—the venue didn't really matter, as long as there were lots of people in a confined space. And then? Then he'd keep shooting until he ran out of ammunition or was cut down himself.

He looked into his own eyes again, fascinated with the reflection. Had incarceration made him vain, or would the novelty wear off soon?

The face had to change, along with the clothes. That death row mug shot would be everywhere once the story broke—and it would, sooner rather than later. But equally, he couldn't simply trim his hair and go clean-shaven either, because they'd also run his service photo—twenty-two-year-old Caleb Wardell in his BDUs, seated demurely in front of the Stars and Stripes. They'd be looking for him both ways: bearded serial killer, or clean-shaven, buzz-cut Captain America. A happy medium was required. He lifted the nail scissors he'd bought in the store and began hacking away at the beard, laying the groundwork for the shave.

Ten minutes later, he'd been transformed. He hadn't cut the hair, but had instead pulled it back tightly from his forehead, tying it in a short ponytail using an elastic band he'd found in the Ford's glove box. The straggly beard had vanished, trimmed down to a neat goatee with razor edges. He looked a little pale, a little gaunt, a little older than he remembered, but otherwise pretty good. The hair and the goatee was an entirely new look for him, and he thought it made him look a little like an indie movie actor, or perhaps a beat poet. The important thing was that he looked nothing like a convict or a soldier.

So what's the next step, soldier?

He knew what the next steps were: target practice and scores settled. He had a list now, having had time to think about it. It was a list he could keep in his head—there were only four names on it so far. But that was okay; there was plenty of room for more.

He put the sunglasses back on and went back outside. There was a pay phone on the wall. It was the kind with rudimentary Internet access, which gave him an idea. He inserted some quarters and set up a basic webmail account with an anonymous name. Then he put in some more change and made a five-minute call to a number he'd memorized.

When he was done, he looked around, surveying his position. The restrooms were out of the line of sight from the gas station, so the clerk wouldn't be able to see his new look, but he kept his head down and walked away quickly anyway. He crossed the parking lot in the direction of the blue Ford. He opened the rear door and reached inside to grip the handles of the black duffel. He'd found it in the trunk earlier, and it was surprisingly roomy. After some thought, he'd left the original contents—a towel and athletic clothes—inside, to add bulk and to prevent the bag settling around the rifle. He hauled the bag out and closed the door. There was no need to lock it this time. He walked away from the Ford and climbed the steep grassy slope to the tree line, emerging on the side of the highway. He squinted east into the sun and saw the glass and aluminum of the small provincial bus station glint in the light two miles distant.

Time to get moving.

8

12:05 p.m.

I had never known the soldier's name, and so the name Caleb Wardell had meant nothing to me when it was splashed across all those front pages all those years before.

Although I'd probably seen the mug shot a couple of dozen times in the media, I'd never taken a closer look. Not just because of the beard and the prison coveralls. But because, from a cursory glance, it looked like all the photographs of that type do: It looked like a man who was crazy and dangerous and pleased with himself. The killer's name and the picture that went with it were unwanted background noise—like a summer pop song, or a ubiquitous commercial. They didn't belong to the world in which I lived and worked, and so I'd never had a reason to take a closer look, to scratch below the surface, to see the familiarity.

But the old photograph in the file left no doubt. There was no mistaking the smiling young Marine in front of the flag that stared out at me. No mistaking those eyes.

Mosul. 2008. It was 112 degrees in the shade. Too many foreigners there for too many different reasons. By then, it had been a long time since Saddam had fallen, and whatever goodwill that had generated among the locals had long since evaporated like piss on hot sand. They didn't want us there. They sure as hell didn't want the insurgents there—particularly those who'd taken it on themselves to come on vacation from Pakistan to wage their holy war in somebody else's backyard.

The resentment wasn't just projected across races or

nationalities; it was internecine too. The military didn't want the CIA there, sneaking around, probably starting shit that would make life harder for the grunts. And neither of them wanted the mercenaries there: those Blackwater assholes making big trouble and small fortunes in equal measure.

And as for us? Nobody wanted us there either. As usual, nobody knew exactly who we were or why we were there. They didn't need to know in order to form an opinion about us. I guess most people figured we were with one of the other groups. Some of the CIA guys had an inkling, had heard one or two whispered code names for something that had no name. They knew enough to know how much was being kept from them. And that was why they *really* hated us.

Mosul. Summer of 2008. Muhammad Rassam. A routine assignment, the best-laid plans royally fucked up by one rogue element with two cold blue eyes.

I'd looked into them and realized the owner didn't give a shit whether I pulled the trigger or not. Those eyes conveyed no fear, no emotion, only the cold single-mindedness of a great white shark.

A dozen dead civilians. One dead million-dollar asset. All because of this cold killer. But I'd followed my orders, and now ...

"We're here."

I looked up to see Agent Banner staring across the narrow aisle of the Learjet at me. "You ready for this? You don't look too ... alert." She was looking at me in the manner of a big sister forced to take her kid brother along to a party.

"Just thinking. Let's go."

She held my gaze a minute longer, skeptical. Then she shot a wary glance at Castle, who was already heading for the open door of the jet. She looked back at me. "You mind if I drive?"

I shook my head and looked back down at the file in my hand.

Caleb Wardell. I knew his name now. And twenty dead civilians and counting said I should have put him down when I had the chance.

9

12:22 p.m.

Banner kept her eyes on the road for the most part, occasionally flicking them to the right to see what Blake was doing. He was still reading the Wardell file, seemingly deep in concentration. He hadn't spoken since the plane, hadn't even glanced out of the window as far as she'd noticed. If not for the whisper of paper as he turned a sheet every few seconds, she could almost forget he was there at all. In the silence, her thoughts shifted to her daughter. Helen—her sister—would be picking Annie up from school as usual, but it was looking likely that she'd have to call and ask her to keep her overnight. Again.

She shelved the familiar concerns for the moment to focus her attention on overtaking a giant semi. The midmorning traffic was moderate. Although they'd yet to hit rain, they seemed to be chasing it, since the road ahead was perpetually glistening.

This had been Castle's idea, her driving from the airport to the crime scene with Blake. He'd taken her aside as they exited the conference room. Personal animosity had temporarily disappeared from his voice—from his point of view,

43

she was on his side for the moment. As he watched the other three men, he kept his voice low. "Keep an eye on him," he'd said. "See if you can work him out."

Work him out. She'd agreed readily enough back in the corridor, but thinking about it now, that vague instruction seemed to Banner to carry a lot of demands: Can he help us? Is he going to get in the way, or worse? And can we trust him?

Who is he?

So far, Banner had carried out only the first part of Castle's request: keeping an eye on Blake. Not exactly an achievement, given the fact they were side by side in a gray Bureau SUV doing eighty on the highway. As for the second part, she was no wiser about Blake than she had been when they left the building.

Initially, her strategy had been to give him the cold shoulder. Perhaps that would encourage him to open up. Blake would probably want to get Banner to warm to him, if only to make her easier to work with. Her strategy had failed miserably. Either he was playing the same game—and doing it a good deal more effectively—or he really was as engrossed in that file as he seemed. Reluctantly, she decided to attempt conversation. It felt like a small defeat, like she was blinking first in a staring contest. "Doing your homework?" she asked, making sure to keep her tone cool.

Blake raised his head from the file. He looked slightly disoriented for a second, as though he had just awakened from a trance, and she knew then that his silence had not been part of a strategy. "Sorry." He smiled. "I get tunnel vision sometimes."

Something in his smile managed to pierce her guard a little, and Banner realized that she had been wrong before: He didn't look nondescript at all. Sure, the impression his appearance left you with was "everyman," but now that she'd spent a little more time with him, she couldn't help notice the determined line of his jaw, the striking green eyes that seemed to gaze through to your innermost thoughts. She turned her own eyes back to the road quickly. "I don't care if you don't say anything at all."

If Blake noticed the slight, he didn't let on. "Just getting caught up on Wardell. Some piece of work, huh?"

His accent was another thing about him that was difficult to place. Not that it seemed out of place, exactly—more that it was difficult to pin down to any *one* place. Blake's voice usually had a generic East-Coast cadence, but occasionally it sounded as though it hailed from farther afield, with an almost British feel. It was the voice of someone who had not grown up in a single, settled community.

Banner nodded curtly at Blake's assertion. She hadn't worked the original Wardell case; it had been a long, stiflingly hot summer that year, and she had been working bank robbery. But of course she'd followed the killings with the morbid fascination that everyone else in the Bureau had. Everyone else in the country, for that matter.

"I thought you jacked in the death penalty in Illinois," Blake said after a minute.

"We did," she answered. "The state did, I mean. But one of the charges Wardell was convicted on was kidnapping. That allowed the DA to bundle everything in as a federal case, which meant he was eligible for death."

"Eligible for death," Blake repeated thoughtfully. Then he shrugged and looked back down at the file. Banner kept looking at the road. The sun found a gap in the clouds and flashed dazzle off the wet road. Banner reached over and located a pair of sunglasses in the glove box. Blake turned more pages; the odometer notched up another three miles before she gave in again and looked at him.

"You're familiar with the original case?"

"Just what was in the papers," he said. He didn't look up from the file, but she could see the edge of a small smile that told her he knew how much that counted for. "I was out of the country at the time."

Out of the country doing what? was the question that occurred. Instead, she asked: "So what do you think now? Could you have caught him any faster?"

Blake looked up. Banner looked back at the road. He waited ten seconds before replying, and she realized it was a technique. He was letting the animosity drain out of the question before answering it at face value.

"I'd have done some things differently," he said. "But I think you would have, too."

"Would I?"

"It was a multijurisdictional mess. Throw in media hysteria and some lucky breaks for the killer, and you people were up against a practically impossible task."

Annoyingly, his assessment was correct, fair-minded even. The hunt for the man the papers had inevitably dubbed the Chicago Sniper had been characterized by interdepartmental wrangling, political interference, and screwups at both bureaucratic and operational levels. The media, initially supportive, had grown impatient as the bodies piled up. When Wardell was finally run down, they had turned nasty, especially once it emerged he was the ex-boyfriend of the first victim. He was also a disgruntled ex-Marine, to whom the psych profile of the killer fit like a wet suit. Just to ice the cake, the son of a bitch had actually been *interviewed* live on CNN as a horrified witness in the aftermath of the tenth and eleventh shootings.

When you added those facts to the public infighting and some well-publicized slipups, the consensus opinion of the

46

national media and a few million armchair sleuths was that a ten-year-old child could have put a stop to the killings as soon as they'd begun.

Never mind that the family of the ex-girlfriend—Mia Jennings—had never met Wardell and didn't even know she had a boyfriend. Never mind that his home town was Birmingham, Alabama, and that there was nothing on record to place him in Chicago. Never mind, either, that he was a professional killer doing what he was trained to do, with the deck stacked squarely in his favor. None of that mattered, because it complicated the narrative the media had decided on—that the cops and the feds and the governor had screwed up, and nineteen people had lost their lives because of it.

In the end, it had been a veteran city detective who had made the breakthrough, tying Wardell to the killings and enabling the task force to make the arrest. They hadn't expected to take him alive, so it had been a surprise when Wardell had held up his hands and gone quietly. Thinking about it, it was Banner's opinion that his surrender had been part of the problem. If he'd fought back, gone down in a hail of bullets the way everyone had expected, it would have been a more satisfying resolution for many. Some of the shortcomings of the investigation might have been forgiven in return for a dramatic conclusion. But the bastard had just put up his hands and turned himself in, like it was all a game. Which only reinforced the belief among the media that the authorities had screwed up, rather than that Wardell had carried out his campaign so effectively. The unspoken question in the news reports and on the talk show monologues was *How hard can it have been?*

"How about you?" Blake asked after a minute. "Were you involved?"

Banner shook her head. "Agent Castle worked the case."

Blake looked away from her and watched the road. "He doesn't seem to relish the thought of another go-round."

"No, he doesn't."

"You don't like him." An observation, not a question.

"He's an excellent agent," she said, realizing immediately that by evading Blake's point she'd merely confirmed it.

More silence. Banner used it to think about why she didn't like Castle, or more accurately, why he didn't like her. It all went back to Markow, last year. What had happened there hadn't been her fault; she was sure of it, but Castle disagreed. Another four miles passed. It was Blake who spoke first this time.

"I don't get how this happens."

Banner looked at him, waiting for him to continue.

"How he escapes, I mean. Only two guards in the van, pretty minimal security, really."

"It shouldn't have happened," Banner agreed.

"Which leaves only two options."

"Yeah," she said. "Somebody screwed up, or somebody was paid to screw up."

"Any bets?"

Banner grimaced. The answer to the question was obvious, but she knew he was more interested in how candid she'd be than her opinion itself. "Those Russians knew exactly where to be."

"I agree. But knowing how it happened doesn't exactly help us. Just like knowing where to be didn't help the Russians in the end."

That made Banner consider an angle she'd overlooked. "What do you think their boss will do about this?"

"Korakovski?" Blake shrugged. "I doubt it registers as more than an inconvenience. He wanted Mitchell dead;

mission accomplished. Unlike the old-time Mafia, these guys are not noted for their sentimentality."

"Wouldn't it be a respect thing, though? Wouldn't he want some kind of payback for his men?"

"Maybe if we were talking about a rival outfit, but we're not. Wardell's a force of nature they happened to run afoul of. An unforeseeable consequence. Like ... bad weather. No insult taken."

"Bad weather," she repeated, thinking that was exactly what was ahead of them, literally and figuratively.

There was another lull in conversation. That's what it was now, a conversation. Progress, but she still didn't know anything new about Blake, other than that he'd spent time out of the country and seemed familiar with the group psychology of the Russian Mafia.

"You 'find people who don't want to be found,'" she said, giving the quote a singsong inflection.

"That's what would be on the business cards. If I had any."

"Been doing it long?"

"Feels like it."

"Have you always worked for yourself, or did you start out someplace else? The Agency, perhaps?" It was a shot in the dark, and she didn't hold out much hope that it was on target. Banner had met and worked with a number of CIA operatives, and Blake didn't fit the profile.

Blake smiled and shook his head, as though brushing off an unintended slight. He took a pair of sunglasses from inside his coat and put them on. Banner wondered if his intention was to shut out the glare from the road, or something else.

When he didn't answer, she probed further. "Is the money good?"

Blake took in a long breath through his nostrils, as though

giving the question great thought. Finally he nodded. "Depending on the client."

"And who are your clients?"

"Anybody who wants somebody found."

She glanced away from the road to give him a sarcastic look.

He tilted his head in mild apology. "Sometimes it's police, or government. Sometimes big companies. Sometimes individual people."

"Individual *rich* people," she corrected.

"I do some pro bono. It's not just about the money."

"Then what? The challenge?"

"Yeah. Among other things."

The first roadblock came into view ahead of them, and as though choreographed, they finally hit the rain they'd been chasing. It was fairly light, but quickly misted the windshield. Time up. Banner was frustrated at her lack of progress: She still knew next to nothing about this guy. Least of all, whether she could trust him. She flicked the wipers onto intermittent and slowed as they approached the county police units blocking the road, reaching into her jacket for her identification.

"In that case," she said, nodding at the Wardell file, "you're going to enjoy yourself on this case."

10

My first thought was that the kill scene was just about perfect for the purpose for which it had been selected.

I surveyed the parking lot of the strip mall. It was square, surrounded by trees on two sides, the highway on the third side, the cluster of modestly proportioned stores lined up on the fourth. Although the lot was packed full of cars—every one of them now held temporarily hostage by the authorities—it was effectively a wide-open space. A person standing anywhere in the lot, even between two cars, would be completely exposed from the chest up. The orderly grid of parked vehicles dictated movement as well, made a pedestrian's motion predictable by limiting it to the aisles and spaces in between. The trees provided excellent cover for a man patiently selecting and acquiring a target, as well as for his subsequent escape. They also acted as an effective windbreak, not that the wind would have posed a professional like Wardell any problem.

Yes, it was a virtually perfect small-town killing ground, suggesting that this was a case of a random victim selected for his presence in a specific location, rather than a random location to kill a specific victim. In my mind, the information I'd absorbed from the file had already begun coalescing into the beginnings of a theory, a prediction of events to come. This development didn't directly contradict that line of thought, but it didn't exactly support it either. I reminded myself to concentrate on the present. The big picture would take care of itself in time.

The entire parking lot was sealed off right up to the tree line and the road and up to the storefronts on the far side. Banner flashed her identification at a female cop manning the perimeter. The cop gave us a mildly resentful glare but stepped aside, and we ducked under the yellow tape. Clearly, the Bureau had already reassigned the locals to guard detail.

"I didn't even know we had a Cairo in Illinois," she remarked, saying it like the Egyptian capital.

"Care-oh," I corrected. "This one's pronounced differently."

"He's right," the female cop said, keeping her back to us.

"How the hell did you know that?" Banner said.

I shrugged. It was just one of those things I happened to know. I'd worked in the Egyptian Cairo a few years before, and I found it difficult to imagine two places more different.

"Care-oh," Banner repeated thoughtfully.

We began crossing the lot, moving roughly diagonally in a staircase pattern dictated by the parked vehicles. Every bay was full, some cars had taken impromptu spaces on grass verges. The rain was so light that it was more like mist. I glanced side to side as we walked, taking in the scene.

Police cars lined the highway bordering the lot. There was a large crowd gathered outside the row of stores, as close to the tape as they could get. It comprised about equal parts civilian gawkers and uniformed workers from the stores smoking cigarettes. I wondered if the stores had been evacuated, or if this level of excitement triggered a de facto town holiday. The audience was crowded behind a barrier at the small staff parking area, below a number of big red signs offering grave warnings about unauthorized parking. A burly cop stood in the one vacant staff bay, keeping a close eye on the crowd, as though he expected them to surge forward at any moment.

Within the taped-off area, the focus of activity seemed to be a spot near the entrance to a supermarket. Suits and uniforms were crowded around something on the ground. Close by, an enormous blue and gray FBI mobile command center truck was taking up the entire delivery bay. Banner was making a beeline for the area.

She moved surely through the glass and aluminum maze, not once glancing behind to check whether I was following. One of the news helicopters hovering a couple hundred feet above adjusted its insectlike gaze to follow the two new figures advancing across the lot. I turned my face downward, away from the cameras, grimacing as the downdraft created its own windchill, unfettered by the trees.

A dark-suited agent greeted us as we reached the crowd of cops and feds. He checked Banner's ID again and eyed me suspiciously when she said, "He's with me." A gap in the outer ring of people opened up, and we stepped through it into the core crime scene. There was a smaller ring of people within. I saw Castle, another agent, and a couple of crime scene techs in blue jackets. They were grouped around the first victim. Grimly, I acknowledged to myself that this was exactly how I was thinking of this one: only the first.

It was the corpse of a big man. He was wearing tight tan chinos, a brown shirt, and a baseball cap that had toppled off his head, either as he fell or on impact with the ground. He was lying faceup, eyes staring with disinterest at the overcast sky, two entrance wounds in his upper body. One of them, evidently the fatal one, had drilled dead center through the breast pocket on the left side of the shirt. Because of the way the man had fallen, the scene didn't look too bloody. I knew that if the body was rolled over, a much bigger mess would be evident. Big, fist-sized exit wounds would be punched through the victim's back.

One of the crime scene guys noticed my stare, read my thoughts: "What you'd expect: high-velocity rifle round. Looks like a 7.62 NATO, or similar. Lot of damage. The first shot wasn't immediately fatal, but it probably would have been in a couple of minutes."

"Because of the blood loss."

"That or hydrostatic shock," he agreed. "You catch one of these suckers, you ain't coming back."

Banner had gone straight to the body and crouched down beside it. She examined the wounds first, then the face, then did a quick survey of the body.

"Have we ID'd him yet?" she asked nobody in particular.

The agent standing beside Castle answered her. "Terry Daniels, forty-four years old, wife and four kids."

"Any doubt whatsoever this is our boy?"

Castle shook his head in response to Banner's question. "We've shut everything down within a thirty-mile radius. Local cops, county sheriff's department, and our guys are all over the area." He looked down at the body and shook his head again. "Of course, if he has a vehicle, all of that came about an hour too late. But if he's on foot, he might still be inside the net."

I was busy examining the two gunshot wounds. If it was Wardell, this was a first. I gestured at the victim. "Two shots this time."

Castle shrugged. "Maybe he's getting rusty."

"I knew there had to be some good news," Banner said.

I shook my head, thinking about the nineteen perfect kills the first time around. Nineteen shots, nineteen kills—an outstanding ratio, even for a Marine Corps sniper. I'd only scratched the surface of the psych profiling, but that statistic told me all I needed to know about Wardell's likely reaction. "It's not good news. Now he has something to prove."

"I'm so glad we invited you along," Castle said dryly.

I ignored him, my mind suddenly a few thousand miles and a few years away. Wardell being led away, throwing a look back in my direction, a look that said *I'll be seein' you.* A man who settled his scores.

"This is a warm-up," I said. "He'll move on to specific hits soon. His enemies. People who he thinks have wronged him."

Banner was still crouched next to the body. Her eyes flicked up to me, and for the first time I heard irritation in her voice. "Were you paying attention to the file? That's completely inconsistent with the established MO."

"It's not inconsistent at all," I said. "And the conditions on the ground have changed. He's a soldier. Soldiers adapt."

"Wardell's an indiscriminate killer," Castle said. "We won't catch him with *who*; we have to think about *where*. Maybe you need a little more time to catch up, Blake. I'm sure we can find you someplace quiet to study."

I glanced at the body again. "The last thing Wardell is," I said, "is indiscriminate. You believe that, you're making a big mistake."

Castle took a step forward. "Excuse me?"

Banner sighed and stood up, smoothing the front of her skirt down and subtly moving between us. "So what do you think?" she asked me. "Is he still in the area?"

I looked at the corpse again. It partially obscured the phrase NO PARKING, painted on the ground in white foot-high letters. "I don't know," I said slowly, thinking. I knew I was missing something, something potentially important.

Castle was looking at me with open contempt. "Wonderful."

"So for now," Banner said, "we focus on the thirty-mile radius."

"All we can do," Castle agreed. "We're looking in every

55

backseat and trunk of every vehicle leaving the area. No reports of any stolen cars anywhere in the vicinity this morning. We've got people making house-to-house inquiries, roadblocks, air support. In the meantime, if anyone has any idea how we get the media to not notice a fucking state-wide manhunt, I'm all ears."

That was when I realized what was wrong. It was right there in front of me, painted in white foot-high letters.

"Has anybody talked to the stores?"

"You mean for witnesses?" the young agent asked.

I shook my head. "About their employees. Did anybody not show up for work today?"

Castle was losing patience. "I think they might have a little more on their minds than one of the bag packers taking a personal day. Have you seen those people?" He waved a hand in the direction of the crowd. "It's like the goddamn circus is in town."

"I've seen them," I said. "And they're standing over by the staff-only bays, right by what is literally the only empty space in this lot."

"Meaning?" Castle snapped.

"Meaning there's a good chance that spot was vacated around the time of the killing, right before the police locked everything down. And meaning there's a good chance that whatever vehicle was in that spot belonged to a member of staff, one who hasn't reported—or who hasn't been able to report—their car stolen."

I half expected Castle to shut me down, but in this I was pleasantly surprised. Castle thought it over for a couple of seconds. Beneath it all, maybe he was too much of a professional to discount a possible lead, however much he might dislike its source. His voice was cautious when he spoke. "Not necessarily."

"No," I said. "But possibly."

Castle turned in Banner's direction, mouth open to say something. But she was already gone.

11

1:57 p.m.

"Got it." I looked up at Banner as she appeared, seemingly out of nowhere. She was smiling, carrying two steaming cardboard coffee cups. I had left the tent and the body of the deliveryman to gather my thoughts and was sitting against the hood of a silver Toyota, watching Castle pace back and forth a hundred yards away, talking animatedly on his cell phone.

"Must be good coffee," I said, taking the cup she offered.

"Sandra Veldon. Assistant manager in the doughnut place. Didn't show up for work today."

"Habitual absentee?"

Head shake. "More like employee of the month: every month. She calls if she's going to be five minutes late. Today? Nothing."

"Car?"

Nod. "Dark blue 2009 Ford Taurus. Got the plates from the DMV already, got the BOLO out."

I nodded and looked at my watch, impressed. "All this and coffee."

Banner shot me a warning look, rebuffing the pat on the head. "I can hold up my end. But you helped us along. She might not have been reported missing until tonight. Maybe you're not as much of a waste of time as I thought you were, Blake."

"Thanks."

"Don't get ahead of yourself. I said 'maybe.'"

"It's a hunch," I cautioned. "Looks good so far, but it might not pay off."

Uninvited, Banner moved closer and took a perch next to me on the hood, taking a sip of her own coffee. "Good at finding people," she said. This time she said it like it was a world-famous corporate motto: like *good to the last drop*, or *king of beers*, or something. "So what makes you so sure he'll pick specific targets this time?"

"What makes you so sure he won't?"

She shrugged. "Doesn't fit with what we know about him. With what he did before."

"It fits," I said, thinking about Mosul. "I know the type."

Banner said nothing for a minute, then she asked, "Anything you don't know?"

I smiled, because that exact phrase and the expression on her face brought back a memory of someone else. A far more pleasant memory this time.

"Plenty of things," I said.

"Why are you smiling like that?"

"You just . . . reminded me of someone for a second."

I looked back in Castle's direction again. He was still on the phone, still pacing. The young agent was approaching him, a pained look on his face. I lip-read "I gotta go," saw Castle hang up.

The agent began talking to Castle, his hands held out defensively like he was negotiating with an aggravated suspect armed with a chain saw. Banner had been looking at me, but now followed the line of my gaze.

The young agent was pointing in the direction of the

mobile command center. After he finished speaking, Castle took off at a run.

Banner and I both slid off the hood of the car and jogged after the two men. My mind was racing, trying to predict what had happened. Another shooting, almost certainly. Maybe they'd found Sandra Veldon's body. Whatever it was, the urgency meant one thing: Somebody new was dead.

But this time, I was wrong.

We reached the door to the command center and stepped up and inside. There was a bank of flat-screen monitors on one wall, all eyes fixed on the one that was tuned to CNN. Nobody had thought to turn up the volume, but perhaps that was because they didn't need sound.

The screen was split into panels, like a comic book page. Two small squares on the left, one long vertical rectangle on the right. Top left: aerial footage of our current position. Bottom left: a county cop manning the barrier in a field somewhere, almost certainly the scene of the prison escape. Right-hand side: Caleb Wardell's mug shot.

Bottom of the screen, two words, white on red: BREAKING NEWS.

12

3:02 p.m.

To my surprise, Castle took the latest development pretty well. After the initial shock, after the questions about who had leaked the story and why, he, Banner, and everyone else seemed to be able to let it go and get back to the task at hand. I decided that made sense—the media blackout was not a natural facet of the manhunt, but rather a complication that had been imposed from above. From that perspective, the media getting ahold of the story was almost a blessing. It took unnecessary pressure off, meaning the task force no longer had to operate with one hand tied behind its collective back.

And, as the day progressed, it became apparent that the story hadn't been leaked at all. The story had broken first on the website of the *Chicago Tribune*. A staff reporter named Mike Whitford had received a call that morning from somebody purporting to be Caleb Wardell. And if it hadn't been Wardell, it had been somebody equally well informed, because one thing was clear: Whitford had his facts straight in the story. Everything from the details of the escape to the position of the shot that had killed the deliveryman. The detail was accurate, the message concise and pitched perfectly to a mass audience: Wardell was back. Five men dead already, and he was just getting started.

Castle spoke to Donaldson at length by phone. The SAC was not happy. But there was work to be done, and so it got done. The focus of activity had switched to locating Sandra Veldon's Ford Taurus, but everything else that had been set in motion was still ongoing, with an added load of media briefings.

Two spent 7.62 cartridges were recovered from the wooded area overlooking the lot, validating the forensic guy's guess. A thumbprint found on one was quickly checked and matched as Caleb Wardell's, to the surprise of no one. Good work from all concerned, but crime scene work wasn't what I had been brought in for. To do that, I needed three things: a little time, a little space, and a lot of information. I caught up with Banner outside in the parking lot as she finished a call on her cell.

"Yeah," she said in acknowledgment. She delivered the word flat: not a question or a challenge, sounding neither impatient nor pleased. She did not seem in any mood to be standing around shooting the breeze, so I cut to the chase.

"Listen, I know bringing me in on this wasn't exactly your idea, but I think I can help you."

Banner turned away, staring into the distance and looking like she was thinking of all the things she ought to be doing five minutes ago. Then she looked back at me. "But first you need something from me?"

"Bingo."

I asked Banner to have everything on Wardell e-mailed to me.

"You already have the file," she said.

I shook my head. "That's the *Reader's Digest* version. I mean the big file. Everything."

"Everything," she repeated. "More homework?"

"Something like that."

A pause, then she said: "All right. I guess Castle would say it'll keep you out of the way."

I didn't rise to that. Being honest, it did feel a little against the grain, to retreat to desk work when there was a killer on the loose, but it was all part of my system. The game was on, and if I was going to play my part, I was going to have to know my quarry inside out. The task force would take care of chasing up leads, coordinating dragnets and searches, warning the populace—all of the thousand and one other concerns. In the meantime, I had to forget about all of those distractions and get down to business. My business.

Banner didn't complain about having to take the time out to make the calls, didn't ask what I was planning to do. Most of the material was available electronically, but she had the remainder faxed through to the command center. While I was waiting, I bought some maps from the supermarket.

When it was done, I thanked her. I meant it, because she didn't have to help me. It certainly wouldn't increase her standing with Castle.

She brushed it off. "No need to get all warm and fuzzy. Let's just say I'm hedging my bets."

By three o'clock, and with no small amount of difficulty, I had located what seemed like the last motel room in town that had not yet been snagged by an incoming journalist. I checked in as Jerry Siegel: an assumed name to hide an assumed name. The room had cable, Wi-Fi, and a desk: everything I needed. I switched on one of the news channels and muted the sound; then I set my laptop up on the desk and got to work.

13

4:10 p.m.

"Agent Banner?" Banner started a little at the sudden voice and looked up from her phone, on which she'd been reading a terse e-mail from Donaldson. The expression on Agent Paxon's face told her this wasn't another shooting, not yet. That news wouldn't come to her in person. When it happened, the first sign would be the ringing of multiple phones.

Kelly Paxon had to be in her first or second year with the Bureau, Banner guessed. She wore a dark skirt and jacket, white blouse, only a little makeup. Her strawberry-blond hair was tied back, and she wore glasses with thin, dark red frames. She was nervous. This was evidently her first time in the midst of one of the really big cases and she, like everyone else, had probably been yelled at a couple of times today by stressed-out superiors.

Banner smiled reassuringly. "What have you got for me?"

"Marion."

"Wardell's prison?"

Paxon nodded. "We've gone over every piece of paperwork on the transfer. Looks like Wardell was a last-minute substitution."

"He wasn't meant to be transferred?"

"It was scheduled, but he was meant to go on his own. Death row transfers are almost always solo. A bunch of the guards called in sick—stomach flu epidemic. They tagged him along with Mitchell, who was also meant to be moved alone."

Banner massaged her right temple with her index finger in slow circles. "A celebrity serial killer and a Mob witness. Sounds like they were playing pretty cavalier with the star attractions."

"It seems so, ma'am."

Banner hated being called ma'am. She knew it was a chain-of-command thing, but it set her teeth on edge every time. It made her feel about a hundred and five. "But why didn't they have an escort?" she asked.

Paxon looked uncertain, as if she were somehow personally to blame for the lapse in security. "The original paperwork has Mitchell's transfer coded 1AA. That means silver service—outriders, chopper, decoy vans, the whole ball of wax."

"So what happened?"

"Somebody recoded it the day of the transfer. It was downgraded to regular security only. Mitchell went from VIP to standard class."

Banner was incredulous. "'Somebody'? Wouldn't something like that need to be signed off on by a bunch of people?"

"In theory, yes. In practice ... maybe not. This time it seems to have gone unchallenged."

"So who made the call?"

"The relevant document is signed by the prisoner transfers coordinator, Paul Summers."

Banner opened her mouth only for Paxon to answer her question before she'd voiced it.

"Summers didn't show up for work today or yesterday. We've got an address; he lives just outside of a town called Janson. It's about twenty-five miles north of here."

"Good work. Do we have anybody out there?"

Paxon shook her head. "We only just got the heads-up."

Banner looked away from Paxon and at the busy scene around them. Castle was on the phone; Blake was nowhere to be seen. Chances were she'd have to head back to Chicago soon. The consensus at Quantico was that Wardell would be heading back to familiar ground. In the meantime, there wasn't much she could do here until Sandra Veldon and her car were accounted for. Banner dug the keys to the gray SUV out and jiggled them in her hand. "Come on."

"To Janson?" Paxon sounded surprised.

"Where else? Let's see what Paul Summers has to say about all this."

14

4:42 p.m.

Paul Summers lived off the beaten path, in a farmhouse about three miles off the old Highway 51. Banner and Paxon missed the turnoff the first time. On the second pass, they saw that the sign for Whitecart Farm had been obscured by bushes.

Paxon was driving, so Banner had been the one to answer the call from one of the other agents chasing up the Summers lead. It turned out his bank account had been credited with a hundred thousand dollars from a bank in the Caymans the previous Friday afternoon. That made it official: The escape hadn't simply been a matter of the Russians getting lucky.

Not that it really mattered anymore: Caleb Wardell had personally tied up virtually every loose end on that particular case by killing Mitchell and his would-be assassins. Running down Summers and whoever else had been involved in downgrading the transfer was a side project. The real issue was the genie they'd inadvertently let out of the bottle.

As Paxon negotiated the narrow, rutted dirt track that led up to the house, Banner ejected the magazine in her Glock, checked the load, then slapped it back in.

"Expecting trouble?" Paxon asked.

"No guts, no glory," she replied. "But I'll be happy to be disappointed."

They knew something was wrong as soon as they heard the barking. They heard it a good thirty seconds before the house came into view. It got louder as they approached. Paxon steered through a wide-open security gate and into the yard in front of the house.

It was a conversion that must have been done twenty or thirty years before, and on a tight budget. The farmhouse itself was ramshackle, with a roof that buckled in places. White paint peeled from every wall. There was an extension on the south end that wasn't in much better shape: a one-story timber structure that tapered off to a covered deck area. The dog was tied by a length of chain to one of the posts supporting the roof over the deck.

It was a big German shepherd, virtually wolflike in proportions. It had been pacing from side to side, but angled itself toward the interlopers as they opened the car doors. The barking increased in intensity, and the chain stretched tight as the animal strained to get at them.

"He's starving," Paxon said, a lilt of sympathy in her voice.

Banner was focused on the spot where the chain had rubbed against the wooden post, noticing that it had worn down an inch deep or more. "Why do I get the feeling he's visualizing a couple of roast chickens in office wear?" She was glad she had the Glock in her hand. "Come on."

They headed for the front door, giving the dog a wide berth. Banner kept a wary eye on it as Paxon rapped on the door. She wasn't a dog person at the best of times—her parents had told her that, when she was a toddler, some idiot's rottweiler had gotten off the leash in the middle of the street and had tried to get to her in her stroller. Thankfully, her father had beaten the dog off before it could savage her, receiving a couple of nasty bites for his trouble. Banner had no memory of the incident, but she didn't doubt it was the reason behind her aversion to canines.

Paxon knocked again, harder. They waited another thirty seconds. Banner shrugged and reached for the handle. It twisted down and the door swung open.

66

"Unlocked," Paxon said.

"No," Banner said slowly. "It was ajar. Right?"

"Of course. My mistake." Paxon drew her own gun, and they stepped through the doorway and into a hallway. It was warmer than outside, but not by much. There was a stillness, a silence that spoke of uninhabitation. The only sound was the muted barking from outside, which suddenly sounded much farther away than it was.

The hall was narrow, with two closed doors on the right-hand side, a steep flight of stairs to the left, and a glass-paneled door at the far end that looked like it would lead to a kitchen. A light was burning in the room beyond, visible through the frosted pane.

"FBI agents," Banner called out. "Be advised we are armed."

There was no response. They advanced down the hall, and Banner noticed there was a slight incline, probably indicative of the house settling. A breeze from the top floor whispered past them, and Banner looked up the flight of stairs to where it ended in a half landing. She was considering ascending the stairs when they heard it.

It was a low, intermittent scratching sound. Quiet and tentative. It was coming from the kitchen.

"What the hell was that?" Paxon whispered.

Banner didn't answer. She changed direction and moved to the far end of the hall. The carpet was so old and so cheap that she could feel the lines of the floorboards through the soles of her shoes. One of the boards creaked loudly as her hand touched the kitchen door handle, and the scratching stopped. They exchanged a glance, and Paxon raised her gun to cover the door.

Banner let out a tiny breath and pulled the handle.

A dark shape flashed out of the kitchen, glancing off

Paxon's calf. She let out a restrained yelp, and they both turned to see the German shepherd puppy as it scampered the length of the hall and out into the yard.

Paxon let out a nervous laugh and put her free hand over her heart. "Jesus."

"Look," Banner said, indicating Paxon's leg. There was a smear of blood on her right thigh, just below the hem of her skirt.

Paxon looked down, confused. She touched a hand to the crimson stain and withdrew it as though she'd touched something hot. Something told Banner that it was the exact opposite of that. They exchanged another glance and both looked toward the open door to the kitchen.

A sweet, decaying stench emanated from within.

The kitchen was a square, low-ceilinged room. At the far end was a long rectangular window and a wooden back door. Grimy venetian blinds were drawn shut along the length of the window, but anemic gray daylight peeked through here and there where the slats had warped. There was a worktop along the entirety of one wall, from which a wooden service island jutted like a peninsula. There was blood spatter on the worktop, more of it on the cupboard doors above, dark and congealed. A shoeless foot protruded from the other side of the service island.

Banner stopped and let her eyes read the room, confirming there was no immediate danger, nothing important she could miss in her urge to find out who was attached to that foot. When she was satisfied, she approached the service island, gun level on the foot as her line of sight changed to reveal a leg and a body. When she saw the rest, she knew positive identification would be a job for the experts.

She turned at the sound of a stifled noise that was pitched midway between a gasp and a gag. Paxon's free hand was tight over her mouth. "Jesus Christ," she said. It came out muffled by her fingers.

"Messy," Banner agreed, holstering her weapon. "At least we know why the puppy wasn't hungry."

She turned back to the body, concentrating on what could be seen below the neckline. The body was that of a Caucasian male, probably of early middle age. He was dressed in plaid pajama pants, no shirt, an open blue terry-cloth robe exposing a pale, lightly haired chest and paunch. He was on his back. Presumably, the Colt .45 lying a foot from his right hand had fired the fatal shot. The postmortem injuries also spoke vividly for themselves.

"Summers?" Paxon asked after a few moments, reluctantly pulling her hand from her lips.

"Your guess is as good as mine," Banner said. "He's the right age and build, and given that he's in Summers's house wearing his pajamas ..."

"So where does that leave us?"

Banner reached for her phone and thumbed through the recent calls to dial Castle. "At a very definite dead end, I'm afraid."

15

10:00 p.m.

It didn't take long to work out why the FBI file I'd been given that morning had seemed so condensed. If Donaldson's file on Wardell had been the CliffsNotes, what Banner and her people had dug up for me was more like the Library of Congress. Thousands of pages of notes from the original sniper case, crime scene pics, interviews with hundreds of witnesses and suspects, police interviews with Wardell. Psych interviews with Wardell. Documents from the trial. Wardell's Marine Corps record. Medical records. Dental records. Everything back to his high school reports.

I worked through the material quickly and methodically, pausing every twenty minutes or so only to glance at the muted television screen. No more killings so far, but that wasn't unexpected. Wardell, for whatever reason, preferred to kill in the morning. There were deviations, but not many. Most of his kills had taken place before nine a.m.

Sometimes, the faces appearing on the screen would coincide with the people I was reading about in the files or the reports: people like Ed Randall, the governor then and now. John Hatcher, sheriff of Cook County, where Wardell had first struck. Hatcher was the man who'd taken the most credit for catching Wardell but whose actual contribution to closing the case was negligible, from what I'd been reading. Some old scores for Wardell to settle back in Chi-town.

With that in mind, my number-one pick for Wardell's first specific target was a bust: Detective Adam Stewart, the man who'd broken the case, had succumbed to a heart attack two summers before and had gone to his grave leaving his wife the contribution from the Police Benevolent Association and not much else.

Revenge wasn't the only factor that made me think Wardell would eventually head back to Chicago. His initial spree had been building in intensity before his capture. It was obvious he'd been working up to something big, even if he himself didn't know what that something was. Unfinished business would bring him back to Chicago; the profilers were dead right about that. But where I parted company with Quantico was with the timing. I had a strong hunch that Wardell would avoid the Windy City to begin with, and not just because it was where he was expected.

At nine o' clock in the evening, the news took its first extended break from Wardell coverage to focus on the final week of buildup to the midterm elections. It looked like another longstanding grudge match was approaching its conclusion in Chicago, with Governor Randall in an unexpectedly close race for the mansion. I wondered briefly if the political action might draw Wardell in before deciding it likely wouldn't make a difference either way.

By ten o'clock in the evening, the desk, the bed, and every other flat square foot of the motel room was covered in paper: files, printouts, maps. I was unaccustomed to having such a wealth of material available, and the sheer volume was both an advantage and a drawback. The immersion of myself in a suspect's life was a proven way of getting results. Somehow, by tracing a man's movements, words, and actions, I could begin to get under his skin. Predict what he might do, where he might go.

This target, however, was proving elusive in more ways than one. The more I read about Wardell—be it first-, second-, or thirdhand—the more I felt the essence of the man shift, contort, slip from my grasp. The one constant was my memory of the look in his eyes back in Mosul, the absolute knowledge that he would not and could not stop once he got going.

Raised in suburban Alabama by a single mother, Wardell had been a bright but quiet child, with few friends. As a young man, he'd been a gifted student, outperforming his peers both on the football field and in the classroom. He'd won a scholarship to the University of Alabama at Birmingham but dropped out in his junior year. It wasn't for lack of ability; his professors reported that he'd just gotten bored. He signed up for the United States Marine Corps in 2004 and volunteered for Force Recon. He excelled on the rifle range and snagged a place at Scout/Sniper School. He passed the Scout Sniper Basic Course with flying colors and quickly proved his mettle in combat operations in Iraq, with twenty confirmed kills. That total included an astonishing head-shot takedown of an RPG-armed insurgent at nine hundred yards.

His combat record was excellent—early on, he was touted for the SEALs—but he didn't socialize much with the other men. They found him distant, aloof. One quote put it more bluntly: "a creepy bastard." Perhaps that explained why he'd stalled at lance corporal, when his work on the ground ought to have made him a sergeant, or a full corporal at the very least.

His third and final tour had brought him to the banks of the Tigris: to Mosul, the capital of the Nineveh Province of Northern Iraq. And that was where, for the briefest of moments, our paths had crossed.

16

10:12 p.m.

I was running an asset named Muhammad Rassam at the time. He was deep undercover in the insurgency and about to bring me within striking distance of one of the major local al Qaeda franchisees. I was thirty-six hours away from nailing my quarry, maybe less, when Wardell put a bullet in Rassam's forehead.

We postmortemed the operation afterward and discovered that the catalyst was a pair of ambushes carried out in the space of a week on US patrols. A couple of well-liked men had been killed, and word had reached their unit that Rassam had been the prime mover on the ambushes. I was 90 percent sure Rassam wasn't the guy. And even if he had been, too bad—he was too valuable to lose. Wardell's CO had been instructed not to pursue the issue. Wardell had ignored the order and organized himself a little extracurricular hunting trip. We were tipped off, but too late. When I made the scene, Wardell had already executed Rassam and a couple of others from long range. Then he'd moved in and massacred eight members of Rassam's family and four of his neighbors. I found him putting a bullet into the back of a woman's head. When he saw me, he dropped his weapon, smiled, and raised his hands, almost mockingly.

I had been a quarter-inch pull away from ending his life right there. I'd like to be able to say it would have been for the dead civilians, but that was only part of it. The other part was the six months of my life Wardell had just wasted.

Cassidy had already been yelling in my ear for a few seconds before I even registered it. "Stand down, back the fuck off, and clear the scene. We do not want to have to explain your presence to JSOC, and we sure as goddamn *fuck* don't want to have to explain a fucking premeditated blue-on-blue."

I eased off the trigger as a Humvee pulled up and disgorged a crew of shell-shocked-looking Marines, including a sergeant I took to be Wardell's CO. I didn't stick around to answer questions.

And that was it, apart from the hard look that passed between the two of us as I cut my losses and left the Marines to clear up the mess their boy had made. Or so I'd thought.

17

I picked up the rest of the thread from the postverdict Wardell biographies that had appeared in the national papers.

The massacre went down on the books as accidental. Wardell was quietly sent home and dishonorably discharged. The next anybody heard from him was when a SWAT team dragged him out of his warehouse hideout and he was revealed as the clinically accurate serial killer who'd been terrorizing Chicago over a four-week period.

Nothing seemed to shake Wardell out of his cool detachment: not trial on multiple counts of first-degree murder, not even the resulting death sentence. In all of the TV footage and news pictures, he wore that same knowing smirk, that same faraway look in his gray-blue eyes. He looked like he knew something you didn't.

The defense team tried the obvious, of course, playing up the highlights of his military career and glossing over the dishonorable discharge. They tried painting him as a poor Southern hick who'd been scarred by his experiences in that hellish desert conflict and just didn't know any better. Tried to convince everybody he was just another victim of PTSD who'd simply snapped one day.

Nobody bought it. Because Wardell was a little too clever for his own good. He liked to talk, to boast. And when you heard him talk, two things came across: He certainly wasn't dumb, and maybe, just maybe, he wasn't even crazy. Not that kind of crazy anyway. Reading the psych reports from the court case—prosecution mostly but even some from the defense—I got the sense that they were all dancing around one unscientific, unsubstantiated, but unavoidable conclusion: Caleb Wardell was just plain bad. He hadn't been scarred by the war; he'd sought out the war because he wanted to kill people, and when his war was over, he'd brought it home, because he wanted to keep killing people.

In all of the interviews and court transcripts, I could find only one instance of Wardell losing his cool.

His father, who'd abandoned the family when Wardell was three months old, had crawled out from under whichever rock he'd been hiding when the story broke about his infamous son. Before, during, and after the trial, Wardell Senior busied himself giving out interviews to anybody with a checkbook. Literally never having known his child hadn't seemed to prove a barrier, either to him or to the numerous news outlets that took him up on the offer. The funny thing? He seemed almost proud. Like his long-lost kid had won an Oscar, or a gold medal at the Olympics.

When one of the prison shrinks had broached the topic, asked him about his relationship with his father, Wardell had snapped for real. Maybe for the first time. He'd leapt over the table and attempted to throttle the shrink with the link chain on his cuffs. It took four guards to separate them, by which time the shrink was unconscious. The whole time, he kept repeating a five-word phrase. Not yelling or screaming, just in a conversational tone that jarred with his actions.

I don't have a father.

Throughout the whole thing—the month-long reign of terror, the arrest, the trial, the conviction, the sentencing, it was the one time Wardell had acted in a way that could be termed as out of control.

I was thinking about that when my cell rang. The display screen told me the caller was Banner. The way her voice sounded when she asked if it was me told me something was new.

"What is it?"

"We found Sandra Veldon."

"Her body?"

"She's alive."

"Alive?"

"Yeah, but maybe only thanks to you. They found the Ford parked in a truck stop over the Kentucky state line. Veldon was in the trunk, bound, gagged, and terrified. It was Wardell, all right. She said he wanted her to pass on a message. I guess he was gambling we'd find her before she died of thirst or exposure."

"A message?"

"He told her to tell everybody: 'Killing season's open.'"

I paused. "Shit."

"I know," Banner agreed. "The delivery guy definitely wasn't a one-off."

"Trail?"

There was a pause at the other end of the line, and I could tell she was thinking it over. "Actually yes, a surprisingly clear one. The convenience store at the truck stop has security video of him picking up a few supplies. Some food and drink and some clothes. Including—get this—a lime-green T-shirt. Forty-five minutes later, a Greyhound driver bound for Chicago remembers a guy in a lime-green shirt boarding his bus at the station a couple of miles down the road."

I sighed. "Too obvious."

"That's what I thought," Banner said. "It's a bluff."

"And what does Castle think?" I asked carefully.

She was equally careful in her reply. "Castle thinks it's a good lead. He's making sure we follow up on everything, so we're looking at the possibility that it was him. God knows we need to cross the T's and dot the I's on this one."

"Media giving you a hard time already?" It was a rhetorical question, since I'd had the television on the whole time. You didn't need sound to catch the outrage over the attempted news blackout.

Banner laughed dryly. "You'd think we'd shot that poor guy ourselves. Jesus. It was a stupid fucking move though. A case like this, we need to keep the press on our side."

I didn't say anything, quietly grateful that of all the difficulties I encounter in my line of work, having to give a damn what the public thinks isn't one of them.

"You hear about Paul Summers?" Banner asked.

"I saw that. News is saying it's a suspected suicide."

"That's the way it looked," she said.

"Doesn't mean anything. It's not too difficult to make it look that way."

Banner cleared her throat at that and started to say something, then changed her mind. "So what do you think about Chicago?" she said after a few seconds. Her voice sounded casual enough, but I could tell she was hoping for something. Maybe just that I was thinking along the same lines she was.

"I think that at this moment, he could be anywhere *but* headed to Chicago," I said. "Assuming he did take a bus, what are the other options?"

There was a pause as she consulted something: a printout maybe. I pictured her holding the phone between her neck and shoulder.

"Lucky for us, it's a quiet station. Just a rural feeder site. In the two hours after he was caught on tape, we've got a half-dozen buses departing. Three for Chicago, one for Kansas City, one for Cedar Rapids, Iowa, and one for St. Louis." She paused, waiting for a response. "You still there?"

I had crossed the room to the bed, swept a pile of papers onto the ground to clear space for one of the maps. "Yeah, just a second."

I took the lid off a red Sharpie with my teeth and spat it on the floor, started drawing lines and dots on the map. I consulted my watch. "What time did the Cedar Rapids bus leave?"

A pause while she checked. "Eleven forty."

I looked from the map to the screen of my laptop. "He's in Iowa."

"Cedar Rapids?"

"No. Not anymore. Say ... Des Moines by now. No— someplace smaller, but nearby. Indianola, Fort Dodge maybe. He'll stay there tonight, rest up, kill somebody in the morning before he moves on."

Banner didn't say anything for a moment or two. I wondered if she was deciding whether to be impressed or to hang up.

"Castle thinks it's a double bluff. He thinks Wardell's heading back to his old hunting ground," she said.

"Castle's looking in the wrong place."

"The guys at Quantico agree with him. They say he'll want to revisit the scene of past glories. They're pretty sure about it."

My eyes were drawn to my watch again. The second hand marched onward, implacable. A new day was coming, as surely and as inexorably as a 7.62 NATO round.

"Maybe they're right, but first he's going to take care of some business, and Iowa's on the way."

"On the way to where?"

I drew another line right to left, across the Iowa state line. I circled the town of Lincoln. "Nebraska."

78

Banner sounded unconvinced. "What kind of business?"

"Family business."

18

10:33 p.m.

The father. He was going to kill his father first.

Wardell's head start was twelve hours and growing. If I wanted to have a prayer of intercepting him in time, I'd have to drive through the night. I didn't bother to clear up, just snapped my laptop closed and slid it into its leather case as I left the room. A minute and a half later, I was settling the bill with a bemused clerk at the front desk.

"Funny time to check out," she commented. She took the cash and looked at the bills with open suspicion.

"Turns out I'm not tired."

As I pushed the exit door open, the chill in the air caught me by surprise after a day confined in a slightly overheated hotel room. I breathed cold air in through my nostrils, letting it wake me up a little, bring me back to the present. I'd left the car back in Chicago, so the first order of business was to find a replacement.

Banner had listened. I gave her that. But in the end, I hadn't been able to convince her. Her final words came back to me as I stepped out into the night:

I can't just toss everything else out of the window to focus on a hunch.

But I can, I'd said after a beat. *It's what I'm here for.*

The motel parking lot was an unevenly patched square of

asphalt, about fifty yards on a side. It was half full, evidently oversized for the hotel's occupancy, and lit by the yellow glare of sodium lights. I was halfway across before I noticed the guy in the black coat with the beanie hat shading his eyes.

He was at the far side of the lot, leaning against the short wall that marked the hotel's property off from the highway, right beside the entrance.

A number of warning signs lit up for me: his demeanor, the attempt to hide his face, the fact I could see he was concealing something inside his jacket. But it was his position that really made me alert. Because, unless I wanted to turn around and walk back into the hotel, the only way I could leave this lot was to pass within a couple of feet of this guy. And before I got to him, I'd have to pass between two high-sided vehicles: a minivan and a chunky SUV.

The guy in the beanie stayed put as I paused midstride. He didn't look up. I kept watching him—stared at him for twenty seconds. I caught the slightest hint of a head movement, as though he'd glanced to his left. That meant someone was behind the parked van. Possibly more than one someone.

I understood the scenario. It was something I ought to have expected: a sudden, violent event that had disturbed the small-town ennui and gotten everyone excited, quickening the pulses of the local tough guys. Put that together with an influx of journalists with expensive phones and iPads and minds on other things, and you have the perfect opportunity to mix business with pleasure.

I considered my options. I knew one thing for sure: If I carried on between the two parked vehicles toward the exit, two, maybe three people would attempt to mug me. The smart thing to do would be to walk back inside the hotel and either find another way out or call the police.

I didn't have time to do the smart thing.

I glanced around to check there was no one else lurking around, then started walking, quickening my pace and aiming directly for the guy in the beanie. He stiffened slightly but didn't look up. I rolled my shoulders as I walked, limbering up. As I reached the spot between the minivan and the SUV, the guy finally looked up at me, jutting his chin in my direction defiantly.

"Give me the bag and your wallet."

I didn't break stride. I could feel the weight of the Beretta where it was strapped across my chest. I resisted the temptation—I knew taking it out would mean having to use it. I tightened my grip on the handle of the leather laptop bag.

The guy blinked as I closed the gap between us, obviously unsure as to why I hadn't stopped. "Give me the fucking bag," he repeated, angry now. I kept coming and he opened his coat, pulling out a baseball bat. The minivan was parked six inches farther from the wall than the SUV, giving me a good idea of the direction from which the first attack would come. As I drew level with its rear fender, I brought the laptop case up to shield the right side of my head. Another bat swung from behind the van, slammed into the padded leather. The case stopped it easily; whoever it was hadn't overcommitted to the swing. It didn't help them. The point of impact allowed me to triangulate the position of the assailant, so that the sole of my right foot was planted square in his solar plexus before the bat had stopped moving on the deflection. The connection was solid. I felt the kick go deep into a fleshy midsection. I didn't bother looking at the guy I'd just incapacitated. I was too busy with the next guy. Not the guy in the beanie, front-row-center, but the third guy, coming at me from left field.

This was a wiry younger man with a blond buzz cut. He

was almost albino-blond, a blade in his left hand. That was annoying: I hate fighting southpaws. He looked a little surprised: The three of them had obviously worked out a game plan that was predicated on me being hit in the face by the bat first. I'd messed that up, and now I was going to take full advantage of the two seconds of confusion I'd caused.

I gripped the handle of the laptop bag with both hands and slammed it against the albino's head so hard that the handle snapped and the zipper broke open. Albino lurched backward, stunned but not down. The padding on the case had worked against me this time, cushioning the blow.

Beanie was coming for me now, a little hesitantly after seeing what I'd just done to his buddies, but I gave him credit for trying anyway. I reached between the zippers, gripped the hard edge of the laptop itself, and let the busted case slide off it, like some rectangular reptile shedding its skin. I stole a glance at the first one I'd hit. He was a balding fat guy, on his knees, trying to force some air into oxygen-starved lungs, the bat by his side. Beanie tried a couple of jabs with his own bat, using it like a spear, trying to keep some distance. I dodged the jabs easily and got in closer. Too late, he swung at me one-handed. I leaned in to the swing, caught his forearm under my left arm, and jerked my whole body back. He let out a high-pitched scream as his radius and ulna snapped like firewood.

I knew I'd left the albino unattended for too long. I released the beanie guy and spun, holding the laptop up to cover my midsection. I was just in time: The point of his blade caught the laptop and scored a trench in the plastic casing, nearly amputating two of my fingers as it slid off the side.

I heard a scuff behind me as the beanie guy made a half-hearted follow-up. I turned my body sideways and kicked him hard in the groin. Not exactly subtle, but put together with the broken arm, it would be more than sufficient to discourage him from another try.

The albino was coming for me again, jabbing with the knife. He knew how to use it—wasn't extending too far, using his right hand to feint effectively.

I stepped back from two fast swipes of the blade and used the laptop to block a quick stab. The point of the blade caught it straight-on this time and penetrated, the tip of the blade going through and coming out the other side. I wasted a moment being glad I always worked off a flash drive, then punched the albino hard in the face while he was still in range.

He shook it off and came at me again, aiming at my fingers, around the edge of the laptop. I faked as if to fall back and then went on the offensive, slamming the hard corner of the laptop into the nerve cluster in his left shoulder. It worked: He dropped the knife and his arm hung limp. I blocked a wild right hook and jabbed the laptop into his face, catching him right across the bridge of the nose. His working arm came up to cover his face, and I swung the laptop as hard as I could from the opposite side. The casing shattered across the left side of his head, the screen ripped free of its hinges, and the albino went down like a rag doll.

I turned my attention to the other two men and saw that they were already across the road and running. I looked down at myself, examining my arms and center mass for injuries I might not have felt in the heat of combat, but found nothing. My computer, alas, was another story.

I dropped the remains of it next to the unconscious albino and walked away quickly. I didn't have the time to waste on this situation, but something was niggling at me, and it wasn't just the loss of my computer. I'd beaten off an attack by three armed thugs in less than a minute, but that was the problem: It shouldn't have taken me that long. The albino had displayed skills, discipline. Either he was made of sterner stuff than your usual street tough, or I was getting rusty.

It was a question for another time, though. I had a far more pressing concern, and he'd be resting up already, getting ready for a new morning. Less than ten hours until first light and six hundred miles to go.

DAY TWO

19

As soon as I passed the legend that read *Welcome to Fort
Dodge, Iowa*, I knew I was in the right place. I didn't know
why, exactly, but the moment the white wooden sign appeared in my high beams was when a strong hunch trans-
mogrified into something like a hard certainty. The process
of predicting how far and in which direction Wardell might
have traveled had been a combination of solid theory and
intuition, but I was at a loss to explain quite how I *knew* my
quarry was in this town.

Once I'd decided where Wardell was headed, it had simply
been a matter of plotting a likely route and taking into account a number of factors: like the assumption that he had
indeed taken the Cedar Rapids bus and whether he'd kept
using public transportation or found a car, either by hitchhiking or stealing one. Wardell wouldn't rush. If I was right
about his eventual destination being Lincoln, Nebraska, then
it was a little too far to make the journey in one day. He could
make it most of the way across the state before nightfall, but
he'd want to get some sleep, having been awake for nearly
two days straight.

Des Moines had sounded good at first, but it was too big
a city. Wardell would know that the cops would be on alert
in major population centers in any of the states bordering

Illinois. That probably wouldn't bother him under normal circumstances, but he was tired and I guessed he'd want to rest in relative safety on the first night. Looking at the other midsized towns he could have reached in the same time frame, I had decided on Fort Dodge. It was small enough, at a population of twenty-five thousand, but at the same time large enough to provide a choice of kill zones and cover to slip away.

So there it was: Fort Dodge. Had to be. When you laid it out like that, it was almost like a simple mathematical equation. Or perhaps that was all just bullshit. Perhaps it was just a plausible-sounding way of justifying an informed hunch. I often wonder about that. If I'm superstitious at all, it's about the process. I never want to analyze it too closely.

I shifted my mind away from the unknowns to the knowns. If Wardell was keeping to his established MO, he'd want to rise early and kill again before he resumed his journey. I was almost certain of this for two reasons: one, his message about 'killing season' being open, together with his contacting the media, said that he meant business—he wouldn't want to let up on the pressure. Two, he'd screwed up on yesterday's shooting, requiring more than one shot for the first time in his career. He'd want to strike again quickly, to prove that it had been a one-off. In fact, I had worried that Wardell might not want to wait for the morning, might act sooner. If that had happened, at least it would have confirmed his direction of travel. But it hadn't, so here I was, in Fort Dodge, Iowa.

But where to look in Fort Dodge? That was the question I'd been mulling over while I made the long drive north. Finding a vehicle had proved slightly more difficult than expected, since Cairo had not counted a car rental company among its amenities. I'd found a place in the next town that was almost out of stock, and settled for the one thing they

88

had left: a silver Cadillac DTS luxury sedan. It had a 4.6 liter V8 engine, leather seating, and a moonroof, whatever that was. Yes, I'd settled for it the way Arthur Miller settled for Marilyn Monroe.

I'd driven through the night, made Fort Dodge a little before seven in the morning. It was a busy town, nestled in the gently rolling hills of the Des Moines River Valley, about ninety miles northwest of Des Moines itself. From here, it was another hundred and sixty miles to the Nebraska state line, assuming you took the most direct route to Lincoln.

There were a few major hotels and plenty of smaller places where one could check in unobtrusively. It would take a man working alone a full day to check them all, and that would be operating on the shaky assumption that Wardell would even use a hotel. He was a Marine Corps Scout Sniper who'd endured three deployments in Iraq and five years in the United States Supermax Prison at Marion, so I guessed he was used to forgoing home comforts. I made a round of the big hotels and a handful of the smaller guest houses anyway—just to cross the T's, as Banner had said. As I'd expected, I came up with nothing.

So I cruised the predawn streets, looking for nondescript cars parked alone in empty malls and office parking lots, cars that might have out-of-state plates or contain a sleeping occupant. Nothing. Clearly, this wasn't one of those jobs that would be resolved through dumb luck.

As the first light of dawn began to creep hesitantly over the eastern horizon, the sun glinting off the frontage of a place called the Red Ball Café caught my eye. I parked outside and bought a newspaper, as well as a black coffee and a donut to raise my blood sugar. I took them out to the car and scanned the headline story on Wardell in twenty seconds, lacking the luxury of more time to waste on it.

I once read that you'll find at least five mistakes in any given news story if you know enough about the subject. From a cursory glance, the *Des Moines Register* was way ahead of the curve in terms of inaccuracy. They had the broadest details right, but everything else was a mix of rumor, speculation, and good old-fashioned sensationalism. For all that, though, the media was doing exactly the same thing I was: waiting for the next one.

I discarded the paper on the passenger seat and unfolded the map I'd bought from a gas station on the edge of town. In my head I went over the top three kill zones I'd identified.

On the face of it, the most likely option was a mall on the eastern edge of town, one that offered near-identical conditions to the shooting Wardell had carried out the previous morning. Another large open space offering a choice of unsuspecting targets, again providing plenty of cover and a choice of exfiltration routes.

Then there were a couple of spots in the center of town: Central Avenue would offer the single greatest amount of targets during rush hour and had a certain symbolic value: the beating heart of a small heartland city.

Five minutes' walk away, City Square Park provided almost as many targets. It wasn't the biggest of the city's parks, but it would provide more viable positions from which to take the shot than any of the others.

I juggled the possibilities in my head as I sat in the parking bay outside the Red Ball, sipping the coffee and watching the morning traffic picking up. I'd developed a feel for the place in the last couple of hours; I guessed I knew the town about as well as a rookie cabdriver would. And even with the morning traffic approaching its zenith, the place was compact enough to be easily navigable. The three potential kill zones were all within easy reach of my current position. The mall was half a mile away. I estimated I could make Central Avenue in four minutes. City Square Park in seven. The only problem? I couldn't be in all three places at once.

I eliminated the mall first. It was an ideal setup, and it was what Wardell had done yesterday; but that was why I found it so easy to discount. Five years before, Wardell had been scrupulously varied in his choice of both locations and victims.

Down to two strong possibilities, then: Central Avenue or the park. I drained the last of the coffee, keyed the ignition, and pointed the Cadillac south, toward the center of town.

Exactly four minutes later, I was headed west along Central. Full daylight had taken its time to arrive. Maybe it was as reluctant as anybody else to begin a cold day in late October. Rush hour was in full swing, which in a town this size, wasn't saying much.

I covered the length of the town's main street with relative ease, stopping only at a broken signal when instructed to by a traffic cop. As I waited for my stream of traffic to be granted permission to move on, I scanned the roofline on either side of the street. Nothing more threatening than pigeons. The big clock on the county courthouse at the top of the street was ten minutes slow. I peered up at the bird-festooned parapet on the roof of the building. It would make a dramatic vantage point for a shooting, albeit with some logistical drawbacks. Then again, it didn't offer any intrinsic advantage over the open window on the sixth floor of the office building across the street, or indeed, the small park at the other end.

I took a right at the cross street after the courthouse, then zigged a left and zagged a right, to bring the car out on the east side of City Square Park.

The park was the width of two blocks. Commuters

crisscrossed the green space, heading for offices and stores and schools and the big public library building. The square was flanked on all four sides by six-story buildings, all uniform and all with accessible-looking flat roofs. The sun had not yet risen above the level of the surrounding buildings, meaning the park was entirely in shadow and a gunman could aim from any of the overlooking rooftops without having to face into any glare.

I scanned the skyline. I saw nothing, but then I hadn't really expected to. Wardell was hardly likely to be perched on a parapet with his legs dangling, rifle in one hand, latte in the other as he picked out his next target. They drum that kind of behavior out of you at the sniper academy.

I spotted a couple of open windows here as well, despite the fact the temperature was just a hair above freezing. It meant nothing. Although I've never worked in an office, I've visited a lot of them in my time. While waiting for appointments, I liked to kill time by making observations in the manner of a visitor to a strange land. Observations like the fact that people who work in offices don't pay the utility bills, so when the heating is on a little too high, they just open a window rather than turning it down.

I made a circuit of the park, looking for potential positions that Wardell might have chosen—street level as well as above. It was a good site, but no better than Central Avenue had been.

A green sedan pulled out of one of the parking bays at the side of the road ahead of me, and I steered the Cadillac into the gap. I got out and made a slow three-hundred-and-sixty-degree turn, surveying the park without any of the obstructions you get inside a vehicle.

Damn it.

I needed more time. And, unusually, I needed more people.

More often than not, in my experience, other people get in the way. But in this situation, more people could be useful; they could be in multiple places. I spent a second wondering if I should have tried harder to persuade Banner to join me. She'd seemed a little more receptive to my methods than her colleagues. Then I dismissed the idea. She'd never have gone for it. Not yet, not while I was an untested resource. If she was going to trust me, I'd have to be right about this.

I scanned the line of rooftops again. It was possible that Wardell might use a position nearer to the ground, but I was betting on a rooftop or a high window. The statistics were on the side of this probability: Thirteen of Wardell's nineteen kills the first time around had been from an elevated position.

I glanced at my watch: 8:55. Wardell was going to strike soon, within the next hour for sure, and probably sooner rather than later. It was going to be soon, and it was going to be from an elevated position, and it was going to be here, in this town, in one of two locations. *But which one?*

The squeal of tires and the sound of a powerful engine accelerating told me I'd picked wrong even before I heard the siren scream to life. Five seconds later, the police cruiser streamed past on the opposite side of the park, not having to slow much to negotiate the traffic. It kept going, headed east. Headed in the direction of Central Avenue.

Damn it.

20

Wardell took a deep breath of the chill morning air, feeling it invigorate him. He held it, then breathed it out through his nostrils, making a miniature cloud that rose heavenward. Then he turned his eyes down to watch the commuters below him on Central Avenue, scurrying like ants to their meaningless destinations.

In the early days of his first killing spree, the reporters had clambered over one another to be the first to come up with the nickname that stuck. "Sudden Death," "One Shot," "The OSOK Killer"—for "one shot, one kill." Wardell hadn't paid undue attention to the media coverage, but when they settled on the boringly prosaic "The Chicago Sniper," he couldn't help but feel a little disappointed. Accurate, yes. But not exactly up there with the Night Stalker or Jack the Ripper.

His personal favorite from those early candidates had been "The Rush Hour Killer." He'd always liked that one. It wasn't strictly accurate, but close enough—since the majority of his kills were carried out between seven and nine a.m., and so it followed that many of his victims were commuters. To start with, that hadn't been a conscious choice. He'd always been an early riser; one of the philosophies impressed upon him by his mother was that if there was a job to be done, it was best to get it done first thing.

As the kills mounted up, however, Wardell decided that rush hour was actually the best time of day to strike for maximum effect. After all, what was more routine, more

94

predictable in your average dead-eyed citizen's life than the daily commute, the morning rat race? Wardell's morning kills smashed that soulless routine like an express train hitting a stray animal. He closed his eyes and replayed some of his favorites in his head: the legal secretary he'd picked off through the window of the seven forty out of LaSalle Street Station, the cyclist cut down in front of Madison Plaza, the articulated truck driver he'd blown away on the 290. They'd all been on their way somewhere, all taken it entirely for granted that they'd get there. And Wardell, like a wrathful god, had punished them for their complacency, rerouted them to the afterlife with the squeeze of a trigger. A couple of weeks in, nobody took the morning commute for granted.

By the time his body count reached double figures, Wardell had begun to realize that he relished the effect his work had on the populace at large as much as, perhaps even more than, he did the shootings themselves. The fear, the hysteria, the mass panic ... knowing that it was all down to him had an effect that was better than the most potent drug ever concocted.

But Wardell had been wary of becoming complacent and hidebound by routine himself, so he had mixed things up with targets selected at other times of day: the executive sitting by the picture window in Paperino's halfway through a business lunch, the teenage girl working the night shift at the McDonald's drive-through window, the two evening joggers in McKinley Park. He didn't want people to think they were safe merely because they'd managed to make it to the office, or because morning rush hour had come and gone.

But still, he liked to kill in the morning best of all.

And this was an important morning for him. He wanted to get on the road as quickly as possible, but first he had yesterday's mistake to atone for. A session of target practice before he moved on to greater things. He'd been building up to something special before; if he could surmount the next hurdle, he could do it again. To require more than one shot this time, or—he barely dared consider this—to actually *miss*, would be shameful. In that event, he questioned whether he'd be able to carry on at all. Better to quit than to limp along like an athlete past his prime, a shadow of his former self. Wardell took pride in his work. He could never understand why pride was one of the cardinal sins, but then there were many things about mainstream morality that he didn't understand, or care to try.

Make or break time, then. One shot, one kill.

The town in which he found himself this morning had a motto that seemed appropriate. He'd seen it emblazoned in a font imitating handwriting on the sign at the city limits: *Fort Dodge, Frontier of the Future.*

He was crouched on the roof of the county courthouse, the H&K PSG1 at his side, leaning against the parapet. He breathed another cloud out and looked down at the busy little worker ants, wondering which one to choose.

There was no point in making things easy on himself, so he'd deliberately picked a challenging setup. The rooftop was fifty feet up and overlooked the town's main thoroughfare. The wind was kicking up, which would take adjustment, and the temperature was hovering around freezing, meaning thermals were unpredictable. He could make the task easier or tougher by choosing between a stationary or moving target.

In purely practical terms, a backup man would have been an asset in this situation. It was one of the reasons modern snipers always worked in pairs: one to relay reconnaissance, one to pull the trigger. The shot itself was a task that required perfect concentration, and that meant it was vital to have somebody watching your back.

There was another reason, however, but not one they'd necessarily admit to in the Marine Corps Sniper School. A sniper's work, put objectively, was murder. A two-man team divided that psychological burden. Needless to say, this was not something for which Wardell felt a particular need. Working alone was one of the best things about going into the murder business for himself.

Time to decide. During his reflection, Wardell had been observing a number of potential targets. There was the cop directing the traffic at an intersection where the lights were out. That would send a message all right.

Or there was the group of three smokers taking an early break outside of a funeral home—he wondered if that was too obvious. Too laden with irony, perhaps? Wardell swept the telescopic sight slowly up Central Avenue. Nobody else jumped out, just hundreds of indistinguishable insects scuttling along, oblivious to his gaze. Perhaps it was time to play one of his little games of chance, like picking the first person he saw wearing pink. Or the first person holding a cell phone in his left hand.

But wait—there he was, his target. Too good to pass up. The man in question had just passed through the intersection with the broken light, traveling on a motor scooter. A moving target, sufficiently difficult to prove his mettle. But what made this moving target perfect was the clerical collar visible below the strap of his helmet. A priest. That would have more of an impact even than shooting the cop; it would demonstrate that he wasn't fucking around.

Wardell got comfortable, rested the rifle on the parapet. His movements were so smooth and natural that the pigeons didn't scatter, just shuffled along for him. He ranged the man of God, leading the target a little to allow for the forward direction of travel. He was moving down the street at a cautious twenty miles an hour, slowed by the other traffic. Wardell placed the illuminated reticle of the telescopic sight in the triangle of opportunity: the zone defined by the prospective victim's head and shoulders.

He had the visor of the priest's helmet locked dead center, his left arm letting the barrel of the rifle come down incrementally to track the forward movement. He breathed in. Let all conscious thought drift away and pressed hold, pressed hold.

His subconscious was working overtime, which perhaps explained why he adjusted his aim down a fraction just before he squeezed the trigger through the final degree of travel.

Six hundred yards away, the 7.62 NATO round found the inch-wide white square on the priest's dog collar, passing through it and entering his throat at the Adam's apple before exiting at the other side, taking a portion of spine and most of the back of the priest's neck with it.

The pigeons took flight, startled by the shot. Wardell closed his eyes and let the breath out. Another perfect wisp of cloud, a kindred echo of the gun smoke. Off to his right, he heard the spent cartridge clink across the rooftop, a good twenty feet away. A military-spec weapon wouldn't have done that—too difficult to sanitize the position. Even though he no longer had to worry about forensics or fingerprints, this irritated him. It was ... untidy.

He took his eye from the telescopic sight and watched as the moped carried on for three or four car lengths before the priest's body realized it was dead and shifted, tipping the scooter sideways between traffic lanes.

Wardell kept watching, hoping that the priest wouldn't be run over—that would muddy the issue.

He was in luck. A taxicab squealed to a halt three feet

from crushing the priest's head like a melon. Bystanders rushed to help. Wardell's mouth creased into an anticipatory grin. Here it came.

He was too far away to make out the exact words contained in the shouts and screams, but he knew the gist: It was evident in the way the Good Samaritans scattered, the way their heads snapped around, looking for danger. He watched the ripple of terror move from the epicenter, the pedestrians reacting, disbelieving, then pushing for the imagined shelter of the storefronts and awnings. He always allowed himself this when there was an audience. No more than fifteen or twenty seconds, that was enough. Any more time spent savoring the scene would be an unacceptable risk. He would have to get moving, clear the kill zone before the authorities could muster a response.

An urge was building, one he had to fight to repress. He wanted *more*. He wanted to take out some of those screaming witnesses as they fled—three, four, five, a dozen. Ride the wave of panic like a surfer on a bloody tide.

That would come, but not yet. First things first. He allowed himself a moment longer to savor the scent of fear like the bouquet of a fine wine, then turned and moved quickly toward the door to the stairwell without a backward glance.

21

"Trust me, Agent Banner. We've got this covered." Banner removed the phone from the crook of her neck, getting ready to hang up. She rolled her eyes at the cockiness dripping from every syllable uttered by the junior agent on the other end of the phone. Jesus, he sounded about fourteen. More and more of them seemed like kids these days. Banner herself was only in her midthirties, but if there had been a transition period from green rookie to seasoned veteran, she'd been too busy to notice it happening.

"I'll quote you on that, okay, Wyacek?"

"Quote me on it? You can take it to the *bank*."

Banner terminated the call without further comment and let her gaze drift back up to the map of the greater metropolitan area, mentally circling the three additional potential strike zones Wyacek had just informed her were under surveillance. Which was not, as she well knew, the same thing as "covered."

She was starting to get the feeling she was on the wrong team.

Castle had seniority, so focusing on Chicago was his call. Would she have made the same decision in his position? Difficult to say. If Wardell was caged early enough, she might get to find out, because she'd be in with a shot of primary on the next high-profile manhunt. Then she'd be the one walking that tightrope: trying to reconcile an open mind and a flexible approach with the hard political necessity of running things by the book.

Certainly, she understood Castle's reasoning. Right now the trail pointed here, to Chicago. And the BS guys at Quantico agreed it was the most likely destination for Wardell. He'd want to return to the old *hunting ground*, revisit the scene of *past glories*. They loved those two phrases, kept using them.

In all, the task force had two dozen priority strike zones under tight surveillance. Parks were closed. Schools were operating under code blue conditions, which meant no outside activities. High-sided vehicles had been commandeered to shield citizens filling up at gas stations.

Chicago was the top priority, but not the only one. Police departments were on alert in the major population clusters in Iowa, Missouri, Kentucky, and Indiana—every state bordering Illinois. All bases covered, with the most resources focused on the most likely scenario. The way it should be.

So why did she feel like she was in the wrong place?

Blake's theory was plausible enough, but hardly a dead certainty. Somehow he'd come to the conclusion that Wardell would go after his father, who was based in Lincoln, Nebraska, the last anybody heard. The FBI's own profilers had considered this too, of course. Family members were generally the first group you looked at when tracking a fugitive—either as potential collaborators or potential victims—but the boys and girls at Quantico had concluded that in this particular instance, it was a low-priority lead.

Calling Wardell's father "family" was stretching the point, in any case. He'd had no contact with his son for the entirety of his life, showing an interest only when Caleb became a celebrity killer. Wardell himself had disavowed the idea that he had a father in the psych transcript Blake had mentioned.

Blake seemed to think that the outburst made the father the priority target. The shrinks disagreed, as did Castle. They thought Wardell would most likely stick to random targets. After all, there was no compelling reason for him to get personal all of a sudden. In fact, the concern was that he'd get *less* discriminating, go for a greater number and frequency of kills now he had literally nothing to lose.

Intellectually, Banner found herself agreeing with their assessment. Wardell's father was a possibility, but not a probability. Not with the facts they were working with. But, because it wasn't an avenue that could be dismissed out of hand, the local police had been asked to put the father in protective custody, and two agents—Gorman and Anderson—had been dispatched to Lincoln.

Blake was probably wrong about the father. And even if he was right, she was at a loss to explain his conviction that Wardell's next kill would be in Fort Dodge—one specific speck on the map in a potential search radius that had reached five hundred thousand square miles and was growing exponentially by the hour. How in the hell could he possibly be so sure?

Sure. That was the word for it, she realized. Banner thought back to the telephone conversation minutes before, to Wyacek's misplaced, exuberant cockiness, and realized that this was the difference. When Blake spoke, he hadn't betrayed one iota of doubt, but he hadn't sounded cocky either. That was it: The man just sounded so damn sure of himself that he'd convinced her, against her better instincts. Convinced her that where she really ought to be was in Fort Dodge, Iowa. The middle of nowhere, instead of the apparent middle of the action. Goddamn Blake and his certainty.

The FBI was the world's largest, best-resourced law-enforcement agency. But even so, it had its limits. Too many limits, according to vocal members of the old guard like Dave Edwards, who remembered fondly the days before counter-terrorism concerns had eaten into their budget.

With a search radius that big, and with a clearly defined high-danger area, they simply couldn't spare the bodies to cover Fort Dodge as well. So Blake would have to cover it on his own.

Enough. She had a job to do. She mentally ranked the top slots on her current list of responsibilities. Besides the fixed surveillance locations, they had rapid-response teams dotted throughout the city, all reporting to her. She was also in touch with the people pounding the sidewalks in the warehouse district, where Wardell had made his hideout the first time around.

Thankfully, one problem she didn't have to deal with was reporters. Castle had been quick to learn the lessons of the botched media blackout. He was currently delivering a briefing in the press room on the third floor, along with the mayor and the police commissioner. The new policy was a complete one eighty: to be as open and up-front as was feasible. That meant they were admitting that the focus of the manhunt was on Chicago and advising caution to all citizens. The usual advice: Keep calm; keep vigilant; go about your usual day; don't panic.

Who knew? People might actually listen for a change. It wasn't like they could hide the focus of their attentions, in any case. Banner hadn't seen this many cops on the street since the Bulls' last NBA championship party in ninety-eight.

The media attention brought with it a host of disadvantages, but also a select few advantages. Like, for example, the blanket helicopter surveillance of the city. She hoped that would plug the gaps in their own coverage. Perhaps it would even make up for the flood of crank and dead-end calls they would now have to wade through.

Assuming Wardell was here—and not in Iowa—she had a sinking feeling in her gut that they weren't going to stop him this early. For all that everyone was talking about nabbing him as soon as he showed his face, deep down everyone knew this operation was more about being ready to go after him when he did strike. If they got him before he killed, it would be great. If not, the idea was they'd be ready to bring him down as soon after the next kill as possible.

And so everyone was holding their breath, waiting for the next one. For the first time this morning, Banner allowed her gaze to linger on the wall clock. It wouldn't be long now.

She had a photograph on her desk in a plain wooden frame. It showed her daughter in a pink coat and matching hat and gloves, building a snowman in the backyard of their old place. It was a couple of years out of date and Annie was still five years old in the picture, but Banner preferred not to update it. It reminded her of happier times. She put her hand on her cell phone to call her sister to check in. Maybe she'd suggest that she bring Annie out of school by the back door today. *Keep calm; keep vigilant; go about your usual day; don't panic.*

The phone started to ring as she touched it. Although she hadn't saved the number yet, she recognized the last three digits of the cell number Blake had given her. She hit the button to pick up.

"Where are you?"

There was a pause. When Blake spoke, the sound of his voice told her everything she needed to know in two brief words. "Fort Dodge."

She closed her eyes. She could hear sirens over street noise in the background. "What happened?"

"I just got to the scene. Looks like one fatality, passersby are saying it was a priest." There was a pause and Banner got the sense that something had caught Blake's attention.

"So you were right," she said, wondering if he'd take the opportunity to say "I told you so."

"Not right enough," he said. "I'll call you back."

The line went dead. And then a dozen more came to life. Desk phones chirruped, cells joined them in a discordant symphony of ringtones and snippets of pop songs.

Banner picked up her own phone, trying to ignore the feeling of illicit relief that today Annie would be able to leave school by the front entrance after all.

22

9:07 a.m.

I hung up on Banner, not waiting for an acknowledgment, and watched as the thin man I'd briefly locked eye contact with turned and melted into the crowd on the opposite side of the street.

The man was around six feet, about a hundred and sixty pounds. Widow's peak, rounded glasses. He'd been dressed for the office: dark suit, white shirt, conservative tie, dark overcoat. Because it was rush hour, there were half a dozen men dressed just like him within spitting distance. But this one looked out of place.

I checked my watch again: 9:07. Twelve minutes since I'd heard the first police siren, so probably thirteen or fourteen minutes since the shooting itself. There were a lot of cops here already, more than you'd think they'd even have on the payroll in a town this size. They hadn't yet had sufficient time to set up a fixed perimeter. Some were crowded around the priest's body, shielding it from rubberneckers; the rest were trying to move the crowds back. When I had arrived, people were still trying to distance themselves from the scene, get away from danger. It hadn't taken long for that impulse to wear off.

The faces in the crowd were pretty uniform in their degrees of animation, if nothing else: shock, fear, bewilderment, curiosity, excitement. That was why the thin man had stood out. Among a sea of emotion, his was literally the only impassive face on the street. That and the very specific way in which he had surveyed the kill scene. It was hard to describe, but he had seemed to be watching with a professional eye. He looked unsurprised, or at least entirely unrattled. Maybe it was noticeable to me because I was doing the same thing. In fact, going by the thin man's demeanor and clothing, I might have made him for a federal agent. But if that was the case, why had he avoided my eyes, then furtively disappeared into the crowd?

If I had wanted to follow the thin man, I wouldn't have been able to. The police presence in the middle of the street that separated us was as good as a twelve-foot barbed-wire fence. Instead, I took a step back, turned my attention away from the killing zone. A quarter of an hour since the shooting, and Wardell would most likely be out of town already.

I surveyed the area again. The buildings were the same, the climate was the same, but it seemed an entirely different place to the one I had passed through less than half an hour before. It was almost like some dark magic trick, the way one madman and one half-ounce piece of copper-jacketed lead could utterly transform a place so quickly and so profoundly. I'd seen it before, seen terror used as a weapon, the ripple effect often more damaging than the original incident.

My eyes scanned the rooftops and high windows again, looking for ... what? A trace, I supposed. Evidence of the magician's passing. I found what I was looking for on the roof of the county courthouse. Or rather, I found an absence of something: birds. When I'd passed through earlier, the parapet had been lined with pigeons. Perhaps that had made me subconsciously discount the spot, but that had been stupid.

There were still birds on the other buildings, but none on the parapet of the county courthouse roof. None at all.

I jogged down the street, keeping my eyes peeled for Wardell, though I knew he'd be long gone. I took the courthouse steps at a run. The foyer was a big, wide space with a marble floor. There was an older woman at the reception desk. I spoke before she could greet me: "You see anybody come by here in the last twenty minutes? Around my height, maybe carrying a long bag or a package?"

The receptionist opened her mouth as if to challenge me, thought again and then shook her head. "Nobody's come by here. What's going on out there?"

I ignored the question. "Have you got a back exit?"

The woman pointed to one of the corridors leading off the foyer. The corridor led back through the big old building, through a series of doors to a black metal fire door with a push bar. I ignored the sign warning of an alarm and pushed the door outward. No alarm sounded. The door opened on a slender alley. I glanced side to side, saw no one and no traces of anyone. I stepped back and examined the doorframe. A cable ran from one of the hinges to a box on the wall. Midway, the cable had been severed. There was a flight of stairs opposite the fire door. I closed the door and climbed the stairs. Thirty seconds later, they brought me out on the roof of the courthouse.

A confusion of pigeons scattered as I paced across the flat roof to the parapet, which gave me an eagle's-eye view of Central Avenue. In the dead center of my field of vision was the spot where the police had set up shop around the body. Something glittered in the cold sunlight, twenty feet to my right. I walked to where the flat roof met the brick of the parapet on the other side of the building and went down on one knee. A spent .762 cartridge. Only one this time.

"Police! Get down on the fucking ground *now*."

I winced at the sudden bark from behind me. I stayed down and put my hands around the back of my head. Slowly.

23

10:49 a.m.

I sat back in the chair and drummed my hands on the tops of my thighs, staring up at the ceiling tiles again. There were fifty-eight of them. Three of those looked like they'd been replaced fairly recently; they were the same make as the rest, but not as yellowed by age and cigarette smoke. There was a clock on the wall, imprisoned behind a square wire cage. The little hand was approaching the eleven. I sighed in frustration and summoned up a mental map. Two hours. Depending on his mode of transport, Wardell might already be in Nebraska. Might be getting ready to take his father out already.

The door opened and Smith entered, the older of the two detectives who'd questioned me. He wore the resigned expression of one who'd just had confirmation that an unlikely long shot was not going to pan out.

"You're lucky I don't shoot you," he said, holding up the key to my cuffs between his thumb and forefinger.

"Don't you mean I'm lucky you *didn't* shoot me, past tense?" That thought had crossed my mind on the rooftop. I'd been grateful the officers had followed correct procedure and waited to ascertain that I wasn't a threat.

Smith ignored my correction, just roughly unlocked the cuffs when I presented my hands across the table.

"I take it you got ahold of Agent Banner," I said.

Smith nodded grudgingly. "And instead of keeping the only suspect in custody, we're to let him go and extend him all cooperation. God bless the FBI."

"Come on, Detective. You know who did this. I was never a viable suspect."

"Maybe not, but you sure as hell were a complication we didn't need."

I pushed my chair back, got up, and perched on the desk. I saw Smith bristle at this and pretended I hadn't noticed. I glanced up at the clock. "So now that we're on the same team, how about an update on the investigation?"

Smith opened his mouth and, although I couldn't quite predict what he was about to say, I knew it would be likely to contain, as Paul Simon once said, words I never heard in the Bible. But then he reconsidered.

"Victim's name was Father David Leary. Killed instantly by a single through-and-through gunshot wound to the throat. No autopsy or ballistics results yet, of course, but the damage is consistent with a 7.62 NATO round." He spoke quickly and in a flat monotone, as if reciting an over-familiar recipe. Exactly as though he were briefing a disliked journalist. "They pulled a good thumbprint off of the cartridge you were kind enough to locate for us on the roof of the courthouse, and it's a match for Caleb Wardell. Amazing how quickly you can get a print back, depending on who's waiting on the results."

"So they're here already."

"The *feds*?" He said it like it was a different four-letter word. "All over it. Might have been handy if we'd had them this morning, instead of now."

"It looked like he was headed for Chicago."

"So why were you here?"

"I had a hunch; the man in charge disagreed. Any witnesses? Anyone see the shooter?"

Smith turned his back, walked four paces, and opened the reinforced door of the interview room, holding it wide. "We're done, Mr. Blake."

"We're working the same case, Detective Smith."

That did it. Smith's face creased and turned the color of a raspberry. "You listen to me, asshole. We aren't working the same case. Because, as of twenty minutes ago, I'm not working the case. All I know is you and your FBI buddies let a killer run free in my town, and now we have to clean up your mess. Everything's 'You don't need to know.' Now, if you knew there was a threat, then why in the hell didn't you contact the department?"

"Would you have listened to me? Would you have known where to look?"

That stopped Smith in his tracks. He changed tack: "We ran your prints too. Know what we came up with?"

As a matter of fact, I did know. That's why I'd been relaxed about providing them. I said nothing.

"A big capital-letter fuck-you from Homeland Security, that's what. Just who in the hell are you, Blake?"

24

"'You don't need to know,'" Banner repeated, unable to keep the grin out of her voice. "You actually said that?"

"Yes."

"Did he hit you?"

"He managed to restrain himself."

"Impressive."

"So how come you're not down here already?" Blake said.

"I'm not coming. The field team's taking care of the investigation of this shooting, but ..."

"But that's just confirming what you already know."

"Yes," she agreed. "This is not a routine manhunt. We're not trying to identify a suspect, just catch up with him. We're focusing on his next move now. By sunup tomorrow, we need to be where he's going, not where he's been."

"He's probably in Nebraska already," Blake said.

There was a pause. "I think that's a possibility," Banner said, a little bit of emphasis on the "I."

"Castle's still not going for it?"

"It's not that. We got a lead on Wardell's mode of transport: Somebody called in to report a man Wardell's height leave the courthouse by the front entrance just after the shooting. He was carrying a long bag. We got a separate call from a news vendor who spotted him five minutes later, a few blocks away. Same description, same bag—he got into a red van parked on Fifth Avenue South and took off east."

"East?"

"I know. It doesn't fit," she said. "That street turns into

Route 20 farther along. We found a security camera in a gas station on the edge of town that covers a little of the road—a red Ford E-Series van passed by about four minutes after the second witness would have seen him. And before you ask, it was a cheap camera, so we didn't get a sniff of the license plate." She paused and gave him a moment to let it sink in. "That's what doesn't fit. If he was headed for Nebraska, he'd have been going south and west."

Blake was silent for a moment as he absorbed the information. The front entrance: That didn't chime with what he knew. Could the receptionist at the courthouse have missed him?

"Maybe he knew he was being observed," he said. "He's trying a misdirect again, like with the green T-shirt. You get names on those eyewitnesses?"

"Our people out there just got done questioning the news vendor. He couldn't give us much more than what I told you, but he was consistent on the details. The first caller didn't leave a name, used a pay phone."

"So that could have been anybody, even Wardell himself."

"Possible. But the details were consistent with the news vendor, and the timings match up perfectly with the first sighting and the security video too."

"Did you bring Wardell's father in?"

Banner put her hand on the APB in front of her. It displayed a two-year-old color photograph of Wardell's father. Inside the investigation, they'd been referring to him as Wardell Senior, but that wasn't really his name. Wardell was the mother's name; this guy answered to Edward Allen Nolan, Eddie to anyone acquainted with him. It was the most recent image they could get ahold of—the man didn't appear to have any family or close friends—and was culled from one of the last interviews he had given before the residual interest in the Chicago Sniper case dropped to a background hum.

The photograph showed a man who looked almost nothing like his son. He was overweight, unshaven, and unkempt. But the scruffy hair was the same dirty blond, the eyes the same cruel shade of blue. The picture showed a porch in the sun, a neglected front yard in the background. Nolan was sitting in a lawn chair on the porch, a hunting rifle across his lap. Banner wondered briefly if that had been the photographer's idea or Nolan's. Either way, it showed some nerve.

"We can't find him," Banner said in answer to Blake's question. "Nobody can. Lincoln PD visited his apartment last night, no answer. Two of our guys went out there today; the super let them in. The place is cleared out—his rent is up to date, but it looks like he hasn't been there in at least two weeks."

"Two weeks," Blake repeated. "Before any of this happened."

"Do you think ...?"

"That there's a connection?" Blake finished. "No. I doubt it. But we need to find him."

"We're working on it," Banner said.

"I'm going to head out there now."

"What about the red van?" Banner asked, feeling like she was saying it only to play devil's advocate.

"He's going after Eddie Nolan," Blake said. "Either I'll find him, or Wardell will. I'll call you when I get there."

Banner replaced the handset on the cradle and looked at the Nolan APB again. She drummed her fingertips on the sheet of paper, then slammed her hand down as she made her mind up. She got up from her desk, exited her open office door, and walked the twelve paces across the open plan to

Castle's office. It was a glass-walled cubicle, like Banner's office but a little bigger.

The blinds were shut tight. She knocked on the door sharply and entered, not waiting to be asked. Castle was on the phone, his chair facing away from his desk at the window. His head jerked around as he heard Banner's entrance. Banner found that a literal open-door policy worked well for her: It relaxed people and encouraged a free flow of information. Castle, by contrast, was the kind of guy who expected you to knock and wait; so Banner was mildly surprised that he didn't look irritated when she walked in. Instead, he looked preoccupied. He swiveled back to face the desk, nodded at Banner, and held up a finger: *Just a minute.*

"Yes, sir," Castle said once, then again after a pause. His mouth stayed half open each time, as though he was trying to get a word in edgeways. *Donaldson*, Banner surmised. It had to be, because Banner couldn't think of anyone else in the world Castle wouldn't talk over to get his point across.

"Sir, with respect—" he began, and was cut off. His mouth closed as he realized he wasn't going to get to say his piece. "Understood." Castle hung up and raised his eyebrows at Banner. "The SAC," he said unnecessarily.

"He's pissed?" she asked, equally unnecessarily.

From Castle's answering expression, she knew that was an understatement.

"He wants the red van, and Wardell, half an hour ago. Do you realize how many red Ford E-Series vans there are registered in Iowa?"

"Actually yes, there are eight hundred and sixty-seven. We're working through the list as we speak, and we've got every cop in the state running stop-and-searches on them." She paused. "Are we going to give this to the media? About the van?"

Castle put his elbows on the desk and clasped his hands in front of his mouth. "I think so. Donaldson thinks they're going to skin us alive for this priest shooting. He keeps bitching about resources, manpower, like that's my fault."

Banner knew that this was the real issue for Donaldson: his own personal public standing. Better that someone like Wardell killed ten victims in secret than one victim that everyone knew about. That had been the real reason for the news blackout: not to free up the investigation, but to cover Donaldson's ass, along with that of the director. Nobody would blame the FBI for the initial escape, of course, but they'd certainly blame them for not catching him quickly enough. And they couldn't assign blame on an operation they were unaware of.

"You think they will?" Banner asked.

"Skin us alive? I don't know. We've been keeping them in the loop since the story leaked. They knew we were focusing here in Chicago, but nobody had any reason to think he'd show up in Fort Dodge."

"Blake did."

Castle's complexion darkened a shade. "Thanks for re minding me. Just make sure that never gets out. We don't need a lucky guess making us look even worse."

"Come on, Castle. You know that's bullshit. Blake called it exactly right. The only reason we don't have Wardell accounted for right now is because we didn't back him up."

Castle kicked his chair back and hauled himself up to his full six feet two inches. "You're out of line, Agent Banner." His voice was just a notch below shouting. "We're chasing a military-trained killer who thinks the entire Midwest is his playground. I don't have the manpower to waste chasing up every goddamn hunch brought to me by every asshole that walks in off the street."

"Off the street? This is what we brought him in for. This is what he does."

"*I didn't bring him in!*"

There was a moment's silence, during which both of them became very aware that the main office chatter outside had dropped away. Only the periodic ringing of phones pierced the quiet.

Castle sat back in his chair and lowered his voice again. "We don't need another Ashley Greenwood on our hands just because you think you know best."

The words hit Banner like a slap in the face, but she didn't show it. She moved in closer, leaned on his desk with both hands. "I'm going to Lincoln."

Castle shook his head, his voice calmer after the outburst. "We coordinate from this office until we get a lead on—"

"He's headed for Lincoln," she said. "I don't care which direction the red van was or wasn't going; the target is the father. Fort Dodge is practically on a straight line to him."

Castle held her gaze, waited for her to finish. "The father is a possibility," he admitted. "But we have agents in the field looking for Edward Nolan. We need to be here, because nobody really *knows* where this son of a bitch is going to strike next. Not you, not me, and not Blake." He spoke the other man's name with mild contempt. "And somebody needs to be manning the helm."

"Not much good manning the helm when the ship's sinking."

Castle just looked back at her. Didn't reply.

After twenty seconds of silence, Banner said it again. Quietly but firmly. "I'm going to Lincoln."

Castle's phone rang. He ignored it for the first three rings, holding the stare, then picked it up and turned back to the window. Banner strode back to her own office, picked up the phone, and dialed her sister's number, steeling herself.

Helen's voice betrayed an undercurrent of disappointment when Banner asked the favor, even though she said it would be fine. Banner had known she'd say that, but she hated to take advantage of her yet again.

· "It's just for a day or two," she said, hoping she wasn't promising something she couldn't deliver.

"It's fine, I guess," Helen said. "And compared to the rest of the brood, Annie is no trouble."

Banner believed that. Helen already had four boys and a girl, with another on the way, and as a group they seemed to get more boisterous with each new addition. Annie could be as much of a handful as any seven-year-old, but she usually behaved herself impeccably at her aunt's.

"You're sure? I really hate to ask again."

Banner heard Helen sigh and then a pause a little too long for comfort. When she spoke again, she'd lowered her voice. "It's not me, Elaine. Annie's growing up. She's big enough to understand that she's being off-loaded."

"Helen, I promise—"

"Stop promising. That's part of the problem. I know about the job. I get that what you do is important. But Annie was really looking forward to going home tonight. I mean, be-tween you and Mr. Big-Shot Ex ..." She paused, and there was another sigh. "I'm sorry, Elaine."

Banner swallowed. There didn't seem to be anything else to say in this conversation.

"Can I talk to her?"

"Sure. Hang on."

Helen put the handset down. In the background, Banner could hear her yelling at one of the boys to put that down *immediately*, and a moment later another voice appeared.

"Mom?" As usual, Annie's voice was level, serious for her

age. Banner felt a pang in her stomach as she realized she couldn't remember when Annie had started calling her that instead of "Mommy."

"Hi, angel. Did Aunt Helen tell you?"

"Yes. You can't come and get me tonight." Annie's voice was matter-of-fact. Did she just expect this now?

"I'll try to be back as soon as I can. How about we go for ice cream when I'm back?"

"Daddy says you give me too much ice cream."

Banner bit her tongue. She was surprised Mark had time to monitor his daughter's junk-food consumption, given how rigidly he resisted seeing her outside of his regular time, every other weekend.

"He's probably right," she said. "Movie instead?"

Annie considered this carefully. "That would be nice," she agreed finally. "Mom?"

"Yes?"

"Are you coming to see my play on Tuesday?"

Banner closed her eyes and fought the easy urge to say yes and hope it would be true. "I don't know, Annie. But I'd really like to go if I can make it."

There was a pause while Annie absorbed this. "Will you come if you catch the bad man?"

"I'll do my best, sweetheart," Banner said, feeling tears prick at the corners of her eyes. "I've got to go now."

"Okay, Mom."

"Be good for your aunt Helen."

"I will be."

"I love you."

"I love you too, Mom."

25

There were two signs. The first one was the approved size and shape and shade of green mandated by federal regulations, and it advised drivers that the town of Stainton was a half mile off the highway at the next exit. That wasn't the sign that caught Wardell's attention, though. The second sign was big and colorful and unconstrained by any style guidelines, and it advertised:

JUBA'S X-PRESS STOP
MAIN STREET, STAINTON
GAS STATION * COFFEE SHOP * CONVENIENCE STORE

Wardell blinked and had time to read the name of the place again before the sign flew by. *Juba.* He glanced at the fuel gauge and saw that the tank was half full. Then again, that also meant it was half empty. No harm in a small detour to top up.

He slowed for the turn and signaled. He had the driver's side window rolled all the way down, enjoying the sting of the cold, fresh air on his face. As a man who'd spent the best part of the previous five years confined to a tiny, airless cell for twenty-three hours of every day, this felt like the lap of luxury.

This was more like it, traveling under his own steam. It was more than worth the risk of stealing the vehicle. The three separate bus journeys it had required to get to Fort Dodge had been uneventful, but there was always the constant nagging pressure that one of the other passengers might recognize him, even with his new look, and make a phone call once they disembarked. Then the game would be over before it had properly begun. Besides, there was something institutional about bus travel that was a little too close to the way he'd been living the past few years. You had to be at a specific place at a specific time to be taken by someone else to a specific destination. There was no room for deviation from the schedule, for detours.

Wardell had a destination, of course. He'd thought about it almost as soon as he'd been freed and had confirmed and finalized those arrangements in the course of the five-minute phone call he'd made the previous morning. But he wasn't on a bus anymore, and he had more than enough time so that he could afford to take a detour.

As promised, Juba's X-press Stop was perched on the main street of Stainton. As far as Wardell could see, it was the only business in what was a minuscule town. He pulled in and parked beside a self-service pump. Before he turned off the engine, he surveyed the area. There was a kid in a red hooded puffer jacket with his—or her, Wardell couldn't tell—back to him, standing over by the ATM that was built into the wall of the store. The only other human in sight was the clerk inside, an overweight man with a thick beard. The man was reading a magazine and hadn't looked up when Wardell pulled in.

There were security cameras, of course, but that was fine. Wardell didn't think his pursuers would have any way of knowing what kind of vehicle he was traveling in. Their attempts to keep up with him had been almost depressingly ineffective so far. He hadn't expected them to fall so completely for the green shirt ruse.

Wardell opened the door, got out, and unlocked the fuel cap. The guy with the beard authorized the pump without looking up. It started with a thump, and the nozzle thrummed in his hand.

Wardell glanced up at the clerk a couple of times as he waited for the tank to fill, but the only sign that he was even conscious was the occasional flick of a magazine page.

"Mister?"

Wardell's head snapped down and he saw the kid in the red jacket staring up at him proprietorially. It was a boy, nine or ten years old maybe. Wardell glanced around again, but there was no one else in sight.

"What do you want, kid?" he asked.

"Are you scared?"

Wardell shook his head briefly and looked away, annoyed. He didn't particularly like kids, especially ones who invaded his space and asked nonsensical questions. When he looked back, the boy was still there, still expecting a response.

"Why the hell would I be scared?"

"Because of the news."

"The news?"

The boy nodded solemnly. "The news. It says people are scared to fill up their tanks. Because of the sniper."

Wardell smiled. Maybe he liked this kid after all.

"I heard about that."

"The lady on the news said people don't want to fill up their cars. 'Case they get shot. My daddy says that's all we need, less customers."

"Your daddy owns this place?"

"Yes, sir."

"Is that your daddy?" He indicated the clerk with a brief nod.

The boy grinned indulgently. "*No.* That's just Phil."

"Right," Wardell said, as though he'd got it straight now.

The pump clicked off automatically as the level of fuel in

the tank hit the sensor in the nozzle. Wardell pulled it out and replaced it in the slot.

"Aren't *you* scared?" he asked the kid as he screwed the cap back into place.

The boy considered this carefully for a moment. "Not really. I'm here to look out for the bad guy. Make the customers feel safer."

Wardell bent at the knees to drop closer to the boy's level. He put a hand on his skinny shoulder and gave it a squeeze.

"You're a pretty brave kid. I bet your daddy appreciates you looking out for the business. A boy should always look out for his pop."

The boy shrugged a little, uncomfortable now. "I guess."

"But I don't think you have anything to worry about."

"No?"

"I mean, look around. There's nobody here. Nobody but you and me. And Phil over there, of course. Why would the bad guy want to come here?"

"But the news says nobody knows where he is."

"Is that right?"

"Uh-huh. So that means he could be anywhere. And if he could be anywhere, he could be right here in Stainton."

"You have a point there, partner. Difficult to argue with that. He could be right here with us." He laughed out. "Why, he could be you or me, I guess."

The boy swallowed and glanced over at Phil, who was oblivious. "I think I have to go in the store now." He tried to move backward, but Wardell tightened his grip on his shoulder.

"Not so fast, partner."

The boy looked back at him and stared, wide-eyed.

Wardell reached down with his free hand, not seeming to disturb the pocket of his jeans. Then his hand flashed up, holding something against the boy's face. He flinched and focused on what Wardell was holding, relaxing a little when he saw it was a fifty-dollar bill.

"I'm in kind of a hurry, to tell you the truth. If you could drop that inside for the gas, I'd be mighty grateful. And make sure Phil gives you the change. You can keep it."

"Thank you, sir," the boy said quickly as he took the bill.

Wardell released his shoulder at last and opened the driver's door. "You know something?"

"What?"

"Even if the bad guy was here, I think he'd leave you alone. I think he'd like the name of your pop's store."

The kid looked puzzled, then glanced up at the sign. "That was just the name when my daddy bought the place. I think Juba's kind of a dumb name."

Wardell smiled and tipped a finger to his brow in a little salute; then he got in and started the engine. As he pulled out of Stainton, he realized that the daylight was already beginning to fade from the sky. He'd find a place to stop soon, somewhere safe to rest up for the night. There was work to do in the morning.

26

9:40 p.m.

The evening was well advanced by the time I arrived in Lincoln, and the clear blue sky of the morning had long since given way to dark gray clouds and then to nightfall. Lincoln was the state capital of Nebraska and the second largest city in the state after Omaha. Nebraska being what it was, that meant the town held a sizable proportion of the total state population.

Eddie Nolan's last-known address was a one-bedroom dive in the Westwood Terrace Apartments, a run-down building located in the part of town called Clinton. Clinton, Lincoln. Being named after two different presidents hadn't helped make the location any more desirable. Westwood Terrace was a dirty concrete block, U-shaped and gathered around a trash-strewn patch of grass. The building superintendent was an obese, husky-voiced man in jeans and a flannel shirt. Although hostile at first, he warmed considerably after I explained I wasn't an FBI agent.

The agents who'd come by earlier in the day had evidently got the super's back up when they'd made him open Nolan's apartment door, so much so that I suspected I could have gained access merely by listening to the guy bitch about their attitude for ten minutes or so. The twenty-dollar bill I produced cut that down to three minutes, which in my estimation was money well spent.

As the super let me in, I noted that the lock plate was shiny, and there was evidence of recent repair to the door-frame.

"The police do that?" I asked, nodding at the lock and the evidence of damage.

The big man shook his head wearily. "That was last week. Lot of people looking for Mr. Nolan."

"Must be a pain in the ass," I said. "Having to deal with this, I mean."

The super shrugged and looked around, as if to say this kind of incident was hardly unusual with his tenants. I guessed the guy was probably just happy the rent was paid up.

The apartment was cramped and smelled of stale cigarette smoke and dampness. Despite the scarcity of furniture, it was a mess, and probably had been almost as bad even before agents Gorman and Anderson had conducted their search. Takeout menus and magazines devoted mainly to guns and barely legal teens mingled with empty beer cans and stained pizza boxes. The agents had gone through the mostly emptied drawers, opened Nolan's junk mail, and moved the furniture around: not exactly what you'd call thorough. Maybe they'd refrained from a more rigorous search because Nolan himself wasn't actually wanted in connection with any crime, and they'd decided he was so tangential to the manhunt that finding him didn't justify much more than the time it took to knock on his door. I thought different, and perhaps that was why I came up with a different result.

In ten minutes, I had kicked loose enough leads to put me on what I thought was the right track. In the otherwise empty closet, I'd found a single clipping from a magazine article about Caleb Wardell. One corner of the clipping was creased over and flattened, as though it had been stored in a box or file under a lot of other papers. Probably a lot of other news clippings in a proud father's collection.

Virtually everything else I needed was in the trash: a bunch of crumpled bookies' slips showing amounts in the high hundreds and a soaked and dried-out again beer mat from a place called Jimmy's Bar and Grill that sported a telephone number scrawled in blue ballpoint pen. The number put me through to one of the bookies represented in the crumpled ball of slips. The sound and manner of the voice at the other end of the line told me it was the kind of operation that would not be above breaking the occasional leg.

Feeling a hunch, I Googled Jimmy's on my cell phone. It was a steakhouse in a place called Allanton, a tiny village in the southwest of Nebraska that seemed to be a popular hunting and fishing location. The bookies' slips explained the busted lock and the absence of Nolan. The beer mat might suggest a possible destination, given what I knew about him from the magazine interviews. Besides being a lousy gambler, Wardell's dad was a hunter. Like father, like son. I just hoped the similarity wasn't too exact.

I thanked the super and went back outside to the rented Caddy. I dialed the number for Jimmy's and waited. I was about due a lucky break—maybe Nolan would be there right now. A deep voice answered on the eighth ring, loud rock music and raucous laughter in the background.

"Jimmy's?" He said it slowly, like he wasn't entirely sure.

"Hi, I'm looking to speak to one of your customers," I said.

"We're not the ..." The voice at the other end paused, trying to think of what it was he was not. "The Yellow Pages, buddy," he finished, sounding mildly pleased with himself. Like a kid who's managed to remember what two and two makes.

I came back quickly before the hang-up I could sense coming. "He told me I could reach him there."

Another pause. When the guy at the other end spoke, he sounded unsure. "Got a name?"

"Eddie Nolan."

I heard a sharp intake of breath. It was as though I'd yelled a four-letter word at a church coffee morning.

"You're gonna need to speak to Brenda."

"Well, can I?"

"Huh?"

"Speak to Brenda?"

"She ain't in. Try tomorrow morning."

I started to ask what time, but the genius on the other end had terminated the call.

I pondered the conversation for a couple of seconds, then took the road atlas thoughtfully supplied by the rental company from the side pocket in the driver's door and worked out the route to Allanton. It was another two hundred and fifty miles to the west. If I was wrong, this detour would send me hopelessly off course. But if I was right ...

It felt right. With everything I knew, Allanton felt right.

Carol's voice chimed in from the back of my mind: *Anything you don't know?*

I glanced down at my phone, half expecting to see the picture from Coney Island. It wasn't there, just a stock image of a dandelion clock.

"Always," I said aloud. There's always something you don't know. But that didn't change my mind about Allanton.

I mulled over the idea of driving straight through before deciding I'd be better off getting some sleep while I could. The genius had said the person I needed to talk to would be in tomorrow morning. Unless the bar opened unusually early, that probably meant Brenda was the manager and that she'd be on site to carry out administrative tasks. That was good; it would mean not having to deal with a bar full of potentially hostile regulars.

I locked the Cadillac's doors, reclined the seat and, despite the discomfort, fell into a deep and dreamless sleep. I woke at four and turned the key in the ignition. I drove south on North Twenty-Seventh Street, took a right on O Street, then merged with I-80 and put the pedal to the floor. By the time the six a.m. news turned all my assumptions upside down, I was two-thirds of the way to Allanton. Too far to turn back.

DAY THREE

27

Four hundred miles southeast of Lincoln, Missouri State Highway Patrol Trooper Abel Williams pulled his cruiser to a halt on the shoulder of Highway 65. He was about as deep into the Busiek State Forest as someone could get without being on his way out again, five or six miles from the nearest streetlight. The remains of the vehicle were far enough off the road that he'd probably have driven right by if he hadn't spotted the last embers of the conflagration.

He got out of the car, withdrawing his gun from its holster. Probably just teenagers down from Springfield, burning a car they'd stolen and taken for a ride. And probably they'd be long gone. Still, it was better to be safe than sorry.

The stink of burnt plastic was carried upward by a chill wind out of the woods. Williams descended the gentle incline toward the dying glow between the trees, unhurried. He unclipped his flashlight from his belt as he walked—it was a heavy-duty Maglite, weighing two pounds and as good as a club as it was as a light source. But he didn't turn it on just yet, even when the branches overhead began to thicken as he moved deeper into the woods.

The wreck was farther down than he'd thought at first; its apparent proximity had been deceptive. Perhaps some kind of optical illusion caused by the position of the trees or the temperature of the air or some other damn thing. Still, he kept the flashlight off and the gun aloft—safety on, because he didn't want to put a foot in a rabbit hole and blow his own head off. He stopped and listened, suddenly feeling very alone and isolated now that he'd walked thirty paces from the car.

He heard nothing—or that is to say, nothing he wouldn't have expected to hear. The wind whispering around tree trunks and between the denuded branches above. The small sounds of woodland animals moving restlessly some way off. Among these the intrusive, alien sounds of the dying vehicle: warped metal ticking and sighing as it cooled in the night air. Williams told himself to ignore the shiver that crept the length of his spine. He reminded himself how ridiculous his fear would seem later, under the cold fluorescent lights of the station. There was nothing to be afraid of here, just a quiet spot in the woods and an abandoned and destroyed piece of some hapless sucker's property.

He threw a quick glance over his shoulder and started toward the vehicle again. As he got closer, he could see it had been on the bigger side: some kind of truck or van. Yes, a van by the looks of things. *A Ford.*

Williams brought the flashlight up and clicked it on, bathing the wreck in a cone of white light. Yes, a lot of the paint had been charred away, but there was enough left around the sills to identify it as a red Ford E-Series van, just like in the APB. A different kind of shiver ran back down his shoulders and settled in his gut. Different, and not entirely unwelcome. The missing vehicle in a multistate manhunt, and the odds were looking pretty good that Abel Williams had found it.

Or were they?

Highway patrol troopers weren't exactly at the top of the

pecking order in such matters, but from the limited intel Williams had picked up, the consensus seemed to be that Caleb Wardell was heading east. That would take him back toward Illinois, not hundreds of miles south to the bottom end of Missouri. And why would he, having somehow eluded the dragnet, choose to abandon his car out here, ten miles from the nearest town—*small* town, at that?

Williams made a slow circuit of the burnt-out husk, keeping his feet just outside the blackened radius on the ground. Sweeping the beam of the flashlight over the almost unrecognizable remains of the driver's seat didn't reveal much, but made him pretty sure there wasn't a corpse in there. Not up front, at least. He slowed as he reached the rear doors of the van, reluctant now to bring the speculation to a close. Stepping inside the charred circle, he holstered his weapon and reached a cautious hand out to test the surface of the rear door. He withdrew his fingertips instinctively, then put them back on. Hot, but not dangerously so.

He hitched up the sleeve of his jacket to use as an improvised oven glove and pulled at the handle. The lock was not engaged, but the door was warped and wouldn't give more than an inch at first. He placed the flashlight on the forest floor, covered his left hand as well, and wrenched. A little later and it would have been futile—he'd have had to call it in and request that Toby or Dave bring a crowbar up here—but as it was, the metal was still just hot enough to be slightly malleable, and the door pulled open with a bereft scream.

He stumbled back, exhaling a long cloud of air after the exertion, and then put his hand down to retrieve the flashlight. He teased it over the open door, then put a boot on the bumper to reach inside and angle the beam over the interior.

Whoever had torched the van had started the blaze in the front seat, so the back wasn't as badly damaged as the front. The body of the vehicle was burnt out, too, but there were identifiable traces of things in the back as opposed to the blackened slag up front. A melted triangle of blue plastic that looked like it might once have been the corner of a sleeping bag. The smoking steel hub of the spare wheel. And something just as unmistakable: the warped barrel and charred stock of a rifle.

Williams hadn't realized there was a wide grin on his face until it was wiped off by the sound of something moving behind him. He spun around, cursing out loud as the flashlight connected with the doorframe and dropped to the ground. He fumbled at his holster, asking himself why in Christ he'd buttoned it. He got the gun out after five or six seconds that felt like a week and a half.

He heard it again, a noise like something moving not too far away. A man-sized something, not some foraging animal. His eyes were still adjusting back to the darkness, so staring ahead was getting him nowhere; it was like standing in a dark room and staring into a closet full of old clothes.

Slowly, aware of his own rapid breathing, he stooped to pick up the flashlight. When he brought it up to bear on the direction from which he'd heard the noise, he saw nothing but trees.

But somehow, he felt the eyes on him. On some primitive, reptilian level, he knew they were there as surely as he'd known the metal doors had been hot.

He wasn't sure how long he stood there, returning the invisible gaze, but after a time he felt that his watcher had gone. He gave it some more time, then started to back away slowly. Stopping every couple of paces to splash light around, it took him ten minutes to get back to the car. When he picked up the CB to call the station, his hands were shaking like he'd just spent a night outside in February.

28

8:17 a.m.

"It doesn't make any goddamn sense," Banner said, kicking a loose branch aside.

"Of course it doesn't, Banner," Castle said abruptly. "He's a grade-A nutcase. You expect him to check in with us? File an itinerary each morning so we can keep in touch?"

"That's not what I meant," she said. She was looking back down the hill in the direction of the burnt-out van. Both of them were assiduously avoiding the unblinking gaze of the news helicopters hovering overhead. Blame either the cold or the frustration, but Banner had a longing for a cigarette almost unequalled in the time since she'd kicked the habit when she and Mark had decided to try for a baby. God, was it really eight years already?

"I know it wasn't," Castle said. The hint of a smile hovered at the edge of his mouth. "For what it's worth, I was starting to think he was headed for Lincoln too. Your boy Blake made a good case."

Immediate evidence to the contrary, Banner thought he still was heading for Lincoln, sooner or later, but she kept that to herself for the moment. Of greater note was the fact that Castle was speaking to her almost like a normal human being. She wondered if it was brought on by remorse over his Ashley Greenwood crack the day before. Banner knew Castle's opinion on the Markow case all too well, but he'd crossed a line with that comment, and she suspected he knew it.

"He's *my* boy now?" she said.

Castle shrugged. "He doesn't seem to be Donaldson's boy anymore. He'd gone cold on him big-time when we spoke. Reminded me he's just an adviser, not to let him distract us too much."

"So pretty much the opposite of what he said two days ago."

"Pretty much."

Banner smiled. "I hear selective amnesia becomes a real issue above a certain pay grade."

Castle didn't return the smile, but he didn't dispute the point either.

"It's the rifle, too," Banner said, returning to the previous discussion. "Why discard a perfectly good weapon?"

"This is America. It's never difficult to lay your hands on another perfectly good weapon when you need one."

"Still, it's too neat. Like he's signposting."

"That may be, but we have to take a look at where the signs point anyway." He checked his watch and changed the subject. "How far did you get? Last night, I mean."

It had taken Banner an hour to stop back at the house to pack an overnight bag, another forty minutes to grab Chinese for dinner, and she'd made good time after that. There wasn't a direct flight to Lincoln until eight forty-five the next morning, so she'd opted to drive. She'd been on I-80, a few miles outside Des Moines, at six a.m. when Castle had called her with the news.

"That's okay, I guess," he said. "At least you didn't have to backtrack. How's the family?"

"She's fine," Banner said shortly.

Castle looked like he was about to say something, then shut up. They stood in silence for a minute, both staring down the slope to where the forensics people were picking over the remains of the car. The rifle had already been recovered, given a preliminary investigation, and rushed to the lab. It would be a while before they'd know if it was even possible to tie what was left of the weapon to the Heckler & Koch PSG1 rifle used in the shootings in Cairo and Fort Dodge, but they could certainly confirm that it had been a PSG1, if not *the* PSG1. She thought about how sure Blake had been and how sure she herself had been of Wardell's likely direction just twelve hours before.

"Maybe it's not him," she said. "Maybe it's not a red van." Castle's brow furrowed in confusion at that. "Maybe it's a red herring, instead."

Castle shook his head. "Be a hell of a coincidence."

Banner realized she'd phrased it wrong. "I don't mean he didn't dump it here, or that this has nothing to do with him. I mean maybe he's trying to throw us off again. Like with the green shirt. That would explain the rifle being here."

Castle's face set hard at the mention of the green shirt. It was still a sore point. Last night they'd managed to finally tie up that particular loose end in the form of a homeless drunk found sleeping among the trash in an alley near the West Harrison Street Greyhound station, green T-shirt still very visible under the puke stains. After being hauled in for questioning, he admitted "some dude" had paid him fifty bucks to swap shirts and take the bus to Chicago. When pressed for a description of said dude, his recollection was shaky to say the least. The fifty dollars had evidently been spent in exactly the way Wardell had hoped it would be.

Banner pretended she hadn't noticed Castle's discomfort and continued. "Just because he's not on a straight-line drive doesn't mean he's not still gunning for Daddy dearest. So either he's doubling straight back to Nebraska ..."

"Or he's taking the scenic route," Castle finished. "Which would involve either laying low for a few days, or killing again down here."

"He'll kill again today."

Castle nodded agreement. "He will. Look, Banner, the father was a good theory. I'll admit it. But we've got no real evidence to suggest that's what he's planning. Not counting the escape, we've got two victims so far, and they fit the established MO like a glove: perfect strangers chosen for convenience." He paused, evidently considering the choice of a priest as the last victim. "Convenience and impact. Today will be the same, unless we get lucky."

"What about Mia Jennings?" Banner said, referring to Wardell's ex-girlfriend and first known victim. "She wasn't a perfect stranger."

"That was different. You read the report from Behavioral Sciences. Jennings was just the spark for the fire."

"That's not what I took from it," Banner said. "It was more like Jennings was the excuse to get started."

"What's the difference?"

Banner said nothing, but she thought there was a difference, and it was an important one.

Castle let the silence hang for a minute and then said, "Random kill, somewhere in this area, within the next two hours. Maybe Springfield, maybe one of the smaller towns." He sighed through his nostrils. "We've already routed teams to every town within a hundred-mile radius of this spot. Everywhere with a population over a thousand." He said this with a slight edge of defeat in his voice. The unspoken rejoinder: What if he picks one of the other places? Castle shook his head in frustration. "The canvas is just too damn big this time: He's only one man against all of us, but he's making that an advantage."

Banner understood his frustration and shared it. Most serial killers operate within much tighter geographical boundaries: choosing their victims within easy reach of their home or base. Wardell was different. Wardell could strike anywhere there were people, whereas they could only hope to cover the areas with the largest concentrations of population, play the odds as best they could. Meanwhile, the bodies would pile up until they got lucky or Wardell got careless.

Banner looked at her watch. Coming up on eight thirty. That meant she'd been up for twenty-seven hours after sleeping three the previous night. It also meant it was peak rush hour, central time: prime time for Caleb Wardell. She looked up at the news choppers.

"When are you on?"

He patted his cell phone through his coat and said, "Anytime now."

"At least people have a rough idea of the danger zone today," Banner said, hoping that was even true. "What are you going to say?"

"Donaldson wants the usual. Stay calm; go about your business; don't panic. The standard bullshit."

"And?"

"And that's not going to do it. They should panic. I'm going to tell people in the area to stay indoors if possible. Don't travel unless it's necessary. Avoid public spaces."

"You think they'll go for it?"

"Some of them. Maybe."

Banner's cell rang; it was Blake. As she hit the button to answer, Castle's phone rang too. The interview, no doubt. In tandem, the two of them turned and walked a few paces apart to concentrate on their new conversations.

Banner didn't bother with hello, just asked, "Are you in Lincoln?"

"I'm headed to a place called Allanton. I was in Lincoln last night. What's happening with the red van in Missouri?"

Banner shot a glance at the nearest news helicopter. "You saw it on the news? I'm there right now."

"Heard it," he said. "On the radio. Castle there?"

"He's getting ready to be interviewed. CNN, I think. You find Nolan yet?"

"I'm working on something. Are your people still up in Lincoln?"

"We pulled them back when there was no trace of Nolan. We've let it be known we're looking for him though. If he sees the news, he might come to us. Assuming he's able to." She paused and said, "Eight thirty already." She didn't have to say more.

"I know."

"We need to catch a break soon."

"I know."

"Blake?"

"Yeah?"

"Be careful up there."

29

8:32 a.m.

It was a wooden shack, long abandoned and forgotten, its rightful owner probably long dead and just as forgotten.

It stood alone in the woods, three hundred yards from the road, barely larger than an outhouse. Decades of long, hot summers and longer, freezing winters had blended it into its surroundings. Ancient green paint peeled back from the damp, dark wood, weaving a perfect camouflage out of the colors and the small ragged patterns. Forget seeing it from the road; you could pass within twenty feet of the shack and not even notice it was there. Unless somebody told you exactly where to look, of course.

Wardell stopped five paces from the door and savored the moment of anticipation, remembering the instructions.

If I'm not around when you get there, the padlock key is in the third tree to the right as you face the door.

Wardell walked to the third tree and circled its trunk. Sure enough, on the other side was a deep knot, just big enough to insert his fingers and thumb. He reached in and felt around until his fingers closed on a cold, hard sliver of metal. He gripped it between two fingers and drew the key out, realizing there was not one padlock key, but two on a ring.

The padlock on the shack door was old and rusty—which fit in with the camouflage—but one of the two keys slid in easily enough, and the lock sprang open with a quarter turn. Wardell lifted it off the catch and creaked the door open. The deep scent of fifty-year rot crept out to meet him. And more recent smells too: oil and powder and gasoline and leather. The floor space inside amounted to not much more than that of the cell Wardell had occupied at Marion. That was all right, because it was clear that the shack had never been intended as a dwelling. It had been merely a storage space for a hunter.

It was still a storage space for a hunter.

There was a ragged hole in the roof in the left-hand corner nearest the door. Diagonally opposite, at the far corner, was a shape roughly rectangular: four feet wide, two feet high and about the same deep, and covered by a green tarpaulin. The tarp was made up like a bedsheet, the excess tucked neatly beneath the shape.

Wardell crossed the interior space in two strides and pulled the tarp off to reveal a large steel trunk. The second key opened the single padlock on the trunk, and Wardell took another moment to savor the anticipation before he swung the lid back on its hinges.

He stood back and surveyed what lay within with approval.

30

8:45 a.m.

I've been to a lot of places in my time. Some of them you'll have heard of, others not. I've worked on every continent. I've worked in countries that don't exist anymore. I've slept on sheets of silk in a Paris penthouse, under sheets of cardboard in a Somali ghetto. I've been all over. But until this job, I'd never been to Nebraska. In fact, just about the only thing I'd known about the state prior to this visit was that it was the title of my favorite Springsteen album.

I kind of wished I had that album to listen to as I crossed the wide, deserted Nebraskan landscape. The title track had strange echoes of the case in hand: a story-song about a spree killer awaiting execution, able to give no excuse for his crime other than, *There's just a meanness in this world*. That made me remember Mosul again: the smell of blood and the killer's eyes. A meanness in this world. That was the truth, all right.

My thoughts turned away from the Boss and back to the red van; the fact that it had been found so far south had taken me by surprise. That there had been two independent eyewitnesses to his departure back in Fort Dodge suggested Wardell had indeed been the man driving the van, and now it looked like he was hundreds of miles away, presumably getting ready to strike again. With an effort, I pushed that thought aside; there was nothing I could do about it now. If nothing else, finding Nolan would tie up a loose end. And if I was lucky, it might even provide a solid lead. Something that would at last allow me to get a grip on this phantom.

The traffic was light to nonexistent on I-80. The vast plains were occasionally interrupted by hills and canyons, but for the most part the country was flat and featureless. The cloud-streaked blue sky above seemed to have more personality.

Even as the hour advanced and I joined Route 183, the company remained sparse. It was early yet. *But rush hour will come*, the voice at the back of my head whispered, and it wasn't concerned about traffic.

It was eight forty-five when I reached the town of Allanton and pulled into the gravel parking lot in front of Jimmy's Bar and Grill. As I'd expected, it was closed. As I'd hoped, there was a sign of life: a blue Dodge pickup parked in the bay nearest an unmarked metal side door that looked as though it could lead to an office.

I rapped on the door and waited. No answer. I tried again. After a minute, I heard a lock click and the door opened a few inches, revealing a heavyset woman aged somewhere between thirty and sixty. Her hair was a copper dye job, and her blue-mascaraed eyelids hung at half-mast, giving her the look of a kid's doll that had been turned halfway between vertical and horizontal.

"We don't open till eleven," she said, and moved to close the door.

I put a hand up to stop it and smiled. "Actually, I'm looking for someone. I wondered if you might be able to help me."

The woman's eyes narrowed still further. "There's just me."

"Oh, I didn't mean here. I'm looking for a friend of mine. We were supposed to meet in the bar last night, but I had some car trouble"—I pointed back in the direction of the Cadillac—"and I forgot to charge my phone. He told me he comes in here a lot. Name's Eddie, Eddie Nolan."

The woman examined me from between the mascara for a long moment. "You a cop?"

Bingo. When somebody doesn't know the guy you're looking for, they tell you so. They don't ask if you're a cop. I shook my head and grinned good-naturedly. "No, ma'am. But knowing Eddie, I can understand why you'd ask me that." I paused, looking her up and down as if trying to remember something, then said, "It's Brenda, right?"

Brenda did not confirm or deny. I could see that she was calculating what benefit this conversation might hold for her. Then she nodded slowly. "Eddie might have been here. Might have mentioned somebody might come by looking for him, as a matter of fact."

I opened my mouth, and she cut me off quickly.

"But he said to expect a tall guy with fair hair and blue eyes. He said not to talk to anybody else who might be asking about him. You're tall enough, I guess, but you don't have fair hair. And if those eyes are blue, I'm Frank Sinatra."

I sighed, but only for effect. I put my hand in my coat pocket, and when it appeared again, it was holding a folded fifty. "Are you absolutely sure about that?" I asked.

Brenda took the bill without changing her expression. Her little eyes were still calculating. "Okay, so you're fair now. Still not sure about those eyes."

I looked at the fifty in her hand for ten seconds, like I was considering taking it back. Long enough to make her uneasy. Then I shrugged and produced another bill of the same denomination. I made a mental note to find an ATM later.

"How about now?"

Brenda's head bobbed up and down, a relieved look on her face. "Ol' blue eyes is back."

31

9:12 a.m.

The log cabins were set on the lower slopes of a ridge a mile outside town, overlooking a small lake. They were evidently built for summer living, which meant they were lying dormant at this time of year. I left the Cadillac at the last blind corner on the entrance road and made for the row of cabins on foot, circling around and climbing the slope, to approach them from the thick woods that lay behind them.

From what Brenda had told me, the cabins all had names: Green Gables, Ocean Breeze, that kind of thing. Some of the owners left a spare set of keys at Jimmy's because they operated a basic spring cleaning service as a sideline. She hadn't known the name of the cabin that could be accessed by the key she'd given to Nolan for a nominal fee, but she'd described it well enough. It was the one with the big front porch and the red door. From the way she'd imparted the information, it didn't sound like Eddie Nolan was the first person she'd sublet to on the quiet.

In any case, I could have picked out the cabin I wanted without any direction from Brenda. It was the only one that didn't have shutters on the windows. I stopped at the edge of the tree line and watched for a few minutes, looking for signs of life. Seeing none, I walked quickly down the slope to the back door. Not hurrying, not creeping. If I was observed, I wanted to look like I had every right in the world to be here.

I reached the door, unholstered my Beretta, and paused for a second to consider my approach. I decided against knocking and tried the handle first. The door was unlocked.

It gave into a long, narrow kitchen that ran the length of the cabin. The kitchen was a good match for Nolan's apartment back in Lincoln. Dirty plates crowded the sink. A half-dozen large pizza boxes were stacked precariously in the corner. A glass ashtray lay on the countertop, vomiting ash and cigarette butts over the surface like a volcano in freeze frame. Next to that, there was a green cardboard box that had contained .300 Win Mag cartridges lying open and empty on its side. Like father, like son.

I heard the sound of whistling from the adjacent room, accessed by a closed door at one end of the kitchen. I moved to close the back door, then changed my mind, pulling it open wide. I went to the blind side of the interior door. The whistling continued. "Moon River." The performer was flatter than unassembled IKEA furniture. He was definitely in the room behind the door, a room that probably covered the entirety of the remainder of the ground level.

I reached out my left hand and gently swiped the glass ashtray off the countertop. It bounced once on the tile floor, disgorging its contents, and then shattered as it landed for the second time.

The whistling stopped. I heard movement, a fumbling. The sound of something metal and heavy being moved from a wooden surface. Then I heard labored breathing on the other side of the door.

146

"Hello?" The voice was cautious, a little scared-sounding. Then, "Caleb?"

The handle turned down and the door swung open.

I stayed put. Waited. I sensed wary eyes taking in the scene: the broken ashtray, the wide-open door. I guessed Nolan was weighing up two likely scenarios: He'd left the door open himself and a light breeze had dislodged the ashtray; or else an intruder had entered and quickly fled.

The muzzle of a rifle appeared at the edge of the door, pointing at the open back doorway. After a pause, more of the rifle appeared. It was a Remington Model 700. It was followed by a hand, then by a blotchy forearm covered with wiry hair.

I reached out and grabbed the wrist holding the fore-end of the rifle with my right hand, pinching the necessary pressure points. As the fingers sprang open, I turned the pinch into a grip, yanking the man all the way into the kitchen. I put my left arm across his throat and put the muzzle of my Beretta against his cheekbone. My grip was tight enough to discourage movement without rendering the subject unconscious. He tensed and dropped the Remington to the floor.

From this position, I could see only the back of my captive: The man was middle-aged, overweight, had dirty-blond hair, and was naked except for a dirty gray vest. His lips sputtered something that sounded like an attempt at *What the fuck?*

"Good morning, Eddie," I said quietly. "If you're willing to cooperate, I'd like to save your life."

32

"You were expecting Wardell."

The older man looked back at me for a moment, then nodded. Contempt in his eyes. A you-wouldn't-understand look.

We were in the front room of the cabin, and it was every bit as well kept as the kitchen. Fast-food containers and crushed cigarette packs were strewn everywhere, mingling with old issues of *Soldier of Fortune* and survivalist pamphlets with titles like "Life After Doomsday." Nolan had been using a big cast-iron stove in the corner for storing his collection of empty beer cans. The owner would probably want their spring-cleaning money back.

At my insistence, Eddie Nolan had donned a pair of sweat-pants. We were sitting opposite each other on matching couches. I still had my Beretta drawn, but I held it loosely, safety on and pointed at the ground. I didn't really need it. We'd already established who was going to come out second in a fight. I'd left the Remington where it had fallen in the kitchen.

"You won't find him," Nolan told me. "He's too good for you."

I didn't see the point in debating the issue. "He's coming to kill you, you know."

The corners of Nolan's mouth curled up. I had seen that smirk before: in one of the news shots of Wardell being escorted into court. It said *I know something you don't know.* Somehow, it was less convincing on the father.

I feigned surprise. "You don't believe me?"

The smirk stayed in place.

"Here's the thing," I continued. "You're operating under a classic narcissistic delusion: You're assuming that, just because you feel a certain way about somebody, they feel the same way about you. I bet it's pretty common in difficult parent–child relationships. But, of course, you're not really a parent, are you?"

The smirk disappeared. "That boy is my flesh and blood," Nolan said sharply, responding to the barb just as I had known he would.

"Sure," I said, letting the word hang in the air for a moment. "Anyway, it must have been something when you found out who your son was. What he'd done. Would have been too much for most parents, even ones who'd been around to raise their kid. But you were okay with it. No, you were *proud* of it."

The knowing smirk was back. Nolan was shaking his head from side to side, not denying what I was saying, just dismissing it as anything worthy of his interest.

"So you keep news clippings. You give interviews. You write fan letters to your son." This last was a guess. Wardell had undoubtedly received letters while in jail—notorious killers always did—but there had been no specific examples in the files. The twitch of irritation provoked by "fan letters" told me I was on the money. "Yeah, that's what they were, Eddie. Fan letters. You're like one of those guys who takes an interest in one of the unwanted pregnancies he was responsible for only when it ends up starting for the Lakers."

"Caleb is my *son*."

"Did your son ever reply to any of those letters?"

Nolan got up from the chair and took a step forward. I left the gun pointed at the ground and stayed exactly where I was, not acknowledging the attempted intimidation.

"I want you out of here, you little prick," Nolan said, sounding like he was struggling to control his fury.

"No."

"No?"

"You're going to help me find your son. And then I'm going to stop him."

Nolan let out a bark of strained laughter. I didn't know which part he found so amusing: that I expected to catch his son, or that I expected him to help. Nolan moved his head from side to side again and this time I saw something in those eyes that told me that maybe I didn't quite know everything, that there was an angle I hadn't considered.

Anything you don't know, Blake?

"Well, I'll be damned," I said softly. "Caleb got the brains from his mother. I guess he got the crazy from you."

Nolan grinned at the slight. "You were right about one thing, punk," he said. "My boy's coming, and when he gets here, we're gonna start with you."

I shook my head. "You think he wants company? You think the two of you are just going to bond over a little spree killing? You're even more deranged than he is. When did he call you? Yesterday?"

Nolan shook his head. "Day before. He's a good boy. I told him to look me up if he ever got out, and that's exactly what he did. Got things all ready for him coming home."

Something about that worried me. The Remington and the survivalist literature indicated a personality that interpreted "getting ready" in a very specific sort of way. Nonetheless, I doubted the homecoming would be what Nolan expected. He had started to back away from me slowly, moving in the direction of the cabin's front door. I jerked the Beretta up, flicked the safety off with my thumb.

"Sit down."

"You ain't gonna shoot me," Nolan said, and I could see that he knew it. "I ain't done nothing wrong. You'd be killing an innocent man. You said it yourself; you're here to protect me." He put his hand on the door handle and pulled.

I stood up. "Close that door and sit the hell down, Nolan. You're delusional."

Nolan swung the door open wide, letting in the freezing morning air. He turned his head to the doorway and closed his eyes, inhaling a lungful of cold through his nostrils. "Shoot me." He chuckled. "You don't know what a killer is, son."

I got out of the chair and pointed the Beretta at Nolan's head, cocking it. "Try me."

"You don't know how ... how goddamn *glorious* it is, killin' a man. A pansy like you couldn't appreciate it." He opened his eyes again and turned his head back to look at me. "I'm gonna go and wait outside for my son to come home. He won't be long. And when he gets here, I'll show you a killer."

I let the muzzle of the gun drop and walked over to Nolan, then put a hand on his shoulder, gripping hard. "I don't need to shoot you to make you do as you're told, old man."

Nolan opened his mouth, but he never got the chance to say his piece.

The right side of his head, the side facing away from the door, exploded like a water balloon in a microwave. I caught an absurdly detailed freeze frame of it: a flap of hair and scalp swinging up, skull fragments and chunks of brain and a gray-blue eyeball and a torrent of blood all expanding out from the epicenter in a multicolored starburst of gore. And then the world was red and I barely registered the crack of the gunshot as it caught up with its work.

33

For a moment, I was senseless. Nolan's blood was in my eyes, my ears, my mouth, my nostrils. The coppery, viscous taste of it brought a series of involuntary gags from my throat. I resisted the overwhelming urge to lose it completely and dropped to the floorboards, praying that I wasn't too close to the open door or to the window. If I was, I was a sitting duck.

I clawed at my face, wiping blood and unidentifiable chunks of Nolan's head away until my vision returned. I managed to hold off until I'd crawled over to the safe side of the cast-iron stove in the corner before I vomited. After a momentary spell of dizziness, my head cleared.

Unbidden, my brain started trying to compute how Wardell was here at this moment when he'd dumped the van seven hundred miles away only a few hours before. Either that wasn't Wardell out there, or Wardell hadn't dumped the van. Explanations could come later, if there was a later. Right now, all that mattered was that someone had me pinned down. I felt my gut sinking as I became aware that my hands were empty. I'd dropped my gun at some point after Nolan's head had exploded, probably while clearing the stupid bastard's blood off of my face. I looked around.

It lay on the floorboards about a yard from Nolan's virtually decapitated body, just outside the still-spreading pool of dark red blood. And, unfortunately, in full view of the open doorway.

I considered my options. The grisly manner of Nolan's

death told me that Wardell—it had to be him, didn't it?—was probably still using the rifle. I had to assume that he knew I was there. He'd probably have seen me through the front window, and besides, it would have been obvious that Nolan had been talking to someone. The old stove would afford some protection, but I wasn't sure it could stop one of those rounds. The biggest thing in my favor was that I was out of the line of sight. The other thing in my favor was Wardell's frugality. He wouldn't want to waste limited ammunition on blind shots. If I moved quickly, I could probably grab the Beretta before he could get a lock on me. Depending on how far away he was, of course.

My only other option was to stay put and hope he got bored of waiting. Somehow, I didn't think that would happen. In a way, the situations where only one realistic course of action presents itself are the easiest. You just take a breath and do it.

I pushed off my right foot, took two steps, and dived for the Beretta. As my fingers closed around the grip, the doorway slid into my field of view and I saw a figure approaching the cabin, a hundred yards away, carrying some kind of assault rifle, another rifle strapped to his back. I tucked my right arm under me and turned the dive into a roll as my shoulders hit the bloodstained wood.

An assault rifle? I rolled past the doorway and up onto my feet in a crouched position as two things happened: A maelstrom of bullets tore into the space on the floor I'd occupied a second ago, and Eddie Nolan's words repeated in my head. *Got things all ready for him.* So much for frugality with ammunition.

As the firing ceased, I gripped the Beretta two-handed and launched myself back the way I'd come, not wanting to give Wardell breathing space. I fired four quick shots at the figure outside, but he was already diving to the ground. Was that Wardell? It was hard to tell at the distance. The height and build looked right for him.

My lunge carried me past the doorway and back behind the shelter of the stove. It looked like he was toting an AK-47—assuming he wasn't tooled up with armor-piercing rounds, the combination of the walls and the stove might be enough to protect me.

Another rattle of gunfire and the beautiful sound of polymer-coated steel jackets ricocheting off cast-iron proved me right.

They kept coming, though. When the hail finally abated, I guessed he'd emptied an entire magazine from that AK, which told me two things: one, that he wasn't short of ammo, and two, that while Wardell was a purist when it came to long-range killing, he could be pragmatic when he found himself in a fight. If I'd nursed a hope that "one shot, one kill" was an absolutism that Wardell applied across the board, and therefore an exploitable weakness, the last thirty seconds had hammered a couple of hundred nails into the coffin of that hope.

I took advantage of the brief lull to dive across the room and slam through what was left of the kitchen door. It wasn't hard to do; the door now had all the structural integrity of a slice of Leerdammer. I kept low as I made the kitchen, a renewed burst of fire punching big holes in the drywall separating the two rooms.

The Remington was still there on the floor. Was it loaded? Going by the ten minutes I'd just spent with Nolan at the end of his life, I thought it was a safe bet. I grabbed it left-handed and glanced at the wide-open back door, praying that Wardell, or whoever the shooter was, didn't have company.

It didn't really matter though. The fact was, there was only one possible way out. I took it.

I hurled myself through the door, aware of another burst of fire ripping through the wall and hearing the dulled impacts on the stove from the next room. Outside, the sky had clouded over. I didn't have time to scan the tree line, but then I didn't need to. If there was a halfway-competent hostile up there, I'd be dead long before I knew about him. I swiveled left and approached the back corner of the cabin. My gun had a seventeen-round capacity. I'd loosed four already, which left me with lucky thirteen, plus whatever was in the Rem.

I took the corner of the cabin low and hugged the west-facing wall. The shooter was still at the front of the cabin. I could tell by the efficient, machined sounds of another magazine clicking into place. There was a pause of twenty or so seconds while nobody shot. Then mother nature decided to bump the table.

A gap in the cloud cover rolled under the morning sun, casting alien, elongated shadows west for the briefest of seconds, like somebody opening and closing a lighted doorway. It showed me the top of the shooter's shadow, putting him around ten feet from the front door, roughly dead center to the house. The inevitable trade-off was that it gave him my position too.

I didn't hesitate, didn't pause for conscious thought, just pointed the gun in the right direction as though there were nothing between us and fired a volley of six shots in a tight circle. The rounds went through my side of the cabin without complaint. I hoped they would pass through the other side as easily.

Fools seldom differ. A trail of exit holes mushroomed in the wooden siding two feet to my right. One glanced off the barrel of the Remington, knocking it out of my loose grip. I fell back to the corner. Stalemate once again.

Except that I had only seven bullets left. My opponent might have a thousand times that. All he had to do was wait me out.

But then I caught a break. As though toying with us, the sun cast its beam over the earth again. Once again it was fleeting, rolling over the dead grass and the sparse trees on the incline before disappearing behind the trees on the western ridge.

But before it did so, it glinted off of a wing mirror.

I squinted and made out a green pickup truck, partially obscured behind trees. Virtually invisible to the casual glance, but clear enough once you knew where to look. I made the range around seventy yards, which meant I hadn't a chance in hell of hitting it with the Beretta. But with the Remington . . .

I glanced around the corner again fleetingly, just in case the shooter was there. It was clear, so I took a longer peek. The Remington was ten feet from my position.

A voice rang out, sure and clear.

"You can come on out, partner. I ain't gonna hurt you." The voice cleared one thing up. The smooth Southern delivery. The "partner" that sounded at once completely natural and carefully studied. It was Wardell all right. "Got to say, though," he continued, "I'd be mighty grateful if you'd toss that weapon first."

I ignored him, knowing that the aw-shucks good humor was about as trustworthy as a crocodile's tears. I got down low and inched around the corner again. My outstretched left hand reached for the Remington. Five feet, three. My fingers closed around the barrel just as a hawk screeched from somewhere back in the tree line. Another burst of AK-47 fire ripped through the siding as I scrambled back for cover. I felt a sting an inch below my right eye and reached my hand up, plucking out a thin splinter of wood half dipped in crimson.

"What happened to not hurting me?" I yelled, covering the noise as I checked the magazine to confirm the Remington had been loaded with the Win Mag cartridges from the box inside.

"My finger slipped. Come on out."

"If it's okay with you, I'll wait a few minutes."

There was a pause, and I wondered if that meant the seed I'd tried to plant was taking root. I braced the butt of the Remington against my right shoulder and found the pickup in the scope. The angle it was parked, I could see three out of four tires. I took a bead on each and practiced sighting and firing. One, two, three.

When the voice returned, it was business as usual on the surface, but something was firming up beneath it. "You're, uh ... you're starting to try my patience here a little, partner."

I didn't answer. Not with words, anyway.

One. Two. Three. All three visible tires on the pickup blew out. I put another round through the driver's side of the windshield and two in the engine block, just for good measure. Six shots, all on target. I was no Caleb Wardell, but it wasn't too shabby.

I hit the ground again and switched back to the Beretta as I heard a surprised curse and the sound of running feet. I swung out from the corner again to see Wardell coming around the side, opening up with the AK. He was expecting me to be higher up, so his first burst went high. I flinched and the five shots I squeezed off went wide too. I saw Wardell roll behind the porch of the neighboring cabin.

"Shit," I said as quietly as I could manage. I was down to two bullets and one hope in hell. "Stick around," I yelled. "I'm beginning to enjoy myself."

No snappy comeback this time, just the still silence of a smart man considering his options. And then the sound of another magazine clicking into place. I flattened against the ground and braced myself. There was a sustained burst from the AK. It was difficult to be sure, but it sounded like it was moving right to left. The poor, abused cabin took a few dozen more hits, the siding splintering a good four feet above my head. He was making no effort to actually hit me, which meant it was covering fire. Which meant that maybe, just maybe, my ruse had worked.

By taking out Wardell's vehicle, I'd turned the tables somewhat, made full use of an information deficit. Wardell had gone from a strong position to one of uncertainty. Without the pickup truck for a guaranteed getaway, he couldn't afford to just wait me out, not when there was no way of telling how far away my backup might be. Maybe that's what I had meant about waiting a few minutes. Maybe I was waiting *him* out.

With an effort of will, I slowed my breathing and kept still, listened. A minute, two, five. I kept listening.

I'm a pretty good listener. With a regular shooter, I'd be one hundred percent satisfied that the scene was clear, but with a Marine sniper, stealth is the name of the game. I started to wonder how long I was going to have to leave it, what it would take to convince me he'd bolted. And then, somewhere in the distance, I heard a starter motor catch and an engine roar to life. A familiar-sounding engine.

Good news, bad news. I was now pretty certain Caleb Wardell was no longer on the scene. I was pretty certain, because the son of a bitch had just stolen my car.

34

Who in the hell was that? The question rode alongside Wardell like a nagging bitch wife as he forced the elegant Cadillac to traverse the rutted country track as though it were a well-used Jeep.

The man in the cabin had been a white squall at the end of a long period of plain sailing. From the moment Wardell had departed Fort Dodge, everything had gone like a dream. Better, in fact. He'd expected that it might be a little difficult getting to Nebraska, that he might be expected when he got there. But no; the feds were apparently hundreds of miles away with their thumbs wedged firmly up their assholes.

So who in the hell was that, then?

Probably not FBI; that was Wardell's first thought. Feds, like cops the world over, traveled in pairs. They tended not to move with such practiced ease under fire, either. Despite all the training, being fired upon just isn't a common enough occurrence for a federal agent to get used to. This guy, though ... this guy moved as though he had been born into a gunfight and hadn't backed out of one since. Wardell had had everything on his side: the element of surprise, a choice of OPs, multiple weapons, and plenty of ammunition courtesy of Nolan. And yet this other man had held his own, put Wardell on the back foot, and achieved a stalemate. Not a fed or a cop, so who?

Wardell put the thought on hold again as he slowed on the approach to a larger road and swung out to the right, the Cadillac's tires gratefully receiving the smooth asphalt. It seemed to Wardell that there were three possibilities.

One: The man in the cabin was completely unrelated to the manhunt. He was meeting with Nolan for his own purposes and just happened to get caught up in the execution of Wardell's business.

Two: The man was a free agent. Some kind of bounty hunter looking to bag Wardell and claim the big reward. Was there a reward? Wardell hadn't had time to check.

Three: The man in the cabin was not FBI, but he was working with them. And, by the looks of things, showing them up pretty handily.

Wardell glanced down at the speedometer, realized that this automobile was deceptively fast. He'd thought he'd been taking it reasonably slowly while he composed his thoughts, but the needle was way past sixty. He took his foot off the gas as he considered his three scenarios.

Option one was probably the most unlikely. He didn't discount the possibility that a man with a gun might have wanted to pay Eddie Nolan a visit—besides himself, of course—but everything in Nolan's life had been strictly small-time, and so he'd have expected a very low-echelon gangster at best. This man had not been that. Besides, how would anyone else have known precisely where to look for Nolan? During the brief call from the pay phone at the Kentucky truck stop, Wardell had suggested an out-of-the-way place for a reason. No, this was not a coincidence.

Option two: a bounty hunter. This was a possibility, but in Wardell's experience, your average bounty hunter had a great deal in common with your average low-echelon gangster: a lot of guns, a lot of unresolved anger issues, not too much upstairs. But still, a possibility.

Wardell's hunch, however, was the third option. An operative working with the FBI, with enough knowledge of the investigation to be able to track Wardell, but without the fast ties to the Bureau that would have seen him dragged down to Missouri with the others. The fact that the man had been alone suggested that either he had kept his paymasters out of the loop, or more likely they hadn't given credence to his line of inquiry. Their mistake, it would seem.

Wardell turned the radio on for some background noise. He found a news station, caught the tail end of a report from Missouri, where everyone seemed to think he was. Wardell hadn't paid much heed to the messages purportedly from him in the media, but by the sounds of things, this red van business went way beyond a simple hoax. He mused on it for a while before deciding to let it lie for now. He'd stay cautious and wait and see what, if anything, developed from it.

A sign for US Route 34 appeared ahead, informing him of the distance to the destinations at either extremity of the highway: Berwyn, Illinois, at 760 miles, or Granby, Colorado, at 320. East or west.

Wardell slowed to a crawl to give himself time to think. The next name on his list wasn't in either direction. The next name was a few hundred miles north. Up until an hour before, Wardell had planned on heading straight on up there. He had felt confident in his plan so far, reasoning that the feds would expect him to head for Chicago and keep picking random targets. While it appeared they hadn't deviated from that expectation, the encounter at the cabin gave him pause. The man in the cabin had been a step ahead, had seen the Nolan hit coming and had managed to track the old man down. The next name on his list was even more obvious—the hunter would predict it easily. It would be rash to proceed. Safer to delay this mission, mix things up with some more randoms. Or maybe even forget about the list and jump straight to the finale, now that he had all of the necessary tools at his disposal.

But then again, he enjoyed a challenge. And if, as he anticipated, the man at the cabin predicted the next target, that would offer the chance of a rematch on Wardell's terms. Only now did he realize that the farther west he'd traveled, the more a sense of disappointment had built. Disappointment at the lack of obstacles, of challenges. When he'd reached his destination back there in Allanton, he'd been downright depressed. Even when he'd squeezed the trigger to end the pathetic existence of his ... of that man ... it hadn't felt like he'd thought it would.

But that cloud of despondency had lifted entirely during the ensuing firefight. And it hadn't returned now, even though the adrenaline had mostly worked its way out of his system. With an alien feeling of surprise, Wardell put a hand to his mouth to confirm a suspicion. He was smiling. And he reckoned he'd been doing so since he'd fallen back from the cabin.

35

12:06 p.m.

The ride up from Missouri in the shiny black Bell 407 was smoother than Banner had anticipated. After she'd gotten off the phone with Blake and realized how she'd be filling the next couple of hours, she'd glanced up at the sky, seen the threatening clouds, and shivered. Banner was prone to airsickness and knew that even a moderately turbulent ride would reduce the chances of her keeping her breakfast down to around zero. But as the pilot upped the pitch of the main rotors and lifted them into the air, the sky brightened a little. It was almost as though the weather had had second thoughts. Banner set her jaw and willed the status quo to remain. *Rain, rain, go away. Come again another day. Or don't.*

The nausea meant she was grateful that Castle was in a reticent mood, barely exchanging four words with her throughout the two-hour flight. She used the time to look back over the Wardell file. She scanned the pictures and reports and interviews, wondering how Blake had gotten so far ahead of the rest of them. She wondered how the hell he—or anyone—was going to predict the bastard's next move. She sighed and put the Wardell section to one side, then opened the victim profiles for the original nineteen.

Whenever a case threatened to overwhelm her, this is what she did: took it back to the basics. The crime and the victim. Just like their killer, every one of the nineteen had a backstory. The accountant celebrating a promotion. The alcoholic fresh out of completing her first successful stint in rchab. Stories cut short for no reason. Lives blacked out on a whim.

Victim number six hit her the hardest. Her name was Emma Durbin, a thirty-two-year-old corporate lawyer recently separated from her husband and raising a young daughter. Banner stopped reading the text and just stared long and hard at the picture of a smiling Durbin at the beach, hugging both arms around her kid's neck as they posed for the camera.

Jesus, Annie.

She snapped the file shut and closed her eyes. Where had the time gone? Her daughter's entire childhood was playing out in the background, drowned out by louder distractions: the fights with Mark, the punishing demands of her work.

And then once Mark had gone, the demands of the job had increased to absorb any breathing space she might have expected.

She took out her phone to call Helen, but it went straight to voice mail. She left a message, asking how they both were and saying that she hoped she'd be home soon. As she hung up, she promised herself it would be different once they caught Wardell. She could take stock, start to prioritize better, focus on what was important. But that was the problem, wasn't it? *Everything* was so goddamned important.

They touched down on the wide, flat plain that separated the line of hunters' cabins from the lake. They were latecomers to the party, and the usual circus of law enforcement, forensics, and media were already entrenched in their traditional positions. Castle leapt from the side door as soon as the skids touched the earth, and Banner followed, ducking down instinctively to avoid the propeller wash.

The center of attention was a cabin that had probably once been fairly indistinguishable from its neighbors, but now looked like it had been transported there from some battleground in Afghanistan. Every window was shattered, lengths of guttering hung loose, large-caliber bullet holes pockmarked the surface like some weird decorative effect. How in the hell had Blake survived this? She wondered where he was now. A couple of states away, perhaps, doubtless hot on Wardell's trail.

The earthly remains of Edward Nolan lay prostrate on the floor of the cabin, half visible through the open doorway. Castle had told the crime scene people that they could do what they like so long as nobody removed the body before he arrived. "Body" was perhaps too substantial a word for what was left of the man. Three-quarters of his head was gone. Wide blood blossoms adorned the rest of his body, evidently the result of getting in the way of automatic rifle fire. The left hand had been blown off at the wrist.

"So much for one shot, one kill," Banner said to no one in particular.

"The kill probably *was* the first shot," Castle said. "But he's upping the tempo, no question."

Banner looked around the sparsely furnished cabin, every piece of furniture and decoration entirely beyond repair. She knew the team would have gone over the place with a fine-tooth comb already and knew that it had likely yielded zilch in the way of intelligence on Wardell.

"The father was the only person close to a relative we knew about," Banner said. "So where the hell is he going now?"

Castle was looking down at the body as though he were a Roman priest attempting to read the entrails of a fresh sacrifice. He breathed a long sigh out of his nose. "Blake." He said the word like it was an admission of defeat. "We need to talk to Blake about where the hell this bastard is going."

There was a cough from behind them and the two of them turned. Blake's hair was disheveled, his white shirt streaked with dirt, and there was a cut beneath his left eye. "I'm afraid, Agent Castle," he said, "that your guess is as good as mine."

36

The three of them were hunched over a large map of the Midwestern states on a small table inside the mobile command center. Blake sipped his third cup of hot black coffee as he indicated points on the map.

"We don't have any more than a day until he kills again," he said. "Probably much less, in fact. So given that he has to keep under the radar, we'll say a five-hundred-mile radius, max."

"Less," Castle said, cradling his chin between the thumb and index finger of his left hand as he considered this. "He's got to dump your rental ASAP and find another vehicle. Did you get the optional insurance, by the way?"

"Always."

Banner smiled. There had been no apology from Castle and certainly no gesture of contrition, but he had quietly dropped his open animosity for Blake. Whether he liked it or not, he had to work with the guy if he wanted to nail Wardell. And he wanted that badly; they all did.

"Say three hundred, then," she said. "What does that give us? We're looking at towns and cities again, since the next one's got to be random. He's out of personal targets."

"Maybe," Blake said. He reached for a pencil, guesstimated a three hundred mile to scale line stretching out north from Allanton, and drew a near-perfect circle on the map. Banner and Castle inclined their heads to look at what that gave them.

"Nebraska, Kansas, Colorado, Wyoming, South Dakota," Castle recited, "or he could double back to Iowa."

"He might want to rest up," Banner suggested. "The nearest big town is Denver."

"Kansas City is almost as close in the other direction," Castle pointed out.

Blake was shaking his head. "Things changed today," he said.

"You mean because you almost got him?" Castle asked.

"It wasn't that close," Blake said. "I was just trying to get out of that situation in one piece. I meant it changed because he's taken out his first predetermined target. Maybe his only predetermined target. And, thanks to Daddy, he seems to have inherited an arsenal. He's ready to kick things up a notch."

Banner tried to swallow, but her mouth was dry. She didn't like to think about what the next notch would be to a guy like Wardell. "Meaning?" she asked after a moment.

"I don't know," Blake said.

"You're right," Castle said after a moment. "Serial killers tend not to keep to their initial pace. They escalate. A lot of the time, that's why we catch them. More than likely, his next move is going to be something big."

"Or some*one* big," Banner said. This chimed with what she'd read in the psych reports. Wardell had never confirmed it, but the shrinks agreed he was working up to a single episode of killing on an unprecedented scale. Something with a lot of people in a confined space. A baseball game or rock concert had been suggested, but it could just as easily have been a hospital or a shopping mall. Wardell hadn't sketched out his plans or written a journal, so there was no way to be sure. That was the challenge about protecting a big city— lots of places with lots of people.

Blake nodded in agreement. "Let's hope we're not there yet. If he sticks with random, we're back to a guessing game. But if we can find a specific target he might want to hit within this circle—or even outside—we could make a guess at his direction at least."

Castle repeated the names of the states that fell within Blake's circle. Banner furrowed her brow in concentration. Nothing stood out. "What towns do we have in those states?" she said, then started picking them out on the map. "Lincoln, Omaha, Wichita, Topeka ..."

"Denver, Colorado Springs, Boulder ..." Castle continued, looking west.

Blake picked up the baton and headed north. "Cheyenne, Rapid City, Sioux Falls ..."

"Wait," Banner exclaimed. The two men stopped, looked up at her, faces questioning. "Rapid City, South Dakota," she said. "Something about Rapid City in the case notes."

Blake snapped his fingers. "Of course. Hatcher."

"John Hatcher?" Castle prompted. "The sheriff?"

Banner nodded. Hatcher had been the newly promoted sheriff of Chicago's Cook County, barely two weeks on the job when Wardell had made his first kill. As the senior law-enforcement representative in the county where Wardell's first two victims had fallen, he'd been heavily involved on the multiagency task force during the first go-round and hadn't been shy with the media. Hatcher had a weird mix of charisma and abrasiveness, which had worked to his advantage during the frequent press conferences. His prickliness and instinctive way with a sound bite had marked him out as a no-bullshit man of action, especially when contrasted with the more reserved FBI agents, including Steve Castle.

It was an entirely false impression. Away from the cameras, he'd contributed little to the case beyond getting people's backs up. But he'd been the only one to come out at the other end with a genuine career boost. It had helped, of course, that it had been one of the detectives on Hatcher's

Special Investigations Division who had made the crucial breakthrough. But Hatcher wasn't slow in taking as much credit for his subordinate's actions as he possibly could.

"What about him?" Castle said.

"He retired," Banner replied. "Departmental regs wouldn't allow him to write a book about the case—you know, *How I Caught the Chicago Sniper*, something like that—so he quit."

Blake nodded. "He did the book. I skimmed it: It was one of those quickie cut-and-paste jobs thrown together in a weekend by a ghost writer. There was nothing new in the book itself, but the 'about the author' bit said he was now living in Rapid City, South Dakota." He paused and narrowed his eyes, and Banner could tell he was running this new variable through the system, looking at what new scenarios it threw up. He looked back at her and said, "Good job, Banner. You've given us the one personal target Wardell could hit in this search radius."

To Banner's irritation, she felt herself begin to flush at Blake's approval. She suppressed the smile and looked skeptical. "It's just a possibility. We can't be sure he knows about Hatcher, or that he'd consider him a target. Like you said, if he hits a random victim, we're back to square one."

"But we can't do anything about that," Castle said. "No more than we're already doing, anyway. This gives us somewhere to focus. Doesn't mean we have to bet everything on it."

Banner turned to Blake, but his head was down again, staring at the map as though he could trace Wardell's exact path on it. "It feels right," he said softly, as though speaking to himself.

"You don't think it'll be too obvious a target for him?" Banner said. "Assuming he even knows about Hatcher, he'll know that we know too."

Blake paused for a beat, considered this. "I think that's why it feels right, Banner."

"I'm not sure I follow."

"I think I do," Castle said. "He wants to prove he's the best. That's been his mission statement since day one. How better to prove it than to take out the very target we're expecting him to?"

At that moment, Banner's phone issued a brief fanfare, signaling a received text message. She took it out and read the message, which was from Kelly Paxon. Although she'd eschewed text speak, it was concise and to the point: *Missouri gun not a match. Will call soon.*

"What is it?" Castle said, noticing Banner's look of surprise.

"That wasn't Wardell's rifle in the van down in Missouri."

"You don't say," Castle said sharply, then murmured a brief apology to Banner. "So we're not talking some half-assed hoax. Heckler & Koch sniper rifles don't grow on trees."

Blake glanced at the map again. "So unless Wardell borrowed a helicopter, there's no way he could have dumped that van as a decoy. Which means . . ."

"Somebody's helping him," Banner finished. "But who? *Why?*" The question was met with silence. It seemed even Blake didn't have an answer for everything. "I'll be back," she said after a minute. "I'm going outside to call Paxon."

"I'll get things rolling on Hatcher," Castle said.

Banner's conversation with Agent Kelly Paxon lasted five or six minutes, but at the end of it she didn't have any more information than she'd gleaned from the text message. After terminating the call, she sat down on the porch of the cabin neighboring Nolan's and watched the red sun sink over the western ridge, pausing for a breath as the fevered activity of local cops and task force personnel continued to swirl around her.

The forensics team down in Missouri had found no trace of Wardell in the burnt-out van. No trace of anybody, in fact. The few parts of the cabin that had escaped the flames had been wiped down to erase any prints. The rifle was a Heckler and Koch PSG1, all right, but not the one that had killed Terry Daniels or Father Leary. And now Eddie Nolan.

It was an expertly executed diversion, falling apart only at the point of matching the rifle, but by then it had done its work. If the red van lead hadn't been so convincing, the task force might well have followed Blake's lead and Wardell might not have made it past this quiet little hunting town.

Somebody's helping him. Her own words echoed in her head. A careful, professional somebody. But that made no sense—Wardell hadn't had a partner before. He'd gone out of his way to avoid human contact, in fact. No, Banner couldn't see him accepting help, even if it was offered.

Turn it around then: Who would benefit from helping Wardell? Money was a dead end; Wardell had none. There had to be another reason.

One of the other agents, standing apart from the rest of the activity, caught her eye. She realized she didn't recognize the man, was only assuming he was FBI because of the way he was dressed. He was tall and thin, wore a dark suit, a dark overcoat, and rounded glasses. He wasn't a local cop or one of the forensics, so by a process of elimination, he had to be FBI. How else could he access the crime scene?

Banner thought about approaching him, then decided she was just being paranoid. She looked away again, turning her mind back to things of greater importance.

37

Mike Whitford leaned back in his leather swivel chair and yawned, looking out at the cold Chicago night through scrunched-up eyes. Getting on for another eighteen-hour day, the third in a row, and his whole being was starting to feel like an old pair of socks that had been worn for a week. It was worth it, though. For the first time in twenty years, he was looking forward to coming into work every day. He was back, and he still had it. He was feeling so good, in fact, that today he'd forgone most of his usual trips to the bathroom with the hip flask. Hell, maybe once this story had run its course, he would kick the booze entirely. Of course, there was no need to rush into anything. The important thing was he knew he could do it now, because he was back.

You didn't have to take Whitford's word for it, either. You could see it in people's eyes. Mandy on reception. That acne-ridden, college-fresh prick on the sports desk. Even Urich. The grizzled old bastard had fixed Whitford with a stare after reading his latest copy and said, "Good job." Eye contact and a couple of words of affirmation. It didn't sound like much, not unless you knew Urich.

There was a predictable undercurrent of jealousy from some of Whitford's rivals, of course. People who would previously have considered him not a rival, but an inferior. He was big enough to forgive that jealousy, because even he had to admit that an element of luck had been involved in his renaissance. After all, almost anyone could have picked up that ringing phone two days before. He'd hesitated a beat—he'd been on his way to the bathroom—but then he'd gone ahead and picked up the handset on the hotdesk. The calls bounced through to that one when the lines at reception were all busy. And, boy, was he glad they'd been busy. That two-minute phone call had turned his career around, put him right in the middle of a national story. Caleb Wardell, escaped from death row and killing already. Even better: a government-level attempt to cover the situation up. It was manna from heaven.

He'd been skeptical at first, his coworkers even more so. But when they'd investigated a few of the details the caller had provided, everything had checked out perfectly. The clincher was a phone call to the destination Wardell had never reached: the federal penitentiary at Terre Haute. They had quickly issued a terse "no comment," but not quite quickly enough. There had been a stunned pause of no more than a half second, but that had been confirmation enough.

From there on, the cover-up unraveled like a hastily constructed cat's cradle. The FBI had come for him within an hour of the story hitting the networks, but he'd cooperated fully. There was no reason not to. Every detail they needed to know about that two-minute conversation with Wardell was already plastered over every major news website. The agents had made it very clear that they were unhappy with Whitford and his employer, but for the moment, that seemed to be the extent of the situation's downside. He wasn't naive: First Amendment or not, he was sure there'd be blowback later. But later was later.

The telephone rang. His own telephone. It had been doing that a lot these past three days. He gave it two full rings, caught it on the third. He said his name with the confidence of twenty years ago.

The voice was quiet, as though it was coming from a long

way off, or the speaker did not want to be overheard. It said, "Am I speaking to Mike Whitford?"

Whitford grunted in the affirmative. "Make it quick. I'm busy."

There was a low chuckle. "I can imagine. But don't worry. I won't keep you long, partner. I'm also a busy man."

"Who is this?"

"Mike," the voice said, elongating the vowel reprovingly. "Mike, Mike, Mike. You know who this is."

"I've had a lot of people claiming to be Caleb Wardell this week, pal. So far only one of them has been the real deal, and ..."

"Maybe not even one, Mike."

"I'm hanging up now."

"The man I killed today was Edward Nolan. The technical term for what he was to me is 'biological father.'"

Whitford stopped cold. It could be a bluff, but that *was* Wardell's father's name, and your average crank might not even know that much. The name was fresh in his mind because he'd tried—unsuccessfully—to track him down for an interview yesterday. And the Nebraska victim's name hadn't yet been released; the feds were keeping a tight lid on it for some reason. He didn't hang up. His mouth hung half open as he considered what to say next.

"Still there, partner?"

"Still here, still skeptical."

"You won't be tomorrow."

"What's happening tomorrow?"

"Do you know who John Hatcher is?"

"Sure I do. If you are who you say you are, he's the guy who nailed your sorry ass to the wall last time."

There was a pause, and Whitford wondered if he'd gone

too far and touched a nerve, but when the voice returned it betrayed no emotion.

"I'm going to put a bullet in John Hatcher's head tomorrow night. Let's say around midnight."

The cool certainty of the voice chilled Whitford to the marrow. It sounded like the caller was simply stating an inevitability, like the sun coming up. He cleared his throat. "Why would you tell me this?"

"Because you've got a big mouth, Mike, and I can trust you to tell the FBI and their little helper. You'll remember the message though, won't you, partner? You need a minute to write it down?"

Helper? What did he mean by that? "Wait a minute ..." Whitford began.

"You had your minute. Now I got one question for you."

"Yeah?"

"What's your favorite color, Mike?"

Whitford was caught off guard. "My favorite ...?" he heard himself answer before he had time to think about it. "Blue. I guess it's blue."

The line went dead, and Whitford realized everybody around him had stopped what they were doing to stare at him.

38

Wardell replaced the receiver of the pay phone and had wiped the prints off with his sleeve before he remembered that there was really no need. He turned and looked across the empty highway at the thick woods he'd be heading into soon enough.

Hatcher was a good target, one that the authorities would find all too plausible. Wardell had been mildly irritated by the way the sheriff had loudly claimed credit for his capture in Chicago, but he was betting some of the guys who'd done the real work were a good deal more irritated. He'd take Hatcher out if he had the chance, of course, but he was more interested now in the chance to engage his current pursuers on his own terms. And particularly the man from the cabin.

The call to Whitford would ensure that they'd focus their efforts properly this time and not on another distraction like the red van. Now they knew where he was going to be tomorrow at midnight. The stage was set.

Tomorrow at noon, however, was a different story.

DAY FOUR

39

The second voice sounded like it had come a long way, and not just in distance.

"What's your favorite color, Mike?" it said, an eerie crackle on the vowels.

A startled pause and then: "My favorite ...? Blue. I guess it's blue."

And that was all there was, save a couple of seconds of dial tone as the little ball at the bottom of the Media Player window completed its journey to the end of the bar that signified the length of the audio clip.

Castle was hunched over behind the technician at the laptop. As the recording of Mike Whitford's phone conversation ended, he straightened up and looked down at the tech, who was rake thin with curly red hair. Although Castle had known about the existence and content of the recording since the previous night, this was the first time he'd actually heard it.

"Perfect match, sir," the tech said.

"It's him, all right," Castle agreed. He'd spent long enough watching the interview tapes to be able to say for certain.

They were set up in the living room of Hatcher's house, a sprawling faux-rustic executive cabin built on the slopes overlooking Pactola Lake, nestled deep within the Black Hills

National Forest. The house was about twenty miles outside of Rapid City, and the thick, dark pines that gave the Black Hills their name encroached on the structure like a hostile crowd.

The owner of the house was in one of the other rooms berating Dave Edwards about the way the manhunt had been carried out so far. Former Cook County Sheriff John Hatcher had a deep, booming voice and a propensity to repeat himself, so Castle had been grateful for the respite. He turned to the other man in the room, Special Agent Eric Wetherspoon. Wetherspoon had more than thirty years with the Bureau, but had openly disdained the quest for promotion, happy to keep working on the front line.

"What did you have to give Whitford to sit on the recording?" Wetherspoon asked. His arms were folded, and he was leaning against a tall bookcase packed with beautifully bound tomes with pristine spines.

Castle sighed. "A lot more than I wanted to. If it were up to me, we'd just take the little prick into protective custody and lose the key. He gets a one-on-one with me tomorrow." He said it like he wished the one-on-one could be held with the reporter's mic switched off, in a locked room with no windows.

Wetherspoon changed the subject. "Is Agent Banner joining us for the main event?"

"A couple of hours," Castle replied. "She was held up in—"

"Leave my house? Leave. My. Fuckin'. *House?*" The conversation died as Hatcher bulled through the door into the living room, a pair of exasperated agents in tow, plus Dave Edwards. Hatcher was tall, barrel-chested, and bald. He wore slacks and a slate-blue short-sleeved shirt. "You pencil dicks have got a lot to learn about the law of the jungle."

Castle cast his eyes across the tropical hardwood floor to

the triple-glazed French doors and the Japanese reflecting pool beyond, then saw the skinny technician doing the same thing. Some jungle.

"This motherfucker knows I beat him first time around, so he's gotta bring it to *my* house now. He's makin' it personal now. You askin' me to back down from that, *Agent* Wetherspoon?" He used the word "agent" like it was a racial slur. To a certain type of cop, that was exactly what it was.

Whether it came naturally or he'd mellowed with age, Wetherspoon was a man who seemed utterly unprovokable. It was a quality Castle couldn't help but admire, mainly because it was one he lacked. He responded to the question with characteristic calm: "If that's the way you want to dress it up, Mr. Hatcher, that's fine with me." His voice betrayed no irritation, just matter-of-fact. "We just wanted to explain to you how this operation is going to run."

"This operation? Let me tell you something about—" Hatcher stopped, sighting Castle, and strode over to him. He placed his palm between Castle's shoulder blades, as though bringing an ally into the debate. "Steve, you know what I'm talking about. You got half a brain at least, not like these pen pushers. You got some real cop in you."

Castle pushed back from the desk, turning to slide Hatcher's hand from his back. He drew himself up to his full height, which was an inch or two taller than Hatcher, and looked him in the eyes for a moment. *Count to ten*, he thought. If Wetherspoon could do it, so could he.

"Mr. Hatcher," he said. "Agent Wetherspoon has apprised you of the situation. We've identified a credible threat against you from—"

Hatcher's face creased into disgust. "Aw, don't give me that shit."

Castle continued as though there had been no interruption.

"A credible threat that became even more credible when Wardell confirmed it personally. We're asking you to leave this location for your own safety."

"Asking me," Hatcher repeated. "But you can't make me."

Castle briefly wondered whether they could tie Hatcher to a tree out front and hang a bull's-eye around his neck.

Dave Edwards chipped in. Castle was unsurprised: Edwards hated to have his authority questioned. "In point of fact, we *can* make you, Mr. Hatcher," he said. "We'd just rather you went of your own free will."

Hatcher ignored Edwards, stared back at Castle for a good twenty seconds before turning away. "Fine. Piss on you assholes," he said over his shoulder as he walked back across the living room and slapped the door open with his palm. Edwards's face reddened, and for a moment he looked unsure of what to do. Then he just nodded his head, as though the exchange had gone exactly as planned.

He turned to Castle. "Donaldson wants a sit-rep at one thirty. And where the hell is Banner?"

"He'll get it, and Banner's on her way."

Edwards reenacted the imperious nod and exited the room in the same direction Hatcher had gone.

Wetherspoon moved to Castle's side of the room and leaned back against the mahogany desk on which the equipment had been set up. "Well, that went better than I expected."

Castle turned to stare out at the reflecting pool, thinking about Hatcher's display. "Why do I get the feeling he was open to persuasion?"

"I don't know," Wetherspoon said, pretending to give the matter some thought. "Maybe because he's a chickenshit asshole who was looking for the excuse?"

Castle cracked a smile for the first time that day. "Might be onto something there."

40

12:00 p.m.

It was twelve o'clock: high noon. But instead of a blazing sun at its apex, the skies overhead were dull, and coal-black thunderheads were building above the imposing hills on the western horizon. There was an old man at the far end of the lunch counter. He was staring out of the window at the clouds, over the rim of his coffee cup. The man was in his eighties at the very least. His skin was yellowed and scattered with liver spots, and he wore a checkered shirt and thick black-rimmed glasses. He shook his head in disapproval, as though taking the incoming weather as just one more screwup of somebody else's doing that he'd just have to grin and bear.

"Those clouds look like Satan's workin' real hard," he said. He turned to Wardell and nodded grimly.

Wardell's lips curled into a wide grin, exposing two perfect rows of teeth. He returned the nod, fully approving of the old man's homily. "He's about to be," he agreed.

The old man gave Wardell a quizzical look and then returned to looking at the gathering storm.

A twenty-eight-inch flat-screen television was fixed to the wall behind the counter, something that would have seemed luxurious at the time Wardell went inside, but that had apparently become commonplace in the interim. Despite the proximity to the congressional elections, the news was all about one subject: Caleb Wardell. That was one thing that hadn't changed: A good serial killer story trumped just about anything, except maybe terrorism.

They'd announced the identity of the man killed in Nebraska in time for the breakfast news, and that had given the pundits and the criminal psychology experts and the psychics plenty to chew over all morning. Every so often they'd flash up Wardell's mug shot, but he wasn't concerned about being recognized. For one thing, he looked almost nothing like he did in the picture; for another, he had always found that, unless you acted guilty and drew attention to yourself, people were by and large pretty unobservant. You had to signpost something for them to take notice.

Wardell listened to some rent-a-shrink speculate about his Oedipus complex while he finished his brunch: steak, rare, with two eggs and fries on the side. The news cut to yesterday's interview with the FBI agent who seemed to be in charge, the one with the gray hair and the permanently pissed-off expression. Castle, wasn't it? And the pretty brunette occasionally by his side was Banner. The camera liked her.

He swallowed the last bite of steak, positioned his knife and fork vertically in the center of the plate, and nodded over at the waitress. She was quite a looker herself: twenty-something, five two, 110 pounds, wearing painted-on black jeans and a navy blue halter top. A small and tasteful silver cross hung from a chain around her neck, nestling in her generous cleavage. She tucked a strand of blond hair that had strayed from her ponytail behind her ear as she smiled and sauntered over. A name tag reading SUZIE was pinned to the blue halter top. Blue: that reminded him. He had a color, but he still needed a number.

"Get you anything else?"

Wardell looked in her green eyes and remained silent for just a second longer than could have been mistaken for an innocent pause for thought. He didn't leer or anything, didn't look her up and down. He didn't want anyone to think he was some kind of pervert, no matter what the news said.

"I don't know," he said. "What do you have?" He smiled. Not the grin he'd just shown to the old man, but the one that women liked.

Suzie glanced away coyly and cocked an eyebrow. Feigning disapproval but with a half smile to show she didn't really mean it. Light flirtation, the kind any good waitress masters in her first week on the job. "Just what's on the menu, pal," she said.

"Pity," Wardell said. He looked beyond her at the television screen. "Serial killers," he said with a shake of his head. "You ever wonder if anything else is happening in the world right now?"

She gazed back at the screen at the exact moment that Wardell's picture flashed back up, staring impassively down at her. She didn't flinch.

"I don't know," she said. "Nothing that gets this kind of ratings, I guess. My boyfriend says that's why they do it."

Wardell was momentarily confused. "The networks?"

She looked back and grinned, thinking he was kidding. "No, the killers. Like this Wardell guy. They dig the attention. That's how they get their kicks. That's what my boyfriend says—if we didn't give them all this attention, they'd just go away."

Wardell smiled again, playing along that he'd been kidding. Only the smile was a little frozen this time, a little off center. "You think so?"

"Don't you?"

He shrugged. "Maybe some of them. The ones who want to be famous and can't think of any other way."

"Isn't that all of them?"

"No," he said sharply, and something in his voice must

have unnerved the girl, because the breezy good humor seemed to drain from her face.

"So, uh, just the check?" she said, suddenly in a hurry to clear his dishes away. As she stacked Wardell's coffee cup on top of his plate, he saw her steal a glance back up at the television screen. The photo wasn't there anymore; they were showing an old interview with Eddie Nolan now.

Sometimes, Wardell reflected, you could signpost without exactly meaning to. He continued anyway, as though nothing had changed.

"That's not all of them, Suzie. Some of them just like to kill. It's what they're good at."

Suzie was avoiding his eyes now. Staring straight down while she lifted his plate with her left hand to give the counter a wipe with a cloth in her right.

"I'll get your check then, sir," she said, the green eyes darting up to survey the diner and finding it all but empty. The eyes turned to the old man watching the thunderheads and then, with great reluctance, back to meet Wardell's gaze. "Okay?" she added, her voice hopeful, almost pleading.

He kept looking at her. "Did you ever hear that song, 'What if God was one of us?'" he said, keeping his voice amiable.

Suzie swallowed. Nodded briefly.

"I always liked that song," Wardell said. "What about you?"

Suzie swallowed again. "Sure. I like it okay."

"That's why they do it, you know. The killers. Not the sad celebrity wannabes your boyfriend's talking about. I mean the *killers*."

Her eyes dropped to the counter again, as though the effort of meeting Wardell's eyes caused physical pain, like holding a heated pot handle.

Softly, Wardell began to sing the first couple of lines of the chorus.

"Please ..." she began, her voice almost inaudible.

"People sometimes say that killers have a God complex, like they're so delusional. But think about it for just a second: A killer decides who lives and who dies. Life or death, and he makes the choice. Do you honestly imagine that the person who dies can tell the difference between his killer and God?"

"Please just go." She sounded on the edge of tears.

Wardell sat back from the counter and smiled broadly. He took a ten-dollar bill from the wallet that had belonged to the woman with the blue Ford Taurus and placed it on the counter, squaring the edges carefully. "God is one of us," he said. "Remember that, Suzie."

He got up and walked toward the door before stopping and turning around.

"What time do you close?" he asked.

Suzie looked like she was on the verge of passing out. She managed to croak out a single syllable: "Six."

"Six?" Wardell thought about it. "Six it is. *Six* is a good number."

He pushed the glass door outward and stepped out into the street. He knew Suzie would already be on her way to the phone to call the cops, but it didn't matter. They'd be too late. His newest car was parked around the corner, and the guns were in the trunk. If he concentrated, he could hear them singing to him.

41

"It's past noon," Banner said, consulting the time display on her phone. She had gone with a different look today: Her hair was down, and she was looking better than anyone had a right to in a dark blue pantsuit.

"It's nothing to get our hopes up about," I said.

"I know," she agreed. "You think he's actually going for Hatcher, or is it just another misdirect?"

I thought about it. "It's interesting that we came up with the target before he called it in. Part of me thinks that makes it more likely."

"And the other part?"

I shrugged. "Still thinking."

"If he isn't gunning for Hatcher, then who? He's not going to take a day off, is he?"

I shook my head. No rest for the wicked.

We'd stopped off in Rapid City on the way out to John Hatcher's place. Castle was leading the advance guard, and there didn't seem to be much else we could do in the meantime with no other leads, so we'd decided to stop on the way to catch a break and something to eat. And to talk about the coming night, of course. We were sitting in Banner's car, parked on Main Street. Groups of people passed us in both directions, a few carrying groceries, most just looking for somewhere to have a quiet Sunday lunch.

We were both thinking about the same thing: Wardell's telephone call to the reporter. Earlier on, Castle had e-mailed Banner the sound clip, and we'd listened to it as I drove. It had been him, all right, and once again he'd backed up his credentials with inside knowledge of the most recent killing. But something about the call niggled at me, and I couldn't quite put my finger on it. It was as though something was missing. Or maybe the something missing was the lack of a recording of the earlier call to match it against.

Banner had spoken to the agent who'd interviewed Whitford—the reporter—directly afterward, and apparently Whitford had been unsure himself at first. The voice had sounded a little different from the first time around, and he'd assumed it was a crank. "But then," Whitford had said, "he knew all the details. Just like before. So I guess it was him, all right."

The most up-to-date voice-recognition software and my own instincts had backed that conclusion to the hilt. It was Wardell, all right. But it didn't necessarily follow that it had been Wardell the first time around. That time Whitford had blindly answered an anonymous incoming call and had no cause to record it.

But if the first call hadn't been Wardell, how did he know so much about the case? The way I saw it, there could be only two explanations. The first was that someone was working alongside Wardell. Someone who wasn't yet on our radar, for whatever reason. The second explanation was less palatable: The call had come from someone who was working along-side us, either in the Bureau or the police. But why? The questions went in circles, like the current flowing around an incomplete circuit. I just needed one last connection to turn the lights on.

"The favorite color thing," Banner said. "What was that about? Some kind of coded message?"

"Could be. Or maybe he's just trying to confuse us. He knows we'll pore over everything he says for hidden meaning."

"Castle said that." She nodded. "Wardell knows we're waiting for him this time. He needs us to be distracted."

At the mention of his name, I thought about how Castle's attitude to me had softened a little after the Nolan killing. He'd adjusted to Wardell's new MO—that of targeted as well as random killings—faster than I would have expected. I still detected a suppressed resentment in his interactions with Banner, though. Which was why I hadn't been surprised when she suggested I tag along with her for the trip to Rapid.

"He seems threatened," I said.

"By Wardell?"

"By you."

She grimaced, aiming for a puzzled look, but I could tell she knew what I was getting at.

"You're what," I said, "fifteen years younger than him? One rung below him on the ladder. You'll have his job pretty soon."

She sighed and shook her head.

"I'm wrong?"

She gazed through the windshield at the groups of pedestrians and the light traffic on Main Street for a minute; then she turned back to face me. "Blake, do you know the name of the first female director of the FBI?"

I thought about it for a second. "I don't believe there's been one."

She nodded. "Do you know the name of the first female assistant director?"

"Has there been one?"

"No."

"Okay," I said after a second. "You're not going to be satisfied with Castle's job."

She smiled. "I have a plan, Blake. Nailing Wardell will put

me ahead of that plan by five years. And from what I've seen so far, sticking close to you is the best way to get close to Wardell."

"So it's not just my looks and personality, then?"

Banner batted her eyelids exaggeratedly and pouted. "Sorry, Blake. I'm only interested in you for your mind."

"Well, my mind does better on a full stomach," I said, opening the car door. "Where do you want to eat?"

"Anyplace," she said, glancing up at the black clouds rolling in from the west. "As long as it's inside."

We got out of the car and walked east along Main Street. We passed a diner that was empty apart from one old guy by the window. There was a sign in the door advertising a Halloween special: pumpkin pie, naturally. I liked the look of the place. Call me antisocial, but I tend to gravitate toward quieter places: quicker service, less background chatter, space to think. It's also a lot easier to keep an eye on the other clientele. I waved a hand at the door. "How about here?"

Banner said, "Actually, I feel more like Italian. What about there?" She pointed at a pizzeria across the main street. "We can split a large Quattro Stagioni." Her pronunciation was flawless, and I wondered if she had Italian heritage—it would certainly fit with her dark, almost black hair and slightly olive skin tone. Maybe I'd ask her over lunch. We headed for the crosswalk. The street was busy with shoppers and fellow lunchers. People cast nervous glances at the darkening sky and hurried to their destinations.

As we crossed the street, the smell from the pizzeria wafted out to meet us, mingling appetizingly with the ozone smell of the coming storm, and I realized I was starving. I hadn't eaten since a sandwich the previous night.

"Maybe I'll have a large to myself," I said.

Banner turned her head, smiling. She opened her mouth to

say something, and then her features blanked as she flinched at the crack of the first shot.

42

12:27 p.m.

When I replayed those first couple of seconds in my head later, I realized that the first two victims were already dead before we even knew what was happening. Whether it was tiredness or hunger or the smile of an attractive woman, there was no excuse—my head was out of the game. For all my healthy skepticism, for all my warnings to others that we shouldn't take anything for granted, I'd let my attention slip, and I was no more prepared than any of the victims on that cold November noon.

My eyes flashed across the scene, taking in images that seemed somehow tinted and unreal, as though from a dream or a memory. A woman in a leather jacket and a navy blue T-shirt lay sprawled halfway across the middle of the road, blood pulsing and pumping from a hole in her skull like water from a burst pipe. Fifty yards up the street, a man in a jean jacket clutched at a ragged wound in his chest and toppled forward, cracking his face on the sidewalk. The flesh-muffled sound of his nose audibly shattering broke the spell.

Our shared moment of paralysis finally over, Banner and I reacted more or less simultaneously—me with actions, her with words. As she yelled, "Gun! Everybody get down!" I flattened my hand against her back and pushed her down behind the wheel well of a Chevy Suburban that was parked curbside.

I scanned the rooftops, tried to pick out ledges and fire escapes and open windows and other likely offensive positions. Off to our right, a blonde woman in a sky-blue coat who'd been screaming and running suddenly stopped doing either and plunged to the ground, the back of her head missing. Banner had her gun out, but she was holding it aimlessly, her mouth half open as she watched the horror unfold. I tried to focus on the rooftops again. It was no goddamn good. The bastard was taking out a fresh victim every couple of seconds, and even if I could make his position, it would do about as much good as air con in hell.

"Shit," Banner hissed through clenched teeth, her face a mirror of the frustration and powerlessness I felt. Ten feet from where we crouched, an old man wearing tan slacks and a blue checkered shirt stepped out of the doorway of the pizzeria, his mouth open as if he was about to start asking somebody what the commotion was about.

I yelled, "Get d—" But that was as far as I got before a deep red rose blossomed in the center of the old man's chest. He staggered a couple of steps toward us and fell, twisting and landing on his back, halfway across the sidewalk. Without thinking, I ran toward him, crouching. From somewhere far off, I heard Banner yelling something at me. I heard tires squeal and horns blare. I heard another crack as someone else's life ended with no explanation. Some part of my brain wondered if I'd hear the shot when it was my turn.

The old man was holding his chest, blood spraying from between his fingers. He was making wheezing noises. Blood spatter blew from his lips. I went into autopilot. Battlefield medicine, it hadn't been so long.

One of the crowd stampeding by knocked over a trash

can, spewing detritus over me and the old man. I saw the discarded plastic bag from a Subway sandwich. I ripped it down the middle, rolled the old man onto his side and forced his hands from his chest wound. I spread the plastic over the hole in his chest. If the round had gone through a lung, it would stop air being sucked into the wound and hastening the development of the injury. When my right hand found the exit hole in his back, I realized I was utterly wasting my time.

"You're going to be okay," I yelled into the old man's ear, trying to make up with volume what I lacked in conviction. The old guy had a fist-sized hole punched through him; no way in hell he was going to make it. He coughed a couple more times, and his brown eyes searched the sky, alighted briefly on my face, and then focused on something both closer and an eternity away.

I let his body slip from my bloody hands and scrabbled back to the cover of the Suburban. Banner was pointing up at the roof of a brown brick building four blocks away. "There," she said, almost quietly.

It was too far to make out a distinct figure, but I saw the muzzle flash, heard the crack a second later. A girl of no more than thirteen, wearing a translucent blue raincoat, lay on her back across the street from us, dead in the imagined shelter of a shoe-store awning.

Banner took aim at the spot where we'd seen the muzzle flash and fired evenly spaced shots from her Glock until the hammer clicked on an empty chamber. It was no frenzied volley: Her composure was perfect, her two-handed grip textbook. It didn't matter. From this range, she might as well have been trying to take him out with negative thoughts.

She dropped down and reached to her belt for another clip. But she didn't get up to fire again. We just waited there, behind the Suburban, counting heartbeats. When it felt like a couple of eternities had passed since the last shot, I turned my head to her and opened my mouth to say something, I don't know what. Banner was looking across the street at the girl in the blue raincoat. A single tear ran down the plane of her cheek and disappeared under her jawbone.

I reached for her shoulder, and a teardrop hit the back of my hand. And then another and another. They pattered off the awning above us and rattled on the metal of car roofs and soaked my hair and began to stream from gutters, and at some point I realized the tears were not tears at all, but raindrops.

43

11:37 p.m.

"Do you have a message for the killer, Agent Castle?"

Castle's eyes narrowed as he looked back at the reporter. He seemed unsure of how to respond. As though the question were intended to catch him out, somehow. He opened his mouth, but before he could speak, Governor Randall leaned over the microphone. Randall had lost some weight since his television appearances during the first Wardell case. He'd stopped dyeing his hair too. But he was still an imposing presence—a six-foot-four African-American with a deep, commanding voice.

"I have a message for him," Randall said, fixing the camera with a resolute stare as though speaking directly to his subject. "We're going to catch you soon, Mr. Wardell. You're not safe anywhere."

"Governor—"A voice rang out from the assembled crowd, but Randall waved it off.

"That's all for just now," he said, turning away.

Castle nodded. "You heard the man. We'll keep you posted."

The screen cut back to the studio pundits, and I reached for the remote and killed it. The press camp had been set up in a big marquee about half a mile from Hatcher's house. Castle would be heading out to the car that was waiting to bring him back out to us even now. Randall would be headed in the other direction—back to his home state following an unscheduled, but politically valuable, detour in his campaign schedule. I wondered how it would play to the voters back in Chicago. Banner was shaking her head, a wry smile on her lips. "Thank you, Mr. Governor," she said, her brown eyes lingering on the darkened screen. She looked up at me. "What do you think, Blake?"

We were in Hatcher's study. I recognized it from the author photo on the back of his book. The walls were lined with books that looked as though they had been chosen for the color of their spines. I looked back at Banner, then beyond her and through the window at the lake. The light from the helicopter searchlights made it sparkle in the dark with the tiny impacts of a million raindrops. The storm had been building in intensity throughout the day and into the evening and showed no signs of abating. The weather made our job tougher, but if we were lucky, it might cause a few problems for Wardell, too.

"I think the governor's right," I said. "We'll get him. And Wardell knows that as well as anyone. You kill on a stage like this and there's no disappearing act afterward."

"But ..." Banner prompted, sensing what I hadn't said.

"But he'll keep going until it's over. Just a matter of how many more people he can kill before we get him."

"Yeah," she agreed quietly. "It was bad today, Blake."

I nodded, not knowing what else to do. Then I said, "Are you okay?"

"Sure," she answered. Too quickly.

Banner had mentioned having a young daughter earlier. As she looked out into the night, I knew she was thinking about the young girl in the translucent blue raincoat. She'd been twelve, a little younger than my estimate. I thought again about not pulling the trigger in Mosul, about how such a tiny physical action could result in so much death. The Buddhists believe if you save a life, you're responsible for that life from that day forward. I guess that applied to sparing a life too; and I felt the weight of that responsibility grow with every new body.

Wherever the multiple shootings in Rapid City had been reported, the adjective "senseless" headed up the trail with grim inevitability. And they were senseless, in the moral sense. Utterly so. But despite that, the atrocity had accomplished exactly what Wardell had intended it to: He'd demonstrated how powerless we were—to us and to the world. If it was intended to unnerve us for the job of protecting Hatcher, it was working. He'd made a point of telegraphing it in code, like a cocky pool shark calling his next bank shot.

The color blue. The number six.

The last question of his telephone call to Whitford. The last question to the waitress he'd terrified in Rapid City. He'd made a point of doing that, so those particular details would be remembered and commented upon and analyzed for meaning. And then he'd gone out and calmly killed exactly six people, chosen for no other reason than because they were all wearing the color blue. It sent a message. It said, "I control the rules of this game."

And now here we were, in place for the next move in Wardell's bloody game. I wasn't worried about a misdirect anymore. He wasn't interested in giving himself a handicap. He was far too arrogant for that. His play with the waitress was evidence of that: She'd called the cops as soon as he'd walked out of the diner. She'd been far too late to prevent the slaughter on Main Street, but her account of the experience meant we now had an up-to-date, detailed description of his appearance, purely because he'd wanted to show off. But if my instinct about his arrogance was right, then what did that say about the red van?

The door opened and Castle walked in, his hair soaked. He was loosening his tie with his right hand. "How was it?" he asked.

"Fine," I told him, which was the truth. From the perspective of catching our man, it was neither a positive nor a negative. It was just something he'd needed to get out of the way. I understood the need for regular media briefings, but I also completely understood Castle's loathing for them.

"Not bad, Castle," Banner agreed. "You're almost starting to look like you're not in the tenth circle of hell every time somebody points a camera at you."

Castle allowed himself a brief but genuine smile, and I found myself starting to like him a little for it. It vanished from his face as the door opened and a tall female agent entered, her hands filled with three Kevlar vests. "Sir?" she said, as though offering canapés at a drinks reception.

Castle stripped off his jacket and lifted one of the vests. Banner and I followed suit. I looped the straps through the buckles and fixed the Velcro tabs, feeling the weight settle on my upper body.

"Back in the city," Banner remarked as the agent who'd brought the vests disappeared back into the corridor,

"Wardell chose head shots around eighty percent of the time."

"Thanks for the statistic," Castle said.

"Any trace of him so far?" I asked.

Castle shook his head. "We know he's in the area, of course, but it's a big area and there's a shitload of trees out there. Our search helicopters would have their work cut out for them even without this goddamn rain. Rapid City is shut down. Half the state is shut down."

I believed him. Banner and I had driven up to the house following the shootings, and the roads leading out of the town toward the Black Hills had been utterly empty. It was eerie, like the town and its surrounds had been evacuated before an imminent nuclear meltdown.

Castle continued. "The only road in here is blocked at the highway, and we've got surveillance every quarter mile up to the house. For all the good that'll do us."

"It pays to cover the bases," I said.

Like Castle, I doubted Wardell would use the road, not when there was an infinite variety of off-road approaches. The house was built on a plateau midway up a steep incline into the hills, and it faced onto the lake. There were thick woods on the other three sides, encroaching to within a hundred yards of the building—Hatcher had picked an interesting location in which to build his home, given how the profits that enabled it were generated. It was an ideal spot from the point of view of any attacking force. I wondered if any of the multitude of shrinks currently drawing network television consultancy fees had noticed this and what conclusions they might have drawn.

The advantage we had was manpower, and for the first time we had been able to focus that resource on a clearly defined area, one that we could be reasonably certain was the right one. Had we been resisting an attack from an army, we'd have prepared differently—laying fortifications, barricading the doors, arranging a ring of men around the three land-facing sides of the house, patrolling the front with gunboats. But none of that would do any good against a sniper intent on taking out a specific target.

There was a strange atmosphere about the house as the agents on Castle's task force carried out their duties, one that either hadn't been present until tonight, or that I hadn't noticed. It wasn't the usual tension that saturated the preparations for a big event, it was more like the vibe in the locker room of a world champion sports team that finds itself losing badly going into the second half and not knowing quite why. The storm and the claustrophobia of the woods didn't help. Maybe it was the sheer number of kills Wardell had racked up in less than four days, but it seemed like everyone was having to make a conscious effort to remember that they were engaged in a manhunt, not a siege.

The task force had focused on making life difficult for Wardell by boarding up the windows and stationing tactical teams throughout the woods around a half-mile radius. A couple of helicopters circled the lake, casting search beams on the choppy waters as small motorboats swept across the surface. We were about as well prepared as it was possible to be, and now we were going to discover just how good Caleb Wardell was.

There was an antique grandfather clock in the south corner of the study. Banner eyed the clock face as the minute hand clicked up to read quarter to twelve.

"You think he'll really come at midnight?" she asked.

"We're expecting midnight," I said, "so the smart thing to do would be to let us wait, get tired, come in at two or three. But I wouldn't bet against midnight."

Castle's cell rang. He answered it immediately. He listened for a second, asked a couple of questions, and then said he wanted the last of the boards up on the lake-facing windows. The windows on the other three sides had been attended to hours before. A minute later, a dressed-down agent with his sleeves rolled up beneath a Kevlar vest arrived, holding a cordless drill. We watched as he screwed sheets of plywood into the PVC window frames.

"How's Hatcher?" Banner asked.

"Why don't we go see him?" Castle said. "You can ask him yourself."

As the three of us left the study, I cast a glance over my shoulder in time to see the last rectangle of rain-soaked night shut out as the final piece of plywood fitted into place. It made a sound like the lid closing on a coffin.

44

11:57 p.m.

Now, this was more of a challenge.

The rain, the woods, the pursuit, had all created a different environment from that which Wardell was accustomed to. He had experienced similar conditions during basic training in Virginia, but never during actual warfare. In Iraq, rain had been as scarce as mercy. He was no meteorologist, but he guessed it wouldn't be an exaggeration to say that South Dakota had soaked up more precipitation in the last twelve hours than that godforsaken dust hole saw in the average year.

The ponderosa pines closed around him, blotting out the sky and filling his field of vision with shadows and random movement—again, the diametric opposite of the blinding, blazing desert heat. And he was alone. In the war, he'd fought in a small unit, often with just one partner, and that had been against impersonal, almost random targets. Now he faced an army of a different kind. Without backup.

He couldn't think of anywhere in the world he'd rather be.

He'd chosen his observation position that morning, a couple of hours before he'd made his midday trip to town. The spot was ideal: a tiny crevice under an overhang created by the gap left by some long-forgotten landslide. The ground that had given way had exposed the roots of a fifty-foot pine that still stood, reaching out over a sixty-degree incline, defying gravity. Wardell had nestled between the roots, camouflaging his position with sticks and dirt. He'd smeared mud on his exposed skin and around the hollows of his eyes. From the crevice beneath the tree, he could see only the southwest corner of the house. That meant it was no good for taking the shot, but it was an excellent spot from which to sit and patiently survey the feds laying their traps and looking in vain for traces of him.

They were doing a decent job, to give them their due. The FBI tactical teams patrolling the strike zone were well drilled and were leaving no easy gaps. Maneuvering out of range of one team would bring him too close to the next. It was a tight net. They had countersnipers of their own, too. He'd spotted a few of them hunched down in makeshift hides. It had been tempting to kill one or two of them, or maybe a member of a patrol, but Wardell had held off all day, keeping his powder dry. He wasn't hunting brain-dead shoppers now, and taking out one of the feds would put an end to the evening's performance.

They'd made the house pretty secure, all in all. Boarding up the windows—all of the windows—had been an excellent move, if not an unexpected one. It meant he was going to have to find a way of flushing Hatcher out, and perhaps more worthy targets.

More worthy targets; he paused to think about that again. His initial list was getting shorter. Nolan was history, and if all went well, Hatcher would join him within the hour. That left two names, and he'd discovered earlier today that one of them—the late Detective Stewart—was entirely beyond his reach. Room for some new recruits.

Agent Castle from the television interviews seemed like a good candidate, him and perhaps the woman who sometimes appeared alongside him, Banner. Wardell was almost positive that had been her back in Rapid City, the one who'd returned fire from the kill zone. He'd had her in his sights; she was even wearing blue. It was a pity he'd already claimed his six victims. On the other hand, there was always next time. Taking out one of the task force leads would certainly throw a wrench in the works of their manhunt. And then there was the man from the cabin, of course.

He wasn't sure if they'd managed to sneak Hatcher out of the house, but in truth he'd started to question whether Hatcher was even worthy of killing. He was a phony, a minor irritation when you really thought about it. Wardell was more interested in taking out somebody of substance this time, even if it meant relinquishing his stated goal, diverging from the plan. Dwight Eisenhower once said that plans are often useless, but planning is indispensable. Wardell had no great liking for generals, still less for presidents, but as a motto he couldn't fault it.

He'd had the germ of that plan before he'd seen the house in real life. He thought back to the truck stop in Kentucky, the morning after his escape, how he'd flicked through Hatcher's book with amusement.

The selection of photographs reproduced in the middle of the book had been predictable, some from the aftermaths of his shootings intermingled with pictures of the key players and a whole lot of pictures of Hatcher himself. The final one had shown Hatcher in front of his house: a sprawling wood-clad building on the shores of Pactola Lake. Wardell's eye had been drawn by the small outbuilding visible in that shot. Having had time to think and to survey the house, he was convinced that this outbuilding would give him the opening he'd need. But only if he could get a little closer—because this was one task he couldn't guarantee executing at long range.

The major problem was the tac teams. The net around the house was a little tighter than he'd anticipated. That was his own fault, of course. He'd told them exactly where he'd be this time, allowing them to focus their manpower without spreading themselves as thinly as they had before. Had he been overconfident? He doubted it. Confidence and over-confidence were essentially the same thing. It was only after the fact that you could tell one from the other. No, he would adapt and triumph once again. After all, he'd been looking for a challenge this time, hadn't he?

He checked his equipment again. Much of what he'd taken from the steel trunk in the shack was stashed at his camp, deeper into the hills, but he'd brought the essentials. The most important item was, of course, the Remington 700. It was a top-of-the-line civilian model, and Wardell had to admit Nolan had done well on this: It bore a close similarity to the M40 that Wardell was accustomed to from the Corps. Nolan had accessorized it with a high-spec bipod, a decent scope, and a sling, too. Whether or not the Remington was superior to the PSG1 was a matter of opinion, but Wardell preferred it. It just felt better in his hands.

Added to the rifle were tools for a variety of jobs. For close-range encounters, he'd stowed the AK in favor of a SIG Sauer P226, chambered for nine-millimeter Parabellum rounds, which was holstered at his hip. If things got even closer, he had a stag-handled bowie knife strapped to his boot. He was dressed in woodland combat BDUs with a multitude of pockets containing all kinds of useful things, like a compass and utility knife and what they'd referred to in the Corps as a blowout kit: a first aid pack specifically for treating gunshot wounds. In a green waterproof drag bag, he had four decently assembled pipe bombs. He'd inspected all of this equipment earlier, of course, and had concluded with some surprise that Nolan had actually done a pretty good Boy Scout job.

Wardell put his eye to the scope of the Remington again and tracked the closest tac team, weighing up his two options. He'd probably be able to get past them, but it wasn't a dead cert. If they saw him, he'd be a rat in a trap. But even so, he liked it better than the other option, which was to pick off every member of the closest five-man team before the alarm could be raised. He wasn't worried about the shooting, because he knew he could take all five out in three and a half seconds, but there was the rub. Three and a half seconds was a hell of a long time for trained men expecting just this sort of attack. No way he'd get all of them before somebody yelled or returned fire. Once that happened, he'd be faced with two more options: fall back and hope he'd get another chance later, or hold his position and engage the incoming backup teams. Sooner or later they'd pin him down, and that would be that. And Wardell wasn't quite ready for that to be that.

He looked at his watch, saw it was nearly midnight. It looked like he'd have to go with the stealthy approach.

But then providence lent a hand. The leader of the nearest tac team put a hand to his right ear. The body language was crystal clear: Somebody at the command center was giving him an instruction. What followed made the content of the instruction just as clear. For some reason, the tac team closest to Wardell, the one he was most worried about, had been ordered to move out of position.

Scarcely able to believe his luck, Wardell watched as the five-man team moved quietly northeast. He reached for the drag bag, flattened himself to the ground, and began to low crawl down the incline.

DAY FIVE

45

12:02 a.m.

We passed through so many rooms and corridors that I began to wonder if I should have left a trail of bread crumbs. Eventually we emerged into a tall, wide entrance foyer. The polished hardwood floor was covered in the center by a gigantic Oriental rug. Several doors on each wall led back off into the interior of the house, and a big wooden spiral staircase in the center of the room accessed a mezzanine level, on which I could see more doors and corridors leading off at each side. The place had looked big from the outside, but from within it seemed positively cavernous.

Two agents, evidently chosen for their powerful builds, guarded the door leading to the basement level, where Hatcher was hiding out in a games room.

As Castle led us down into the bowels of the building, I was struck by the contrast with the rest of the house. Although the basement space was well appointed with a pool table, big-screen TV, and even a small bar, the decor seemed deliberately unfinished. The walls were bare concrete, and the struts and beams supporting the house above were left visible. As a bunker, it was actually pretty effective, nestled in foundations of three-foot-thick poured concrete. And it was windowless.

Hatcher was a big man, and I immediately sensed that he

was someone used to getting his own way. He was working the pool table all by himself, knocking the striped balls into the pockets with increasing ferocity.

"I thought you guys were moving me," he said again. Castle had told me this was something of an about-face from his earlier requests.

Banner said, "Given the weather conditions and the events in Rapid City earlier, we felt it would—"

"Yeah, yeah, yeah," Hatcher said, cutting her off mid-sentence and holding a hand up as if to ward off further words. "Why don't you—"

"Wardell's out there right now," I cut in. "He's out in those woods and he's ready to put a bullet in you. Any vehicle leaves this place, he's going to know exactly who's in it."

Hatcher snorted and put the cue down on the edge of the table.

"And, in point of fact, you probably wouldn't make it to the vehicle," I continued. "Likely as not, he could drop you as soon as you stuck your head out of the door."

"You know how to put a guy at ease, Agent."

I ignored the assumption. "I don't want you at ease, Hatcher. People at ease take things for granted. They don't look over their shoulder when they walk down the street."

He walked over to a couch pushed up against one of the walls, then changed his mind and paced the other way, scratching behind his ear angrily.

"I gotta get out of here," he said suddenly, turning and heading for the stairs.

Castle put a hand on his left shoulder. "You're staying here."

Hatcher tried to shrug the hand off, then pushed Castle back when that didn't work. "Get the fuck off of me."

A scuffle broke out, Castle trying to restrain Hatcher as the other man tried to connect with a couple of wild swings. I moved to intervene as one of Hatcher's swipes connected with Castle's nose and he yelled in pain. I didn't expend too much effort, just put a couple of smooth, practiced moves into action, and all of a sudden I had Hatcher pinned against the rough concrete wall with his right arm twisted up between his shoulder blades. Hatcher had fifty pounds on me, but he was the one who was doing the yelping.

"Do what we tell you," I said, speaking slowly and deliberately, "or you're dead." It sounded more like a direct threat when I said it, but I figured that wouldn't necessarily hurt.

Banner approached from the side. "I don't want you dead, Mr. Hatcher. It looks shitty on the report." She glanced at Castle, who was holding his bloody nose between thumb and index finger. "You okay?"

Castle nodded. "I hope that fucking hurts."

"Okay, okay, just let me go," Hatcher said.

I held him another few seconds and let him yell again before, warily, I relaxed my grip.

Hatcher stumbled over to the couch and slumped down on it. Then he did the last thing any of us expected. He put his head in his hands and started to cry. There was an uncomfortable silence, broken only by Hatcher's muffled sobs.

"Why me?" he said, then raised his head to look up at Castle, who was still tending his nose. "Why me?"

Castle glanced up at the ceiling, above which the million-dollar house sat. Nobody spoke. Outside, the sound of the rain hitting the ground seemed to get louder, as though the elements were stepping up their assault. Then there was a dull sound like something heavy being dropped, and all of us looked up.

"What was that?" Banner asked.

"Nothing good," I replied.

A minute later, the door at the top of the stairs was flung open.

"We've got to clear the building," yelled one of the big agents from the top of the stairs.

"What the hell is going on?" Banner demanded.

"Fire."

They weren't kidding. You could smell the smoke halfway up the stairs. "What happened?" I said, addressing the agent who'd opened the door as we ascended.

"North side of the building's on fire. We need to get the hell out of here ASAP." He held the door as we emerged into the entrance hall, which was already filling with smoke. As I watched, part of the ceiling at the far side of the room gave way, a shower of flaming debris raining down from above.

I grabbed his arm. "What the hell *happened*?"

"Looks like a fire broke out in the shed containing the gas cylinders. Agent Wetherspoon's out there. He says it went up like the Fourth of July. We have to clear the building, sir."

"That's just what he wants. That's why he started the goddamn fire," I said.

"We secured that shed, right?" Banner said, addressing Castle.

"We had two guys right outside, orders not to move no matter what."

"They're dead," the agent at the door said abruptly.

"What?"

"Park and Cole," he elaborated. "Wetherspoon says they're both down."

"That's impossible," Castle said. "That's inside the ring. If he'd gotten that far, we'd know about it. He'd have engaged one of the teams."

"Looks like he got past them," I replied.

"Sir, we need to—" the agent started, trying to herd us toward the front door.

Castle ignored him. "Something's wrong. This is all wrong."

He was right. A hundred and fifty armed men protecting the building, and Wardell had managed to get close enough to give himself his only realistic chance of acquiring the target, by smoking us out. There was something more at work here. But we would have to worry about that later.

At that moment we had two pressing concerns: to get out of the building before it burned down around us, and to make sure Hatcher didn't leave by the main door. I opened my mouth to say as much, just as a door at the other end of the hall exploded off its hinges, a dragon's breath of fire billowing into the corridor in its wake. Beyond the doorframe was an inferno. The entire north side of the house was ablaze, and it was spreading fast.

The agent who'd led us out of the basement was at the main door, yelling for us to follow.

"Hatcher," I yelled. "Are there any other exits?" Wardell had played an expert hand, but there was still only one of him. He'd be forced to play the odds and cover the main door. Hatcher had a glazed look on his face, as though the fire on top of everything else had caused a sensory shutdown.

Castle looked at the main exit, saw what I meant. He grabbed Hatcher's shirt lapels and pushed him back, slamming him against the wall.

"Hatcher! Another way out?"

Slowly, he got the words out. "Master bedroom. Stairs down from the deck." He started toward the big spiral staircase.

Just then, one of the exposed ceiling joists collapsed

directly above us with a shrieking, bansheelike noise. I wrapped my arms around Banner's waist and dived for the floor, just scraping under the falling beam. Flaming debris showered down after it like confetti. A spark ignited the sleeve of my shirt and I managed to pat it out with Banner's help, but not before sustaining a long burn on my right forearm.

"You okay?" she asked.

I nodded, wincing. "Good thing I'm allergic to polyester," I said, turning to look at the long bonfire that now divided the wide entrance hall. I looked down the length of the beam and saw that the bulky agent was lying dead under it, his skull crushed by the beam.

Castle and Hatcher were on the other side of the flaming beam, both unharmed. The collapse seemed to have snapped Hatcher out of his daze, and he was looking around for an exit. The beam had landed roughly diagonally across the space. Banner and I could reach the front entrance, but not the spiral staircase that led to the mezzanine. Castle and Hatcher were faced with the opposite situation.

Castle pointed at the door. "You go. I'll get him out by the bedroom."

I grabbed Banner by the arm. Front entrance it was, then. Especially since the only other option was going back down to the basement and slow-roasting. I only hoped Wardell wasn't feeling like a consolation prize, because we were about to present ourselves as candidates. As we headed for the door, I glanced up and saw Castle and Hatcher reach the second-floor mezzanine that overlooked the hall. A lone agent appeared from the south corridor, beckoning for them to follow. I turned away and then did a double take. The agent was thin and was wearing glasses. Even through the smoke and the heat haze, there was something familiar about him. Then it clicked. It was the man I'd seen in the crowd in Fort Dodge.

I yelled out Castle's name, but the sound was lost in the roar of the flames as the three men disappeared along the second-floor landing.

"Come on," Banner yelled, tugging at my arm.

"You go," I said, unstrapping my Kevlar vest and handing it to her. "Hold it up like a shield and run like hell for cover."

"What about you?"

I didn't answer. Castle and Hatcher were in trouble, and being trapped in a burning building was the goddamned least of it.

46

12:19 a.m.

I lingered long enough to see Banner bolt through the front door, then waited a couple of seconds. There were no shots, none that I could hear. Encouraged, I turned back to attempt to get past the bonfire, quickly realizing there wasn't a way. The flames had spread rapidly, and the big Oriental rug, together with much of the wooden hall floor, was ablaze. I'd have to circumvent it. There was a big antique cabinet below the mezzanine level, only inches away from the flames spreading from the doorway at the far end.

I took a breath and ran for it, pushing off my right foot, landing atop the cabinet with my left, and then slingshotting myself upward. The mezzanine was a good twelve feet off the ground, so I barely made it. My left hand found the polished wood floor and slipped off, but my right hand caught the bottom of one of the banisters and found purchase. I hauled myself up and over.

The mezzanine was empty—smoke seeping from beneath the doors on the north side. I touched the back of my hand to one of the brass door handles and instantly pulled it away. It was like touching a griddle. The whole place was a time bomb waiting to explode. I ran in the direction Castle and the others had gone, rounded a corner, and saw Castle lying prone on the wood floor.

I rolled him over onto his back to check for a pulse, but he saved me the trouble by groaning and opening his eyes. He touched a hand to the back of his head and winced. "Blake. What ...?"

I started to ask which way they'd gone, then remembered there was only one direction possible—straight ahead. There were three doors at the far end of the hall: one on the left, one in the middle, one on the right. The one on the left was closed and faced north, so it would be a backdraft death trap. The one on the right was open.

I hauled Castle to his feet and we made for the door. Behind us, I heard a *whump* as one of the landing doors exploded outward. I was first through the open doorway and instinctively raised my arm up to cover my eyes from the blinding light flooding the room. Someone had removed the plywood from the big plate-glass window, and a searchlight from one of the choppers lit up the room like Las Vegas. I blinked the flash out of my eyes as the helicopter's beam angled away and was able to make out two blurred figures by the window.

"Hatcher, get down!" I yelled, not sure which of the figures was him.

Just then I felt Castle's shoulder slam into me and knock me off my feet. I heard three shots from a pistol and a yell of pain and anger. As I blinked the last of the stars out of my eyes, I saw Castle charge at the thin gunman and football-tackle him to the ground. Hatcher was standing by the window, watching the two men on the floor. I suddenly realized that this room faced the front of the building. There was no deck out there, which meant it wasn't the master bedroom. The thin man had brought Hatcher in here for the very reason I had avoided bringing him out the front entrance.

"Get—" Before I could finish, part of Hatcher's head seemed to vanish, and there was a puff of vapor that was bright red in the concentrated light. His legs buckled and he dropped to the floor.

I scrambled to my feet and ducked as I heard another shot, realizing quickly that this one had come from within the room. The two men on the floor had stopped moving. The thin man was on top of Castle, slumped and unmoving. They looked like a couple who had just finished lovemaking. I pulled the thin man off, knowing he was dead from the bloody stain over his heart. Castle was still breathing, but it didn't look like he would be for much longer. The vest had stopped one of the rounds, but another had hit between the top of the vest and his throat.

He blinked and coughed blood when he saw me. He said, "Hatcher?" having difficulty getting the word out.

I looked at Hatcher's body, looked back and shook my head.

"Get the hell out of here, Blake," he said, closing his eyes.

I ignored him, busying myself with reaching inside the thin man's jacket. My fingers closed around a leather ID case. There was no time to examine it, so I slid it into my pocket. I looked up at the window with its single neat bullet hole. I heard more shots from outside, but not from a rifle. A pistol this time, maybe more than one. I looked back at the hallway. The shadows of flames danced along the wall. The middle door had to be the master bedroom, the one Hatcher had talked about.

"I'm sorry," I said.

"Don't be. You need a tissue, asshole?"

"No," I said. "I'm sorry because this is going to hurt like a son of a bitch."

I grabbed Castle under the armpits and dragged, knowing I was stretching his wound as I pulled him across the floor, keeping low and out of line of sight of the window. He kept screaming at me to leave him until I reached the door; then he passed out.

The corridor was ablaze, the flames having advanced to within a couple of feet of us. Beyond was an inferno. I dropped Castle long enough to touch the handle of the middle door; it felt cold. I got the door open. The flames behind us lit up a large bedroom that might well have been the last area of the house untouched by fire. Directly across from us was a boarded-up French door. It had to lead out to the deck Hatcher had mentioned. I dragged Castle into the room, one leg of his suit catching fire as the flames reached us, and slammed the door shut to give us another minute or so. I kicked out the flames on Castle's leg and made for the boarded-up door. Three good tugs ripped the board loose from its screws and now the door handle was accessible. Locked, of course. I picked up a small armchair by the window in both hands and swung it. It splintered into firewood against the double-glazed door.

I heard a crackling behind me as the varnish on the bedroom door began to bubble and peel. Reaching into my shoulder holster, I drew my Beretta and fired six rounds in a wide circle as I walked back toward the glass door. Six neat holes appeared in the double glazing, but it held. I kicked the middle of the circle and both panes of glass gave way. The cold night air flooded into the room like the breath of an angel. I ran back to where Castle lay, grabbed him under the arms, and started dragging him toward the outside world.

47

12:24 a.m.

The big house on the lake was dying.

The heat on Banner's face was uncomfortable even twenty yards distant from the house. The blaze vaporized the rain above and around it, creating a fog that drifted out from the building. God only knew how much more quickly the building would have burned without the rain. The scene reminded her of a painting of hell she'd seen years before, in the Louvre on her honeymoon. Watching the flames dance in every window, the intermittent explosions of glass and metal, it seemed difficult to believe she'd ever see Castle or Blake again. And then, of course, there was the danger outside.

Banner tore her eyes from the flames to take in the surrounding area. It wasn't easy; the incandescence of the blaze made everything surrounding it darker. The personnel who'd been inside the house were all outside. The ones who'd made it, anyway. There hadn't been a lot of time: The fire had begun and spread with a vicious enthusiasm. There were around forty agents forming an even semicircle around the entrance at the closest distance bearable. Banner guessed the tac teams were holding their positions around the perimeter. Not that it would do any good, because the perimeter had manifestly been breached. Banner was suddenly aware that the agents watching the blaze presented a target even easier than the crowds on Main Street earlier that day.

She unholstered her Glock and fired three quick shots in the air. That got everyone's attention, reminded them of the other clear-and-present danger.

"People, we are in a shooting gallery right now," she yelled. "Fall back to the trees."

The agents surrounding the blaze snapped out of it, started moving quickly toward the greater shelter afforded by the woods. If Wardell was on this side of the building, he could pick any of them off any old time he wanted.

Where the hell is he? The question returned with renewed intensity as Banner reached the tree line and backed up against the trunk of one of the pines, watching the blaze. Wardell had slipped through the net, flushed them all out. Was he really going to wait around and see if Hatcher appeared before he made any kind of move? It was starting to look that way. But where would he be? How could he be sure of being in a position to see Hatcher? She scanned the faces of the agents around her, hoping Blake or Castle might be among them, that they'd found another way out, but to no avail. Not everybody had retreated as far as the trees. The mobile command center was still parked on the gravel driveway, thirty yards from the house's front entrance. She could see a couple of men silhouetted in the vehicle's cab; another had scaled the side and was crouched on the roof, probably doing the same thing she was: looking for a sign of life.

Something about that thought brought Banner up short. She pushed off the tree, at first walking briskly, then jogging, and then flat-out running toward the command center. She opened her mouth to address the man on the roof, and then she saw the muzzle flash as he fired into a room on the second floor.

"Son of a *bitch*," she said to herself. Then "Drop your weapon" loud, as she leveled her own piece. The gunman didn't miss a beat, didn't even swing the rifle around to point it at her, the way she'd been half expecting. Instead, his left hand dropped from the barrel of the rifle, brushed his side, and came back up with a pistol. It looked impossibly instinctive, like breathing in and out.

Banner saw more muzzle flash even as she felt her own gun kick. She felt the slipstream as a bullet passed within an inch of the side of her face. She ducked and kept firing. There was a grunt of pain and the figure dropped to the roof and slid off on the opposite side. Banner kept the gun level, watching both ends of the command center as she moved toward it. They had him now; no way he could outrun—

That was when the second fire broke out. This one was in the cab, where she could still see the two agents. She ran for the door, gun still in her right hand, and tugged at the handle. It was locked. Two agents caught up with her and wasted another second trying the handle again.

"It's locked. Wardell's on the other side. Go!" she yelled, directing one of the agents. He looked confused, but only for a second, then moved away from the burning cab. Banner could see the two men inside writhing as the flames leapt around them. She could smell burning flesh and hair. The other agent punched through the side window, bare-fisted. The flames lit up his face, showing an expression of panic. He reached in and got the door open. Burning gasoline ran out over the sill like lava. Banner and the other agent leapt back. The man in the driver's seat toppled out as the heat contracted the muscles in his body again, shifting his position. The burning body landed faceup on the grass. There was a dark entrance wound in the center of his forehead. Banner felt something almost like relief for the dead man.

All of a sudden, other people were swarming around. Somebody had a foam fire extinguisher and sprayed the flames out.

"What the hell?"

"What happened?"

"How'd it ...?"

"Something from the house?"

"You okay?"

Banner felt anger, wanted to yell, *What took you so fucking long?* at the others, even though she knew that only a few seconds had passed since she'd first noticed the man on the roof of the command center.

The agent she'd sent after Wardell reappeared from around the side of the command unit, shaking his head.

"Anything?" Banner asked.

"Yeah," the agent said, beckoning. "Come see this."

Banner moved around to the other side of the command center, a few of the other men breaking off to follow her. The first agent was there, pointing up at something on the side.

"Looks like you winged him." He was pointing at a smear of blood down the blue and gray paint of the big vehicle. Banner looked at the smear, then the ground below it. There were no obvious pools of blood on the grass, which meant Wardell might not be wounded too badly. A pity, but it was something. From here, it was a mere twenty feet to the trees.

"Go," Banner said, but she didn't have to. The men who'd followed her around were already running for the woods. A couple of them had flashlights.

"Medic! Need a medic over here!"

Banner turned around to tell whoever was yelling that the two men were way beyond medical help. Then she realized the shout had rung out from farther away, closer to the house. One of the agents was crouched next to a body lying less than ten yards from the burning house. She ran toward them, holding up an arm to block the intense heat from her face. She reached them and looked down at the man on the ground. It was Castle, and he was in a bad way. The shirt under his vest was so soaked with blood that it was impossible to tell how many wounds there were. Banner loosened the straps on the vest and ripped the shirt open. Looked like a gunshot, definitely. She shucked her own jacket off and bunched it up, used it to put pressure on the wound. Castle winced and his eyes flickered open.

"We're going to get you out of here," Banner said. "Just hang on, Castle. Hang on, you stubborn bastard."

She thought she saw the ghost of a smile on his lips. It gave her hope. She kept talking. "Where's Blake?"

With painful effort, Castle raised his left hand a little at the wrist and three fingers and a thumb dropped down a little. It took Banner a second to realize he was trying to point.

He was pointing in the direction in which Caleb Wardell had fled.

48

The chilled, rain-damp night air sucked in and out of my lungs as I ran between the trees. After the burning house, it was beautiful. The rain was still falling fast and hard, but the woods afforded some shelter from the deluge. Wardell was up ahead of me. I couldn't see him, but I could hear him as he crashed through the undergrowth. Brilliant white light sliced through the tree cover and swept in front on me in a wide beam, and I realized Banner or somebody else had called in the helicopters. That was good and bad: good because it meant somebody besides me had seen Wardell escape into the woods, bad because I wasn't betting on them being able to distinguish between the two armed men running in the same direction.

About thirty feet ahead I saw the shape of a man leap an obstruction and then seemingly vanish into the earth, suggesting the ground dropped away beyond. The undergrowth was thick and the going slow; it took me longer than I'd have liked to reach the obstruction—it was the thick trunk of a fallen tree, and sure enough, there was a forty-five-degree incline beyond it. I braced myself on the trunk and felt something tacky in the wetness. Blood. I raised my fingers to my face to try to confirm it, and that's when I heard the click of a handgun being cocked.

"Drop it."

The FBI agent who'd spoken was six feet from my face, the muzzle of his Glock 23 a good deal closer.

"I'm with the—" I began.

"I said drop it, asshole."

I did as I was told, opening my fingers and letting the Beretta drop to the forest floor. I looked at the agent. I didn't recognize him. Maybe that didn't mean much. At night, in a dark blue FBI-branded raincoat and matching baseball cap, everyone looks pretty much identical: man or woman, black or white. But it also meant I couldn't rule him out as being with the thin man.

"I'm with the task force," I said.

"Hands on your head, asshole."

I complied. "You know, my name isn't actually ass—"

"Shut up."

"The man you want is down there. He's getting away." The agent opened his mouth, no doubt to either tell me to shut up again or call me an asshole again, or possibly both, so I cut him off. "Call it in, Agent. Talk to Banner. My name's Blake, I'm a civilian adviser. I'm on your side."

The agent's eyes narrowed and he tightened his grip on his Glock. Then, carefully, he took his left hand off the gun, reached for his cell phone, and hit a couple of buttons without averting his gaze one millimeter from me.

"It's Riley. I got somebody. No, it's not the target. Get me Agent Castle."

That made my mind up. By the time the guy at the other end of the call went looking for Castle, discovered he was out of the action, found Banner, and she managed to convinced him I wasn't the enemy, Wardell would be in the next state.

A lot of people think a gun will go off if the guy holding it flinches. That's not true, not with modern firearms. The standard FBI-issue Glock 23 for example, like the one that was pointed at my head, has three separate safety mechanisms to prevent accidental discharge: an external integrated trigger safety, a firing pin safety, and a drop safety. A lot of safety, in other words.

That means it takes conscious thought to squeeze the trigger, not to mention resolve. All in all, there's a lot less effort involved in knocking somebody's gun aside, especially when you're dealing with a law-enforcement practitioner who's been trained up to the eyeballs to make sure there's a clear threat before firing. The most important thing is not to telegraph the action. So I didn't. I just kept eye contact with the agent, kept breathing regularly, then opened my mouth as though I were going to say something else.

Then I just reached out and punched his wrist out of the way. Before he could readjust, I grabbed the gun with both hands and twisted it down. I felt the bone in his finger snap on the trigger guard. As he opened his mouth to cry out in pain, I yanked the gun out of his hand and slammed my right elbow into his nose. The guy went down as emphatically as the *Titanic*, and a whole lot quicker. I tossed the gun deep into the pines, retrieved my own from the ground, then put my left hand onto the fallen tree and vaulted over and onto the incline.

I scrabbled down the slope, trying to balance speed with some regard for safety. It wasn't easy in the dark; the pines dotting the slope blotted out the sky as effectively as a black-out blind, and I realized why they were called the Black Hills. I could barely make out the ground, never mind what was ahead of me. The incline suddenly became more pronounced, and any control over my speed of descent evaporated. All of a sudden I was running full tilt. And then the inevitable happened: My foot landed on a loose rock, which gave way and sent me tumbling face-first. I brought my arms up around my head as I hit the ground and kept falling. I grabbed around for purchase on a root, a bush, some grass … anything to slow my fall. My right side impacted off something large and unyielding—had to be a tree. It knocked the wind out of me but absorbed some of my momentum. The fingers of my right hand brushed against the leaves of a bush, and I closed my fist around a handful of it. The handful ripped away, but I was moving slower again. I was able to roll onto my back and use my heels and my palms to brake. I caught my breath and looked down.

About twenty feet below me, the trees stopped and the slope leveled out. There was a little more light down there, and I could make out what looked like some kind of weird rock formation in a clearing. I wiped raindrops and sweat from my eyes and took a moment to check myself for injuries. I had an impressive collection of cuts and scrapes, my shirt was ripped in several places, and my side hurt like a son of a bitch, but other than that, I was okay.

I picked my way down the remainder of the slope and emerged into the clearing. I realized that what I'd been looking at wasn't a rock formation at all, but a graveyard. A very old graveyard, by the looks of it. I thought back to earlier, when I'd looked at the house plans, which had included a map of the surrounding area. I remembered seeing something about an old gold mining town, now long gone. At least, the town itself was long gone. Evidently, its dead remained.

I squinted my eyes and peered ahead into the dark. It looked like the clearing occupied a natural plateau on the hillside. Uneven rows of subsiding and fallen headstones marched ahead for a couple of hundred yards before the pines closed in once more. There was a dirt track on the other side that disappeared down a farther slope, probably leading to was left of the mining town. I cast a glance back at the upper slope and realized it had damned near turned into a cliff at the point I'd fallen. It would take Banner's people a while either to find another way down or to rustle up rappelling equipment. That meant there was no point waiting for backup, even if waiting for backup had been my style.

I began my advance toward the dirt track. The rain washed down unabated, turning the earth under my feet to sludge. I thought about the hundred-year-old remains six feet beneath me. I put my hand on a moss-covered marker to steady myself, and my breath caught in my throat as a figure stepped from behind a large monument at the far side of the graveyard.

Wardell. Fifteen feet away. Close enough to speak to without raising my voice, too far to do anything about the rifle that was pointed at my head.

"Evening, partner," he said. His voice contained both tiredness and pain, but also something that sounded like camaraderie. "Persistent, ain't you?"

49

12:40 a.m.

It was him: the man from the cabin. Wardell had known it would be, instinctively, when he'd heard the sounds of somebody crashing down that hill. Nobody on a fixed salary would risk following him down that lethal slalom on foot. He was pleased to see that he didn't appear to have any serious injuries. A man this interesting didn't deserve to go out breaking his neck in a fall. Wardell kept the Remington 700 trained on him, ready to put a round through his right eyeball. So why didn't he? Because he wanted to know who he was first. That was harmless enough, wasn't it? He'd have to kill him soon, before the feds had a chance to catch up, but they had a little time before that.

"Nice weather for ducks, huh?" he said.

The other man just shrugged in acknowledgment. He hadn't put his hands up, hadn't tried to beg or bargain. "We're going to talk about the weather?"

Wardell felt a flash of déjà vu at the sound of the man's voice. It seemed familiar somehow. Or was it the situation that felt familiar? Doubtful: Most of his targets were never aware that he had them in his sights, so this setup was a little out of the ordinary.

"Good to meet you again," he said. "Name's Caleb Wardell."

The other man smiled thinly. "I know."

"Then you have me at kind of a disadvantage, partner."

"And here was me thinking it was the other way around."

"Point taken." Wardell chuckled. "What's your name, soldier?"

"Carter Blake."

"You're not one of them."

"I'm not one of them," Blake agreed.

"I know you, don't I?"

"We've met."

"Refresh my memory."

Blake stared at the muzzle of Wardell's rifle. "This situation was the other way around last time."

Wardell's mouth broke into a wide grin. Of course. *Now* he remembered. Mosul—right after he'd scragged all of those locals. Although it had led to his exit from the military, the episode bore nothing but fond memories for him. A dozen kills: a satisfying mix of distance shots and up-close action. Tying it up with the hit on Rassam had been smart—a legitimate target in the mix turned the civilians into straight collateral damage, gave him the freedom to go as far as he liked. Later, in Chicago, he had never been able to let himself so completely off the leash before they caught him.

"Get out of here! I knew I recognized that uptight face. I bet you're wishing things had turned out different last time, huh?"

Blake said nothing.

Wardell nodded, remembering. Thinking about the non-uniformed man who'd appeared out of nowhere and interrupted his work, stopped him from going house to house looking for more victims. "You weren't with *them* then either, as I recall. So what? Bounty hunter? Spook, maybe? You with Christians in Action?"

Blake shook his head. "Exterminator. They call me in when there's a vermin problem."

Wardell ignored that, flicked his eyes up at the hill and back. "How long do you reckon we have?"

"Not long."

"Pity. You want to know something funny, Blake?"

Blake said nothing.

"I wish I didn't have to shoot you. You were starting to make this interesting."

"I can understand that," Blake said.

"Yeah?"

"Yeah. I'd imagine it gets boring after a while, shooting unarmed twelve-year-olds and octogenarians."

Wardell paused. Spoke more quietly. "And unarmed exterminators. Don't forget those, partner."

"Why do you do it?" Blake said. He was just playing for time, obviously. *Why did you do it?* had been the most frequently asked question of Wardell after his arrest. He'd never given anybody an answer to it before. But now? Why not? It wouldn't take so very long.

230

"You ever hear the name 'Juba'?"

Blake used his thumb and index finger to sweep water from the bridge of his nose. Seemed to consider the question. Then he simply said, "Sure."

"And?"

"Juba was the insurgency's very own Baron von Richthofen. Some kind of supersniper. They say he never missed. He popped up everywhere: Baghdad, Falluja, Mosul, Basra. Took out dozens of coalition troops. Came out of nowhere and vanished back into the desert like a ghost. Or a demon. One shot, one kill."

"Not bad, Blake. Not bad at all."

"There was only one problem with Juba."

"Do tell."

"It was all bullshit. There was no Juba. No unfailing, supernatural assassin. It was a PR thing—every time the bad guys managed to bag one of our people, they credited it to Juba. Built the legend of this ghost killer. Probably worked reasonably well to inspire their own people, the more impressionable ones at least. They released videos of some of the shootings, the way they always do. The guy playing Juba changed more times than James Bond."

Wardell laughed out loud. He didn't let his rifle muzzle waver, of course. "Very good, Blake. Very good. I'm really going to miss you. I mean that."

"So that's what it's about? You think you're Juba?"

"Juba was bullshit, Blake. You're one hundred percent right about that. But all the same, there was something about it, you know? The legend. Your experienced grunts never bought into it, of course. Some of the new guys, though ... you could see it in their eyes even when they laughed it off. There was a little bit of fear there. Just a little bit, but it was real. Like they were trading ghost stories over the campfire."

"Ghost stories," Blake repeated. Still keeping him talking. Wardell didn't mind that. He was enjoying this. It was a shame it would have to end soon.

"Yeah," Wardell said, his mind drifting to the cold, arid darkness of a desert night. "Of course, I never could believe it, not even from the start. Not just because I wasn't a rookie. Juba was supposedly operating in my area of professional expertise, so to speak, so I could never feel it like those younger guys did. Or like the rank-and-file insurgents must have. But right from the beginning, I kind of loved the idea."

"The idea of a boogeyman."

"Exactly. I started thinking, in a weird way, it would almost be nice if it were true. You know what I mean?"

A wide grin broke out on Blake's face, and Wardell thought for a second that he got it, that here was a true kindred spirit. "Wardell, I have absolutely no goddamn clue what you mean."

Wardell nodded, disappointed but not entirely surprised. "No. No, you really wouldn't, would you? Anyway, I got to thinking: If it worked for the insurgents, and if it made some of the guys on *our side* a little scared, what would it be like to do that back home? I mean it's so simple: You pick a city, and you kill a few people, and all of a sudden, you're—"

"Juba?"

"God."

Blake's face broke out in a grin, and he shook his head.

"Something funny, partner?" Wardell asked sharply. Blake didn't seem to be at all afraid of him, and the guy was beginning to push the boundaries of his not-inconsiderable patience.

"It's just, you're describing it like it's a new idea. The way you've been killing."

"Nobody's done what I'm doing, Blake."

"You really think so? Disgruntled Marine sniper comes home and decides, 'What the hell? Why not shoot a few people from a distance?' Just off the top of my head, we've got Muhammad in Washington, 2002. Charles Whitman in Texas in sixty-six. And Lee Harvey Oswald, of course."

"Marksmen, Blake, not snipers. There's a big difference. I mean, Oswald? Not in the same class at all. I wouldn't need three shots to kill a president."

"Why not? You needed two to kill a fat, slow delivery guy."

Wardell shook his head and tightened his finger on the trigger. "Time to say good night, Blake."

"Wait a second," Blake said hurriedly, obviously realizing he'd pushed his luck a little too far.

"You used up your last second, partner."

"The red van," Blake said quickly, giving Wardell a moment's pause. "Haven't you wondered about the red van?"

"Haven't paid it much mind, to be honest with you," Wardell lied. He glanced up at the hill as he heard the buzzing of one of the FBI helos. It sounded like it was a little closer. It was time to get moving.

"I don't believe you. And that first call to the press, the one that blew the media blackout—that wasn't you, was it?"

"Get to the point, Blake," Wardell snapped. "You're trying my patience, and I got places to be." The chopper was definitely getting closer. In another few seconds it would be overhead, and it wouldn't take long to pick them out with the searchlight.

If Blake had noticed, he gave no indication, just kept talking. "Somebody's going out of their way to make things tough for the task force. To make things easy for you. Somebody with connections, inside knowledge."

"So?" Wardell said, growing tired of the conversation.

It was time to bring this exchange to a close. "Somebody's helping me out a little. Maybe he's a fan of what I do. Makes no difference to me."

"Helping you out is one way of putting it. How about looking at it a different way?"

Wardell said nothing, waited for him to continue. Every instinct in his body screamed, *Do it now*. He held firm.

"I don't think you're being helped, Wardell. I think you're being used."

The helicopter broke the cover of the trees at the top of the hill, its beam directed straight into Wardell's eyes. He jammed them shut and fell behind a tall monument as the beam continued its sweep for twenty yards before zipping back to his position as the operator tried to confirm what he'd just seen.

Wardell swore as he stuck his head out from behind the monument and saw Blake too had taken cover. The opportunity for a clean kill had vanished. He'd played straight into Blake's hands. There was one last ace in the hole. Wardell reached into the drag bag and withdrew the last pipe bomb. He snapped the fuse off close to the cap, leaving about three seconds, then lit it and tossed it to Blake's last position.

An orange and black cloud of flame and grave dirt exploded up into the rain, forcing the helicopter to swing back and upward. It would be good enough for a distraction, to allow him to escape the chopper's searchlight. It ought to take out Blake, too. It ought to rip that bastard into a few thousand bloody pieces and wipe that goddamn knowing expression off his face for good. But Wardell wasn't counting on it. He wasn't counting on it at all.

50

Banner stood beneath the shelter of a tall pine as she watched the deluge continue, blurring the blue lights of the fire trucks and ambulances closer to what was left of the house. On the other end of the phone line, her sister's voice was utterly devoid of its usual critical undercurrent.

"Thank God you're okay, Elaine. Is everybody else . . . ?"

Helen's sentence trailed off there, and Banner realized she already knew the answer to that question if she was within sight of a television. It was the reason Banner had called Helen as soon as she could, despite the hour. She had to avoid the possibility that she—or, God forbid, Annie—might hear about this on the morning news and fear the worst.

"No. We lost some people. Good people."

"I'm sorry."

"Yeah."

"I saw on the news about Rapid City. They're saying he killed a young girl this time."

Banner closed her eyes, and the image of the girl in the blue raincoat flashed before them once again. She'd been seeing that image all day. It was one of the ones that would take time to go away, if it ever did.

"That's right, Helen. She was only a few years older than . . ." This time, it was Banner who trailed off, unable to complete that thought.

"Elaine, I don't know what to tell you. Part of me wants you to get the hell out of there. Part of me wants you to hunt that son of a bitch down."

She allowed herself a smile. "Let's go with the second option for now. Tell Annie I love her and I'll call her tomorrow."

There was a long pause; then Helen said, "Okay. Stay safe, Elaine."

Banner murmured a hollow reassurance and hung up. She kept looking at the blue lights in the darkness for a while, feeling a longing to be home, to crawl into Annie's bed and hug her tightly until the morning. This manhunt had taken Banner far from home and might still take her farther, but at least that meant Wardell was far away from Chicago, from Annie. One thing to be grateful for.

She hurried across to the Bureau van that was parked at the side of the access road and climbed into the back. The female paramedic was almost done with Blake. Banner allowed herself a wry smile at Blake's wince as the paramedic tugged a little on the last stitch in the long gash on his forearm. She shook her head.

"You tough guys."

Blake looked up at her, raised his eyebrows questioningly.

"You'll happily get in a gunfight, dive headfirst off a cliff, stand next to a grenade, but subject you to anything medical and you start crying."

"It wasn't a grenade; it was a pipe bomb."

"Whatever. You ought to be dead."

"You can thank Edward R. Garrett that I'm not."

"Who?"

"1837 to 1879. Luckily for me, they built headstones to last in 1879."

"And to absorb blast damage."

"Indeed. How's Castle?"

Banner bit her lip. They'd used one of the search helicopters to transport Castle to the regional hospital in Rapid City. It had reduced their capacity to search for Wardell, but it had saved Castle's life. For the moment, at least. "Critical but stable, is what they're telling us."

"I'm sorry," Blake said.

"Don't be. The only reason he's still breathing is you."

The house was a still-burning pile of rubble, the mobile command center a partially burnt-out crime scene. Wardell had melted into the thick woods after the explosion in the graveyard, and either he'd had a vehicle hidden somewhere off the grid, or he'd stayed on foot. Whatever the case, he hadn't left a trace.

Blake was stripped to the waist, having discarded his torn and soaked shirt. Banner noticed that there was a long, whitened scar running from his left pectoral all of the way down to his waistline. Blake caught her staring at it and looked away. She decided not to ask.

The paramedic finished the stitching and tied it off. Blake flexed the fingers of his hand, testing the strength of the stitches, finding them adequate.

"What the hell happened in there?" Banner asked after a minute. "Inside the house, I mean." Blake had already briefed her on what had taken place down in the old graveyard.

"Somebody was helping Wardell."

"What?"

Blake reached for the blue FBI T-shirt they'd scavenged for him, pulled it over his head. "You people really like this color, huh?"

"What do you mean somebody was helping him?"

He shrugged. "That's the way it worked out, anyway, whether or not it was the intention. But I think it was."

"Hold on a second, Blake," she said, shaking her head. "How the hell would anyone get inside the damn house? We had that place sewn up tighter than—"

"It was one of your guys."

Banner felt like somebody had punched her in the gut. She opened her mouth to tell him he was crazy, or at the very least mistaken. That no one on the task force could have been involved in helping Wardell. But did she know that for sure? Really know it?

Blake's face was sympathetic as he watched her struggle. "Or at least he was doing a fair impression of one of yours. The only reason I knew something was up with him is because I'd seen him before, at the Fort Dodge scene."

"Is that a surprise? We had lots of agents at the scene."

"But he was there right after the shooting, long before your people got there."

Banner suppressed the barrage of questions that welled up inside her, decided to focus on the events in the house. "So what happened?"

"He coldcocked Castle, led Hatcher right into Wardell's sights."

"He was covering the front of the building, just like we thought," Banner said. "Brazen asshole was actually perched on top of the command center's roof. Killed another two of our guys who were in his way." *Our guys*; that brought the question of an inside man back into focus. "What would one of us have to gain from helping?" she asked. "Who the hell is this guy? What does he look like?"

"As of right now? I'm guessing extra crispy. Castle shot him in the fight. We left him in the room at the front, the one where Hatcher died."

"All right. What *did* he look like, then?"

"Like one of you," Blake said. "Like your stereotypical anonymous G-Man. Dark suit, white shirt, quiet tie. Glasses. Tall, with a slight build."

"And our only lead, up in smoke," Banner said, shaking her head again.

"Not quite."

Blake was reaching into the pocket of his pants. He withdrew a small black leather ID wallet and tossed it to her. She caught it one-handed and flipped it open. The object was as familiar to Banner as her own front door. In the bottom half, a metal shield with an eagle and the words "Federal Bureau of Investigation" and "Department of Justice," gold on gold. In the top, a photo ID card.

"Anyone you know?" Blake prompted, adding, "The name's unlikely."

"'John H. Edgar,'" she read from the ID. "I guess J. Edgar Hoover would have been too on the nose."

"Is it a fake? Looks pretty good to me."

"It must be. But you're right; it's a good one. We have guys from all over the country on the task force, way more than a hundred people here tonight. You can't know everybody by sight. In fact—" Banner stopped midthought, looking at the gaunt, balding, unsmiling head shot in the photograph. The man in the picture wore no glasses. "You said he was wearing glasses?"

"Yes."

"I saw him too. Allanton, after Wardell killed his father." She closed her eyes and summoned the memory of the man she'd seen outside Nolan's cabin. It was the same man in the picture; she was almost certain. "Blake, what the hell is going on here?"

Before Blake could begin to answer, a voice rang out from behind them.

"Funny, that's exactly the question I was going to ask."

Banner and Blake looked over to the open rear doors of the van. It was Edwards. He wore a dark raincoat with the hood up, and he looked pissed.

"Edwards," Banner said. She closed the ID wallet and put it in her pocket. "Is Donaldson coming down?"

Edwards bristled at this but didn't answer. He turned his gaze on Blake. "You assaulted one of my agents," he said slowly, as though he could barely entertain the notion that such a thing had occurred.

"That's ridic—" Banner began, the words dying in her throat as she saw the look on Blake's face.

"Actually, it's true. I forgot to mention that."

"He's in the infirmary with a broken finger, a broken nose, and a concussion."

"I'm sorry, but he wouldn't listen and he was in the way."

"He was in the ..." Edwards blinked as though a bucket of water had been thrown over him; then he really lost his temper. "You are in *my* fucking way, Blake. And as of now, you are officially out of my fucking way. You are off the task force and off the payroll, and if you don't get the hell out of my sight in the next ten seconds, I'll have you arrested for the attempted murder of a federal fucking agent."

"Wait a second—" Banner started.

Edwards ignored her. "Get out of here, Blake."

Blake glanced at Banner, then stood up slowly.

"Stay right there," Banner said, then turned back to Edwards. "We need him, sir. He saved Castle; he nearly got Wardell; he—"

"He compromised this operation. He got the person we were here to protect killed, and then he let the target escape. We can do without his kind of help. And quite frankly, Agent Banner, we can do without yours for a while too."

"Excuse me, sir?"

Edwards smiled for the first time. "Castle is out of action. The special agent in charge has reorganized the command structure of this task force. As of five minutes ago, I'm in operational command here. And I think you need to take a step back."

"With all due respect, you need me. And Blake."

"Three days' leave, Agent Banner. Don't force me to make it a suspension. Wouldn't look good on your record, would it?"

Banner opened her mouth to say something, then bit her tongue. She glanced at Blake, who locked eye contact and gave her a barely perceptible headshake. Edwards stared at her, daring her to protest. When she didn't, he nodded.

"Don't worry. You can help with the cleanup after we get Wardell. Good night, Banner." He turned and strode away. "Don't let me see you again, Blake," he called without looking back.

51

2:00 a.m.

Edwards had been right about one thing, Banner thought: She had to take a step back. Even without the enforced leave of absence, she needed time to think, to take stock. She didn't need to ask Blake if he was still in; the look in his eyes said he was down for the long haul, and fuck the paycheck. She thought about that. What was still in it for him? She wondered if he pursued all of his subjects with this kind of relentlessness, or if there was something special about Wardell, something that he hadn't told them.

She had found them a pair of rooms at a motel on the outskirts of Rapid City. They made the first half of the short journey in silence, Banner driving again. The rain had let up, finally, and a bitter, wintry cold had rushed in to fill its place.

"So, where to tomorrow?" Blake asked.

Banner took her eyes off the dark road for a second to glance at him in mock astonishment. "You mean you don't know?"

"I don't *know*," Blake said. "I have a few ideas."

"I thought you might."

"He's hurt, thanks to you," Blake said. "That might buy us a little time."

"First Nolan, then Hatcher," Banner mused. "You were right about him targeting his enemies. Who's next, logically? I'd expect him to go for Stewart, the detective who brought him in, but—"

"It definitely won't be Stewart, because he's already dead."

"You really did do your homework. So who's next? *Where's* next?"

Blake turned his head to look out at the dark landscape as he thought about it. "Who? I think he'll want to hit somebody important. But he'll want to do it somewhere where he can take out lots of other people, too."

"Why so sure?"

"Because of something I said. Or rather, because of his reaction to something I said."

"What was that?" Blake had given her the gist of their conversation in the graveyard—all the stuff about Juba, but not the specific details.

"Basically, I was just trying to keep him talking, because as long as he was talking he wasn't putting a bullet in my head. At one point I pushed his buttons about needing two shots for the delivery guy. I knew right away I'd pushed him too far."

"And then?"

"And then I just said the first thing that came into my head, to make him hesitate. I asked him about the red van. About the fact somebody's been helping him, the thin man."

"And what did he say?"

"He let slip that he didn't know any more about it than we do. I wasn't a hundred percent sure that the diversions were nothing to do with him until that moment, but that reaction convinced me. Then he said he didn't care if somebody wanted to help him out. Like it made no difference to him. And that's when I said it."

"Said what?"

"It hadn't occurred to me before. I don't think I really meant anything by it; I was just trying to throw him off. Screw with his head."

Banner slowed the car abruptly, steered right, and brought the car to a sharp halt at the side of the road. She just looked at Blake, waiting for him to get to the point, not sure whether he was being deliberately infuriating or if he couldn't help it. She realized the irony: This was probably exactly how he'd made Caleb Wardell feel earlier that night.

"I said whoever it was wasn't helping him; they were using him."

"And?"

"And that did the job, really threw him off his stride. He's so arrogant, it was probably the first time it had even occurred to him. And he looked pissed."

"So what does that all mean?"

"I think it means he'll go for another specific target this time. A high-value target. To prove he's his own man. To prove he can do whatever he likes."

"He pretty much did that tonight," Banner said grimly, thinking about the carnage back at the lake house.

"But he only got Hatcher because 'Agent Edgar' set it up. Castle would have gotten him out otherwise. That's going to eat away at him; trust me. He'll go for someone important. He's going to take this personally." Blake stopped and looked ahead through the windshield. A dull red neon glow emanated from a building a mile down the road: the motel. "Earlier, you asked me who and where. I can't get specific on who yet, but I think I know where."

"Have you ever thought about getting straight to the point?"

Blake put his hands up in apology. "Sorry. I tend to talk in circles when I'm thinking. Chicago. I think he's headed back to Chicago."

52

2:11 a.m.

Banner stared back at Blake. Just when she'd thought she had a handle on him, he'd pulled a complete one eighty. He was agreeing with the profilers now?

"What makes you think that?" she asked. "What changed your mind?"

Blake shook his head. "I haven't changed my mind. I always thought he'd aim to end up there. It's home turf, and he'll want to reassert himself. Especially if he's leading up to his big finish. I'm betting being hurt and the fact somebody's muscling in on his show might make him accelerate his timetable."

Banner looked away and cursed. Her first reaction was as

a mother: The monster was coming home. Living in Chicago during Wardell's first spree, she'd felt the same anxiety as everyone else. But it was different now: Annie was no longer a baby, no longer safe and secure in her bassinette.

With an effort of will, she forced herself to snap into professional mode, running through the logistics in her head. "He can't make Chicago tomorrow. It'll take well over a day by road. At least."

"Two days from now will be Tuesday. Tuesday is ..."

"Election day," Banner said, finishing the thought.

"That certainly suggests some interesting targets, doesn't it?"

Banner put the car into drive and pulled out on the highway again, running through this new scenario, trying to figure out what Castle would have done and what Edwards would now do.

"Like I said," Blake continued, "I was just talking, trying to get under his skin. But ..."

"What?"

"I think I might have been right. I think somebody's using him. It's the only explanation."

"For what?"

"For why somebody would help him out without him knowing about it."

"But that makes no kind of sense at all."

Blake just raised his eyebrows, as if to say, *But there it is*.

Banner pulled up in front of the motel and parked.

"I booked us two rooms," Banner said, and then immediately delivered herself a mental kick. Why the hell had she said that? She felt herself flush.

Blake smiled slowly. "That's for the best. We're both going to need the sleep. We need to be on the road early tomorrow."

She opened her mouth to respond—to explain that she hadn't meant anything by that, or to make a joke about it, or maybe to ask just what the hell he meant by "that's for the best."

Instead, she composed herself and said, "Tomorrow? Where are we going tomorrow?"

"New York City."

She fought the abrupt urge to slap Blake. She counted to five and spoke slowly, unable to mask the annoyance in her tone. "You said Wardell was going to Chicago."

"I think he is, but I want to talk to somebody in New York."

"Blake—"

"Sorry, but it's better I'm vague about this one for the time being. You might call the gentleman 'high value.'"

53

3:11 a.m.

Wardell was hurting.

The shot fired by the FBI bitch had grazed him high up on his left leg. He'd been lucky that it hadn't been a direct hit, but it had carved a wicked trench three inches long across the outside of his thigh. He'd lost some blood, but not too much. Despite being slapped on in a hurry, the four-by-four-inch gauze bandage with tie straps from the blowout kit had held. If nothing else, the night had confirmed two more names for his list: Elaine Banner and Carter Blake.

His pack and the rest of his equipment were still where he'd stashed them the previous afternoon: under a camouflage

246

tarpaulin three miles from Hatcher's lake house. It had felt like three hundred miles in the dark, with the leg wound, but the distance had been a necessary precaution, to keep things well out of reach of his pursuers.

He'd stopped hearing the sounds of people searching for him on the ground about a mile from the house, although every so often one of the helos swung overhead, casting its beam over the treetops. That was no sweat. He could always hear them coming a good minute before they appeared, ample time to make himself invisible. He reached camp around three in the morning, allowed himself forty minutes of rest after he'd redressed his wound, then changed out of the soaking BDUs and into a dry pair of blue jeans and a plaid shirt. He'd purchased both from a factory outlet store in Rapid City before he'd gone to the diner.

He kept rubbing the outside of the dressing on his leg compulsively, wincing at the sharp pain each time. To distract himself from the compulsion, he unfurled the tarp again and laid his remaining weapons and clips on top of it in perfectly squared rows. He'd kept the AK and the SIG and the Rem, as well as the Glock 23 he'd taken from one of the feds in the big truck. He arranged each gun in a separate row, with its spare magazines to the left. The rifles at the top, then the SIG, and finally the Glock. The order calmed him, soothed the niggling pain in his leg.

As he worked, he thought about the night. It had not been an unqualified success. He'd killed his stated target, sure, but if what Blake had said was the truth, maybe he'd had inside help.

You're being used.

But used for what? Wardell acted according to his own agenda, killing whomever he pleased, whenever he pleased. How could someone be using him to kill people if he was choosing the targets? An unfamiliar, unpleasant feeling was stirring in his gut. It was like the feeling after he'd missed the outright kill on the deliveryman. Could it be that someone was actually predicting his actions? Somebody who knew how Wardell would act before he himself did? Was it possible that he was that predictable?

He shook his head and felt a new experience: self-doubt. The answer was no; it wasn't possible. Edward Nolan? Sure, he could see how that could have been foreseen. John Hatcher he'd actually gone ahead with *because* it could be foreseen through the combination of shared history and proximity. He'd figured they'd predict him as a target and had even called that reporter about it to make sure they didn't vanish on some wild-goose chase this time. Because he'd wanted the challenge, because he'd wanted another shot at Blake.

But who would gain from the deaths of Hatcher and Nolan? They had nothing to do with each other, beyond their tenuous connections to Wardell. Neither held any real power or influence. And the others, the truly random kills in Cairo and Fort Dodge and Rapid City—who benefited from those deaths? Nobody, that was who.

But somebody had set up the red van as a decoy. Somebody in the know had tipped off the media that he'd escaped.

You're being used.

Wardell grabbed his pack and started jamming spare magazines and supplies into it, trying to banish the doubts with activity. They'd want him to have doubts, would want him to be distracted from his mission. Well, that was too bad. Whoever was helping him or using him could keep on trying. Wardell would do his own thing. He put the SIG in his side holster, tucked the Glock into the back of his belt, and slipped the rifles inside the long bag. He was ready for the hike.

54

6:00 a.m.

I awoke to the sound of the alarm on my phone and hauled myself out of bed with a Herculean effort. It felt as though somebody had borrowed my body during the night and stuffed it into a tumble dryer on maximum spin. I stepped into the shower and turned on the water as hot as I could stand it.

I emerged five minutes later and toweled myself down, surveying my new outfit. Despite being officially removed from the action, Banner still had people loyal to her, and they were continuing to provide assistance below the radar. I dressed in the clothes one of them had conjured up for me: black jeans, black T-shirt, polo shirt—navy blue of course. It wasn't emblazoned with the FBI logo at least, and everything fit me. I knocked on Banner's door at 6:25 and she answered immediately, looking pressed and groomed and like she'd just stepped out of wardrobe.

"Good morning," I said.

"Is it?" Her voice was sharp, like she didn't like mornings a whole lot. "Plane leaves in two hours. Let's go."

55

I drove this time. Things would have been a lot easier had we still had access to the full resources of the Bureau, but Banner's removal from active duty meant we'd have to start making some compromises on convenience. First example: commercial flights instead of the Lear, which meant separate flights and making connections. It also meant passing through regular airport security.

We made the airport in good time and hopped on a short flight to Minneapolis. Banner's FBI badge allowed us to take our weapons, although they had to be stowed with baggage. A thirty-minute layover, and then the flight to NYC would take a little less than three hours. Banner worked most of it on her phone, talking to the people she could trust, getting updates on progress, and keeping tabs on how Edwards was running the task force. She spoke to somebody named Paxon a number of times.

I used the time to do some of my own work: think about the case, let things percolate a little in my brain. The confirmation that there was more at work here than just one madman had thrown up a whole lot of complications that I could have done without. It cast new light on many of the events of the past four days—my attempted mugging in Cairo, for one. I had a few ideas about what might be happening, but so far the only motive I could come up with felt wrong.

At the midway point of the flight, we were served an in-flight breakfast that tasted like all in-flight breakfasts—as though it had been stored for a month inside an old suitcase and then microwaved, still inside the suitcase. The coffee, at least, was okay. I drank three cups in quick succession, sharpening myself up for the hours ahead.

When Banner took a break to drink her own coffee, sensibly forgoing the breakfast, I told her who we were going to see and why we had to go alone. She wasn't exactly happy about it, or convinced about the use of our time.

"What if Wardell hits somewhere else while we're in New York?"

"It's a possibility," I agreed. "But it's the same problem we've faced all along. If we don't know where he's going to strike, how can we do anything about it? Hell, we didn't stop him when we did know where."

She thought about it for a long minute, finally nodding. "You're right, unfortunately. All we can do is identify danger zones and try to cover them as best we can."

"You don't sound like somebody who's off duty."

She smiled. "We have good people on this. With any luck, Edwards won't get in their way too much."

"How's it going, anyway?"

"For a change, it looks like everyone agrees with you: He's headed back to Chicago. We're prioritizing towns en route and covering as many other bases as we can, of course. We're making it really general, telling people anywhere in the area to be cautious, make only essential journeys." She stopped and looked out of the window for a moment, and for a second it looked like she was about to throw up.

"Are you okay?"

She looked pained. "Air sickness. I'll be fine. Christ, it's not like we need to tell people to be cautious. People are scared, Blake. It feels like we're admitting defeat every time we issue one of those warnings, like he's beating us."

I said nothing.

"Why go see this guy now?" she asked, turning the conversation back to our rendezvous in New York. "Why not before?"

"I didn't think he could tell us anything important before."

"Why not?"

I reconsidered. "Maybe important is the wrong word. What I mean is, it didn't seem like I could learn anything urgent. As in urgent to the main task, which is stopping Wardell. If the building's on fire, you ought to spend all your time putting the fire out. You worry about figuring out who started the fire later."

"Appropriate analogy, Blake."

"Sorry."

"All right, so what changed your mind? Why has it become urgent?"

"Because I have a hunch that the person who started this fire is more significant than we thought. And if we're lucky, it might even give us Wardell."

56

2:07 p.m.

We landed at Newark a little after lunchtime. No Bureau car was waiting for us, of course, but in any case we needed to leave as little trail as possible. We took an airport taxi into the city. It dropped us on the corner of Worth and West Broadway. Looking south, it was impossible to miss the brand new World Trade Center towering above its neighbors. It made me think about that Springsteen record again, one line in particular. The line about how everything that dies comes back.

We took a yellow cab north to SoHo, got out on Broome Street and walked a couple of blocks to a tall office building at the corner of Lafayette.

Banner looked up at the glass frontage, reflecting a gunmetal gray sky in the November daylight.

"Here?" She sounded doubtful.

"Here," I confirmed. I took a step forward, activating the sensor for the big revolving door, which began circling demurely. I held my arm out—*after you*—and Banner stepped into the revolving door. It brought us out in an anonymous reception area, the width of the building but only thirty feet deep. The gray of the carpet was not far from the color of the sky outside. A long, high reception desk ran the length of the space at the other side, looking a lot like an airport check-in. A pair of potted ferns provided a splash of verdant color to relieve the austerity. There were two female receptionists at the desk, one young, one in middle age. The middle-aged one was on the phone. The younger one smiled politely as we entered.

I could see Banner reach unconsciously for her FBI identification and touched her forearm to stop her. I didn't blame her. It probably gets to be as reflexive and as reliable as putting your hand out to open a door.

"Good afternoon," I said. "We're looking for Kane Holdings?"

The brunette reciprocated the good afternoon and consulted something on her desk, below the upper shelf visible to visitors.

She repeated the name to herself. "I'm not sure ... Oh, here it is. They're on fourteen. Looks like they just moved in. Can I ask you to sign in?"

I thanked her and signed us in as John and Jane Smith. The receptionist indicated the elevators, and we stepped in and hit the button. When the doors had closed, Banner spoke for the first time.

"You never told me how the hell—"

I shot her a pointed sidelong glance.

"Good at finding people," she said wryly, shaking her head.

"Let me do the talking."

The red LCD counter crept up to fourteen; the elevator pinged and the doors slid open, revealing more gray carpet and a long corridor with a door every thirty feet or so. Some of the doors were unmarked; some had the remains of nameplates that had been peeled off. There was no door marked as Kane Holdings. We heard a click as one of the doors at the far end of the corridor opened inward, and a guy the size and shape of a WWE wrestler stepped out.

He said nothing, just occupied the corridor like a rhino in a supermarket aisle. It was an apt comparison in other ways too: His skin looked gray and dry and tough. We approached him. When we were within a dozen paces, he spoke. He addressed me, not even looking at Banner.

"Mr. Blake." It was an acknowledgment, not a question. The Russian accent was pronounced, the three syllables spaced out and carefully separated.

"Yes."

"Mr. Korakovski is able to give you fifteen minutes."

57

The Black Hills National Park stretched out for sixty miles to the west of John Hatcher's wood and glass monument to his own vanity. As soon as Wardell had discovered that, he'd known the target really was ideal—because it allowed a million perfect escape routes. Unless you were wearing a hi-vis hunting vest and waving at the sky, nobody was going to be able to find you once you got more than a hundred yards into those woods. There were a few small Forest Service roads within easy distance of Wardell's camp and some unmapped logging trails. Wardell ignored these in favor of an eighteen-mile hike cross-country to the point where Highway 85 cut through the woods.

The day was cold, and Wardell wished he had gloves, but at least it was dry. He made good time, reaching the road by just after three o'clock. The highway glided through the woods on a raised causeway of struts and supports, and Wardell had to scale a thirty-foot dirt embankment to reach the crash barrier. He approached the crest of the embankment flat on his stomach, just to be safe, and peered under the steel barrier. Nothing. No police or government cars, no foot patrols, no traffic at all in fact.

He'd expected this to be the case, which was why he'd chosen to exit the woods so far from the search area. Securing the road for the length of its journey through this area would be like securing the border of a small country. He waited another thirty seconds, conscious of the dull pain in his thigh. A car approached from the north, doing seventy or eighty. A station wagon, packed with kids and baggage for a cross-country trip. It shot past him, unaware, and continued on its way down to Colorado or Texas or wherever.

Wardell stood up, slung the pack on his back and placed the rifle bag on the ground by the crash barrier. He waited, rubbing a hand over his goatee and two-day stubble and mildly regretting the fact that they knew what he looked like now. The waitress in Rapid City would have given them an up-to-date description, one that would be corroborated by Blake, if he'd made it. And that meant hitchhiking was risky.

He looked up at the cold gray sky, scanning the hills back the way he'd come, looking for helos. They didn't have the manpower to guard the length of this road, but they could sure as hell run a few flybys. Best not to stay out here too long.

Minutes passed. A couple more cars passed heading south, no other vehicles on his side. He kept ignoring the pain in his thigh, kept watching the sky. He thought about killing Hatcher and thought some more about the two new names on his list.

Wardell had often wondered why individuals in his position never seemed to go after the people chasing them. It was a mystery that it didn't happen more often in fact. It was so simple, when you thought about it. So ... symmetrical? No: *practical*. That was what it was. A kill that was more than just for the buzz.

Practical in the same kind of way he'd most likely have to kill the driver of the burgundy sedan that was now approaching from the south, still about three-quarters of a mile distant. He couldn't afford to be recognized, not now. If Wardell stuck his thumb out and the guy in the burgundy car just blew by him without a second glance, then both he and the driver could live with that. If the guy stopped? Great. They'd take it from there. But if the guy took a good look at Wardell and *then* kept going, he would be signing his own death warrant.

Without taking his eyes off of the burgundy car, Wardell crouched to the rifle bag and snapped the zipper back the full length. The Rem 700 was on top, ready to reach down and grab.

The burgundy car was about half a mile away now. He was cruising around seventy. Twenty-six, twenty-seven seconds maybe. Wardell rehearsed the action in his head: As soon as the car passed him, he'd have the Remington in his hands in less than a second. Up to his shoulder and taking aim in one point five. Locking the target and squeezing the trigger in two. Two seconds after the driver passed Wardell, even assuming he maintained his current speed and didn't slow to get a better look, he'd be seventy yards away. No challenge at all. Wardell could blow out one of the rear tires, chase down the car as it slewed onto the shoulder, and put the second round in the back of the driver's head. Then it would just be a matter of fitting the spare and dumping the body off the side of the road. Simple. *Practical.*

The burgundy car was eighteen seconds away, seventeen. Wardell angled his body sideways, kept his head down, and held out his arm, thumb pointing in the direction of travel. But as he turned his body, something caught his eye on the edge of his peripheral vision. Approaching from the east, hovering over a patch of forest ten miles back. A black helicopter.

Shit.

No time for changing a tire now. From that altitude, they'd know for sure something was happening out on the road, which would be enough reason to come investigate. But wait—the driver of the burgundy car was already slowing. Wardell could see him peering out at him. The burgundy car swept past, its speed cut to thirty, now twenty-five, brake lights glowing in the dull midafternoon light. Wardell had caught another break: Whether he had to kill this Good Samaritan or not, there would be no need to change the tire now.

58

3:45 p.m.

The office was unoccupied, illuminated only by the dull light sidling in between gray vertical blinds.

Banner's first thought was that it was laid out like a spacious waiting room. Two wooden-framed, padded chairs in front of a wide, low coffee table, both angled slightly inward to face a third chair on the far side. After consideration, she rethought her initial impression. It wasn't a waiting room. It had been set up for a meeting. This meeting. Almost certainly the only meeting that would be held in this office under its current lease.

A side door opened and a man in a black suit and a dark gray open-necked shirt stepped into the room. It took a second, but then Banner recognized the face from blurry surveillance photographs. She wasn't altogether convinced she would have, had she not known whom to expect.

Korakovski was in his late fifties and had about him the air of a European statesman. He was around six feet and slim, with black hair streaked with silver and a mildly tanned complexion. In stark contrast to his henchman, he didn't look like a gangster. In his own way, he was as unassuming on first glance as Blake. Banner realized that this case had opened her eyes to some strange subworld of nondescript killers, of quiet, dangerous men who blended in.

Korakovski crossed the floor and nodded at both Blake and Banner, unsmiling. He shook hands first with Banner and then with Blake. His handshake was light and gentle with Banner, but she saw his fingers grip tightly as they closed around Blake's hand.

"Mr. Blake," he said, an accent barely discernible. "You come highly recommended."

Banner shot a glance at Blake, remembering his admonishment to let him do the talking.

Blake smiled briefly and perfunctorily. "Yuri is too kind."

"I think he—and, of course, his daughter—would disagree, but I applaud your modesty in any case." His eyes flicked over to meet Banner's, and she saw recognition there. Castle had been the FBI's public face on the task force, but she'd been in the background of enough newscasts over the past couple of days. And then there had been that interview with the *New York Times* last year, of course. Just ten minutes ago, she wouldn't have thought of pegging a brutal Russian gang lord as a *Times* reader, but now she wasn't so sure.

"And I'm pleased to make the acquaintance of your friend. Agent . . . ?"

Banner said, "Elaine. Just Elaine." She didn't elaborate. She wasn't thinking of Blake's advice anymore. She was too busy trying not to think about what Donaldson might say if her attendance at this—meeting? Summit? What the hell was it?—ever got out.

Korakovski kept looking at her, unblinking, as though testing her resolve. She didn't blink right back at him. Eventually, he said, "Good, good."

He snapped his fingers and the rhino-sized flunky shuffled to the side door and opened it again. Immediately, a petite, dark-haired women in her twenties stepped through carrying a tray: coffee in a French press and three china mugs, along with a sugar bowl and a small jug of milk or cream. She avoided making eye contact with anyone in the room. She set the tray down on the low table as the three of them took their seats: Blake and Banner on one side, Korakovski on the other. Without asking, Korakovski reached out and poured coffee into the three cups. First Banner's, then Blake's, then his own. The small woman slipped away without an apparent signal and closed the door softly behind her. The rhino moved back into position behind Banner and Blake.

Blake ignored his coffee, fixing Korakovski with a stare. "We'd like you to help us make a couple of clarifications."

"I see. And this would relate to ... ?"

Blake paused and smiled. "To the ambush on a prisoner transport vehicle your men carried out in the course of an assassination attempt on one of your former employees."

Korakovski didn't blink. Banner wondered if he ever blinked. She couldn't remember it happening since he'd entered the room. He took a sip of coffee.

"I'm afraid I don't know what you're talking about. Perhaps you have, as you Americans say, the wrong guy?"

"Perhaps."

Thirty seconds of silence, easily, as both men stared at each other.

"You're aware of the Caleb Wardell situation," Blake said finally, reaching for his coffee for the first time.

"It's difficult to miss. You have quite a voracious appetite for the exploits of murderers in this country."

"And yet we always seem to have room to import more. Like the three men you lost to Wardell."

260

Korakovski leaned back in his chair, spreading his arms. Amused, not offended in the slightest. "Again, I have no idea what you're talking about."

"Of course not. But Clarence Mitchell, he worked for you, right?"

Korakovski sighed. "Sadly, yes. A regrettable fact of business: When one unwittingly employs a criminal and then terminates his employment, he must expect the criminal to spread lies about his entirely legitimate activities."

"So you must be happy he's out of the picture."

"It makes certain things simpler; you are correct."

Blake watched him for a minute. "I need to know how the hit was set up. I need to know so I can catch Wardell. We're not interested in anything else right now."

Korakovski's stare flitted to Banner again. She returned it. He looked like he was going to ask her a question, but then changed his mind and turned back to Blake.

"If I were able to cooperate with you, to offer my advice on a purely hypothetical basis ... perhaps you could do a favor in return for me."

Banner breathed in through her nose, watching Blake carefully. This was the moment when the devil produced the expensive fountain pen and asked you to sign on the dotted line. She wondered how he'd handle it.

Blake shook his head slowly. Like Korakovski, not angry but amused. "The favor has already been done. Your debt to Yuri Leonov is wiped clean from today."

For the first time, Korakovski showed some teeth, a wide grin that defied Blake to blame him for trying.

"Fair enough," he said. "As you say, a fair return on a modest investment, in this case information that costs me nothing. And, of course, I'm always delighted to help the authorities."

"Aren't we all?" Blake asked.

Korakovski looked at Banner again. Sensing that now was the time to speak, she reiterated what Blake had said. "We're not interested in anything else at the moment. In fact, we're not even here at all."

He nodded, seeming to find this acceptable.

"The man you mentioned, Mitchell, was, as you say, a potential thorn in my side. We'd been trying to ... reach out to him for some time. To convince him of his mistake. Initially, it did not prove easy. We were told that this particular goal was impossible to satisfy."

Banner was pleased to hear it; it showed witness protection did some things right. But she wondered what he meant by "initially."

"And how did you change that situation?" Blake said.

"We didn't. We were approached by a man who proved to be most helpful."

"Paul Summers?" Blake suggested.

The prisoner transfer coordinator—the guy who'd shot himself. Or had he? Banner was beginning to question everything about this setup.

Korakovski shook his head. "No. We did speak to Mr. Summers later on, but this first man was someone else."

"Did he have a name? Who was he working for?"

Korakovski spaced his hands apart. "Names and jobs do not interest me. The only thing that interests me is what someone can do for me. This man promised he could deliver something considerable."

"Clarence Mitchell on a silver platter."

Korakovski nodded. "We were furnished with all of the intelligence we needed. We were also assured that the path would be cleared for us. That was when we were put in touch with Mr. Summers."

"And you paid him a hundred thousand dollars. Why did you do it so obviously? I mean, a wire transfer into his regular bank account? That can't be how you generally do business."

For the first time, Korakovski looked mildly irritated. It seemed you could impugn his character, but not his professionalism. "It is not how we do business. We did not pay Summers a hundred thousand. We did not pay him anything."

Blake's eyes narrowed. "What?"

"Summers was already fully cooperative. He needed no persuasion. We assumed he had been appropriately compensated, or persuaded, by the other party."

"And you didn't think that was strange?"

"Come now, Blake. Do you forget my background?"

Banner thought about that, sized him up. If Korakovski was in his late fifties and had arrived in America within the last two decades, that meant he reached adulthood well before the final decline of the Soviet Union.

Blake was nodding, interested. "Go on."

"Citizens in my country were and are, even today, strongly discouraged from questioning the activities of the state. Sometimes the Kremlin and the KGB allowed certain activities to proceed that benefited their long-term interests. I was not interested in their motives then, and I'm not now."

Banner couldn't hold it in any longer. "The state? Surely you're not suggesting—"

"I suggest nothing, Elaine. I'm speaking figuratively. I'm speaking about power. The state. The Kremlin. The US Government. The police. The media. The so-called Mob. All powerful forces—nothing more, nothing less. Occasionally their goals ... converge."

"Except this time they didn't," Blake said. "Not quite.

Whoever greased the wheels for you wasn't interested in a hit on Mitchell. Mitchell was just the carrot they dangled in front of you to get you to carry out the ambush."

Korakovski just looked back at Blake. Not offering confirmation, but not looking as though this came as any kind of revelation to him.

"You don't like being used."

"I am a realist, Mr. Blake. We are all used by forces greater than ourselves from time to time." He paused and pointed a finger at Blake's chest. "Even you."

Blake said nothing.

Korakovski continued. "I entered into a business arrangement, and I gained what I wanted out of it. However, the party with which I entered into this arrangement was not entirely candid with me, resulting in the loss of three valued members of my staff. While this was still a net gain, I would not be ... displeased if problems were caused for the other party." He drew himself back up in his chair and looked at both of them. "I hope this meeting has been useful to you."

Blake said, "It has. One last thing."

"Yes?"

"The first man, the one who approached you. Did you meet him in person?"

"On two occasions."

Blake produced the picture card from the FBI identification he'd taken from the body at Hatcher's house. He held it up for Korakovski to examine, covering the half that said FBI. The Russian stared at the picture for a moment and nodded.

Blake put the photograph back in his pocket and stood up. Banner followed suit. Korakovski stayed seated. As they turned to head for the door, he stopped them by speaking Blake's name.

"Yes?" Blake said.

"Notwithstanding the arrangements you made with Leonov, I would be most interested in retaining your services. From time to time, I have need of certain talents that you seem to possess in abundance."

Blake shook his head, almost amiably. "Sorry, Korakovski. No deal. I don't work for bad guys."

Korakovski seemed to think about it and then shrugged. No harm done. The rhino scowled and opened the door for the two of them.

"Then I apologize. I was misinformed," Korakovski said in parting. "Perhaps I too have the wrong guy."

59

4:17 p.m.

Interstate truck stops: just about the only place you could reliably expect to find a pay phone these days. Wardell didn't suppose it would be hard to get hold of a cell phone, but then he only needed to make the one call.

Unlike the one he'd used to call Nolan the other day, this pay phone didn't have Internet access, but that was fine. He dialed the number from memory. It was answered on the second ring.

"Bellamy."

"Is Mike Whitford there?"

"Who is this?"

"His great-aunt Petunia. Put Whitford on the line."

Wardell heard a muttered *asshole* and the sound of the receiver being passed to someone at the next desk.

"Whitford." The voice sounded anxious, on edge. Like he knew who'd be on the line and why he'd avoided calling Whitford direct.

"What'd you think of Rapid City, partner?"

There was a pause. "I thought you said you were just going to kill Hatcher."

"Just Hatcher? When did I say that? Come on, partner. Nobody minds getting a little extra value, do they? Thanks for the color, by the way. Good choice. I'd have been screwed if you'd said lilac."

Wardell heard the hint of a trembling intake of breath. Like something was weighing on Whitford's conscience.

"I never wanted you to kill those people."

Wardell feigned surprise, mild indignation. "Oh, I'm sorry. I thought that's what sold your newspapers. Maybe I was mistaken." Whitford was coming across even softer than Wardell had anticipated, and he wondered if maybe they'd tapped his neighbor's phone too, just to be safe. It didn't matter. If Wardell's estimation of Whitford was correct, nobody would get to listen to a replay of this call.

"What do you want?"

Wardell couldn't help but grin. Whitford was trying to sound as though he was so disgusted with Wardell that he could barely stand to keep speaking to him, but it was no good. His desperation to have his question answered showed through like a pornographic magazine covered by tracing paper.

"What do I want? I want you to relay another message for me."

"Yes?" Pathetically eager.

"Whoa there. Not so fast. This is becoming kind of a one-way street, don't you think, partner?"

"What do you mean?"

"You know what I mean. You talk to me, I give you something and you get your story."

"And you get the attention you want, right?"

"Well. Ain't neither of us averse to that, are we?" When there was no reply, Wardell continued. "Yeah, I thought so. I want you to do something for me, Mike. You do it right, I'll call you back. I'll call you with the big one."

"The big one?" Whitford repeated before remembering the first part of what Wardell had said, his voice switching from intrigued to suspicious. "Do what for you?"

Wardell counted to five in his head, let Whitford sweat. "Maybe you're not interested. I'm sure Gabrielle Wood over at the *Sun-Times* would be ..."

"No!" Whitford said quickly, then seemed to regain his composure. "I'm interested."

"Good. That's good, Mike. You got a pen?"

"Of course I have a pen. I'm a reporter."

"Careful, Mike."

Wardell heard an audible swallow at the other end of the line as the other man remembered there might be worse consequences to displeasing Wardell than a hang-up.

"Sorry."

"That's okay, Mike. I understand. We're all on edge here. Write this down." He gave Whitford the webmail address he'd set up back at the truck stop in Kentucky. He repeated it to make sure he'd taken it down right.

"You want me to e-mail you something?"

"You're on fire this week, Mike. I want you to find everything you can on a couple of people who've been causing me some problems. Special Agent Elaine Banner and another guy who's been helping the feds. Goes by the name of Blake."

"Wait a minute. I can't—"

"I'm not asking here, Mike."

"You don't understand ..."

"No, you don't understand, Whitford. You do what I tell you to. You don't do it, and I'm not just going to cut you off, I'm going to find you and I'm going to cut your fucking throat. Do you believe me when I say that?"

Another swallow. "Ah ... I ..."

"Do. You. Believe. Me?"

"Yes."

Wardell hung up without another word.

60

4:29 p.m.

"That wasn't exactly what I expected," Banner said as we stepped out onto the street and began walking east.

"What did you expect?" I asked. "A vodka bar above a strip club in Little Odessa?"

She thought about it and the ghost of a smile appeared at the corner of her lips. "Yeah. I guess that is what I expected."

While we'd been inside the building, the sky had grown dimmer and the volume of traffic had intensified. Diagonally across the street from us was a jewelers with a big, ornate clock hanging outside it. Half past four. We both stopped to look at it, then turned to each other.

"We have to get back to Chicago," Banner said, reaching for her cell phone.

We decided to take a single cab the whole way to the airport this time. The unbroken journey would give us time to discuss how Korakovski's story had changed the dimensions of the game.

"So what do we know now?" Banner asked as the cab pulled away from the sidewalk. She kept her voice low enough to sail under the talk radio show the driver was listening to. They were replaying the clip of the governor at the press conference the day before: *You're not safe anywhere.*

"You know what we know," I said.

Banner looked back at me. "Wardell's escape was no accident. Somebody specifically wanted him broken out."

I nodded. "Who?"

Banner thought about it, looked out at the darkening rush hour streets as they crawled by. "Somebody very well resourced. Somebody connected."

"Connected is an understatement," I said. "They played Korakovski. They got to Summers. They infiltrated your task force."

Banner visibly bristled at this. "I got a call earlier about our Mr. Edgar. They weren't able to identify him from dental or from facial recognition from the ID photo. But he wasn't one of us."

"You're sure about that?"

"Based on the autopsy and the photo, we came up with a list of current agents fitting Edgar's stats: approximate height, weight, age. There are a couple dozen names—all of them are accounted for. We have dental records for them all, too. Have to. Bureau regs."

"He was able to pass as one of you," I said. "That demonstrates resources and connections again. Whether he was actually a paid-up agent is basically irrelevant."

"It's not irrelevant to me."

"I know that."

"Do you think he was working alone?"

I shook my head. "Not a chance. This is too big."

"But it doesn't make any sense," Banner said. "You're talking about some big conspiracy to break Wardell out."

"You don't think there's a conspiracy?"

She looked irritated, but she knew it was pretty hard to deny that now.

"But to what end? Who benefits?"

"That's the problem I'm having," I admitted. "I stopped thinking Wardell's escape was just happenstance two days ago, after the red van decoy. But the best explanation I can come up with doesn't wash."

"Let's hear it," Banner said. "It's got to be better than nothing."

"That's just it. It *is* nothing." I stopped and tried to arrange hours of brainstorming into some kind of coherent stream. "Okay. Let's start with why somebody would want to break a clinically psychotic murderer out of death row."

"Exactly. Why the hell would they?"

I shook my head. "You're still thinking motive, Banner. Think about it literally."

She paused, furrowed her brow, shrugged. "To kill people, obviously."

"That's right. And that's what's happened. Wardell was freed a little less than five days ago. Since then, by my count he's killed eighteen people."

Banner motioned for me to continue. "Go on."

"All right, go back to what we know about whoever set this up."

"Well resourced, well connected."

"That's what they are, yeah. But what's the only other thing we know about them? What do they do?"

Her brow furrowed again. She didn't take long. "They use people. Korakovski. Summers. This 'Edgar' guy, maybe.

And—" Banner stopped midthought and looked at me. "And Wardell himself. Like you told him in the graveyard."

"Bingo," I said. "So what's the logical conclusion?"

"They're using Wardell. They're using him to do the one thing they know for certain he'll do. Which is kill."

"That has to be it," I said. "That's why they went to such lengths to break him out. That's why they misdirected the media and the task force to guarantee his safe passage."

"Wait a minute," she said, holding up a hand to stop my flow. "Why does it have to be him? Hired killers are a dime a dozen."

"Not professionals of Wardell's caliber," I said, "but point taken."

"It's a hell of a lot of trouble to go to when other options would be available."

"Agreed," I said. "For some reason, it's important that it's Wardell. We don't know what that reason is yet, but that's not the main problem with this theory."

Banner played along, refusing to cave in and ask me straight out. She ran through the problem in her head again.

"Who's the target?" she said after a few seconds, her tone conveying her full knowledge of the implications of that question.

"Exactly."

"Whoever it is broke Wardell out because they wanted him to kill someone. They knew it would all look like a coincidence, like it was all fallout from the Russians' ambush. It's a great idea, when you think about it. You want someone out of the way, what's the best camouflage? To have them fall victim to a crazed serial killer. Nobody looks for another motive."

"It's tried and tested," I said.

"Sure," she agreed. "People try it from time to time. They

271

want their spouse offed, so they make it look like it's part of a random series. The guys in Behavioral Sciences call it a 'leaf in a forest killing,' as in the best place to hide a leaf is in the middle of a forest."

"But this would be even better. Not just making it look like a serial killer did it—actually having the serial killer do it for real."

"Except there's one big problem with that theory, Blake."

I held up my hands. "Your killer is unpredictable," I said. "You know he's going to kill, but you don't know *who* he's going to kill."

"So we're left with this: Somebody broke Wardell out of death row to achieve an objective. The objective was to kill someone. That objective is not yet complete."

"That's about the size of it," I agreed.

"Then we have to forget about the motive for just now and come at it from the other angle. Who might be next?"

"And as we said, we have some candidates, given what day tomorrow is."

"Good candidates," Banner said. "With money and power and influence. And one of them as good as challenged Wardell to a fight yesterday."

I nodded. "So how do we get a meeting with the governor on election day?"

61

Banner and Blake touched down at O'Hare a little after nine p.m., the beginnings of a plan for the following day agreed. Blake had reclined his seat and caught a catnap, while Banner made a few more calls in-flight, talking to agents she trusted to keep quiet about her inquiries and getting updates on arrangements across the states in Wardell's predicted path.

Unsurprisingly, the search had yet to turn up any sign of Wardell after the graveyard. Going by his track record so far, he could be traveling by bus or another stolen car. A car was the more likely option, given that they now had a much better idea of his current appearance and a pretty good composite had been splashed all over the news. They were chasing up all reported vehicle thefts within four hundred miles of Rapid City. No firm leads as of yet, although one report of a car stolen from a truck stop outside of Sioux Falls sounded promising.

The bulk of Banner's phone time had been consumed securing a brief slot to meet with the governor. It hadn't been easy, but she'd managed to get ten minutes with him before the rally. Naturally, she'd omitted to mention the fact that she was not officially on the case anymore.

They landed at one of the outlying runways, far from the terminal, and climbed into the back of a waiting sedan. The driver of the sedan was Kelly Paxon, who was officially off duty for the night. Banner made brief introductions, last names only. Paxon smiled thinly in acknowledgment and shut the hell up.

"You got a place to stay?" Banner asked as the sedan pulled out and headed for the security check.

Blake paused in the middle of fastening his seat belt, as though he hadn't considered the matter, then said, "I think I'll find someplace that serves coffee and doesn't close, go through some of the background on Randall and the other guy. Congressional candidates too—I'll see if anything chimes with Wardell. You should go home, get some sleep."

Banner smiled and shook her head.

"The office, then?" he asked.

She shook her head again. "I'm on leave, remember? We'll go to my place." She paused. "Don't worry. I have a comfy couch."

62

10:31 p.m.

As Banner turned the key in the lock of her apartment, she silently gave thanks that the cleaner's day was a Friday and that she hadn't been home since. It meant she avoided the embarrassment of empty pizza boxes in the kitchen and a teetering ironing pile.

She kicked off her shoes and turned on the lights in each room of the apartment—habit, ever since she'd been living apart from Mark.

"Nice place," Blake said, hovering in the doorway.

"Thanks. Feels like I'm barely here, even in a normal week. Have a seat," she said, indicating the living room.

She went through to the bedroom, quickly changing out

274

of her suit and into sweatpants and a gray Northwestern University T-shirt. When she went back to the living room, Blake was on the leather couch by the window. Looking at him, she remembered it was only a two-seater, which meant that while it was indeed comfortable, it was probably better if you were five six or shorter. Blake had picked up the framed photo from the table beside the couch. The one that showed her—smiling, with her hair down—shoulder to shoulder with Mark—tall, serious-looking, dark suit—each of them with a hand on their daughter's shoulders.

"That's Annie," she said.

He looked up. "She's beautiful."

Banner swallowed. All of a sudden an urge hit her like a physical blow, the urge to drop everything, to forget about Wardell and go and be with her daughter. Forget about protecting the city and focus on protecting Annie.

Blake caught the look on her face. "You okay?"

"Fine. It just feels like I'm barely here for her, either."

"Is she with her father right now?"

Banner shook her head. "My sister. She's been really great. Oh *shit*."

"What?"

"I'm going to miss her school play. *Calamity Jane*. Annie's playing Adelaid Adams. I said I'd try to be there."

Blake looked sympathetic, but like he didn't know exactly what to say. It was the look of someone who'd never had a family. Banner decided to test the waters again, see if he was ready to open up a little more.

"How about you, Blake? Any kids? Anybody special?" As she said the words, she remembered Blake's involuntary smile four days before, when she'd asked him if there was anything he didn't know. There was somebody special, all right. Somebody in the past, Banner thought. But if she was a memory, it was a fond one.

He didn't answer for a second, thought about it, then shook his head and looked away again. "Nobody special. Free agent, remember?"

"Makes work easier, I guess."

"I guess."

Blake put the photo down next to a glass paperweight Annie had brought back from a school trip to the Museum of Science. He glanced out of the window at the view. He didn't volunteer any personal information whatsoever.

"So where do you live, Blake?" she asked, needling him just to try and get a rise. "You got an apartment somewhere? A house? Motor home perhaps?"

"I move around a lot."

Banner waited for elaboration. When none was forthcoming, she shook her head. "You are *impossible*."

He turned back to her, looked honestly confused. "What?"

"Fine, let's talk about the damn case." Banner reached for the remote and turned on CNN, muting the sound. The Wardell mug shot stared back as though taunting them.

Blake's eyes narrowed, then he turned his head from the screen. "Wardell's coming back to Chicago and he'll be arriving tomorrow."

"If you're right."

"I'm right. It's election day and he wants to make an impact. That's why Governor Randall is the most likely target."

Banner sat down beside him. "And we have a six o'clock appointment with him. But what if it's not him? What about the challenger, Robert Weir? Or the congressional candidates, for that matter?"

"It's a possibility, but I'm factoring in Wardell's history.

Randall was pretty visible during the original manhunt and the trial. He was scheduled to attend the execution, in fact. He's like the next level up after John Hatcher."

"How does this fit in with your theory? About someone using Wardell, I mean?" It was the first time she'd brought it up since the plane. They'd both found it easier to focus on Randall as a likely target than banging their heads against the brick wall of figuring out the motivation behind Wardell's escape.

"Randall makes a lot of sense as a planned assassination. He's not like the other people Wardell's killed up until now. We're talking about a man of consequence. You remove a governor from the equation and somebody somewhere will benefit."

Banner shook her head. "I don't buy it."

"You don't?"

"I mean yes, I agree he's the most likely target, assuming Wardell is coming to Chicago on this day of all days. But it doesn't solve the major problem with this theory: Wardell's unpredictability."

Blake sighed in frustration. "It's like we can see the left side and the right side of the puzzle, but we have a bunch of pieces missing from the middle."

Neither of them spoke for a full minute. The news switched to an interview with SAC Donaldson from earlier in the day. He looked calm, but Banner knew his body language well enough to see he was making some kind of forceful point to the interviewer. She turned her head from the screen and gazed out of the window at the lights of some faraway vessel on the surface of Lake Michigan. She turned to Blake when she realized he was looking at her, those searching green eyes alighting on the curve of her neck. He looked away and looked back, as though catching himself out.

"Hey," she said.

Blake opened his mouth to say something, but was cut off by her cell phone ringing. Both of them cleared their throats and sat up straight. Banner got up and walked across to the table where she'd left the phone and checked the display. It was Donaldson, and she knew whatever it was, it wouldn't be welcome news. She hit the button and said her name.

"Banner, it's Donaldson." There was a pause. Something in his voice that she didn't like. "I know Edwards has recommended you take a couple of days ..."

"What's wrong? Is it Castle?"

There was another pause that confirmed what she was about to hear.

"Castle went into cardiac arrest forty minutes ago. He died on the table."

"God ..."

"Banner, this doesn't change anything. I don't want you—"

She swallowed. "It's okay. I won't do anything stupid. Thanks for letting me know."

There was another pause, a different kind of pause, and she could tell he was weighing up whether to say more. Eventually he just said, "Bad situation, Banner. Take it easy and we'll talk soon."

Banner hung up. Blake was staring at her.

"I'm sorry. He was a good man."

She didn't say anything for a moment, turned to look out the window at the lights of the city and the black void of Lake Michigan beyond. She said the name quietly, so quietly that Blake had to ask her to repeat it.

"Eric Markow," she said again. "You know who he is?"

Blake thought about it for a second. "The guy who kidnapped Ashley Greenwood."

"The guy who murdered Ashley Greenwood," she corrected.

It had been the big news story of last year, the biggest to hit Chicago since Caleb Wardell, in fact. A photogenic millionaire heiress abducted and ransomed for two million dollars. The father paid up, but Greenwood wasn't released. The FBI tracked them down, but Markow had already killed her, cutting her throat. He blew his brains out when he knew he was cornered.

"You worked the case," Blake said. "I remember Donaldson mentioning it in the briefing."

"You asked me why Castle doesn't—didn't—like me. Markow's the reason."

Blake didn't say anything, just let her talk. Banner's throat dried up as she remembered that rain-soaked night. It was the first time she'd spoken about it out loud to anyone, other than in the dry, official context of a formal report.

"He was running the task force on the kidnapping. Castle was, I mean. We supervised the drop of the ransom. Markow was pretty clever about it, very well organized. He led us a merry chase through the city. My job was to tail the father as he made the trade, but not to be seen."

"What happened?"

She shrugged. "I don't know. Greenwood was eventually instructed to get on the last carriage of a train at the station on Ninety-Fifth Street, leave the bag, and step off right as the doors closed. He was supposed to get the location of his daughter after that—instead, nothing. Castle thinks Markow made me. He'd said no cops."

"What do you think?"

She shook her head. "He didn't see me. The inquiry confirmed that later on, but it wasn't good enough for Castle. Either Markow changed his mind and wanted more money, or something went wrong. We nailed him a couple of weeks later. I got a big promotion out of it. But of course we were too late for Ashley Greenwood." She swallowed and blinked a tear out of her eye. "Too late," she said again, thinking about the present now.

"We'll get him, Banner," Blake said quietly.

"You sound so sure."

"I am sure. We'll do whatever it takes to run Wardell down."

"You mean you will. You'll do whatever it takes."

"I will."

Banner tossed the phone on the coffee table and sat down on the couch, next to him. "Why are you still here? You're not getting paid. You can just walk away. Why put yourself in harm's way for no reward?"

"I can't for the same reason he can't."

Banner watched him, but he avoided her eyes. Hiding something? Still?

"You prefer it this way, don't you? No rules, no procedure. You don't understand what it's like for—"

"I understand rules fine. I understand why they have to be there. And when they have to be broken."

There was another long pause, but neither of them looked away this time. As though impelled by magnetic attraction, their faces had moved closer together, their lips almost touching now.

"Blake . . ."

He pulled back from her at the last second. "This is a bad idea."

"Why?"

"I'm not here to stay. I've seen this one before: We get close, things happen, then we stop the bad guy and I'm gone before the dust settles."

Banner said nothing for a second, then smiled out of the corner of her mouth. "Promise?"

Blake blinked.

"I'm not looking for a lifelong commitment, Blake. I'm not searching for a new father for my daughter, and if I were, no offense, but ..."

"None taken."

"I need to keep my real life separate. I need to keep Annie away from ... all of this." She sighed and closed her eyes. "I just want ..."

"Want?" Blake whispered.

"To break the rules."

Their lips met, and Banner felt an electric jolt go through her body as Blake pulled her close. They kept kissing as their hands explored up and down and around. After a minute Banner broke the kiss and opened her eyes. She tugged Blake's shirt up and he raised his arms to let her haul it over his head. The long white scar caught her eye again. She put the tip of her middle finger on the raised tissue, traced it from his upper chest down to where it disappeared beneath his belt. Her eyes moved up and met his. He didn't say anything. If she'd expected an explanation for the scar, she should have known better by now. She pulled her own T-shirt over her head, and Blake moved in again, hands around her ribs, picking her up and pushing her gently but firmly back on the couch.

63

The needle hovered around a safe sixty. The dashboard clock clicked up another digit closer to midnight. Wardell gazed ahead and watched as the broken white lines marking each lane were swallowed up by the hood of his car. He wondered how many of those lines there were between here and Chicago. Tens of thousands. Hundreds of thousands, maybe.

He'd make the Chicago metropolitan area by dawn if he didn't stop. And he wasn't going to stop. No more sleep. Never again. He ought to have been exhausted. Instead he felt reinvigorated, utterly alive.

He'd come to a decision after the call to Whitford. Detective Stewart was dead, leaving just one name from his original list. In a perfect world, he'd have liked to go ahead with it, but he had come to realize that that name did not fit the wider plan anymore. He wanted to engage Banner and Blake, to beat them before he killed them. To ensure that could happen, he'd found a new name to replace the old one.

He let his right hand slip from the steering wheel and fall to rest on top of the cheap notebook he'd laid on the passenger seat. It contained all the intel he'd need for the next twenty-four hours.

DAY SIX

DAY SIX

64

Mike Whitford opened his eyes. Sluggishly, he came to, realizing that he'd dozed off on the living room couch, still holding his coffee-stained Boston Celtics mug. He'd been working on the latest Wardell story through the night, and it looked like the Irish influence in the coffee had momentarily won the battle against the caffeine. Although it was technically morning, it was still pitch black outside. The story was pretty much ready to go, pending a few important details. Not bad, considering Wardell hadn't yet been back in touch to give him the details of his next hit.

He supposed that a layman might be surprised by that. That you could write most of a story about a planned event that had yet to happen and for which you had none of the details. But that was the way it worked: A story like this, direct contact with a celebrity killer, it was all about atmosphere, setting the scene. Whitford could make up the quotes out of whole cloth. All he needed to do was plug in the details as soon as they were made available to him. Whenever that was.

That Wardell hadn't gotten back in touch yet really surprised him. He reached for the laptop and opened up the Hushmail account he'd created to send Wardell the information he'd requested. He'd chosen Hushmail for the strong

285

encryption it offered, and picked an utterly anonymous alias—jim23456@hushmail.com—from which to send the documents. In the unlikely event that Wardell's own anonymous webmail account was discovered, there'd be nothing leading back to him. Just to be on the safe side, he'd dispose of the laptop as soon as he could. He clicked on his in-box and saw for the hundredth time a pristine screen, unsullied even by spam.

Maybe Wardell had forgotten about him. Or maybe his e-mail to Wardell hadn't sent right. For the fifteenth time he clicked on Sent Items. There it was, just as it had been the fourteen previous times: a single e-mail with a modest attachment size sent to the Gmail address Wardell had provided him with. The phone at the office was on a redirect to his cell phone, and he'd bought a second throwaway cell after Wardell's call, the number of which he'd provided in the e-mail. He'd dispose of that too, of course. He had to admit that a part of him was enjoying the clandestine precautions he'd been forced to take as soon as he'd crossed the line and journeyed far beyond a breach of journalistic ethics.

And there was absolutely no mistake about that, about crossing the line. The line was now a distant memory left at the border of a far-off country. Sending that e-mail was obstruction of justice at the very least, possibly even conspiracy to commit murder, depending on how a prosecuting attorney was feeling. And that went way beyond career-ending. It meant heavy jail time became something of a best-case scenario.

An icy sweat broke out on his brow. Whitford scrunched his eyes shut as though that action could pinch off the perspiration and the feeling that came with it, like closing a valve. He reached for the bottle of Scotch and took a good long slug. It did the trick, burned off the sharp edge of anxiety.

But there was nothing to worry about, really. It wasn't like Wardell would be sticking around to update people on his contact details. Whitford had a hunch Wardell wouldn't be doing much of anything twenty-four hours from now. It was election day, and that meant Wardell was most likely going for a big political target. Probably one of the candidates for congress or the governorship. And if Whitford was thinking it, then the cops and the FBI were thinking it too. Whitford got the feeling—maybe from tracking events with a professional eye, maybe from the steely undertone in Wardell's voice that last time—that tonight was going to be the big finish. That had to be why he'd contacted Whitford again, right? To advertise the big finale. When you came right down to it, Wardell fucking *needed* him.

So where the hell was his e-mail? Why the fuck wasn't he calling?

Whitford hit refresh on his e-mail screen again. Checked his phone. Checked the throwaway cell. Each was as empty as his Celtics mug. He tucked the new cell phone into the pocket of his sweatpants and got up on rubbery legs. He lifted the mug from the arm of the couch and pointed himself at the kitchen. He'd make another coffee. By the time he got back, Wardell would have called. Or e-mailed. For certain.

He reached for the light switch. His fingers made it halfway before they were frozen by a single-syllable utterance.

"Don't."

Whitford didn't drop the mug. He felt a nanosecond of inane self-congratulation for that. There was a man standing in his kitchen. And not just any man. He knew that without having to turn the light on. All of a sudden, Whitford's mouth seemed drier than the inside of a toaster oven.

"Mr. Wardell?"

"My, haven't we become formal."

"I thought ..."

"I know, partner. But isn't a home visit so much more ... personal?"

Whitford cleared his throat and swallowed. The saliva tasted like copper.

"I did what you asked me to," he said. When Wardell said nothing, Whitford felt the urge to keep talking, to fill the terrible silence. "As I said in the e-mail, it was kind of a tall order. Gathering intel on a federal agent is difficult enough, but with this other guy, this ... Blake, I got—"

"Absolutely nothing."

Whitford cleared his throat again. "That's right, and I'm sorry. His name was mentioned in relation to some Russian thing a year ago, but the details have been wiped, if it was even the same Blake. There's a driver's license, but the address is a dead end—looks like a virtual office in New York. Other than that, there's no record of him anywhere: no social security number, no criminal record, no nothing. This guy's a ghost."

Wardell kept staring at him unblinking.

Whitford thought about continuing to talk, then decided against it.

Finally, Wardell spoke. "I'm disappointed, Mike."

Whitford opened his mouth to apologize again, but this time his voice failed him, his lips mouthing the words as though somebody had hit the mute button. Wardell smiled.

"I'm disappointed," he repeated, "but I'm not exactly surprised. Don't worry about it. I can make sure he'll be there tonight."

A surge of relief engulfed Whitford. Five seconds before, he'd been absolutely convinced he was going to die. Like the incorrigible optimist he was, Whitford switched from terror to hope with nothing in between. What did Wardell mean by the last thing he'd said, about making sure Blake would be there tonight?

Whitford's lips pulled back across his teeth in an uneasy smile that was a little too wide. "So, I still came through for you, right? On Banner? There wasn't a lot of background on her either, but you got what there is. I guarantee it."

Wardell seemed to think about it, nodded slowly. "It was enough. The *Times* article was particularly interesting."

"Great, great," Whitford said, not bothering to mention that this had been by far the easiest piece of information to find. The real work had been getting things like her address and unlisted phone number. "So ... you're still going to help me out now?"

Wardell took a step forward. "Help you out? Oh yes."

"Great ... Do you, uh, do you want to do the interview in here? We can sit down in the living room if you'd prefer."

Wardell had taken three more languid steps forward in the time Whitford had been speaking. They were now within touching distance.

"Here's fine," he said, putting a hand on the kitchen worktop where Whitford was standing.

"It is?"

"It's perfect."

Whitford didn't like the sound of that. But of course it was far, far too late. Wardell's hand brushed against his leg and came back up with some kind of hunting knife. As Whitford was still thinking about moving, Wardell slammed the knife up to the hilt in his chest. The last thing he heard was a sound like somebody punching a watermelon, and then everything went away.

65

Wardell let go of the handle of the bowie knife and let Whitford's body drop to the tiled floor like a sack of hate mail. It landed awkwardly on its side. A little blood trickled from the wound, but not much. A hard stab directly to the heart like that killed instantly, stopping the heart in the most direct way possible, limiting blood loss.

"No muss, no fuss," Wardell said mildly as he regarded the dead man's wide-open eyes. A cheap cell phone lay on the floor beside the body. Wardell supposed it was Whitford's throwaway. He picked it up, removed the battery, then put both in his pocket. A phone would come in handy for later. Then he drew the knife out carefully and carried it to the sink to wash the blood off.

The killing hadn't been strictly vital, he supposed, but it tied up a loose end. He didn't need Whitford or the media anymore. And besides, it would not hurt to have gotten in a little more practice on killing up close and personal.

He had a feeling that was the way it was going to be with Blake.

66

Darkness. And Carol's voice. Gently teasing.

"Anything you don't know, Blake?"

Carol couldn't be asking that. Carol was gone.

I opened my eyes and the light burned into me. Something was wrong. Something was very, very wrong.

The midday sun beat down relentlessly from an azure-blue sky, but somehow I was shivering as though in the midst of the longest winter. I'd never felt so cold in my life. And then I realized, with the twisted logic of dreams, that I was cold because someone was blocking out the sun. The silhouette of a man towered over me, and though it was impossible to discern the features or even the type of clothes, I knew it was him: Murphy. And I knew exactly what he was going to say.

"Sorry, hoss. You know this is nothin' personal."

And then something shifted and the low, earthy chuckle began and I realized I'd been wrong. It wasn't Murphy at all, not anymore. It was Wardell. The chuckle rattled itself out.

"Aw, who are we kidding, partner? It's always personal."

That was when the explosion began. But instead of a blinding flash bang, it moved slowly. Silky tendrils of flame flowed lazily out to meet me, caressing my skin, burning me slowly . . .

My eyes snapped open and the hellish vista was replaced by blue moonlight and Banner's concerned face.

"Jesus, are you okay?"

The here and now ebbed back. Wardell, Chicago, Banner's

place. Banner's bed. She was sitting up next to me, one arm coyly crossing her breasts.

"What's 'Winterlong'?" she asked after giving me a moment to come to.

I looked back at her.

"You were talking in your sleep," she explained. "Right before you started having what I'm guessing was a doozy of a nightmare."

I sighed and wiped a sheen of cold sweat from my brow. "It's nothing," I said. "It doesn't exist. Never did."

She didn't break eye contact. "You know him, don't you? Wardell."

I stared her out for a moment, considered lying, then relented. "I don't know him. I ran into him once. In Iraq. I could have stopped him."

"It's not your fault. You couldn't have known."

"I did know. Not about all of this, but I knew. I knew if ever there was a man who needed killing, then it was him."

She didn't say anything for a minute. Then, "You really think the target is the governor?"

I shrugged. "Right now, it's more of a best guess. I do know one thing though."

"What's that?"

"Wardell will want us to be there. The people who have gotten closest to stopping him. The people who have hurt him."

"So we can see him beat us, right?"

"That's part of it, yeah."

"But not all?"

I shook my head slowly. "He'll want to make sure we're there to know we're beaten. And then he'll want to kill us. Both of us."

67

5:49 p.m.

The roads were cut off for blocks ahead on the approach, some intentionally by police roadblocks, some merely as a by-product of the early-evening rush hour. We left our cab and walked. The gradual pace gave me time to take in the sheer scale of our destination as it loomed ahead out of the urban sprawl.

The monolithic James R. Thompson Center was planted in the heart of the Loop, the commercial core of downtown Chicago. The JRTC, as it was known, occupied the entire city block bounded by Randolph, Lake, Clark, and LaSalle Streets. The all-glass exterior rose seventeen stories high, sloping upward from street level like some kind of round-edged pyramid. It was an utterly imposing building—dominating its environment, radiating power. I could see why so many of the governors of the past quarter century had chosen to locate their offices here, rather than in the state capital of Springfield.

A harassed campaign worker in short sleeves led us across the marble floor of the impressive atrium, already filling up for the evening's event. The atrium acted as the focal point of the building, all seventeen floors of government offices layered around the open space beneath an immense glass-paneled ceiling. Although I was glad the governor's rally would be taking place inside, and theoretically under more controllable conditions, I wondered about those open balconies on each floor. Seventeen floors, thousands of feet of open space. All of a sudden, I felt more exposed than any time I could remember.

We rode up to the fifteenth floor in one of the glass elevators. The campaign worker led us to the governor's office, knocked briskly on the door, opened it, and then shooed us in, not entering himself. My first thought on entering was that Governor Ed Randall looked like a pale shadow of his former self. Watching the press conference the other day, I had noticed he'd lost weight, but the difference was more dramatic away from the cameras.

Randall had been a first-term governor at the time of Wardell's original spree, and he'd appeared with some regularity in the news reports from that time. In common with others who had found brief national fame during that heated four-week span, he was a larger-than-life figure. He'd spoken in a deep baritone and had favored Armani suits and expensive hair dye, judging by the way that his convincingly jet-black hair belied his sixty years.

Unlike John Hatcher, Randall had avoided grandstanding or issuing direct threats to the killer at press conferences, but had instead struck a balance between caution and reassurance, facing up to the situation with quiet resolve rather than macho posturing.

I found it impossible to reconcile these images of Randall with the slighter, smaller, grayer man who sat behind the desk in front of us. For a moment I wondered if there had been a mix-up, but then he opened his mouth to greet us and the low, mellifluous voice familiar from the news broadcasts set me straight.

"Good evening, Agent Banner, Mr. Blake. I hear this is important."

Banner took his outstretched hand and shook it. I did likewise. The skin felt papery, the bones beneath fragile.

"Life or death," Banner confirmed as we sat down on the opposite side of the desk.

Randall smiled. "Important enough to lie your ass off to as many people as it took to get you this meeting."

I looked at Banner. She opened her mouth to say one thing, changed her mind and then said simply: "Yes."

Randall nodded. "I called your boss, Walt Donaldson. Asked him what he knew about this agent who was so desperate to see me. He didn't know a damn thing about it."

Banner swallowed. "Then why keep the meeting?"

"I knew I was going to spend eighteen hours straight shaking hands and figured I'd be ready for a break right about now."

"Seriously?"

Randall leaned back in his chair and sighed. "I've been hearing a lot about Caleb Wardell this week. A lot of people are fretting I'm going to be next on his list. You're the first person I've spoken to that sounded like she knew what she was talking about."

I leaned forward. "Wardell's coming back to Chicago. He may be here already. I think he's planning one last hit."

"And, it being election day, you think it's going to be me."

"Your prior involvement with the original case makes you the most likely high-profile target, sir," I said. "And it's possible he could have interpreted your comments at the press conference as a challenge."

Randall raised an eyebrow and seemed to slump back into his chair. He looked tired, beat. For his sake, I hoped this wasn't the body language he employed for his television spots. "Maybe that makes me less likely. Have you considered that? This boy has a habit of throwing curveballs. Particularly lately."

"That's just it," I said. "Curveballs. Sometimes he hits an entirely random target; sometimes he goes for exactly the person we expected him to. He's got the task force chasing their tails."

"But not you, as I understand it," Randall said, his eyes flicking to Banner. I realized she'd been talking me up during the phone calls she'd made to secure this appointment.

"Blake has been consistently ahead of the game," she said. "If his advice had been followed from the beginning, I believe we would have Wardell back in custody."

"Is that true?" he said, the dark brown eyes swiveling back to me.

"More or less."

Randall sighed and brought his elbows onto the desk, clasping his fingers. "So what is it you want me to do?"

"We'd like you to consider scaling down your event tonight," Banner said.

Randall's face stayed impassive, but there was a glint of amusement in his eye. "Agent Banner, please, it's not an *event*. It's a *victory party*."

"That's fine," I said. "But can you celebrate in a less-open space? Close friends and family?"

"Out of the question."

"You're too exposed out there," I said.

"We have security on every floor. *Extra* security."

"You have thousands of feet of open balcony overlooking that atrium. Hundreds of people in the crowd. You're going to be the only person standing in the center of a well-lit stage. They can't guarantee your safety under those conditions, no matter what your security people are saying."

He considered this, made a reluctant concession: "My people have raised the idea of bulletproof glass at the podium."

"That's great," I said. "Unless he has armor-piercing rounds."

296

Randall grumbled. "Why don't you just load me into a giant bulletproof hamster ball, roll me on there?"

"Or why don't you just scale down the event?"

Randall said nothing, looked to Banner for support and found none. I pressed the point. "If Wardell is gunning for you, and if you make it this easy for him, there's nothing we can do."

Randall was quiet for a few moments, his mouth half open as he considered what he was going to say. When he finally spoke, it took us both by surprise.

"Has either of you ever had cancer?"

Banner and I exchanged a puzzled glance. It seemed like a non sequitur for the second before I realized why his appearance was so different from before.

"No. Don't answer that. I can tell you haven't. You're both too young, and more important, you look it. Anyway, I'd have to say I don't recommend it. I was diagnosed the day after we caught that little bastard Wardell. Stomach cancer. I went through eighteen months of chemotherapy before I got the all clear. I underwent four major procedures. They removed several feet of my large intestine. The docs said I had about a fifty-fifty chance, back when they originally found it. I'd ignored the warning signs for a while, and so I'd let the tumor get to be the size of a tennis ball. I gave it a name. Do you want to know what I called my tumor?"

"Wardell," I said after a moment.

"Very good, Blake. I called my tumor Caleb Wardell. I thought it was appropriate, with the timing and all. Because that's what he is, you know. A cancer. An ugly little malignant mass of tissue that gets a foothold in a basically healthy place and just keeps on spreading. It's been a few years since he was on the loose the first time, and every time I see a documentary on the son of a bitch, I always take a look.

Can't help myself. They all focus on the bottom line: nineteen kills, nineteen shots. But the worst of it is that isn't close to the sum of the damage he caused. The killings, the fear, it infected the whole damn city. People were afraid to go outside, to let their kids play, to fill their gas tanks. He made people in this city afraid, and we had to hold our hands up and tell them they were *right* to be afraid. That they were *right* to hide indoors. *Right* to think that we couldn't do enough to protect them." He punctuated each "right" by slamming his hand on the desk blotter. "And this time it's even worse, because it's not just one city. It's America. People are scared out there, and the fear is spreading from state to state every time he makes another kill. He's a cancer. We fought him into remission last time, but he's come back more aggressively."

"I did eighteen months of chemo. I went through four procedures. Maybe I was slow to getting around to facing it, but that's how I dealt with cancer. I didn't beat it by running away from it. And I won't run away from this pathetic little psychopath."

A heavy silence filled the room like a tangible thing. I held Randall's gaze for a long minute.

"I'm sorry," I said. "When did it come back?"

Randall leaned back in his chair and breathed out a long sigh. "Maybe it never really went away. I went for my six-month checkup in September. They told me it's back and this time there's too damn much to cut out of me." He let out a low, dark laugh as a thought occurred to him. "Maybe I should have seen that as some kind of . . . omen."

Banner swallowed. "I'm sorry, sir. How long do you have?"

"Not long. Six months, a year at the outside. Long enough to get reelected, maybe even to do a little good, I hope."

"With all due respect," Banner said, "that makes it even more important that we keep you safe tonight."

"Then do so, Agent Banner. Catch this killer. But I will not cancel the rally. I'm not afraid of death, and I'm sure as shit not afraid of Caleb Wardell." He looked us both straight in the face in turn, holding our eyes and daring us to offer resistance. "All right?"

Banner said nothing.

"All right," I said.

"Excellent. Now if you wouldn't mind, I have an election to win."

68

6:17 p.m.

I watched the red neon digits descending, feeling Banner's glare burn into me. I watched from floors fifteen to eight before I relented.

"What?"

"Why did you let it go?"

"Didn't seem like we had much of an option, short of hitting him over the head and locking him in the trunk of your car."

"Wardell's going to kill him."

"Not if I can help it."

"And how are you going to help it?"

"I'm not convinced he's the target."

Banner blinked in surprise. "You're not?"

"No."

"If anything, I'm more convinced he is now," she said.

"How so?"

"We're working on the assumption somebody is using Wardell, that they're hoping he takes out someone important. Like you said, Randall is the best target on paper for this day and this location. But after speaking to him, it seems even *more* likely. You heard him. He's got nothing to lose. Politicians like that scare the crap out of vested interests."

"But his cancer isn't public knowledge. Nobody knows about it."

"His doctors know. Maybe he's told other people. Come on. You have to admit it. After meeting him in person, don't you see Ed Randall as being more worthy of assassination?"

"Banner, that is the both the strangest and most sincere compliment I've ever heard paid to a politician."

"Well, don't you?"

"Yes," I allowed. "But I'm starting to wonder if we're wrong about what Wardell wants. And it's something Randall said that's got me wondering about it. Wardell doesn't care about politics; he cares about only one thing: fear."

Banner looked up at the ceiling. "Then maybe Randall still fits. The man sounded like he'd declared war on fear."

And that was when the circuit clicked into place and the lights began to come on in my head. The elevator pinged and the doors opened. Banner started to step out and stopped when she saw I hadn't moved.

"What is it?"

"Say that again."

"War on fear?"

"That's it," I said. "Like War on Terror or War on Crime."

Banner was searching my face for clues, her brow furrowed. I made another few mental connections and knew what the next step had to be.

"Banner, I need you to get me something. A list of dead FBI agents going back for the last five—no, ten years."

"Slow down, Blake. What—" she began, stopping as my cell phone beeped to indicate a text message received.

I tapped on the animated envelope and read the message. *Somebody's been digging. Will call soon.*

"Who is it?" Banner asked.

"A friend."

She glanced at the text, read it out loud. "What does that mean?"

"I don't know yet."

69

6:20 p.m.

Wardell sat with his back to the wall and closed his eyes, focusing on the murmur of the crowds arriving below. Although there were no windows, he knew that darkness had fallen outside. It was pitch black in this small space, just as it had been when he made his entry, nine hours before.

It had been easy enough to gain access to his chosen vantage point, but then he hadn't expected otherwise. There was an extractor vent in the ceiling. Through it, he could hear the soporific noise of the traffic. He wondered how many of those commuters out there were thinking of him right now. How many were sitting hunched down in their seats, one eye on the fuel gauge hoping they could make it to their destination without having to stop and leave the imagined shelter of their cars to fill up.

Listening to the talk radio stations in the car that morning, Wardell had been mildly amused that he was expected here in Chicago this evening. Mike Whitford had never had the chance to file his story this time, of course, but somehow the media and the populace had managed to intuit the stage for this final act of the drama. Perhaps some eventualities were just inevitable—like a final face-off against Blake.

Circumstances had clicked into place perfectly for that, and now Wardell knew how to make sure they were in the right place: both Blake and the FBI bitch. He'd make his initial kill; then he would take out Banner. After that, the location was perfect for one last dance.

Wardell spun the cap off a bottle of water and took a sip. The Remington 700 was set up on its bipod, trained on the stage. He squinted through the scope and swept it over the kill zone once again.

As he watched, two techs wandered across the stage, ticking off positions of cables and checking that everything conformed to safety regulations. Wardell closed his eyes and savored the anticipation. Not long now.

He watched the crowd as it built, waiting until that one very special person took to the stage.

Not long now.

70

6:42 p.m.

It wouldn't be long now. *One way or another*, Banner thought, *it ends tonight.*

She took her eyes from the crowds milling around the atrium and raised them to the sky. Or, more accurately, to the vast glazed ceiling. The lights inside rendered the sky beyond a thick, tarlike black, dimming the clouds and the stars to nothing at all. She had caught herself doing this more and more often over the past few days—looking up.

With Caleb Wardell, death came from above and with no warning. She understood the practical reasons behind shooting from an elevated position, but part of her couldn't help but wonder if Wardell struck from on high so regularly because it tied in with his god complex. Earlier in the day, she'd finally listened to a recording of the waitress from Rapid City being interviewed. Her recollections of what Wardell had said had chilled Banner, knowing what had happened less than twenty minutes after he'd left the diner.

With a conscious effort, Banner lowered her gaze to take in the ground level. The great and the good of the party were gathering in their hundreds. The quality of their suits marking them apart from the federal agents and security personnel, who were almost as numerous. Although she was technically no longer on the task force, none of the agents had raised an eyebrow at her presence. If they knew she wasn't supposed to be there, they hadn't let on. Paxon was there and had told her Edwards was at HQ with Donaldson, coordinating things centrally. Banner hoped that would continue.

For once, it looked as though the task force had sufficient manpower, at least in theory. Chicago was virtually on lockdown tonight. The JRTC was one of the high-priority locations, of course, but it was far from the only one. The FBI had their own countersniper teams on rooftops overlooking another six focal sites throughout the city. The Chicago PD's overtime budget was being maxed out tonight, and police departments from as far afield as Philadelphia had sent over reinforcements to help out. Spot-checks of vehicles were ongoing, and seven and a half miles of downtown Chicago had closed down.

All of this for one man.

Except, that wasn't the whole truth, was it? The road closures and the extra police and the state-of-the-art riot gear weren't for Wardell. Nobody Banner had spoken to had said it out loud, but it was clear that the authorities were focusing on another danger. It was like Randall had said: People were scared, tense, waiting for things to come to a head. Nowhere more so than right here in Chicago. The town was a pressure cooker, and they were trying to keep the lid on with brute force.

The fact that Wardell hadn't struck since Hatcher's house gave credence to the belief that he was headed back to Chicago. The media knew it; the public knew it; the FBI and the cops knew it. This time, Blake's hunch was in step with popular opinion. Although nobody had come out and said it was a sure thing, the broad consensus had allowed them to scale down their contingency presences in other states and had enabled them to bring the bulk of resources to bear on the city. Donaldson had been interviewed on television the previous night, making the case that Caleb Wardell was just another symptom demonstrating the need to roll back budget cuts to domestic law enforcement. And based on the number of federal wing tips in evidence on the ground tonight, it felt to Banner as though his pleas were having an immediate effect.

A large stage had been erected on the north side of the atrium. At midnight, Governor Randall would make a speech, either to claim victory or to concede defeat. Watching the people gathering, Banner wondered if any of them could have guessed the man they had voted for might be dead within six months—or six hours.

A local band who had recently had a fair-to-middling-sized national radio hit were currently playing the stage. Later, the lineup was scheduled to include various minor celebrities and party bigwigs. The organizers had already had a few cancellations, and Banner wondered how many more they would get due to unforeseen diary clashes. It didn't take Banner's inside knowledge of the case to know that this rally was a strong potential target, and not everyone shared Randall's desire to place themselves literally in the spotlight this night.

She squinted into the distance in the direction Blake had headed a couple of minutes before. He'd received another text message and gone to make a call. That meant he hadn't had time to explain why he was suddenly so interested in the dead of the FBI. Did he think there was some revenge angle on the events of the past week? And if so, how exactly would that tie in with Wardell?

"Banner."

She turned at the sound of her name and saw Dave Edwards pushing through a knot of crowd on his way toward her. *Shit*. A tall guy with close-cropped hair in a pinstripe suit looking aggrieved at being bumped out of the way opened his mouth and then shut it reluctantly when the lady he was with put her hand on his arm and gave him a cold stare. Oblivious, Edwards carried on his way. Banner blinked, sure she was mistaken, but no—he was actually smiling at her.

"I thought you were taking a couple of days," he said.

She pointed at the stage. "I'm here for the band."

"Sure," he said. "How's it going?"

"Fine," she said warily, waiting for the other shoe to drop. Had he spoken to Donaldson? "You?"

"Good, good," he said, and it dawned on Banner that he really wasn't going to yell at her or order her off the scene.

Perhaps he was just happy that Blake wasn't around any-more. No, it was more than that. He seemed ... cheerful.

"You see Donaldson on the news last night?" he asked.

"I caught the end of it."

"I know. Great, wasn't it?"

That was the moment when the atmosphere on the floor changed. The civilians wouldn't have noticed anything, but to Banner and Edwards it was obvious in the way hands jumped to ear pieces and radios. Edwards was reaching for his phone as it rang.

He located it, said his name and listened, said, "Okay," and hung up.

"What's happening?" Banner asked.

"A nine-one-one call. Caucasian male—six one, two hundred pounds—with a gun at the Art Institute in Grant Park."

"That's four blocks south of here," Banner said.

A nearby cop's radio crackled: "Shots fired at Grant Park scene; repeat shots fired."

Banner's stomach tightened. *Shit*. Was this it? Another curveball? More random victims?

"Looks like this is the genuine article," Edwards said. "Let's go, Banner."

Banner followed Edwards at a run, heading for the nearest idling cop car. As she moved, she scanned the crowd again for Blake. There was no sign of him. She'd have to call him on the way to the scene and hope that Edwards didn't realize whom she was calling.

71

Somebody's been digging.

Somebody had indeed been digging, and I was beginning to get a picture of who and why. The voice at the other end of the line belonged to an acquaintance of mine in the CIA. The type of acquaintance who specializes in noticing suspicious patterns and unusual requests. The type of acquaintance who owes me.

"From time to time, administrators sometimes accept bribes to search the open personnel database," he explained. "It's usually difficult to identify, because thousands of records are accessed legitimately every day. But certain names are flagged, because we want to know when somebody runs a search for that name. Carter Blake is one such flagged name."

"I'm honored," I said.

"Don't be. It's not necessarily a compliment. We hauled the administrator in. He was like a rabbit in headlights, admitted everything before we'd asked him to take a seat. Sounds like it was your standard fishing expedition, trying to get some intel on you. Needless to say, he came up with zilch."

"And who was doing the fishing?"

"His name's Mike Whitford. He's a reporter for the *Chicago Tribune*."

"Whitford," I repeated. "He's the guy Wardell contacted."

"Could be it's just background."

"No," I said. "I don't like the timing. Right after I had my chat with Wardell." I thought about it for a second. "Did

307

Whitford ask your guy to search for intel on anybody other than me?"

There was a pause. "How did you know that?"

"Don't tell me. Special Agent Elaine Banner."

"That's the one. Like I said, a fishing expedition, because we don't have much on her beyond what you'd expect."

So Whitford might have gone elsewhere for information on Banner, I thought. Maybe to a similar source in the FBI itself. Maybe even a more obvious source. I asked my acquaintance if he was in front of a computer.

"I'm always in front of a damn computer."

"Good. I want you to search for anything on Banner."

"I told you, we don't have—"

"Not your database. I'm talking about Google."

There was a short silence punctuated by rapid keystrokes.

"Not much. The Bureau's website, of course, a few mentions in local news reports. Wait a minute . . ."

I waited, holding my breath.

"She was interviewed last year by the *New York Times*. For their Sunday supplement. Part of a big feature on successful women in traditionally male-dominated industries. She was representing law enforcement."

"Damn it," I said.

"That a problem?"

"What's the article look like?" I asked. "Lots of human interest, day-in-the-life stuff? Balancing the demands of work and family, that kind of thing?"

There was a pause as he skimmed the article on the computer screen.

"Sounds about right," he confirmed.

"Thanks. I owe you a drink next time I'm in Washington," I said, terminating the call without waiting for him to respond.

I took off at a run, weaving my way through the crowd, heading back to the spot I'd left Banner. She'd gone. The phone was still in my hand. I called her number. Straight to voice mail. *Fuck*.

I heard a loud crack and ducked instinctively. The hundred or so people nearby did exactly the same thing. The abrupt silence turned to uneasy laughter when a shower of foil confetti to the left of the stage signified the source of the noise: a prematurely activated celebration. As the babble of conversation resumed, the forgotten confetti danced in the floodlights and fell to the ground. I saw puzzle pieces fall into place.

Wardell was going to make a statement all right, and he was going to make sure we were there. For the aftermath, if not the act itself. But the first victim of the night would not be Ed Randall, and neither would the victim be chosen randomly. It was still personal with Wardell. It was always personal.

I knew exactly who he was going to kill.

72

6:57 p.m.

There was a black-and-white outside ready to go. Banner and Edwards climbed in with a Chicago PD sergeant. He punched the lights and they hauled out along one of the cleared routes that had been cordoned off to allow the authorities free movement. Banner hit redial a couple of times on her cell, found Blake's number busy both times. She thought about leaving a message, decided against it. It wouldn't be too difficult for him to figure out where she'd gone. He was good at finding people, after all.

Small, intermittent drops of rain spattered on the windshield as they headed south on LaSalle and then east on Jackson, reaching the Art Institute in less than three minutes. Even so, it was like being the last to arrive at the party. There were at least a dozen more police cruisers already there, parked haphazardly across the street in front of the neo-classical facade of the original Art Institute building. The police vehicles intermingled with shiny Bureau sedans and a couple of ambulances. Cops overtook them on foot, running toward the building. Banner opened the passenger door as they slowed to a crawl and jumped out. Her eyes followed the direction of the tide of running uniformed figures and she saw what they were homing in on.

The barricades were already up, a clear space extending a hundred yards out from the twin bronze lions that flanked the entrance. Knots of pedestrians were being shepherded farther away down Adams Street, none of them needing much in the way of encouragement. An ambulance started up and pulled out, its lights and siren kicking in as it passed by. A helicopter hung in the air at rooftop level, its searchlight sweeping back and forth over the second floor of the building. The beam focused primarily on the gallery above the entrance doors: an open space bounded by stone balustrades and divided into bays by three grand arches separated by Corinthian columns.

All eyes were on the gallery. A hundred yards wasn't a safe distance, of course, Banner thought, not even close to safe. They were relying on the threat of superior firepower: a hundred of their guns to Wardell's one. Certain death if he started shooting. It was a false sense of security—if he was still up there, he had nothing to lose. Edwards hung back, making sure to keep low and behind the cruiser they'd arrived in. Banner crouched a little and moved across to the nearest uniformed officer, her eyes never wavering from the three arches where the spotlight played. She tapped the cop on the shoulder and held up her ID, which was barely glanced at.

"Special Agent Banner," she said. "I'm on the Wardell task force."

The cop nodded. He was a young Hispanic guy, mid-twenties. "You came to the right place."

"Is the building evacuated?"

"Uh-huh. SWAT just entered the building around the back," he said. "We think he's up there," he said unnecessarily, pointing up at the second-floor gallery.

Banner risked a glance behind her, in the direction the ambulance had gone. "Who was the vic?"

The cop shrugged, still not looking at her. His voice was tense, distracted. "White female. Teens, early twenties I guess."

Banner's brow furrowed. It sounded like another random target. "Dead?"

Head shake from the cop.

"What?"

The cop turned to look at her for the first time. "She wasn't dead. Not yet, anyw—"

The unmistakable snap of a bullet breaking the sound barrier stopped him in the middle of the word. The snap heralded an inevitable sequence of signals, unfolding so quickly that they appeared to be simultaneous, but not quite: the louder crack of the rifle, the bright muzzle flare in the darkness behind the balustrade beneath the left-hand arch, and finally the startled yells from the crowd.

Banner had time to wonder who'd been hit, and if it could be her, before she heard the rotors of the helicopter screech as it banked sharply and rose up and back from the facade of the building, recoiling like a dog getting too close to an open fire. As it banked away from the building, she saw a big crack spider-webbing the glass on one side of the cockpit.

Less than two seconds had elapsed since the shot, but it felt like an eternity before the return fire began. Bullets peppered the building's facade from a dozen different angles and as many calibers. Stone chipped and windows smashed and lights winked out. The onslaught lasted ten or fifteen seconds before enough senior officers yelled it to a halt. Relative silence descended, undercut by the rotors of the retreating helicopter and the wail of far-off sirens.

Banner looked around for Edwards, finally located him about thirty yards away, standing with a group mostly dressed in body armor behind a van emblazoned with the word SWAT. She crouch-walked over, and Edwards nodded in acknowledgment. He was standing next to a tall, athletically built man with graying hair she took to be the SWAT commander. He and the two men around him were gazing intently at a tablet computer, evidently running a live video feed from the team inside the building.

"You think we got him?" Edwards said.

Before Banner could answer, the tall man's right hand shot up to quiet them, his left pressing the earpiece of his headset deeper in to pick up what was being said more clearly. "Second floor is clear; they're about to go out on the gallery."

Banner tensed, heard breaths being taken in from the others gathered. An interminable pause followed, though it could have been only a matter of seconds.

Finally, the tall man closed his eyes and nodded. "Suspect is down. Confirm, suspect is down. Good job, fellas."

Banner was shaking her head even as smiles broke out on the faces of the men around her. "It's not him."

"What do you mean?" Edwards asked.

"The victim's not dead. If nobody's dead, it isn't Wardell."

"Banner, did you just see—"

"She's right."

They both turned to look at the SWAT commander, who was holding his earpiece again. He spoke into the mouthpiece part of the headset again. "Miller, can you hold on the suspect's face?"

Then he turned the tablet around to show them the video feed from the team up on the gallery. The image itself was shaky, obviously being broadcast from a helmet-mounted camera, but the conclusion was high-definition: the unconscious or dead man lying on the ground beside a discarded rifle was not Wardell. The shooter was a skinny kid of no more than twenty, maybe a college boy. Shoulder-length dark hair pooled around his head on the ground like a dark halo.

"Holy shit," Edwards remarked. "A copycat?"

Wonderful, Banner thought. With the blanket coverage and the building tension, she supposed it had been inevitable that Wardell's spree would provoke something like this before too long. Either this kid had been inspired to carve out his own piece of celebrity, or it was something more calculated: an attempt to kill some enemy or ex-girlfriend and pin it on Wardell. It really didn't matter. The only thing that mattered was that Wardell was still out there somewhere.

The rain began to fall, fast and hard. The SWAT commander departed and Edwards followed in his wake with barely a nod to Banner, no doubt to make sure he'd appear in the news coverage. Banner looked around for the cop who'd given her the ride from the JRTC but was unable to pick him out from the dozens of other uniformed officers. They'd all be kept busy here for some time, meaning it would be quicker to make the trip on foot. She started across the road, heading for Adams Street, checking the display on her cell as she walked. One missed call, one voice message received. She speed-dialed voice mail, heard Blake's voice.

"Banner, it's Blake. I know where he is, and you need to know I'm on my way."

The full message lasted twelve seconds. Banner listened to the remainder, feeling the bottom drop out of her world.

73

7:01 p.m.

It was almost time.

Strictly speaking, the first one would be the only necessary kill. The first kill would bring Blake and Banner running. Wardell smiled, because he knew there was no need to hold back this time, nothing to be gained by resisting the urge for more.

There: the target had taken to the stage, finally. Wardell put his eye to the scope, tracking her as she moved about the stage. He adjusted the focus a little, to the point where he could see the individual curls of dark hair on her forehead. Something about that brought a realization: This would be his youngest victim to date. The realization came unencumbered with any kind of trepidation or remorse, but merely the mild interest of a sociologist noting a minor new statistical trend.

Annie Banner was dressed in a purple dress and matching

hat. It was a miniature, stylized version of the kind of flouncy apparel favored by well-turned-out ladies in the Old West.

Wardell relaxed his arms and let the crosshairs float across the stage with her, keeping her head in the dead center. He blanked his mind, breathed in and out. In and out. The kid paused, stage right, held up her hands in an exaggerated fit of pique. Wardell put his finger on the trigger, breathed in, and pressed hold. Pressed hold.

74

7:01 p.m.

The rain battered down on the windshield and was swept aside by the wipers to form twin waterfalls on either side. The waterfalls flashed red and blue in time with the siren. Given that I'd already punched out a federal agent, I was betting that stealing a police car probably couldn't make things appreciably worse for me.

I ran another red light, swinging a little wide to avoid the grille of a slow-to-react bus crossing North Franklin Street. The needle dipped down to forty-five as I took pressure off the gas pedal, and then it climbed again as I cleared the cross street and continued west, crossing the Chicago River. I took the on-ramp for the 90 at close to seventy, then put my foot all the way down as I swung across to the outside lane. I risked taking my eyes of the road to check the GPS on my phone and saw the red dot representing my destination creep in at the top of the screen.

I cursed myself again for taking so long to identify

Wardell's target, for taking so long for it even to occur to me. Wardell didn't care about taking out a politically important target. He cared about impact, sure, but it was still personal. It was always personal. Killing the seven-year-old daughter of a federal agent would have all the impact he was looking for, but it would also guarantee Banner and I would come running, ready to be next in line.

I saw the sign for my exit ahead, slowed to a marginally less-insane speed as I hit the surface streets again, and found the road I was looking for. A minute later, a sprawling red-brick building hove into view on the left-hand side. I saw a free-standing sign that labeled it as Barkley Elementary School.

I prayed for two things: first, that I wasn't too late; second, that the person I'd spoken to had taken my warning seriously and had acted exactly according to my instructions. I knew the second prayer had been granted as I reached the front entrance of the school, braking hard and slewing to a stop in the middle of the road. An ancient-sounding school bell was sounding an insistent, pulsing ring as perplexed groups of parents and children spilled out onto the sidewalk. I allowed myself a scintilla of hope at that: perplexed was good. Perplexed wasn't terrified.

I opened the door and got out, reaching for my Beretta as I faced the front entrance.

75

7:03 p.m.

Two things happened.

First, the image of Annie Banner's little head vanished from the scope. Then, an ear-splitting clanging cut through the quiet of the projection booth like a three a.m. phone call. Wardell flinched, his finger instinctively moving back from the trigger.

He opened his other eye and moved his head away from the scope. That was when he realized that there was no problem with the scope itself. The gym hall below was in utter darkness. The stage lights had all been extinguished, the black felt curtains holding out any glimmer of light from the outside world.

The clanging kept on, a short-long pulse vibrating in Wardell's skull. The goddamn bell must have been attached to the outside wall of the booth. He could make out the hint of sounds from below, where two hundred or so people scrabbled in the dark. Chairs scraping loudly, the scuffle of feet, children crying. Mass confusion, just like Wardell had wanted.

No, not like he'd wanted, because it wasn't on his terms. The confusion enveloped him too; he didn't soar above it. Wardell clicked the night vision back on, but the scene had shifted unrecognizably. The stage had cleared. People were pushing and shoving in the direction of the exits. A few of the adults were trying to direct the crowds in the darkness. People were already beginning to find their way out, moving with urgency but without real panic. Once the doors were open, it wouldn't take long to clear the hall.

He could just start firing, of course. It would be the easiest thing in the world, a turkey shoot. But he needed Banner's daughter.

Plans are often useless; planning is indispensable. Wardell made a snap decision. The situation had shifted, but was still eminently salvageable. He needed only to secure a handful of hostages, Banner's daughter among them. That meant he would need to descend to the hall. He laid the Remington down and selected a handgun—the Glock—from the canvas duffel. He reached down to the floor to open the access panel.

The hall beneath him was still in darkness, but his eyes were beginning to adjust to it. Below him he could make out figures fumbling around in the dark. Wardell stepped through the hatch and slid down the sides of the ladder. A woman brushed past him, apologizing briskly. Others passed by, wondering aloud what was going on. Still plenty of people, plenty of potential hostages.

Just a minor setback. There was still time to turn it into a positive.

76

7:11 p.m.

People were still flowing out from the main entrance, adding to the swelling crowd outside the school. Many of them looked back at the building as they exited, evidently expecting to see smoke or flames or some other reason for the interruption to their evening. A couple of children were crying, but the presiding air seemed to be one of bemusement tinged with irritation. A tall, bespectacled woman in her early thirties with long strawberry-blond hair and a red skirt was holding one of the main doors open, ushering people out and looking official about it. I pushed through the mass of disgruntled parents and excited kids and tapped her on the shoulder.

"Do you know if Miss Bass made it out yet?"

The woman broke off from hollering instructions and looked me up and down. "You're looking at her."

"I'm Blake," I said. "We just spoke on the phone."

She stared back at me, "I seem to recall that," she deadpanned.

"Thank you," I said with sincerity.

"No sweat, but I have to say, even though I'll be in trouble, I sure hope you're wrong about this."

I indicated the doors and the stream of refugees from the school, a stream that appeared to be slowing. "Many more to come out?"

"Hard to say. After what you said was about to happen, I didn't think we had time to take attendance."

"You cut the lights on the stage?"

"Uh-huh. Every light in the gym. Fire alarm virtually simultaneously. There was one right next to the fuse box." She paused and looked at me over the rims of her glasses. "What?"

"Nothing. I just don't generally meet people this ... efficient."

"Mister, I teach drama in an elementary school. Those little bastards will eat you alive if you don't have your shit together. Pardon my French."

I put a hand on her shoulder as I moved past her and through the door. "Miss Bass, I'll pardon you pretty much anything."

I moved through the doorway and into a wide foyer, about a hundred feet square. The foyer was low-ceilinged with ancient polystyrene tiles. At the far side of the scuffed linoleum floor was a glass case displaying various cheap trophies accumulated for soccer or cake decoration or whatever the hell students compete in these days. The space was entirely empty of people. Which meant that either the flow of families leaving the gym had naturally petered out, or it had been stemmed. Two corridors led off the foyer at either side. A sign on the right-hand wall sported blue arrows labeled for various classrooms, upper levels, cafeteria, and a couple of other selections. There were only two arrows on the left side: small gym hall, large gym hall.

I approached the corridor slowly, conscious of the thick silence between the urgent clangs of the fire bell. The familiar school smell of pencils and disinfectant seemed ridiculous in the situation. I reached the wall at the edge of the corridor and backed against it, pausing for a second to listen between clangs. I stuck my head around the corner in time to see twin wood and glass fire doors slam outward, rebounding violently off whitewashed cinder-block walls.

Half a dozen kids ran toward me. It was difficult to guess what ages they were. There was a foot in height variation from the tallest to the smallest, and they were decked out in costumes from the show. Every last one of them was terrified. The first couple of them blew past me, apparently not even seeing me. I grabbed the upper arm of the tallest kid as he swept past. His momentum actually took his feet off the ground as I gripped him. He turned around, letting out a scream that would have impressed Janet Leigh, struggling to get loose.

"It's okay. I'm with the police," I said. Not true, but a scared child doesn't often need to hear the truth. "What's happening?" I said, indicating the direction from which they'd come.

The kid was around ten or eleven, wearing blue jeans, a checkered shirt, and a black waistcoat. I guessed he'd lost the Stetson somewhere back along the corridor. He stopped struggling a few seconds after he realized it wasn't making any difference and turned his tearstained face up to mine.

"Please, mister, let me go."

"Sure. Just tell me what's happening."

"A m-m—ma—" he stuttered, either through fear or inability to get the word out through the sobs.

"A man? With a gun?"

The kid swallowed and nodded fiercely.

"Is anybody else back there?"

The kid was trying to pull away again, his head moving side to side. I didn't think that was in response to my question, but more a denial of the whole situation. I glanced back down the corridor. The double doors had settled back into place, guided gently by torsion springs. The two wire-glassed windows in the doors showed nothing in the corridor beyond.

I tightened my grip and pulled him closer, hating the anger in my voice as I growled, "Listen to me, kid. This is very important. Is anyone back there?"

He blinked tears out of his eyes and seemed to calm himself for a moment, my words having the effect of a bucket of cold water. "Yes, sir. Annie Banner and Mr. Bence. The m—the m—" He stopped, blinked again. "He wanted us all to stay, but we ran. Please."

I relaxed my grip. As I felt my fingers slip from the kid's arm I knew I'd probably added a pretty good bruise to his night of trauma. "You did great. Thank you. Now I want you to run outside and tell Miss Bass exactly what you told me. Make sure nobody comes back in."

His head bobbed up and down gratefully. "Where are you going?"

I looked back down the corridor. "To get Annie and Mr. Bence."

I moved down the cinder-block corridor toward the double fire doors. Behind me I heard the exit door open and slam shut again. A niggling, doubting voice in my head whispered three words in the space between fire alarm clangs.

Last one out.

I answered the voice by telling it to go fuck itself.

The doors parted before me, and I was reminded of saloon doors in an old Western. Through them was another forty feet of cinder-block walls that sank into darkness as they entered the part of the school where the power had been cut. I ran toward the darkness, the soles of my shoes cracking off the linoleum and bouncing back to me off the walls.

Then I heard another noise, coming from up ahead. Sharper than the cracks of my footsteps. Louder than the clang of the fire bell. A sound that I knew better than my own heartbeat.

And then I heard it again.

77

7:15 p.m.

It took only until the first intersection for Banner to realize she'd made a bad choice of vehicle. The Bureau Sedan had simply been the nearest available car after she'd picked up Blake's voice mail. Only as she slowed for the red light and started slamming the horn with the heel of her hand did she realize she should have had one of the uniformed cops drive her in a black-and-white.

Wardell's going after Annie. He's at the school.

Blake's words were so clear in her head it was as though it were being relayed through the car's speakers on a loop. She nosed out into the intersection, giving oncoming cars space to swerve, if not stop completely, then pushed through the gap. She yanked the wheel right to duck in front of a braking taxicab, ripping the left side of her car across its bumper. She was in luck. Nothing caught. The car rocked on its tires a little and fishtailed as she came through the intersection and back onto the road west.

A clear patch of road emerged with half a block to go before the next set of red lights. Banner realized that she hadn't taken the time to tell anybody else about the new threat, about Wardell being at Annie's school. As far as she knew, the only people who were aware of it were herself and Blake. Which was exactly what Wardell wanted, of course.

She would call Donaldson from the school, as soon as she knew Annie was all right. Right now she needed a quick response. She took her eyes off the road to hit 911, jamming the phone in the crook of her neck and raising her right hand again, poised to start pummeling the horn. Then the traffic light ahead flicked to yellow and she put the hand back on the wheel and the gas pedal back on the floor.

"Nine-one-one emerg—"

Banner cut across the operator. "This is Special Agent Elaine Banner, FBI, with the Chicago field office. I have just received credible information that Caleb Wardell has been sighted in the Barkley Elementary School on North Western Avenue."

There was a pause, and Banner knew exactly what was coming next.

"Could you repeat that information?"

"Barkley Elementary. Wardell. Now. Get some fucking cars down there."

She cut the call off and let the phone drop. The next red light turned green again. Another break. She made herself focus on the lights. They stopped her from thinking about Annie.

The next intersection was a hundred yards ahead, the light switching from green to yellow. Beyond was the on-ramp for I-90. She leaned on the horn and kept the gas pedal down.

Don't think; just drive.

78

7:22 p.m.

The corridor dipped into darkness, but beyond the point the lights were extinguished there was still enough backlight to see where I was going. I ran toward the sound of the gunshots, knowing I'd failed. The corridor hit a T junction. Straight ahead were the doors to the main gym. They were the same wood and glass doors that I'd encountered throughout the school, but the little windows were covered on the inside with red curtains.

I hesitated at the doors, glanced left and right along the new length of corridor. There was another set of doors to the left, a flight of stairs to the right. The stairs would probably lead to the stage. I thought about taking the time to climb the stairs and enter the hall from a less obvious direction. After a moment I discounted the idea: A direct entrance was riskier, but it would save precious seconds. Depending on what I found behind the door, those seconds could mean the difference between life and death.

There was no prospect of sneaking in, so I just barged through the doors, ducking and rolling to my left, coming up on my heels. From three o'clock and a little above me—the level of the stage, at a guess—I heard a female scream and the sound of a door slamming shut. The slam echoed in the vast stillness. As it dissipated, I became aware of another sound: small and wet and insignificant in the space. I recognized it. It was the sound somebody's breathing makes when they're hurt very badly—the sound that suggests the breathing isn't going to continue for much longer.

Almost unconsciously, I held my breath and walked in the direction of the sound. The pupils of my eyes had dilated all the way, just enough to make out the shapes of over-turned chairs and avoid them. It was useless to worry about whether Wardell was watching me through a scope with a night sight. There was nothing I could do about it. In any case, I didn't think he'd settle for such an easy kill—or at least I hoped not.

The edge of the stage was five feet off the ground and marked with white fluorescent tape, making it stand out like a beacon. I put a hand out and touched the line of tape. The raspy breathing had reduced in volume and frequency to the point where I could barely discern it from the silence. I put both arms on the stage and hauled myself up. By the time I'd gotten to my feet, the breathing had stopped entirely, replaced by a long, rattling wheeze.

Hesitating briefly, I took my phone out and tapped it to activate the flashlight. The illumination cast a bright, narrow beam a few feet in front of me. I moved it around a little and located a foot in a leather shoe. I angled up and found it attached to a leg, and then a body, and finally a bloody face. There was a bullet hole in the forehead, the diameter of the wound and the powder burns telling me the weapon had been a handgun at point-blank range. The death rattle petered out as the flashlight beam passed over the eyes of the dead man. A tall man, balding and in his late forties. His comfortable slip-on shoes and V-neck sweater marked him out as a quasi-off-duty teacher. Mr. Bence, most likely. I swept the beam around, highlighting frustratingly small patches of the stage at a time. I hoped I would find nothing, but I'd heard two shots. I knew there was at least one more body to locate on this stage.

I walked forward slowly and closed my eyes as the beam caught first a pool of red and then curls of dark hair on the boards. The framed picture of Annie from Banner's apartment flashed in front of my eyes. I followed the dark hair and found another head, facing away from me. Gently, I reached out and felt for a pulse in the neck. Finding nothing, I moved my fingers below the jaw and gently moved it so I could see the face. The eyes were closed as though sleeping. The bullet hole was in the right temple this time.

It wasn't Annie.

79

7:24 p.m.

The body that lay before me was a good deal older. A petite woman in her midtwenties. Maybe another teacher, maybe a parent. But not Annie.

Not yet.

I sprang to my feet. The kid outside had said Wardell had Banner's daughter. Two shots fired, two more bodies on my conscience. But it meant Wardell had spared Annie for the moment. She was his ace in the hole—he knew the building would be surrounded, knew nobody would enter right away if he had hostages. Nobody but me or Banner.

I closed my eyes and replayed the scream and the slamming door I'd heard on entering the hall, lined it up with my current position and scrabbled across the stage to get there, colliding with a couple of upturned pieces of stage furniture on the way. I found a brick wall, moved my palms around it until I found a metal door with a push bar. The door creaked open and dim light returned. I was in another cinder-block-walled corridor. This one had small plastic skylights that let in dirty streetlight.

The stage door exited adjacent a blank wall, so there was only one way to go. I gripped my gun and ran along the corridor until I reached another door. The clanging fire alarm grew louder as I approached another wall-mounted bell. I pulled the door open and found a stairwell. Which direction? Experience said up. Wardell liked high ground. I stopped and listened between the clangs of the bell.

Ring riiiiiiiiing.

Ring riiiiiiiiing.

Ring riiiiiiiiing.

There. I heard the sound of someone crying out, suddenly cut off, as though somebody had clamped a hand over their mouth. The cry had lasted a heartbeat longer than the end of the last pulse of the bell. It had come from below.

80

"I'm sorry, ma'am. I can't let you go in there."

Banner produced her badge. "I'm FBI. It's Special Agent Banner, not ma'am. And you're not going to stop me." Banner's sharp tone was directed at herself as much as the young officer blocking her way to the front entrance of the school. If she'd been thinking, she'd have realized that this was the downside of summoning backup. Regulations, procedure. Due process.

Law enforcement had been stretched to breaking point across the city for election night. Officers from across the state and farther afield had been drafted in to cover the identified danger zones, the highest-profile areas where it was thought Wardell might choose to strike. Unsurprisingly, nobody had thought to include a small elementary school on that list, and so the full response was taking a while to mobilize. There were only three police cars, and the half-dozen cops were manfully dealing with the task of herding the crowds to the opposite side of the street so a perimeter could be established when reinforcements arrived. That left this one officer as the only thing standing between Banner and the school, and to her surprise and irritation, he wasn't getting out of her way.

"I'm sorry, Agent Banner. FBI or not, nobody's going in there. We've got reports of an armed suspect who's taken some hostages. Ain't nobody going in there until we get a negotiator down here."

Banner put her badge away, looking around the scene. Still only those half-dozen first responders, though she could hear approaching sirens from multiple different directions. Within a minute, maybe less, there'd be a whole lot more obstacles in her way than this one cop.

"My kid's in there," she said simply.

The cop glanced at the school entrance, turned back to her. He shook his head in sympathy, spreading his hands. "Ma'am ..." he began, forgetting her earlier admonishment and falling back on a half-assed recollection of whatever crowd control course he'd attended at the academy. He didn't look like a guy who was comfortable with thinking for himself, or making exceptions to the rules.

The sirens were getting closer. Banner put a hand on his shoulder and said, "You're going to have to shoot me."

The cop looked like she'd slapped him.

"Now hold on ..."

Banner walked quickly past him, up the steps, and pushed the door open. She glanced back and saw that the cop wasn't even watching her. He was too busy looking around to see if anyone had seen him fail to stop her getting past.

81

7:33 p.m.

Wardell had dragged the brat down three short flights of stairs. The last flight had been a narrow steel stairway that had brought them down to the basement level—the boiler room, he guessed. The space was wide and low-ceilinged. Though it spread virtually open plan across the old building's footprint, it was cluttered with thick pipes and abandoned crates and storage lockers. Steel uprights supported the ceiling, evenly spaced out. The power was on down here, but the illuminations were few and far between. Grimy fluorescent tubes unevenly spaced along the wall emitting little more than candlelight.

Wardell was pleased that the brat was presenting no major difficulties so far. After he'd shot the two teachers on the stage, she'd screamed at first, but then she'd gone quiet. Almost eerily quiet. He guessed she was in shock. Even so, he kept his right hand over her mouth as he put the gun down on top of a tall packing crate and reached for Whitford's cell phone. Time was of the essence. He didn't know how many of the escapees from the hall would realize exactly what was going on. That meant he couldn't be sure anybody knew that he was holding hostages. Part of him relished the idea of a last stand against an entire SWAT team. In time, it would probably come to that. But for the moment, he certainly didn't want just anybody barging in here. When he thought about the opportunity gone forever—all those people in that crowd—he felt it like acid burning through his guts.

He slotted the battery back in and switched the phone on, then dialed 911. The beeps of the phone seemed to rouse the girl from her state of shock. She began to squirm again and Wardell tightened his grip.

A male operator answered the call with the standard greeting, and Wardell said, "You record all of these, right?"

"This call is being recorded, yes, sir. What is the nature of your emergency?"

Wardell laughed. "Better men than you have tried to work that one out, partner. This is Caleb Wardell. No, this is not a hoax. I know you're probably going to have to get people to check this out, so I'll be brief and to the point. I'm at Barkley Elementary School. I'm armed and I have three hostages: a man, a woman, and a little girl. I'll kill them all unless I get what I want."

"Sir—"

"I didn't ask you to contribute, son. Now, this last part is very important. I will not negotiate with anybody but Carter Blake or Elaine Banner; they're on the FBI task force. Anybody else tries to do it, I kill a hostage. I want Blake and Banner—just them—to enter the building. If they try to talk to me from outside, I kill a hostage. You got all of that? Good."

Wardell ended the call and tossed the phone over his shoulder. That ought to do it. He reached to pick up the gun from the top of the packing crate, and as he did so, the angle of his right hand, the one over the kid's mouth, shifted. Wardell grimaced as a sharp pain gripped his hand. The little shit had sunk her teeth into the webbing between his thumb and index finger. He felt the teeth meet in the middle, piercing all of the way through. He grasped at her as she started to wriggle loose, managed to slam her against the wall so that her jaws relaxed. The kid cried out and Wardell backhanded her across the face with his wounded hand, spraying his own blood over her and the wall.

"You goddamned little whore!" he yelled, wincing and realizing the strike had only made the pain in his hand worse. After the lights had gone out, he'd changed his mind about killing the kid before Banner got here. Now he was changing his mind back again.

The girl was scrabbling to her feet, sobbing. Wardell lunged for her as she fled, catching the edge of her flouncy costume dress with his good hand and tugging it so that she fell down. He dragged her back across the dirty concrete floor and hauled her to her feet, wrapping his left arm around her midsection—making sure to keep his hand away from those goddamn sharp teeth this time.

Out of breath, he carried her bodily back to the packing crate and reached for the gun. As his fingers closed around the grip, he heard another gun being cocked from above him.

He raised his head to see Carter Blake at the top of the metal stairs—a lot earlier than expected and drawing a bead on Wardell's head.

"Drop the kid and put your hands on your head."

Wardell froze; then the surprise abated and he hugged Annie tighter to his body. A grin broke out on his face. Maybe the situation called for a poker face, but he couldn't help it. Blake had nothing. Okay, he had the gun, but he wouldn't use it, not with the brat this close. Slowly, he shook his head.

"Second time you've made that mistake, Blake. Second and last."

Wardell's fingers closed around the butt of the gun on top of the crate. Blake tightened his grip on his own gun but did not fire. He was less than fifteen feet away: literally a can't-miss. Wardell moved in one smooth, practiced motion without hesitation: He raised the gun, pointed it in the middle of Blake's face, and fired.

82

7:37 p.m.

Instinctively, I lunged forward. But even as I did it, I knew it was futile. There was no way he could miss me, not from this distance. The crack of the gunshot was fierce in the low space. I saw the muzzle flash as I fell forward and wondered how long it would take me to feel the pain.

But then the pain didn't come. I continued my tumble forward, losing height as I dropped from the top of the metal stairway. Wardell was wincing, and I registered that his right hand was covered with blood. He'd missed me. He'd actually *missed me*. He'd hurt his hand somehow and it had thrown his aim off. Not by much, maybe just enough to foul the last-moment adjustment he'd made as I jumped—so that my reflexive lunge had let me pass under the path of the bullet. He was still holding Annie, though, and still holding the gun, despite his obvious pain. But I was still falling forward, and I wasn't about to stop.

My left foot landed square on the third step from the bottom and I sprang off it, diving right at Wardell as he brought the gun to bear on me again. I caught him high and to his right side, contacting my shoulder with his head and grabbing his wrist with my hand, so that the second bullet went high too, the gunshot just about rupturing my eardrums as it did so. The momentum knocked Wardell over backward, and he let go of Annie to free up his other hand to try and break his fall.

We slammed onto the concrete floor, me on top. Annie rolled as she landed and scampered back from us as though distancing herself from two wild animals fighting over a piece of meat. My right hand was trapped beneath Wardell's back. The impact had made me drop the gun. My left hand kept hold of his wrist. With both of our other hands pinned, it turned into an arm wrestle. I dug my fingers into the flesh of his wrist and tried to lock my arm. He pushed back, edging the gun back down toward my face. It was a fairly even match. Fairly, but not exactly. I was in good shape, but Wardell had spent the last five years with little else to do but build muscle. Little by little, quarter inch by quarter inch, I was losing the struggle. I felt the muzzle of the gun bob against my hair. Wardell's face, a mask of concentration up until now, started to twitch into an anticipatory leer.

I relaxed my grip on his wrist abruptly and simultaneously smashed my forehead into Wardell's nose. I felt rather than heard the crunch of bone, and Wardell roared in pain. I took advantage by sliding my hand over the muzzle of the gun and yanking it down. Faced with a split-second choice between letting go of the gun or retaining his grip and allowing his trigger finger to be broken, Wardell chose the first option. I yanked the gun back and started to pull my right arm out from under Wardell as I adjusted the gun in my left, intending to turn it on its former owner.

I didn't get the chance. Wardell brought his knee up dead center toward my groin, causing me to roll to the side to avoid an injury that would take me out of the fight. He balled his fist and batted the gun out of my hand sideways. It flew from my fingers and sailed into a pile of machine parts beneath the metal stairway. We broke apart and staggered back a couple of steps, like boxers. Our eyes locked for a heartbeat, and then as though choreographed, we both looked down, remembering my gun. It lay between us, equidistant. We came together again, more like sumo wrestlers this time, pushing against each other hard, neither giving ground.

Wardell tried my own trick on me, dropping one hand so that I lurched forward, then bringing the hand back as a fist. I angled my body to catch his forearm between my arm and ribs and used his momentum to swing him into one of the steel pillars. I relaxed the grip so that I could bend for the gun on the floor, but Wardell was already countering, slamming his fist into my back and knocking me off course. I ignored the sharp lance of pain in my lungs and pivoted, grabbing him at the shoulders and blocking his lunge for the gun. Over his right shoulder I saw Annie backed into a corner and staring at the scene, wide-eyed. That made up my mind: I liked my own chances better with the gun in play, but I couldn't risk a stray bullet finding her.

I feinted as though I were going to pull the head butt move again and then renewed the pressure and kicked the fallen gun hard with the side of my shoe. It skittered side-on across the floor, disappearing beneath a stack of wooden pallets. Wardell laughed and pushed back off me, dancing away and wiping blood from his broken nose with the back of his hand. I took a step back, feeling more than a little unsteady on my feet. I hoped it didn't show. Wardell looked entirely unruffled, despite the blood flowing from his hand and his nose.

"Better this way," Wardell said, nodding in the direction the gun had gone. "You know, I don't usually like to get my hands dirty. With you? I'm glad to make an exception."

I shook my head. "Bring it on, psycho. I know you can't handle it up close."

He didn't respond. Not with words. He took a step toward me, feinted, and then nailed me on the shoulder and the side of my head before I saw his hands moving. It felt as though I'd stuck my head out in front of a subway train. I shook the starburst out of my eyes and resisted the temptation of a blind charge. I hung back and let the shock drain out of the head blow, allowing the pain to rush in to fill the void. I grinned it out. "Weak. Don't give up the day job."

Wardell returned the grin, saying nothing. He came close again, feinting with the left this time. I was ready for it, blocked the true swing from the right and drove my fist into his gut. It hurt him, but it hurt my fist almost as much. It was like punching a car tire. I took a lucky gamble on a right cross from Wardell, blocked it with my forearm, and slammed my elbow hard into his already-broken nose. The cry of pain was louder this time and angrier. He fell back a step, coming up short against a low workbench. His right hand fell back to steady himself and, too late, I realized I'd pushed him back into a virtual hand-to-hand armory. His fingers swept over an array of hammers, saws, and chisels. I charged him as his fingers closed around a heavy monkey wrench.

He was too fast for me, already swinging it at my head by the time I got anywhere near. I ducked, the cruel mouth of the wrench just clipping the top of my scalp. Continuing on its swing, the wrench crashed into one of the steel pillars, making a noise like the dinner gong in hell.

Wardell moved while I was off balance, sweeping his right leg across the backs of my knees and dropping me onto the concrete. He grabbed the wrench two-handed and raised it above his head, as though intending to cut me in half with it. I rolled to the side and felt a sting on my arm as the wrench smashed a concrete chip out of the floor. Every cell in my body told me to roll again, get as far away as I could from the next swing of the wrench. I stayed put. I might dodge the next one, and maybe even the one after, but sooner or later, the realities of my position dictated that I had only one tenable defense.

Wardell brought the wrench down again, launching his follow-up strike with supernatural speed. I saw the blunt, rusty steel head of it closing in on my face and knew that if I didn't have perfect timing, I wouldn't have anything at all. I heard the beginning of Annie's scream. I brought both hands up from each side and caught the wrench between them, feeling the jolt travel all the way up to my biceps. A flicker of confusion crossed Wardell's face, and I milked it to the full, pulling him off balance with the wrench and kneeing him hard in the solar plexus. He wasn't ready for it this time, gagging as the breath was forced out of him.

I kept pulling him down and got up on one knee, bringing the wrench across his throat and pulling his body back against me. He coughed and gagged again, fingers scratching at mine. I pulled harder. His body convulsed and he tried to shake his head from side to side. I grunted and increased the pressure. From somewhere far away, I heard somebody screaming. It was Annie. I felt Wardell's fingers relax a little on my grip on the wrench and felt the beginnings of relief myself, knowing that the last of his strength was beginning to ebb away.

I was wrong.

Wardell's right hand dropped to his side, and a heartbeat later I felt a white-hot pain in my thigh. Although I couldn't see it, I knew I'd been stabbed. Stupid. I should have known he'd always have a backup. I gritted my teeth against the pain and increased the pressure again. The gash in my leg sang out another chorus of agony as I felt the blade twist and draw out. Wardell's hand swung dazedly outward, and I saw the steel of the blade winking out from under a thick shroud of my own blood. He brought the knife back toward us and I felt a stab in my right side.

This one didn't feel white-hot, just the opposite: like a perfectly formed sheet of ice had been slid into my abdomen. I felt a sickly numbness and was aware of my own blood soaking into my clothing and running down my leg. My grip on the wrench relaxed just enough, and Wardell was able to squirm out from under.

I fell back, holding my side. A second later I realized with surprise that I'd fallen to the ground. Wardell was still on his feet for now, but he didn't look like he'd be far behind me. He was staggering in a circle, holding his throat with one hand, the blade in the other. His breath rasped out. It sounded like I'd broken something important in there. I didn't feel any remorse. He looked down at himself and saw dirt, sweat, blood—his and mine. His face contorted into a mask of revulsion. For a fleeting moment, I wondered if he might save me some trouble and die of fastidiousness.

I struggled to one knee and tried to get up, pressing harder on my side and feeling blood seep between my fingers. Wardell looked at me, then at the blade in his hands. From between his teeth, he issued one word: "Kill."

"Freeze, FBI."

The shout from behind Wardell stopped both of us as though we'd been flash frozen.

"Mommy!"

I looked at Annie, then followed her gaze to see Banner edging down the stairway, her gun gripped in both hands and aimed squarely at Wardell.

"Drop it," she said.

Wardell turned slowly to face her.

"Last warning," Banner snapped before he'd completed the rotation. "I will shoot you."

Will you? I wondered. *Because I really think you're going to need to, Banner.* Something about Wardell's movements told me he was thinking the same thing. It didn't reassure me in the slightest when Wardell appeared to comply, dropping the knife to the floor, where it made a dull clink.

Banner was at the bottom of the stairs now. Wardell was opening his hands in a gesture of surrender. I didn't buy it for a second.

I tried to say, "Shoot him," but I couldn't seem to get it out. My lips were moving, but there didn't seem to be anything left in me to force the sound out. The room was starting to spin. The neon tubes on the walls were casting out rainbows that I was pretty sure hadn't been there before.

I knew I couldn't pass out now, because somehow I had to

stop what was going to happen next. I knew what Wardell was going to do because we both knew what Banner was going to do, and in this situation it was entirely the wrong thing to do: follow the rules, follow procedure.

If you carry a badge, you're trained to observe certain rules of engagement in situations like this. Rules like not discharging your weapon unless you are absolutely certain there is a threat to your life. Like not shooting an unarmed suspect. Like ensuring you give him time to surrender. Those rules were about to get Elaine Banner killed, because despite his injuries, a moment's uncertainty was all Caleb Wardell would need.

He was going to wait another second or two, because he knew that would only move Banner that much more out of the heat of the moment, and then he was going to rush her. Banner's gun was a Glock. Three separate safety mechanisms to prevent accidental discharge. She might get an accurate shot off in that split second, but if she didn't, that would be all she wrote.

Banner was speaking again. Her words sounded echoey, like she was half a mile away at the end of a drainage tunnel. "Get down on the floor, Wardell."

Wardell was nodding, moving his arms as though he were about to do just that. I opened my mouth again to try to warn her.

Then something confusing happened. Wardell tensed and stepped back. What seemed like a long time later, I heard a shot. And then two more in quick succession. Wardell stepped forward, then pinwheeled, falling hard to the concrete floor and landing crooked. His head was angled back toward me, his sightless blue eyes staring back at me from an inch below a weeping entrance wound in his forehead.

I closed my eyes for a second, but the image stayed there,

like a strobe flash. I felt myself being rocked and opened my eyes. Banner was above me, Annie clinging to her side. She was shaking me and saying a word I couldn't understand over and over again. It took me a second to realize it was my name.

"I'm okay," I said.

A wave of skepticism crossed Banner's face, but she did a good job of getting rid of it. "Hang on, Blake. Help's on the way."

I looked over at Wardell's body. I was pleased to see it hadn't moved. "I thought you were supposed to ..." I began, and then had to pause to get my breath. Banner understood anyway.

"Yeah, well," she said, glancing back at the body. "He shouldn't have tried to shoot my daughter."

I started to laugh, but it came out as a coughing fit. The coughing hurt. It seemed like hard work, and yet somehow I couldn't stop. And then I stopped feeling the pain. I slipped blissfully into a dark, warm pool of something.

TWO
WEEKS
LATER

83

"You look good, Blake. I mean, better than I'd have expected, anyway." Edwards's tone was one of pleasant surprise, artificially so, since he'd received the call alerting him to my visit five minutes before.

"I heal fast," I said, keeping pleasantry scrupulously absent from my voice. I glanced at Agent Paxon, who'd escorted me up to the tenth floor of the FBI building. She got the message, nodded at Edwards, and stepped back out into the corridor, closing the door behind her.

That damned grin. It was there again, smeared all over his face as he came out from behind the desk to shake my hand, physically grasping it when it wasn't offered.

"Good to see you, son."

I winced as the unexpected movement jolted the stitches in my side. Edwards didn't notice.

"Donaldson's in Washington," he said.

"That's okay," I said. "I didn't come here to see Donaldson."

His face blanked for a moment—though the grin stayed in place, naturally—and then the lightbulb went on. "Of course. I've got what you're looking for right here." He crossed back to his desk, opened a drawer, and pulled out a large manila envelope. "Half on completion, just like we agreed," he said. "We didn't have an address to forward it to, so to tell you the truth, I was kind of hoping you'd drop by. And here you are."

"Keep it," I said.

"Excuse me?" He waited for a nod or a smile or something from me. I kept him waiting. He shrugged, sat back down, and put the envelope back in the drawer.

"We're very grateful for your help, you know. Me, Donaldson, Banner, the whole Bureau. Hell, the whole country would be, if they knew what you'd done."

I sat down in the chair opposite Edwards's desk. Apparently, this move was unanticipated, because he sat back a little. Clearly, he'd been hoping the act of producing payment would make me disappear like a rabbit in a hat.

The desk was mostly clear, with only a couple of papers, an expensive fountain pen, and a folded copy of today's *Chicago Tribune*. There was also a vintage baseball sitting on a little slate plinth, the indecipherable name of some now-retired ball player scrawled across it in Magic Marker.

After another ten seconds of uneasy silence, Edwards spoke. "We thought it was only fair to ensure you received the full payment we'd agreed upon. Despite the ah ... problems that were encountered."

"Very generous of you," I said.

"But that's all in the past now. And I'm not going to sit here and say we could have done it without you. You helped us get our man, and that's exactly what you said you'd do."

"That's right. And I got him despite your best efforts."

That didn't leave him much option but to willfully misinterpret me, and he didn't disappoint. "Now, come on, Blake," he said, the smile still in place. "That's just not fair. You know we have to play it by the book. We just don't have the luxury of going off the reservation like you do. Even when it does get results." He kept talking, carrying on in this vein for another minute, talking to fill the silence. I tuned out and looked beyond him at the gray late-afternoon sky. The clouds were pregnant with snow. It looked like the weather forecasts were on the money. When Edwards finally ran out of platitudes about working within the rules, I looked back at him, nodding at the *Tribune*. The headline was about the reelected governor's announcement that he had terminal cancer. The sidebar was *House Votes to Increase Appropriations to DOJ*.

"I gather election season went well," I said.

He looked down at the paper and shrugged. "I guess you could say that. Looks like thinking is finally turning back our way."

"How so?"

"Well, spending on law enforcement, of course. And I mean *real* law enforcement, not this terrorist crap. For the last decade, all the money's been going to hunt down fruitcake jihadists in caves in Pakistan. Meanwhile, we've taken our eye off the ball back home. The country's been going to hell."

The way he was speaking now was in marked contrast to his prevarications only a moment before. He sounded confident, authoritative, on comfortable ground.

"You really think it's going to hell?" I asked.

He widened the grin and this time it looked quite genuine. "How can you even doubt it? Look at Wardell, at what just one man like that can do."

"Look at Wardell," I repeated slowly, as though considering it for the first time.

"We've seen real cuts in genuine law-enforcement budgets—local and state cops, prosecutors, the Bureau—since the early nineties. Now a lot of people who ought to know better think this is just fine. And why not? Crime rates are down. They've been falling since ninety-one. It's like the way they cut military spending to the bone after the Berlin Wall came down."

"The peace dividend?"

"Exactly." Edwards pointed at me, delighted. I realized he wasn't just on comfortable ground. This was a kind of religious fervor. "Well, this is more like ... more like a 'safety dividend,' I suppose. Crime's falling, so we don't need as many cops, so why not spend the money on schools, hospitals, tax cuts, whatever."

"Sounds reasonable."

"No." He almost yelled the word, slapping the desk.

"No?"

"No. Because here's what nobody seems to be thinking about, Blake: *What if it isn't a decline?* What if the fall in crime rates is just a blip?"

I furrowed my brow as though concentrating on keeping up with him. "You're worried about a sudden upswing, that we'd be caught with our pants down."

Edwards nodded vigorously. If he was suspicious about the fact that I'd suddenly become such a receptive listener, he didn't show it. "Exactly. Read the runes, Blake. The economy's in the toilet; unemployment's rising. It's a damn tinderbox out there. The right spark and the whole damn country goes up in flames. And we won't have the manpower to put it out."

"I see where you're going. We needed a wake-up call. As a country, I mean."

"Bingo."

"And you decided Caleb Wardell would be the perfect candidate to make that call."

Edwards's mouth hung half open for a second, on its way to another approving affirmative. His mouth twisted into the beginnings of several other words before he settled on a simple, "What?"

I leaned forward in the chair and put my elbows on the

desk. "I underestimated you, Edwards. When I worked out what was happening, I thought it had to be Donaldson who was behind this."

Edwards tried a bemused smile on for size. It didn't match the look in his eyes.

I continued. "From almost the beginning I knew there was something else going on. It just took me a while to figure it out. Some of that was because the motive was obscured by Wardell's random killings, but some of it was because the motive was so goddamn insane to begin with."

"I ... I don't ..."

"I was trying to see a pattern in the victims. A pattern in the *predictable* victims. I thought that would give me a motive. If I could identify a specific target that someone could know Wardell would pick, then that would give me the motive and the motive would give me the mastermind. It got me running in circles looking for something that wasn't there. And then I realized I was looking at it the wrong way: Wardell wasn't released to kill anyone specific, but just to kill *anyone*. It was Banner who made me see it. It was impossible to predict exactly who he'd kill. The one thing someone *could* predict was the basic fact that Wardell would kill, and do it in a way that attracted mass media attention."

"Now, hold on a second, Blake."

"You wanted to reverse the trend. The decline in spending. Lobbying was getting you there, but too slowly. You needed a nudge. A big media event to push it over the edge, right around election time. Like the way Hoover used Dillinger and the Lindbergh kidnapping to justify the War on Crime back in the thirties. The Markow kidnap, the ransom drop that went mysteriously wrong—that was you too, right?"

I stopped for breath and waited for Edwards to say something: confirmation, or more likely more denials. He just sat

347

there looking back at me. The oleaginous grin banished at last. I decided to play my hole card to shake him up. It didn't seem like much. Just two words.

"Martin Bryce," I said.

It worked. Edwards flinched in his chair as though I'd touched a live wire to the metal armrests. He moistened his lips and opened his mouth, but nothing issued forth.

"Yeah, I know about Bryce," I continued. "Or 'John Edgar,' as you were calling him lately. It was Bryce who approached Korakovski and told him which transport to ambush and how. Then he bribed Paul Summers to switch Wardell to the transport Korakovski's men were going to hit. Then he killed Summers to cover his tracks. It was a nice plan, I have to admit. It never occurred to anyone to question the timing of Caleb Wardell's escape because from the outside it looked entirely coincidental."

Edwards had given up on denials. He just looked utterly bewildered. "How did you ...?"

"It was the only way it could have happened," I said. "Bryce was there in Fort Dodge and in Nebraska. He was there at Hatcher's place. He was always one step ahead of me and two ahead of the task force. Which means you must have found a way of tagging Wardell after you broke him out. Something on his clothes wouldn't have worked, because you knew he'd ditch them, so I'm betting the rifle was bugged. How am I doing?"

Edwards said nothing. He didn't have to. The look in his eyes said it all.

I continued. "So you have a fake agent who's working on the flip side. Keeping tabs on Wardell for you, but also enabling him when he needs help, like with the phony tip on the red van, or putting Hatcher in his sights. I'd hazard a guess he set up the mugging attempt on me in the motel parking lot in Cairo, when you realized I was getting a little too close a little too soon.

"This guy is not on staff at the FBI, and yet he has inside knowledge of the investigation. He could move freely among the task force; he has a look and a bearing and identification that are all good enough to fool any real agent. How is that possible? Because he's not fake at all. He's the real deal. Like I said: the only way it could have happened.

"I had a long time to think about it in the hospital, and I kept coming back to that conclusion. So how come he didn't show up in the system? I asked Banner to get me ID photos for every male agent in the Bureau who died in the last ten years. Some of those were killed in the line of duty, but I didn't spend too long looking at them. I was interested in people who'd died unrelated to the job. Over the entire United States, that fit less than two dozen men in the period. Few enough that I could really focus on those faces. It didn't take too long to find the one I wanted. He had a little more hair and contact lenses, but there was no mistaking it: Martin Bryce, who was supposed to have been killed in an automobile accident in San Diego three years ago, somehow shows up as John Edgar two weeks ago. The dental records were different, but if you can fake an FBI ID, dental records are a piece of cake. We did a little more digging, and guess what? Bryce was assigned to your team back when you worked Organized Crime, which would have brought you both into contact with Vitali Korakovski. Quite a coincidence. How many more John Edgars do you have, Edwards? How many ghost agents working behind the scenes?"

Edwards had managed to compose himself. When he spoke, his tone was as dark and pregnant as the clouds outside the windows. "Martin Bryce was worth ten of you, you goddamned mercenary. Look at you, sitting in judgment of men like us. Who are you? Martin Bryce was a patriot. A man who sacrificed everything for the greater good."

"Why is it that people who talk about the greater good have usually just killed a bunch of people?"

"We did what needed to be done. This country—"

"This country has enough maniacs. You unleashed one of the worst just to scare people, to build hysteria to fit your agenda. A dozen innocent—"

"Lives will be saved—"

"A dozen innocent people," I repeated, "men, women, and children, are dead because you thought it would be a good way to cap your fucking PR campaign."

We were practically butting heads over the desk. Edwards opened his mouth to respond and then just shook his head and lowered himself back down into his chair. Slowly, he brought the grin back. Something twisted in my stomach that felt worse than Wardell's blade had done.

"So what?" he said. "You've got nothing. There's nothing at all to tie Martin Bryce to any of this. He died three years back. It was a tragic accident. You already know the dental records in his file aren't going to match up with the body they pulled out of Hatcher's house. All you have is a crazy conspiracy theory. Nobody's going to listen to you. You'd be laughed out of court."

I stayed on my feet. I looked at Edwards until the grin began to fade.

"That would be true," I said. "Except for one thing." I reached into my coat and took out a folded piece of paper. I tossed it on the desk in front of Edwards. He looked down at it, then back at me. Warily, he reached out and took the paper, unfolding it.

"What the hell is this?"

"It's an address." I let him read it, saw the recognition

in his eyes. "Bryce's address, right here in Chicago. The second-floor walk-up on West Twenty-First. Not the nicest neighborhood, but fine as a base of operations."

Edwards's eyes narrowed. "Bullshit. You're bluffing."

"You know I'm not." I smiled and shook my head, as though in regret. "It's what I do for a living, Edwards: I find people. Even people who are dead twice over."

Edwards kept his eyes on me. He crumpled the paper in his right hand and dropped it on the desk, as though the act of doing so would make the problem go away.

"Bryce was a methodical thinker," I continued. "I guess he had to be. He kept plans, notes, receipts. Even a journal."

Edwards was searching my eyes for a tell, hoping against hope I was bluffing. Beads of sweat blossomed on his forehead. "You're lying," he said. "No phone calls, nothing in writing, that was the rule. Bryce knew the rule."

"Maybe Bryce thought it was safe. Nobody knew he existed, so nobody would go looking for his apartment." I shrugged and pretended not to notice the way his hand had started inching toward the top drawer of his desk. "I don't think that was it, though. Notes are one thing, but keeping a detailed journal?" I paused for effect and then shook my head slowly. "An insurance policy. Against you throwing him to the wolves if things got messy."

Edwards swallowed. "If this were true, if you had anything, you wouldn't be talking to me."

"This is a favor. Not for you, for Banner. She still believes in the Bureau. She can't stand what a scandal like this is going to do to it. Banner is the only reason I'm here: to give you a choice."

Edwards digested that and then flinched visibly. "A choice? You mean ..."

"They say it's painless."

He nodded slowly, as though coming to a decision. Then his right hand jerked the top drawer of the desk open. I was across the desk before he could bring his gun to bear on me. It wasn't the standard Bureau-issue Glock 23, but the smaller, more compact Glock 27: his backup piece. I grabbed the gun with both hands and started to pull down. Edwards struggled and tried to push me off with his left hand, but I held firm. Then he tried pulling the trigger anyway, but I was putting too much pressure on his hand for him to keep his finger on it. After Caleb Wardell, overpowering this guy seemed about as challenging as wrestling a vanilla pudding.

He forgot about the gun and looked up at me, eyes bulging as he realized I wasn't going to stop until I snapped his wrist. The fight evaporated from him, and I took the Glock, stepping back. I picked up the balled-up piece of paper with Bryce's address on it, then walked to the door. When I turned back, Edwards was watching me, cradling his hand. There was a pleading look in his eyes.

Without taking my eyes from his, I used my shirtsleeve to wipe the grip and the barrel; then I bent one knee and placed the Glock on the carpet. I opened the door and stepped back into the corridor. I closed it behind me, being careful to wipe the handle down.

By my watch, it took me four minutes and eighteen seconds to reach the sidewalk taking the route Paxon had recommended, avoiding both of the security cameras on the tenth floor. Paxon herself would not remember my visit. The call to alert Edwards of my visit had not, in fact, come from reception. According to his schedule, Edwards was entirely alone.

I turned around when I reached the neat waist-high steel fence and looked up at the tenth floor of the building on West Roosevelt Road. I counted along until I located Edwards's window. I waited for him to appear there, for a shiny, ashen face to look down to see me, but it never came. And then it was impossible to see anything, because the glass turned red. There was just a small, insignificant pop, barely audible over the traffic.

I thought about Rapid City. I thought about the little girl in the blue raincoat. Then I turned and walked away.

EPILOGUE

I met Banner twenty minutes later, a few blocks from the FBI building in an anonymous coffeehouse that looked out on Addams Park.

I glanced at my watch and wondered if they'd found him yet. I ran through the duration of the encounter in my head and satisfied myself that I hadn't left any prints, or anything else to connect myself to the scene. With Edwards alone and only his own prints on his own gun, it ought to be an open-and-shut suicide verdict. I sipped a double espresso. Banner hadn't ordered anything.

"He killed himself?" she asked, her tone cold.

"Yes."

"You knew he would, didn't you?"

"I think you knew too."

Her eyes dropped to regard the tabletop. "How did you know he'd believe you?"

I thought back to the previous night. The apartment on West Twenty-First. As empty as a nun's little black book. Bryce had been as good as his word: nothing in writing. Nothing at all.

"I know the type. Edwards didn't trust anyone, not really. Not even Bryce. That's why he bought the story as soon as he knew I'd found Bryce's apartment."

"We had nothing on him," Banner said quietly.

"He admitted it, if that makes you feel any better."

"I suppose it ought to."

"We did the right thing," I said. "There was no way to get him. Not within the rules."

Banner shivered and folded her arms around herself, avoiding my gaze and instead looking out at the street.

"That's what they thought," she said after a minute. "Edwards and Bryce. They thought they had to break the rules to make things right. What makes us different?"

I took another sip of coffee. "Maybe we're not."

She turned back to me, didn't say anything.

"Banner, if you want to wallow in guilt about what we just did, be my guest. Edwards and Bryce freed a serial killer in the certain knowledge that he would kill innocent people. We didn't kill any innocent people. You don't have to feel great about yourself for this, but I think that's kind of an important distinction, don't you?"

"I'm sorry, Blake. This ..." She shook her head and looked away again, lowering her voice. "Damn it. This isn't why I joined the Bureau."

"Then forget about it. Move on. This thing is done now. Go back to what you do: catching bad guys. You're good at it. First female director, remember?"

She smiled sadly and shook her head. "Donaldson can't actually fire me just now because I got Wardell, but he's not happy with the way I handled things. I'm not promotion material anymore, not the way I wanted. I have a bunch of very well-paid PR engagements in my future, and that's pretty much it."

"I'm sorry."

"Don't be. What I used to think was important doesn't seem so important anymore."

"How's Annie?"

"Holding up. Considering."

"I'm glad. Tell her thanks for the get-well-soon card."

She nodded. "So what about you?"

"I'm leaving. I think I'll go someplace warm for a while, let the sutures heal. And then I'll go back to what I do."

"Finding people who don't want to be found."

"That's what it would say on the business cards. If I had any."

She leaned across the table and kissed me on the mouth. It was a long, searching kiss. I didn't need much persuasion to return it. She broke the kiss after a minute and drew back, opening her eyes and staring into mine. She'd never looked at me like that before. It was like she was seeing something in my eyes she hadn't noticed before. Or hadn't wanted to acknowledge.

"Goodbye, Blake. Please don't come back."

I looked back at her for a moment and then nodded. I slid five bucks under my coffee cup and stood up. Banner stared straight ahead, not watching as I left. I pushed the glass door open and stepped out onto West Fifteenth Street. As the weathermen had predicted, it had begun to snow. I thought about warmer climes, pulled my jacket closed, and walked away.